a Wolf *in* Duke's Clothing

SUSANNA ALLEN

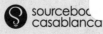

sourcebooks
casablanca

D0311537

Published by Sourcebooks Casablanca, an imprint of Sourcebooks
P.O. Box 4410, Naperville, Illinois 60567-4410
(630) 961-3900
sourcebooks.com

Printed and bound in the United States of America.
SB 10 9 8 7 6 5 4 3 2 1

One

IT WAS A VERITABLE CRUSH.

In the year 1817, with the Napoleonic Wars well and truly won and the American Colonies well and truly lost, nothing less than an utter squeeze would do, not when the hostess was the Countess of Livingston and well able to put the wealth of her husband's earldom on display. The ballroom was spacious, framed by its gilded and frescoed ceiling; impressive with its shining wall of mirrors; fragrant from the banks of hothouse flowers set about the vast space; and yet... Nothing about it was unlike any other ballroom in London, where hopes and dreams were realized or dashed upon the rocks of ignominy. Packed to the walls with the great and good of the English *haute ton*, the society ball was as lively and bright as any before it and any that would follow.

Despite having traversed a well-trod path of lineage and reputation all their lives, the guests gave themselves to the event with an abandon that appeared newly coined. They came to the dance, and to the gossip, and to the planning of alliances and assignations with the energy of girls fresh out of the schoolroom and young lords newly decanted from Eton and Harrow. Those undertaking the lively reel threw themselves into it as though it were the first opportunity they had to perform it; the watchers congregated at the sides of the dance floor observed it as though they'd never seen such a display in all their lives. Though the room was lit by more than two thousand candles in crystal chandeliers, shadows lurked in the farthest corners; the gloom was not equal, however, to the beauty of the silks and satins of the ladies' gowns or to the richness of their adornments. As the multitude of jewels and those eddying skirts caught the light, the setting looked like a dream.

Unless it had all the hallmarks of a personal nightmare. Alfred Blakesley, Seventh Duke of Lowell, Earl of Ulrich, Viscount Randolf, Baron Conrí, and a handful of lesser titles not worth their salt, found the Livingstons' ball to be an unrelenting assault of bodies, sounds, and most of all, scents. This last was a civilized term covering a broad range of aromas that encompassed the pleasant—perfumes, unguents, and those hothouse arrangements—to the less so, among them the unlaundered linen of the less fussy young bucks and the outdated sachets used to freshen the gowns of the chaperones. If he wouldn't look an utter macaroni, he'd carry a scented handkerchief or, in a nod to the Elizabethans, an orange studded with cloves. Whilst either would save his sensitive snout from the onslaught of odors, it would defeat the purpose of his presence this evening.

As usual, said presence, after an absence of five years, was causing a flurry of gossip and conjecture. With jaded amusement, the only amusement he was able to muster these days, and without appearing to do so, he eavesdropped on the far-ranging theories regarding his person that were swirling around the ballroom, much as the dancers spun around the floor itself. If the gossips only knew how acute his hearing was, they might hesitate to tittle-tattle…

"My Lord, he is divine," last year's premiere diamond of the first water sighed.

"That chiseled face, that muscular form." Her friend, at best a ruby, fanned herself vigorously.

"If only my dear Herbert would grow his hair until it touched his collar," Diamond said.

"If only my Charles would pad his jacket. And his thighs. And his bum!" Ruby laughed wickedly.

"I doubt very much that there is any padding on the duke's person," Diamond said.

Ruby peeked at him over her fan. "If only he would stand up with one of us so we could get a hand on those shoulders."

Two bucks of vintages separated by at least twenty years waited out the current set. "He may be among us, but he will not stay as much as an hour. My valet would thrash me did I not pass at least three hours allowing the entire *ton* to remark upon his prowess," the aging young buck opined.

"And yet, he is dressed to a turn, his linen pristine, his coat of the latest cut," the actual young buck replied.

"His linen may be," scoffed his elder, "but there is something queer in the lineage."

"Lineage!" One old gent bleated to another as they made their way to the card room. "Hodgepodge more like. A ragbag of dependents of no known origin, a mishmash of retainers, a mélange of—"

"Yes, yes." His companion flourished his cane. "My own family claims quite a healthy acreage near to Lowell's shire, and ne'er the twain shall meet, I can tell you."

"I do not take your meaning," Gent the First said.

Gent the Second put his hand on his friend's arm and leaned in. "My nephew's housekeeper's brother's wife's granddaughter is from the neighboring village and says there is never a house party, never a ball, and never a need for outside help. And we all know what that means."

"Penury."

"Not a groat to his name."

Along the mirrored wall, an older matron rustled her organza. "He is rich as Croesus, although the origins of the fortune are suspect."

Her bosom friend gasped. "Surely it does not come from trade?"

"He keeps no sheep, he tends no crops—well, he has no people to do such things. Even he is not so far gone to propriety to engage in animal husbandry firsthand."

"Some say the entirety of his holding is a gold mine, a literal gold mine." Bosom Friend looked ecstatic at the notion.

"Hardly," Matron replied. "There's not a nugget of gold on this island; the Scots mined it eons ago."

A merry widow and her ardent admirer lingered near the drinks table. "No one I know has had him, and I know everyone who has had anyone of import," Merry grumbled.

Ardent moved closer. "Is he...?" He gestured to a group of *very good* male friends clustered in the corner.

"*Quelle tragedie*, if so," said Merry. "It is true that he is seen nowhere without his steward, Bates, by his side."

"He, too, is a favorite amongst the ladies."

"No one's had him, either."

And so the ton *sups from the same old scandal broth*, thought Alfred. He'd heard every word without having moved so much as an inch from his place near the entrance to the ballroom. No creature with hearing such as his would need to do so. The rumors and speculation built in strength the longer he did not take a wife, but it was not merely a wife for whom he searched.

Searched he had, far and wide, all across Europe, as far as the Far East, a duke of the realm wandering the earth like a common journeyman—but it had to be done, for no one could find his lady for him, identify her for him, take the place of her. He found himself back in England after five years of endless travel, thwarted yet somehow not disheartened despite being here again. Here, almost to the man and woman, were the same faces he'd seen upon entering society after coming up from Oxford, faces that were beginning to resemble one another; he feared they'd all been intermarrying rather too closely for comfort.

His own family line was a different breed, and to explain his clan's uniqueness to most in this room would result in panic, fear, and an atavistic desire to obliterate any trace of him and those like him, for all time. To expose their distinction would put all under his care in the most perilous danger—a paradox, as that difference made him more powerful than any human being.

Yet, here he was among them, bracing himself for the possibility that the one sought by him and his inner creature, his essential self was of their number. His wolf stirred within him, impatient, vexed by the delay in finding their mate, held in check when all it wanted to do was hunt and hunt until they found the one whose heart and soul called to them, belonged to them, whose presence would set things right at Lowell Hall.

"Your Grace." His steward, Matthias Bates, appeared at his shoulder.

"Animal husbandry…" Alfred murmured, and Matthias gave a low laugh. Alfred regarded his closest friend and right-hand man—the perfect second-in-command, aligned with him in thought, yet with enough independence of spirit to challenge Alfred as needed. Bates stood as tall as he, at several inches over six feet, although the steward was blond where he was dark, lean where he was excessively muscular. None of the gossips had gotten around to that criticism this evening: What well-bred male of his status sought to gain such brawny proportions?

"I believe the *haute ton* needs to stop marrying itself." Alfred began to wander, Bates at his side.

"Indeed," Bates replied. "And it is, of course, a discussion relevant to your own situation."

A sigh soughed through Alfred's entire being. "It is enough to make one wish to take a ship and sail far, far away—had I not already done so and visited every corner of the globe."

"There are always the Colonies."

"The United States of America," Alfred corrected. "I am not well acquainted with any of our sort from out that way, despite their being one branch from whence we all came. My sister has not written to me of discovering such, in any case."

"One imagines such outliers to be as poor a choice as one of these women."

The air around the two men became oppressive, as though all

the heat of the room had coalesced to envelop Bates. He struggled for his next breath, and his body trembled as he fought an outside force for control of it. It did not affect Alfred, as this elemental energy generated from him; known as the *dominatum*, it was the ultimate expression of his power as Alpha of the Shifters of Lowell Hall. This power was his and his alone, the essence of his authority, the manner in which he held sway over the beasts within his people, the way in which he protected them from outside aggressors, and if need be, from one another. To him, it was akin to the dynamism of the Change: held entirely within and called upon with a thought. Its use was judicious, never mindless, but in this instance, it was excessive; he blamed his wolf, who was surging under his skin, seeking release. Even the slightest insult to his future mate was enough to incense them both, and at this precise moment in time, when the search looked to be a failure, he did not need the reminder that his true mate was no longer likely to be one of his kind.

Bates was not the only one to experience the potency of the emanation. Though invisible to the naked eye, it had an intensity akin to a lightning strike; the ladies who had ventured closer, hoping to catch the eye of the duke, came over rather faint and repaired to the retiring room. Nor were the men unaffected: the more delicate youths swayed as though they had visited the punch bowl several times too many. Alfred's face showed no effect or exertion but for the tightening of his jaw and an increased ferocity in his gaze.

"Your Grace." Bates managed a stiff bow and turned his head, baring the side of his neck. "I misspoke. We will welcome any female you bring to us as your bride, regardless of her provenance." He held his posture until the pressure receded but still did not meet Alfred's gaze.

"What must be done, must be done," Alfred said, and they continued their perambulations. "The issues that arise when lines too closely related produce offspring is, in the case of the *ton*, a weakness that expresses itself in illnesses of the body and of the mind. This is happening far too often amongst our own branches of society, and it must be addressed. The bloodlines of our…family must be strengthened, and our only hope may be found by my marrying one of 'these.'"

"Which will endow permission to do so for those among us who also wish to marry and to be, er, fruitful," Bates replied.

"Permission must be endowed sooner rather than later. Enough time has been wasted in my jaunts across the Continent. The continents, in fact. My wish to marry one of our own is not to be. I despair I have wasted time and endangered our people in trying to do so. I wanted my ma—my wife to be of our lineage."

"Alpha—" Bates dropped into another bow. "Alfred, that is to say, Duke, Your Gr—"

"Matthias." Alfred reached out and touched his steward on the arm, bringing him back up to full height. "If a secure future for our people is achieved through marriage to a society lady, then any sacrifice will be worth the cost." He swept his glance around the room and met a domino-effect of lowering glances. *How difficult this undertaking will be,* he thought, *if she won't look me in the eye… But surely the one meant for me is as strong as I, no matter her genus?* "My entire existence walks this fine line between our ways and the ways of society. The paradox is that in choosing my bride from the *ton*, I will have to hide my true self from her, regardless of our customs."

"Impossible," said Bates. "You will no more be able to hide your true self from your wife than the moon could fail to draw the tide."

"That sounds almost romantic, my friend," Alfred teased.

"Certainly not." Bates's offended expression inspired Alfred to indulge in a short bark of laughter. "It does not fall to me, thank all the Gods, to subscribe to this fated-mate nonsense." He coughed and lowered his voice. "But the notion you could spend a lifetime pretending to be something you are not? The expense of energy this would require?"

"I have neither the time nor the energy for romance."

Which he would feign, like it or not. His interactions with the ladies of the *ton* had always been marked by a social duplicity that was anathema to him: the little white lies, the sham emotions, the manners that in fact betrayed a lack of gentility and integrity. But there were far too many in his care, and they had gone too long without a strong sense of cohesion and community for him to indulge in stubbornness. He must lead the way, though it seemed unlikely he was to find happiness on his path.

Happiness! Had he ever thought happiness was in his future or was his birthright? In every clan he met, of every breed, he saw what a world of difference it made when they honored the ways of their kind. When a pack or a clowder or a flock were led by an Alpha pair who were *vera amorum*, they thrived, and it pierced his heart with regret, even as it strengthened his resolve. His mother and father had lied about their status, claiming one another as true mates, and the reverberations of that falsehood were still serving to hurt his people and endanger their future.

"I will do what is needed, whatever that may be." He took the glass of champagne that Bates offered, and both pretended to drink. "I will find a lady before the Feast of Lupercalia, and we shall go forward from there."

"Your Grace, I must remind you of what O'Mara made plain upon our return to England. Nothing less than a love match will satisfy your people." He sounded dubious; since puphood, Matthias had scorned the tendency of their breed to mate for life. "As well, you will have to proceed as a male of the *ton* and observe the customary formalities."

Alfred half listened to Bates prose on as regarded the necessity of *billets-doux* and floral tributes and wooing and instead assessed the women who came close, but not too close, to him.

They treated him as though he were unapproachable when all he wanted was to be approached; unlike the majority of the young aristocratic males in the room, he yearned to marry. A failed pairing could destroy the morale and robustness of a pack—he had only to look at his parents: the disaster that was their reign had all to do with disrespecting Fate and allowing their ambitions precedence. And yet, he dreaded the notion that he might not find her by the Feast day and would thus be consigned to searching one ballroom, one garden party, one Venetian breakfast after another, for another year, all in the hopes of discovering—

He thrust his glass into Bates's hand and froze, nostrils flaring. There. Where? He let his instinctual self scan the ballroom, his vision heightening to an almost painful degree even in the soft candlelight, his focus sharp as a blade. He fought to turn without the preternatural speed with which he was endowed and struggled to align the rest of his senses. His ears pricked, such as they could in this form: he heard laughter, a note of feminine gaiety that made his skin come out all over in gooseflesh, a sound that landed into the center of his heart as would Cupid's dart. His inner self rolled through his consciousness, eager to explode into life, and he held it at bay.

The set concluded; the next was to be a waltz, and the usual flutter of partnering unfolded around him. That laugh rang out again, and he turned once more in a circle, uncaring if anyone noted the oddness of his behavior. It was as if every one of his nerve endings had been plucked at once, as if a bolt of lightning were gathering its power to explode down his spine. He scented the air again, and between the candle wax and the overbearing scent of lilacs, he divined a hint of vanilla, an unexpected hint of rosemary, a waft of sweet william…

"We are very near the wallflower conservatory," joked Bates as he set their untouched glasses aside. "Shall you pluck a bloom from there?"

Alfred held up a hand and focused on the wall of palms screening the corner in which the undesirables mingled and hid, homing in on a bouquet of fragrance he'd despaired of scenting, a combination of familiar elements he may have experienced singly but never before as one, not with such rapturous force. He turned to face the greenery; Bates moved to protect his back. He inhaled, and yes, there it was, a collection of mundane notes that combined to create a glorious symphony of attraction, desire, lust, yearning, and possibility; a concoction of lush skin, that hint of sweet william, fresh air, horses—and an excessive amount of lemon? His heart beat like thunder, and as the violins tuned for the upcoming dance and the crowd's murmur built into a roar, he swept, heedless, through them to reach the source.

Two

IT LOOKED TO BE A VERITABLE CRUSH, AT LEAST FROM THE VIEW behind the palms. It had taken the Honorable Felicity Templeton far longer than usual to claim her place away from the superior gaze of society. As she had resolutely edged around the dance floor, she nodded and distributed faint smiles to those who exerted themselves to obstruct her path. Did the Incomparables and Corinthians and rakes force her to arduously achieve the anonymity of the fronds out of spite? They certainly cut her, if not directly, then with just enough acknowledgment of her person to imply that her person required very little acknowledgment at all.

She had held her head high as she maneuvered past the simpering maidens and their vigilant mamas; past the knowing widows and their fluttering fans; past the tabbies and the tartars and the dragons clustered in strategic positions around the dance floor so no one and nothing would escape their notice; past the leering elderly gents keen on finding their umpteenth wife; and past the young bucks who insinuated their bodies against her softer parts without fail or shame. She was no one, after all; there was no one to give redress.

And yet, they gossiped about her. The *ton* would gossip about a fly on a wall, never mind an oddity that debuted at the grand old age of twenty and after five seasons had failed to secure an offer, much less a husband, a young woman with only an uncle and two cousins to her name—and were they first cousins? She'd best marry one of them, should they be further removed along the bloodline, as beggars could not be choosers, even if they were Cits. She had, of course, tragically lost her parents one after the other, but that didn't excuse her sad lack of style. Her uncle, Ezra Purcell, must have the funds to hire his niece a decent companion. It was a scandal she went about with no companion at all!

What would they say if they knew that every misstep she took was made with purpose? That she was on a mission to remain unwed? They would collapse in a heap of disbelief.

Once installed in the area meant to screen the less fortunate ladies from the gaze of their betters, Felicity let down her guard, safe for the moment from the talk and the laughter and the whispers; from the overwhelming colors and scents; from the vertiginous sensation of the dancers swirling near to her and then away; and from the sensation of being surrounded, about to be drowned in humanity. She was also secure in the company of her friendship with Lady Jemima Coleman, who had run her own gauntlet to escape the protracted notice of the *ton*.

Both ladies had collected as many cups of lemonade as they could carry so that they might be refreshed throughout the interminable evening without needing to leave their camouflage. Felicity sipped from her second serving, cautiously. "This tastes rather unusual."

"I believe it has been concocted from actual lemons," Jemima replied. "As well as with a touch of honey, as my grandmother used to make it." Her robust Northumberland cadence, earthy and rough around the edges, came as something of a surprise from as petite and delicate a lady as she appeared—a surprise the year's swains did not find enchanting.

Nor did they find Felicity's strapping, sun-kissed person to be in any way intoxicating. Standing eye to eye with most of the men of her class, Felicity was not suited to the high-waisted, wispy fashions of the day, which did not show her bosomy figure to its best advantage. The short-capped sleeves made her arms look positively muscular, and the roundness of her face was exacerbated by the severity of her topknot. Such fashionable deficits would send many a maid weeping into her pillow at night, but not she. If anything, she ensured that her dress and toilette were done to her disadvantage as rigorously as possible.

For Felicity had a plan, a plan that would turn into a dream come true.

"Do you yearn for your homeplace?" She rearranged a few fronds to shield them further from the gaze of the ballroom's denizens.

"I do not." Jemima delicately sipped from her cup. "Most especially not since having made your acquaintance."

"We are friends, Jem, for the love of—galoshes."

"We are, we are," Jemima replied. "And it's grateful I am for it. I have received the welcome to be expected for a nobody from near enough to Scotland to be vulgar and uncouth, and yet it has transcended even the worst of my imaginings."

"The slightest intimation of difference sets this lot off like hounds on a hunt." Yet, Jemima was everything Felicity herself was not, far closer to the *ton*'s ideal of femininity, and she couldn't imagine why her friend had not "taken." Fine-featured and slim yet with an ample bosom, pale-skinned, with smooth, dark-brown hair, Jemima's appeal was perhaps undone by her gray eyes: too perceptive, too observant, and thus disturbing, as there was oh, so much that was required to remain unseen in high society.

"I can only imagine the things they're saying about me." Felicity waved her cup airily toward the crowd. "'Why, she's as sturdy as those columns she prefers to hide behind—I wouldn't give even the tweeny one of her gowns—that hair of hers is positively red—I do believe she has been out in the sun without her bonnet!'" She sighed. That hadn't been as amusing as she had intended.

"If they knew the truth about you, their tongues would fall out of their heads from wagging." Jemima reached out to touch Felicity's elbow. She was demonstrative and a frequent giver of soothing pats and bolstering squeezes.

It had the desired effect. Felicity smiled and could feel the vitality of her vision surge through her like it was a living thing, a thing that was strong of spine and stance, beautiful and glorious and fierce. The mere thought of her passion filled her entire being with life and hope and joy.

"Bedamned with them," she said, with conviction.

"Your language becomes dangerously coarse these days, friend."

"Due to frequenting the stables and the sales." Felicity smiled into her cup, hoarding the dregs of her treat.

If the *ton* only knew how conversant Felicity was in matters regarding the stables and the horseflesh sales. What would her parents have thought, were they alive? But were they alive, she would not be on this path. She would have been brought out at the proper age of seventeen, when she was still dewy and naive; perhaps dewiness and naivety would have garnered her a decent match, but as time went on, Felicity doubted she had ever been as fetching and credulous as any of the debutantes she'd come across.

Her parents' marriage hadn't been in the usual run of things: they had fallen in love at first sight and damned the consequences—one of which was Felicity, born rather hale and hardy for a child delivered at seven months. Had they truly known each other before they'd let their fascination for one another sweep them away from family and friends? Upon their elopement, her mother had been cut dead by her family for a time, which had amused her father, as it was the aristos who indulged in that sort of nonsense. For Felicity's mother was the daughter of a merchant, and her father a baron, and the twain had met, heedless of all societal strictures, for better and for worse.

She'd also been aware of her father's dislike of her mother's horse madness, of her mother's laughing disdain of his fears, but when she'd died due to that passion, the grief proved too much for her remaining parent, and he soon followed his love to the grave.

Two bereavements hard upon the heels of each other had forestalled any chance of a debut, and as the years passed and her heart healed, Felicity was certain she had missed her chance. It had been a dream she had shared with her mum in happier times, just before it was time for her to lengthen her skirts and put up her hair: of standing at the top of a sweeping staircase, clothed in a diaphanous, white gown, waiting to be announced, all the while turning heads and smiling down upon the beaux who swarmed to meet her as she descended.

That dream was long gone. Notions of a match made locally were scotched thanks to her father's dramatic decline into debauchery following her mother's death, and she lost face with the neighboring gentry despite being of the highest status in the locality. Or so they were in their part of Kent, at any rate; her mother had spoken of a duchy over the border, but Father had no interest in taking hat in hand and pursuing an acquaintance. For what had the Quality ever done for their family? They had looked down upon his wife and laughed at him for daring to have wed beneath his station, choosing love and passion rather than lineage and bloodline.

Ironic, then, that all that Felicity cared about now were bloodlines. For years, she'd thought her legacy consisted of a pittance doled out from her late maternal grandmother's estate and the harem of seven high-strung mares her mother had collected. Eight years on, their blood ran true and made them difficult mounts even for the most experienced of riders. With the skills she'd learned at her mother's knee, Felicity had such experience and also the ambition to found a line from a cross with sturdier stock under her own auspices. When her maternal uncle Ezra had inexplicably decided she would make her bow at the ripe old age of twenty and had taunted her with what he considered would be the devastating conditions of the inheritance left for her in her father's will, she had found a new lease on life. She would focus only on her aims. She would indulge in the joy she found in those stables and at those sales, and she'd be *damned* if they took that away from her.

"I learn more and more on every visit," Felicity said. "And that scheme of yours worked a treat. I move without restriction throughout Tattersalls dressed in the widow's weeds you created for me. No one is the wiser."

"And how does your stud?" Jemima asked, sending them off into snorts of subdued laughter.

"Himself is still refusing to cover my mares." More snorting, which in Felicity's case ended in a frustrated sigh. "Delilah near to kicked him into uselessness." She raised a hand. "Do not say it. I am aware that he is not entirely useful at the moment, but he is what I envisioned. His conformation, his lines, the heaviness of his bone…"

Jemima once again placed a hand on Felicity's arm, offering the comfort of a friend able to read between the lines. "You will succeed. It is a noble Undertaking, and the realization of a Dream is rarely straightforward." A devotee of the Gothic novel, Jemima's speech often gave the impression of being riddled with initial capitals. "The pursuance itself is an Art."

"The breeding of horses is indeed an art," Felicity replied, "but there is science involved as well. Biology, in fact." More snorting, this time behind their fans. "You are the true artist between us, Jem."

"If only you would accept the wardrobe I have made for you, then you would honor that art." She plucked at the drape of Felicity's gown, an uninspired, pale peach that clashed with her complexion. "This *peau de soie* has not been cut correctly, and it is puckering like a toothless old woman. And the waistline is far too high. If only you would wrap a sash around your waist, your figure would show to great advantage."

"That is not the plan, Jemima." Felicity was gentle with her friend—dressmaking and all that went with it was the lady's consuming passion. Jemima was a genius, and her own understated but cunning frock was a testament to her talent: despite adhering to the style of the day, Jemima's use of fabric and embellishment was striking, too striking for the sticklers, who found her garb to be bordering on salacious in a way they could not articulate.

"When your plan comes to fruition, you must look the part," Jemima insisted. "In fact, you ought to look the part before it does. You must lead the way, Felicity, be the inspiration to others like you, like us. The way I would dress you…none of this straight drapery and insipid palette and fussy sleeves and lace and wisps." She moved around Felicity like a bird of prey. "Bold blues and violets and greens, rich textures, a tight waist and deep décolletage, shawl collars and tiny diamanté buttons and ribbons threaded through, perhaps, perhaps…"

Felicity was both enthralled and slightly frightened. "I do not have the countenance to carry off such a departure from the norm." Not as regarded her figure, in any case. "I have neither the influence nor the infamy attached to my name."

"May I at least gift you with a new style of hat I have created? It would suit you down to the ground. It dips low over one eye, rather along the lines of the Paris Beau."

"A man's hat? You shock even me, Jem." Nevertheless, the notion thrilled her to her core. "It sounds quite dashing."

Jemima's hands fluttered, almost dislodging her fan and reticule. "It is infinitely dashing. Yet feminine. You are my inspiration for it, Felicity, as you are both."

"I will remember you said as much, the next time I feel less than either." She took a small notebook and stick of graphite out of her reticule. "'Jemima insists that I am dashing and feminine.' There. That's on my list to remember when I am covered in muck and hay and despairing of ever getting my stud to do his duty."

"I have a notion to make a clever little holder for graphite and suchlike." Jemima took the stick of lead wrapped in cloth and turned it around in her hands. "Something perhaps that has a chain to connect it to the notebook so it is always to hand."

"It's only a book of my lists, but I do like to keep them near."

"This one is almost entirely crossed through. Is that promising?"

"It is not, I'm afraid." Felicity took back the graphite and thumbed over another page. "I have been seeking a solicitor who might review my father's will for me, but none will consent to meet with a mere woman. Even the widow's garb only gets me so far. And I cannot secure a response from the firm that originated the document, which is peculiar and worrying."

"Perhaps they have disbanded? Shall we hire a hackney and call upon them in person?"

Felicity reached out to squeeze her friend's hand. "Thank you for offering, but a subtle querying of my cousins has revealed the address to be in the stews, of all places. I would not risk our safety in such environs, nor can I expect my cousins to accompany me without having to explain the reason for the journey. Why would my father consult in such a low place?" She picked up another glass of lemonade. "How infuriating this is, to be so uneducated in the ways of the world. I must discover how the terms will be made good, as I am so close to my twenty-fifth birthday. It is in less than a fortnight—eleven days, in fact."

"Many, many happy returns." Jemima snapped open her fan for emphasis.

"I shall accept your congratulations on the day itself, with a champagne toast to coming into my freedom and womanhood." Felicity closed her eyes at the thrill of it. "And then I shall begin to wear those gowns of yours. I promise."

"What is the first thing on your list you will do? When the terms of the will are met?"

"Which list?" Felicity laughed. "I have many, many lists."

"The whimsical one." Jemima flapped her hands as a demonstration of frivolousness.

Felicity shook her head. "I have no such list. My wishes to eschew marriage and motherhood are eccentric choices as they are."

Jemima set her delicate jaw. "Why must we choose? Why must

we have only one thing and never the other? Why should my art and your craft prevent us from havin' a man and wee childer?" She caught herself descending into her rustic dialect. "It is unfair. All of society's dictates show preference for the man's lot over the woman's."

"I…regret I will not have a family," Felicity said. "It was once my dream, as any girl might have. My intentions now preclude me from such, for no man would support the business ambitions of his bride. But surely your dream is not beyond the pale?"

"Because it is mere fripperies and trinkets? Woman's work?" Jemima scoffed. "I do not merely huddle on the floor with pins in my mouth. I create! And as such, I am too much for a man who seeks a broodmare. No offense intended."

"None taken." Felicity took a turn in touching her friend's arm. "I myself do not believe we can have both. And since we are both considered the Antidotes of the century"—at least this made Jemima smile—"we must not devote even one iota of our passion and vision to something that cannot occur. While we may not know what will happen in regard to our dreams, at least we will have the capacity to adjust and change them. People are not so easy to change. May I present as exhibits Odious Rollo and Querulous Cecil? My cousins and keepers, navigating the shoals of society with little grace and much dissipation."

It did not surprise her that Rollo had gone down the road to ruin, but that Cecil, who had once been her friend, was so lost to sober behavior…it was deeply disappointing. In their youth, their families had briefly reconciled, and they had become fast friends but had not met again until her debut. She had hoped they would renew that friendship, but Cecil's loyalty was entirely with his father and brother, despite the ill-treatment he often received at their hands. "Neither honor me as a relation, much less a woman. I know how to school a horse," she concluded, "but I have no idea how to deal with the likes of them."

"I am imagining them with bits in their mouths," Jemima joked.

Felicity let out a hearty peal of laughter—yet another fault in the eyes of the young bucks. "Indeed! And I am holding the reins in one hand and a long whip in the other." She laughed again, and she and Jemima toasted with their last cups of lemonade. "I often marvel that we are related," Felicity said.

"You may be of their bloodline," Jemima said, "but you are of different stuff altogether. A weave runs true in the hands of the weaver, not in the thread or the wool."

"We will make of ourselves what we choose," Felicity concurred, "and the dev—the doodle take the hindmost."

Suddenly, the usual murmur and shriek of the ballroom reached an almighty roar, like the sound of the sea at high tide in a hurricane, and was remarkable enough in volume to reach the ladies in their secluded corner.

"Must be rather a big fish swimming about," Felicity said, bestirring herself enough to part the fronds. "Thank heavens the supper dance is next; then I shall spirit myself away for another night. Eleven days to go…" she whispered.

Jemima peeked around a palm. "Oh, dear, is that Querulous heading this way?"

"Blast! No, that is Odious, about to introduce another one of his prospects." Felicity stashed her cup in the pot of one of the palms and considered fleeing through the French doors.

"I admit I yearn to waltz," said Jemima.

"If I thought you were lurking here on the fringes in order to keep me company, I should be very cross indeed," said Felicity, yanking her gown into an even more unflattering aspect.

"Perhaps it is you who are keeping me company." Jemima waved her fan about like a tiny wing. "I have no chance of acquiring a partner. This is why it is known as yearning."

Odious and his companion went in and out of sight as they wove through the crowd, which was feverishly pairing up for the final dance before the meal.

"It makes no sense that my cousins insist on matchmaking. They have no right to my money, so why should they be so intent upon my marriage?" Felicity groaned. "And look whom Odious is bringing me. Waltham! His nose will be level with my bosom, and he has pustules on his scalp. Rollo is a beast, if that is not an insult to beasts."

Jemima's throaty laugh rang out, full and with an undercurrent of roughness, like the grit in an oyster crafting a pearl. Felicity found it infectious; she turned her back to laugh into the wall so she would not be perceived to be amused by her cousin's attempt to fob her off on Waltham. As she composed herself, giggling and sighing, she turned to her fate and ended up face-first in a Cravat of Perfection.

Three

IT HAPPENED IN A HEARTBEAT: ONE MOMENT SHE WAS NOSE-deep in a neckcloth that smelled of starch and sunshine, the next she was being led into the ballroom, a strong hand at her elbow, a warm, deep voice sounding well above her ear. Along with the scent of clean linen, she caught a whisper of vetiver, of soap, and of male—male? What was *male*? It wasn't a fragrance she could recall identifying before, but if masculinity could be bottled and sold on Bond Street, it would be redolent of this man.

As she fought against the slight slide of the marble floor under her slippers, she managed to sort through further sensory information: the sound of Odious's protestations, of Jemima's gasp, of Waltham's blathering, contrasted with the current silence in the room, a silence pregnant with astonishment; she shuddered, and the hand gripped her arm with authority. Chills cascaded through her veins; the hold did curious things to her person. As did the heat coming off the body that was turning her to face it; as did the feel of the muscular shoulder under her hand as she took the proper position, with her other hand engulfed in a firm grasp; as did the knowledge that this man, whoever he was, was tall enough to be looking down at her. All this hurtled through her mind and body before she had so much as taken a glance at him, all this before she had managed to look up into his eyes.

Icy-blue warmth. A paradox, to be sure, but his eyes were the hue of winter light and yet burned as they gazed upon her. Who would have fancied that eyes such as these would look upon the Honorable Felicity Templeton and burn? It was almost too much to bear, and she sundered the contact to focus upon the Cravat of Perfection. His hand flexed around hers as though…crestfallen.

This made no sense. Why should she be able intuit a complete stranger's emotion through as mundane an action as the squeeze of a hand? She felt the urge to assuage the disappointment and so lifted her chin and looked him in the eye.

The hand flexed again, the thumb stroking her knuckles with relief. It was a ridiculous conclusion to draw, but she was as certain of it as she was of that burning gaze. The entire situation was absurd, that she should be standing up with the likes of him, so far above her touch—whoever he was. Felicity was about to say as much when the violin drew its first note. His right hand nestled itself on her upper back, and she was swept, with elegance and authority, into the waltz.

God—galoshes, he was glorious. His clothing was in the first stare of fashion, yet he didn't give the impression of having been wrestled into his coat. The broadness of his shoulders was unheard of in a nobleman—did he toss cabers as a pastime? His dark, unruly hair would torment even the least haughty of valets, but it suited the hewn quality of his face. She, who never took vapors, felt exceedingly vaporous. It was time she asserted herself.

"We do not have an acquaintance, sir." She congratulated herself on her observation of the proprieties, however delayed they might be.

An effortless turn took them around a corner. "Had you been longing to gaze upon Waltham's pustules?"

She refrained from smiling, much less laughing, as she yearned to do. "I do not know to what you refer."

"He is famous for his scabrous scalp. Has been since Eton."

"I find it difficult to believe you and he are contemporaries." *Much less of the same species*, she thought. "I would hazard he is greater in age than you are."

"Not at all. Perhaps the disparity in our apparent youth or lack thereof can be accorded to the possibility that my family's exquisite breeding has nullified the occurrence of erupting carbuncles."

Felicity fought to turn her giggle into a cough, but then

thought coughing was unrefined and ended up making a noise that sounded as though a fox was being drawn through a wringer.

He didn't smile, not in the conventional sense, but his eyes shone as if she had given him a marvelous gift. He drew in a deep breath through his nose—had she examined his nose in detail? It was the pattern card for an aristocratic appendage, straight but very large and yet appealing. If she didn't know better, she'd think he was *smelling* her. Her horses exhibited the same flare of nostril when they were making olfactory investigations of their surroundings. But he was clearly a lord of some stripe and likely didn't go around sniffing strange women.

What to say, what to say...did not the burden of chitchat fall upon the lady? If only she had social graces! If only she'd had a governess or a companion...or her mother. Her breath hitched with sadness, and the hand at her back gave her a comforting pat. What in the world was happening?

"Quite the crush, sir, I am sure you will agree." There: benign, with a touch of frost. Impersonal. A comment any of the other ladies in the room might deliver.

"Your Grace," he said, executing another flawless maneuver around the next corner.

She snorted and consigned to oblivion any chance of being confused with a lady. "I am not a duchess."

"But I am a duke."

Bloody hell! "Of?" There: even chillier, and disdainful. As if he were a duke of no account at all. She didn't know what she was doing or why she was doing it, but there was nothing to be done but to brazen it out.

"I am Lowell."

"I am unfamiliar with the name." Which wasn't a lie.

"Haven't memorized your *Debretts*, then?" He sounded pleased.

"I am shocked that I am unfamiliar with the name of a duke of the realm." As if it were his fault.

"I do not go about indiscriminately in society," he replied.

"I am not indiscriminate in my going about, but the notion that one of the highest in the land would be unknown to even one of the lowest would be ridiculous on any account." *What* had she just said?

The hand that had caressed her upper back now laid itself on her side and slid up a fraction, and back down. "If I may make myself known to you, I am Alfred Blakesley, Seventh Duke of Lowell, of Lowell Hall, Tandridge, Surrey."

"Tandridge? Surrey?" This could not be… "My family home is in Kent, near to the village of Edenbridge, which marches along the border of Tandridge."

"Of course it does." The hand caressed her side again. "And all my efforts these past five years were an exercise in futility." He swung her around a corner of the dance floor. No explanation followed.

"I do not know of what you speak."

"You will, ere long," he murmured, nostrils flaring once more.

"Sir! Your Grace. I must object to this repeated inhalation of my person."

And then he smiled—oh, not the kind of smile that a jolly person might assay, full of teeth and creased eyes, but the merest, slightest quirk of the lips. Had she examined his lips? It seemed outrageous and unfair that a man would have a mouth like that, full and plush and yet chiseled and manly. The smile teased out crinkles at the corners of those breathtaking eyes, which made Felicity misstep and fall against his chest—had she examined his *chest* in detail? She couldn't bear to, it was all too much: the glorious handsomeness, the effortless dance… She swayed, and he bolstered her, without exertion, and the first part of the set came to an end.

All at once, she became aware of her surroundings, of the susurrations of gowns and the murmur of voices around the room as innuendo was sown hither and yon. Self-consciousness descended upon her like a heavy cloak, and she wanted nothing more than to flee. How dare he do this to her, make a show of her in front of what she was coming to believe were not the cream of society but the dross? The only thing worse than being made a spectacle of by another was to make one of herself, and so she remained, even as the duke's hands tightened on her person, as if he sensed her impulse to abandon him. The next set began; he swept her around again, and Felicity refused to be powerless.

"Quite the stir you've created," she said.

"Have I? Created a stir? A stir, of all things." His mellifluous voice betrayed mirth.

"Oh, yes, well, may you be amused, Your Grace," she replied. "As you do not go about, you may not know I number among the most legendary of Antidotes that the *haute ton* has ever seen."

"I have often thought little of the opinions of society," he said. "I find no reason to revise that impression, under these circumstances."

"Which are?"

"Dancing with you. Holding you in my arms. Feeling your heart beat"—he drew her closer, and a wave of whispers threatened to capsize her composure—"as we move through the waltz."

She, who had taught herself to waltz based on illustrations in *La Belle Assemblée*, who had never expected to make use of that knowledge, was floating around the ballroom as though she had enjoyed instruction from the *crème de la crème* of French dancing masters. Lost to the music, to the feel of his hands holding her rather closer than was permissible, she took a turn in breathing in his scent, and her old visions of ballroom triumph reawakened—until she looked about her, just for a moment, and saw the spiteful smiles and the fans concealing mouths that dripped venomous *on-dits*.

"I suppose it's an interesting strategy." She pretended to muse, looking away from the crowd and focusing on his perfect cravat, a vision of enviable elegance.

"Strategy?" He brought her even closer to That Chest.

"You have done your duty standing up with a wallflower, have made a beneficent showing, and can therefore take yourself off without falling into the grasp of the fortune-hunting mamas or the wily widows. After all, no one would believe"—she made herself laugh—"that you have an interest in me. I am Miss Felicity Templeton, if I may make myself known to you. An honorable, of which you would not have been aware unless I told you. Which I have. Had you any curiosity as to who I was?"

"I know who you are." He growled in her ear. Growled? In her *ear*? She pulled back but moved only as far as he allowed. Rather than take fright, she became angry. That half smile, the single most charming, delirious thing she'd ever seen, only served to infuriate her further. It appeared he could divine her feelings as she did his, and the more fractious she became, the more pleased he seemed.

She bristled. "If it would not create even more of a scene, I should leave you here in the middle of the dance."

"Should you? Dislike the odd scene now and then?"

Were dukes always this impertinent? "I have had quite enough of this, Your Grace, and I do not appreciate being made to be a figure of fun, or worse."

"It is not my intention to do so, I assure you."

"And who will assure the *beau monde*? On the very rare occasions I have been led out, it has been with partners culled from the worst of the *ton* by my cousins, who seem determined to make a mockery of me. They fill my dance card with the halt, the lame, and the aged to highlight my inability to attract partners for myself, though I have no desire to attract any at all. None of these likely fellows ranked higher than a baron, and on the occasion they'd fetched me an earl, the gossip lasted for a fortnight. How dared I reach so high? But perhaps you have done me a favor. I have plans to remove myself from society forever, and I believe you have made my exodus that much simpler."

"*Pardon* me?"

"I shall be nothing less than a laughingstock, and receive the cut direct for daring to dance with a duke. I must thank you, Your Grace." Her voice dripped with sarcasm and the tremor of failing bravado. "You have made me notorious."

He sighed. "Oh, my dear. I can do much better than this."

Again, without volition, Felicity found herself being taken elsewhere: no longer on the dance floor, headed for her erstwhile hiding place.

In a clutch of heartbeats, Alfred swept Miss Templeton off the floor and back behind those palms he'd found her hiding amongst. Her fluttery friend had flown, as had the other wallflowers who had been cowering there. He could feel her pulse racing, could scent her anxiety, but it was lacking the astringent overtones of terror.

"You are unafraid." He released her and nodded to Bates; having stood sentinel near the edge of the dance floor, his steward now bowed and disappeared.

"I am not unfamiliar with the capricious antics of large creatures." Felicity unfurled her fan with little panache and wafted air over her flushed cheeks.

"I should be very interested in hearing such tales." He reached out and tucked a wayward curl behind her ear, taking the opportunity to edge her toward the French doors.

She put both hands on his chest and, with elbows bent, pushed back, preventing him from going farther. *Horses*, he thought and allowed her to believe she'd stopped him in his tracks.

"We may part company here," she said. "No one need be the wiser, and I am certain I can rely upon the gossips to shred my reputation to flinders by dawn."

"I suspect it is in tatters even as we speak. For the whole of the *ton* must know that we are here, alone." Alfred moved to her left, putting the doors at his back. As he suspected she would, she turned to face him. *I won't kick out at you,* he thought, amused, *but best to keep me in your sights.* "Can you be sure that this transgression is enough?"

Miss Templeton snapped her fan closed and slapped herself on the thigh. "It is sufficient unto my own ends, sir. Your Grace."

"Ah, but insufficient unto mine." He moved forward, and she moved back; he shifted to the left, and she spun and backed toward the doors. Much like the waltz they'd just shared, he was invigorated, and for the first time in years, full of hope. "For my ends rely less on gossip and more upon Fate."

"Fate! I believe in choice, although choice is as elusive to women as is the opportunity to address the House of Lords."

He moved again, but she had divined his intentions and edged away from the doors. With regret, he drew down the power of the Alpha, snared her in his gaze, and exuded the inexplicable puissance of the most powerful of his kind, that forceful, compelling energy that none could resist, much less a *homo plenus.* He could feel the characteristic compression of air all around him that caused those less dominant than he to experience difficulty in drawing breath and inspired the precipitous constriction of personal will and movement; it was a pity to use his power in this way, so soon upon meeting her. He lowered his voice. "Fate has favored you, and as you will soon see, the only choice to be made is to be—"

"Are you snarling at me?" Miss Templeton rapped him on the shoulder with her fan, hard. His hand went to the spot, shocked not from the strike—its force was nothing to one of his constitution— but by the fact that he was unable to overwhelm her. She held his gaze, pink of cheek, firm of jaw, unafraid, and euphoria exploded in his chest. He could see what the *ton* saw, a fleshy woman who was perhaps too fond of being out in the sun without her bonnet, who was not suited to the current mode of fashion, who was less than a diamond of the first water, but he saw beyond their narrow-minded, idiosyncratic prejudices to the fiery highlights of her hair, to the voluptuousness of her figure, the brightness of her eyes. He imagined taking down her russet-colored tresses, the waves of it caressing her glorious shoulders in company with his hands, hands that would roam over every delightful curve to both their infinite pleasure... He inhaled deeply again, imprinting her very essence upon his soul, frantic to indulge in her fragrance from head to toe. This was she, finally, after all the years on his increasingly desperate search, his *vera amoris*, the one he'd nearly sacrificed his entire pack to find—the one he feared did not in fact exist. Here she was standing before him, and his wolf howled to take her, mark her, so that none could dispute she belonged to him—

"Your Grace, I cannot promise I will remain ladylike if you insist upon smelling me."

"Magnificent thing, noses," he mused. Her eyes darted toward the dance floor. "No, I'm not mad. You are extraordinarily calm, aren't you? I've had ladies of the highest bloodlines trembling in my grasp because of who I am. It would take rather a lot to unnerve *you*."

"This is improper in the extreme, Your Grace."

"Is it? Hmmmm." He inhaled again, so close to her neck, she backed herself right out the doors and onto the terrace, all the way to the balustrade. The moon was new; all was darkness around them, with only the faintest light spilling from the mansion—yet he saw her clear as day. "Noses. I discern your gown has been in sachets of sweet william rather than lavender, an unconventional choice. You bathed with vanilla-scented soap, and the top note of your perfume is rosemary, yet another uncommon combination. You are something of a devotee of lemonade, and I detect a generous dollop of honey. Delicious," he murmured. He heard her heart race once more, and he scented the beginnings of arousal. "But I digress. Were we to go about this in the way of the *ton*, I would ask to whom I would apply for permission to court you."

"Permission! Courting? I do not intend to marry, much less wed someone who despite the loftiness of his birth is little better than a ruffian cozying up to a doxy—which I am not, and as such, I am insulted beyond measure by this treatment." She shivered, and he stepped closer; his heat enfolded her, and the gooseflesh on the upper parts of her arm disappeared.

"It is clear that you are a woman of substance," he said, not understanding why she flinched. "And that you are due all the respect of your station."

"If that is the case, then I insist that you respect my decision never to court, much less marry." Did he detect the slightest waver in her voice, of disappointment—of sadness? What in the world could have put it there? Nothing he had said, surely.

"Never to court?" he whispered, lips against her ear, and this time her gooseflesh was not the result of the frosty air. He indulged in another inhalation of her glorious elixir, and she melted against the railing. "Never to marry?" He tickled her cheek with his nose, ever so lightly, and whatever unhappiness he inspired dissipated and transmuted into desire. His ran his nose over to her ear, and rubbed beneath it; he breathed onto her neck, and her hands clutched at the front of his coat.

"Please…" she sighed.

"Tell me what you require," he murmured.

"It is past time I returned to the ballroom." She tilted her head so that her nose was a breath away from his.

"I yearn to fulfill your every desire." He allowed their noses to touch, a paltry contact that nevertheless set his inner beast alight. He stepped back and offered her his arm. "Even those that seek to part you from me. Only allow me to call upon you in the morning as propriety demands, so I may begin to learn every wish of your heart."

She stared at his mouth. "I—my heart? Every wish?" She swayed forward—an inch, a breath—and it took all of his strength to resist what she unknowingly offered. He laid his hand over hers over his forearm, and his wolf, who had been purring like a kitten, pricked up his ears. His attenuated hearing discerned whispers in the ballroom rising in volume and movement sweeping toward the doors to discover them in what the *beau monde* would deem a scandalous assignation.

Ah, well. There was nothing for it, then.

"My dear Miss Templeton." He smiled again. "I believe we will soon find ourselves on the sharp end of convention. Though it aligns with my own wishes, I must ask in advance that you pardon me."

He leaned in and took one more whiff of her ambrosial piquancy. She lowered her lids and licked her lips—*minx, there will be time for kissing later*—and he threw an arm around her waist and took them both over the marble railing, into the garden, and beyond.

Four

SHE HAD BEEN PREPARING HERSELF TO BE KISSED; WHILE SHE found herself in his arms, the world blurred past her at a speed that put the swiftest thoroughbred to shame. It was as though they were skimming over the ground, aloft, at a rate that would cause even a horsewoman of her abilities to tingle with apprehension. In less time than it took her to draw a breath to protest, they reached a large, luxurious carriage boasting four horses in harness. The coachman nodded to them as they approached; how he could see them, even with the side lamps lit, was incomprehensible. A door bearing the duke's arms swung open, and she was deposited onto decadent squabs upholstered in lavish velvet; there was room enough for her long legs, those of His Grace, and the equally lengthy limbs of two more occupants.

The blond, green-eyed, and lean gentleman who sat in the backward-facing seat was the antithesis of the duke not only in aspect but also in effect: of powerful build but less hard in his bearing. His dress was subdued but nowhere near as fine, the out-fitting of a well-off younger son or a lesser-titled employee.

Joining him on the bench was a woman wearing trousers.

Despite the events of the last hour—less than an hour, per-haps only three-quarters!—this woman in full male regalia set Felicity back on her heels. The ensemble would give even the daring Jemima pause: not only did this person wear trousers, but also a frock coat and a waistcoat. She stopped short of a cravat, but even so, her scarf was thrown about her neck with masculine élan. Felicity recalled the hat Jemima mentioned; it would be the crowning glory to this rig-out.

The woman was as lean as the man by her side and as tall and as blond as he, except her eyes were a deep brown, limpid, and almost too large for her face. She exuded the same ineffable aura of power as did the men, the same vitality that was both invigorating and intimidating. It was, oddly enough, the same essence that drew her to the horses, what drew her to her stud, the chestnut she'd named Himself: oh, how the established breeders would scoff, but she intuited something about him, something uncommon, something noteworthy, an unknown quantity begging to be discovered, something that went beyond the run-of-the-mill into the extraordinary.

"If I may make known to you my heads of staff. Bates is my steward and O'Mara is my...chamberlain." Bates secured the door and rapped on the roof, and they were off.

"The difference between the two is so slight as to be negligible," Felicity said. "But a female chamberlain. How revolutionary. How do you do?"

They murmured and nodded. The duke took a sharp breath, and what followed was akin to the strange vitality that emanated from him in the ballroom and on the terrace, similar to the gathering of energy that might presage a storm, a pressure in the air that produced a tingling on the skin. She thought she had imagined it, and while finding it odd and inexplicable, it had not affected her unduly. His people reacted rather differently—their bodies looked as though paralyzed, their demeanors froze; they were held in suspension until they did something truly bizarre and bared their necks to the duke. The pressure receded somewhat; only when they made what she perceived to be excessive obeisance did the oppressive quality recede completely and allow them to move at will once more.

She turned her head toward the window, the flocked fabric that covered it finer than anything she'd ever worn, much less seen hung in a vehicle. She nudged it aside only to be faced with indecipherable darkness. "Where are you taking me? How dare you carry me off with no respect to my person. Turn this carriage around, this instant!"

"That would be a pointless endeavor," the duke replied. "You are now ruined. By society's dictates, you are for all intents and purposes my wife."

"Your wife! Are you mad?"

"Not mad," he replied. "Merely intent. Merely determined."

That voice was like the indecipherable darkness incarnate. Nevertheless, she was not afraid, only frustrated, and if she were being honest, curious. She supposed a man of his station was accustomed to getting his way, but he was going above and beyond the necessary to secure her ruination. It made no sense. He was gorgeous and wealthy and titled and yet… She saw his fist clench, saw it slide down the front of That Chest, and she had the daft notion he was nervous. That he was as oppressed as he was oppressive. She sensed a darkness in his being—what might that darkness yield in the light?

She shook off such ridiculous thoughts. "Determined and intent upon what? I am no one of any account at all. I cannot be ruined."

Bates cleared his throat. A gentle clearing, she thought, a reluctant one, as though wishing not to offend, but also laced with some impatience and a touch of peevishness. How she knew this was beyond her. She didn't make a habit of parsing another's emotions in a heartbeat through the merest sound any more than she was expert in discerning the meaning behind certain people's flexing of hands.

Bates spoke. "The Honorable Felicity Templeton, daughter of the late Anne and Benjamin, left motherless at the age of sixteen, fatherless at the age of twenty. Ancestral home: Templeton House, which has run on a skeleton staff since the unfortunate demise of the baron, by the order of the lady's uncle, her mother's brother. Uncle is Mr. Ezra Purcell, of the City, cousins are Rollo and Cecil. Miss Templeton is in receipt of a minor legacy from her maternal grandmother. Since making a very late bow in society, she has been conveying between the family home and Purcell's townhouse in Finsbury Square, where she has spent most of the last year. Rumored to have been left undowered by her father's will, she nevertheless was presented to the Queen and has been escorted these past five seasons by said cousins, who go about society, it is to be presumed, on her coattails. You are, ma'am, very much a lady of the *ton*, and as such, can indeed be ruined."

"For all you know, it may have been my goal in life to cast aside my reputation. Didn't find that in your consultation of *Debretts*, did you, Mr. Bates? If only one was permitted to enhance some of the biographical information in that tome. Why, it would be as compelling as a Gothic novel." Felicity turned on the duke—a colossal mistake. He lounged in the corner of the carriage, confident, relaxed, self-satisfied, his gaze warm upon her. "Do not sprawl so, Your Grace. Ruined or not, I demand the respect you would show to any lady in your presence, as I appear to be one, by your man's account."

O'Mara took a deep breath. "Ma'am, all will be well," she soothed. "May I secure you another brick for your feet? We think only of your comfort. It has been rather a shock, and it is understandable that you may be out of sorts—"

"Do not address me as though I were a child, Miss O'Mara."

Bates looked down at his dancing shoes, and the duke crossed his arms over That Chest, his eyes gleaming with satisfaction.

"O'Mara is sufficient, Your Grace."

"I am not Your Grace. I am, as Mr. Bates so helpfully pointed out, an honorable, and despite being the lowest of ranks, it accords me a level of respect that has been denied me from the outset of my dealings with all of you! Do not chuckle, Duke. I loathe chuckling."

"I have never chuckled in my life." He blinked at her slowly, and if the novels Jemima insisted she read had the right of it, seductively. "In actual fact—"

Felicity cut across him. "How dare you make a spectacle of me before the entire *ton*, how dare you waltz with me only to abduct me? How dare you threaten to court me, to marry me?"

O'Mara leaned forward, murmuring.

"Desist with your tranquilizing tones, *Miss* O'Mara. I am enraged! I am justified in my rage. I had a plan. I had ambitions."

"Well may you scoff, sir." She turned on Bates, who had done no such thing. What he did do was drop his chin to his shoulder, exposing the side of his neck to her, as he had done with the duke. "A low-ranked, unwed woman of society must yearn only for the solace of husband and family. Not I. I had dreams, and now they are crushed. All that effort spent on Himself, wasted. What will he come to without me?" She turned back to the duke. "If only you'd thought beyond your own ends, perhaps you would have considered that more than one future would be destroyed by your selfishness. And how dare you push these horses beyond their strength? I insist your coachman slow down, straightaway."

The duke nodded; Bates thumped on the roof of the coach and the speed decreased to a trot. Felicity wedged herself into the farthest corner of the carriage and presented her back to the author of her downfall.

The carriage now rocked at a brisk rather than ruinous pace. Felicity fought to sit up straight, as she had been exhorted to do since she could remember being sat on furniture, but here, there was no one to scold her, no one to impress—why should a ruined, aging virgin not let herself relax? She leaned against the side of the conveyance and allowed her spine to curve, her head to loll against the wall, her weight to fall on her right hip, and she slumped against the velvet squabs. It was a feeling of such bodily freedom, she sighed and sank further into the corner.

As she rocked to and fro, she gave her mind free rein, and thinking back, realized that she'd seen more than she'd thought as the duke swept her onto the dance floor: Jemima's face, white with

shock, to a degree that seemed all out of proportion to the event;
Odious's gaping dismay was overwrought in the circumstances—
was he in cahoots with Waltham? Was he angling for a percent-
age of her nonexistent bride price? Why would he think she had a
dowry when, as her Uncle Ezra said, she did not? If Bates had heard
the rumors, then her own cousin was apprised. Her eyes fluttered
shut... That horrible, wonderful day when her uncle told her the
truth about her future... She stifled a yawn... How uncharacteristic of Uncle Ezra it was to address her about anything at all...

A beleaguered footman told of her the summons: her uncle had
arrived at Templeton House from Town and was desirous of her
presence in her father's study. As she rushed down the stairs, she
could not fathom what had brought him to the place he openly
despised more than any other in the whole world. This loathing
for her father's ancestral home was demonstrated by the meager
funds provided for the wages of the reduced staff and her own
provender. She used her grandmother's legacy to feed her mother's mares and chafed at the lack of warning that her uncle had
descended; there was no opportunity to warn the stable lads to
hide the herd in the holiday field.

At the bottom of the stairs, she took a breath, composed herself, and went into the study.

"Good day, Uncle." Her curtsy was rather perfect if she did say
so herself, which she had to, not anticipating compliments from
her relation.

She stood, her head bowed by the weight of his stare. Her mother
often laughed when speaking of her brother's stern demeanor, putting it down to the pressures of his work in the City and his deter-
mination to secure the Purcell family fortunes for posterity. To
Felicity, it was intimidating. Avuncularity never entered into any of
her cursory dealings with him, and today, so soon after the death of

her father, his presence was more oppressive than ever. Out of the corner of her eye, she could see the beloved portrait of herself and her parents, painted in her youth, the day itself a blur of color and cuddles that had gone some way to alleviate the boredom of sitting still. Each time she saw the picture, she remembered her mother speaking of how active Felicity had been in the womb, which made mama blush and papa's eyes twinkle. The sound of her mother's voice and the vision of her father's bright eyes were fading; grief overwhelmed her anew, and she struggled to take courage from the joyful, painted faces and the sweet remembrance of her childhood.

"You will put aside your mourning," her uncle announced, shifting in her father's chair. Her heart pulsed with anger—that he should sit there as though he belonged—and shock at his announcement.

"It has been a mere three months, Uncle. It would be disrespectful to do so." A mistake, inferring that he was unaware how to go on. For someone with as much disdain for formalities as he professed, her uncle was as high a stickler as Lady Jersey. Of whom she knew only from the tonnish ladies magazines. Which she devoured with gusto despite having no real place in society.

"You will do as you are told." He heaved his bulk out from behind the desk. Refusing to cede her ground, Felicity stood firm as he paced around her. "You are to be placed on the Marriage Mart," he said. "That is what you people call it, is it not? Such terms do trickle down to lowly Cits like myself." He gurgled; she assumed it was a laugh of some sort, a chuckle perhaps.

"One wonders at the notion you should be snapped up," he continued. "Did you know your father left you without a dowry? I see you did not. Was it because he thought you so lovely that the young bucks would not require incentive to ask for your hand?" He gurgled again. "Perhaps, on the contrary, he reckoned that all the money in Christendom would not suffice? You are less than ladylike—"

"If only you would allow me a finishing governess, Uncle," Felicity began.

"—and I do not know that you will snare a husband with hay in your hair. How you can remain true to the very beasts that killed your mother—"

"It was not Calliope's fault!" Felicity knew better than to go over this ground; she'd heard her father and uncle arguing for weeks after the terrible event. "The course had not been inspected properly by that old sot Lord Millington, and she spooked at an uncleared ditch—she hadn't expected it and panicked." Her throat closed, and she grieved for her mother, grieved for the horse that had been put down the same day, and once more regretted her mother's penchant for horses with the purest of bloodlines. Would a less spooky mare have handled that ditch with greater aplomb? Would a more sober, steady beast have managed to get them both through safely?

"As if an animal was of equal account as my sister." He stood before her, and she lifted her gaze, held his. "I'd like to know where those beasts got to. That bunch of mares she cultivated? They seem to have disappeared. Were they sold? And if so, why was the fee not reverted to me, as your guardian? Are they still on this property?"

Felicity's brow misted with perspiration even as she wrinkled it in confusion. "I would be more than pleased to walk with you around the grounds, Uncle. But will your gout allow? I take it to understand that you suffer from the disease of kings?"

"I'm sure you'd like nothing more than to lead a sick, elderly man on a wild goose chase."

"I accord you nothing you do not fully deserve." She lowered her eyes and let him chew on that. A quiet part of her mind chided her for her brazen manner; she blamed the horses, having become more assertive every day she worked with them. Could she get word to the yard if he did insist on touring the estate? She had one or two allies left in the house since her uncle had cut the staff and replaced the pensioners with his own people. The boot boy was always willing to run messages for her—

"Do you understand what I've told you?"

Devilment! "No, sir." She'd incited enough discord for one day, and she folded her hands at her waist to project a humbled air.

"Stupid girl." He moved to sit behind the desk once more, and picking up a piece of parchment, waved it in the air. "I waste time making this known to you, but your father's will"—he waved the paper again—"makes no provision for you should you marry. You are dowerless."

Felicity remained motionless; within, it was if every bone in her body had turned to water. "But, my mother's jewels? They were to be left to me—and she said I would receive an endowment that would set me above all other girls, far greater than a common inheritance."

"As for the gewgaws, they are all gone. Sold to pay off your father's debts, perhaps? Drank them away, did he? The diamonds, the pearls?" Her uncle never looked more porcine than when he smiled, as he did now. "Your father, it would appear, lied to your mother."

"He would never." Could a man who gambled and drank himself to death be trusted to do what was right?

"He has done. He has sealed your fate—no husband and children for you, as there is no portion to attract a suitor, my dear." Her uncle made the endearment sound like a curse.

"My father loved my mother and would not insult her memory through me." Would he not? He had certainly insulted that memory through his behavior upon her death.

Uncle Ezra sighed, the exhalation sarcastic. "We will never know. All we know is that he has pledged the entirety of his goods and chattels and income to you, a mere female, should you *not* marry. Is there logic to this? There is, if he expected that your expectations would be nil. It is a terrible thing, for one of your station, is it not? Consignment to spinsterhood?"

"Yes, Uncle. Any debutante would think it a fate worse than death." Felicity lowered her gaze, hoping she appeared abject. Inside, exultation rushed up her spine. She kept her eyes on her toes, and her breathing became labored; he might interpret it as panic rather than excitement. To be left dowerless by one's father implied a lack of worth even beneath the general low value women held in society. Her mother had been certain of the terms of her jointure; had her father changed his mind?

And yet... Was there a gift hidden in her father's apparent betrayal? For no matter how she'd done her sums, her little legacy would not stretch to fund her dream and keep her from penury—or at least beans on toast for the next twenty years. If she gave up the increasingly remote dream of husband and children for the sake of the vision of her breeding farm, she'd be able to achieve something in her life.

"I cannot believe this of my father."

"Can you not?" Her uncle snorted and leaned on the desk. "Can you not believe it of a feckless, intemperate gamester who stole my sister from the bosom of her family by dangling a title before her besotted eyes? A man who could not even bring forth a son, who could only produce one unnatural female? Bah!" His choler rose, and Felicity tore a handkerchief from her sleeve, holding it to her face, as much to avoid the spittle that flew in the air due to his outrage as to shield her emotions.

Uncle Ezra shuffled some papers, peered at them, and slid them into a battered portfolio. "The terms are quite clear. Should you remain unwed upon your twenty-fifth birthday, you will come into a substantial competence. Should you prove immensely popular following this event, all proceeds will, of course, revert to your husband. Your husband, who I am sure was so overwhelmed by your grace and beauty he could not speak for you before you were made solvent." He chuckled again, and Felicity feared she might do him an injury did he not cease making that horrible sound.

A sensible part of Felicity's brain warned her this was all too good to be true. Would a father who had all but forgotten his daughter was alive bequeath her such largess? And who was to say that, like her mother's jewels, he hadn't run through the entirety of their wealth? "I—there must be—this cannot be correct or, or, legal, or…"

"I might be able to discern whether or not it is," her uncle mused, and she peeked out from her hankie. He was smiling again, never a favorable sign. "Were I to seek to investigate the document. Which I will not. It is a foolish will made by a foolish man, and I would dishonor his memory if did I not abide by his foolish wishes. Now, begone, and think upon your fate."

Felicity rushed from the room, her uncle's satisfaction palpable. She continued to clutch her hankie to her face, but if only he'd seen the gleam of triumph in her eyes…if only he'd understood that her sobs were in fact suppressed, giddy laughter—

_____

She woke with a start. Over the past five years, her thoughts had gone again and again to that moment, the moment her girlish dreams of hearth and husband had been put aside in exchange for womanly plans and actions. After that horrible interview, her ambitions had taken flight. She would have the funds to establish a breeding farm that would become known for its sound, safe mounts and its superior bloodlines. Or so she would have done, until this debacle with the duke.

She snuggled against the cushion under her head. What would happen to her band of mares, to Himself? She thought it unlikely that any of the missives from her head lads that had been snuck into Finsbury Square would follow her to…Lowell Hall, she presumed. And as adept and reliable as both lads were, neither got on with Himself to any greater degree than did her beautiful ladies. Aherne and Bailey were nigh on otherworldly when it came to horsemanship and husbandry, but they and the stallion had been at daggers drawn from the start. It was a mystery, as both Aherne and Himself were Irish, after all. But how silly to think nationality crossed species... Felicity struggled to contain a yawn and then thought, *The devil with it*, and allowed herself to yawn with relish.

How long until her uncle heard the news? Would it make any difference? He might exult in her downfall and use it as the justification he needed to cut her from his life, once and for all. Would he demand recompense for her tainted reputation, and by extension, his? Would he come to her rescue, taking it as an opportunity to prevent another society marriage occurring in their family line? One would assume so, but Felicity failed, time and again, to comprehend the way his mind worked. He shifted and changed like a will-o'-the-wisp, never predictable—never logical, if it came down to it.

If only her father's solicitor had answered her queries. It occurred to her that the letters had gone astray since it was her uncle through whom the letters were posted, yet even the missives she'd entrusted to Jemima had been met with silence. Perhaps now that she was social anathema, she could present herself at the address. She would, of course, have to escape the duke first, make her way back to London, sneak into her uncle's town house, change out of her ball gown, pack only what she could carry... With that exhausting rumination, she allowed her eyes to close once more. Between the lateness of the hour, the rocking of the carriage, and the uncharacteristic expenditure of temper, she yawned with abandon; something heavy wrapped around her shoulders; cuddling up against something warm and strong, she succumbed to a dreamless slumber.

Silence reigned. Neither Alfred's steward nor his chamberlain required the repressive look he directed at them. They were four hours distant from the estate, and nothing would disturb the rest of his *vera amoris*, rest he suspected was much needed, were she in truth a horsewoman. Early hours and late nights were the lot of those who tended to *animalis pura* of that species; figure in the entertainments that carried on until dawn during the Season, and it was no wonder his mate was exhausted.

His mate! He inhaled again of her heady elixir. Beneath his euphoria, however, he experienced a frisson of unease. Were she *versipellis* as was he, instinct would prevail and they would be pledged and bonded and marked before sunrise. Since she was *homo plenus*, this was out of the question, and he found himself unsure how to proceed, a circumstance he had not foreseen in all his years of yearning. If only he'd thought to quiz the few Alphas he'd met who had mated humans as to how they'd managed to reveal their secrets to them. Perhaps Bates could be sent abroad to gather information? He negated that notion as soon as it formed; he could not spare him, not at this vital juncture.

He considered his Beta, who reclined against the cushions, eyes shut, arms crossed; Alfred knew Matthias shielded his thoughts from him in this manner—or thought he did so; having been friends since they were pups, Alfred could intuit his Second's mental perambulations. To wit: How could a *homo plenus* be not only their duchess but also their Alpha female? How would she react when it became apparent that all was not as it seemed in Lowell Hall? That its inhabitants were not as *they* seemed? How would they guard against the sort of exposure that had sent their French compatriots to the guillotine at the end of last century?

"You will have your hands full courting her," said Bates, his eyes remaining closed.

"She will see all she is to be mistress of, receive the warmest welcome she has ever known, and the battle will be half won," Alfred retorted.

Bates scoffed, and Alfred sent him a wave of suppression, out of spite. No one knew quite how to wind him up as did his oldest friend. Matthias shuddered but did not open his eyes.

"Miss Templeton's friend…" Alfred began and was surprised to see a ruddy hue overtake his Beta's cheeks.

"I will set out to discover who she is," Bates mumbled. *We already know* what *she is*, thought Alfred, *and it is not solely human.* "Would she have disclosed the truth of her dual identity, do you suppose? As one bosom friend to another?"

Bates opened his eyes. Their green depths darkened; he was ever conscious of holding to the laws of their kind. "Only if she sought to be kicked out of the nest." He grimaced. "If she has not been already. If she is what I think she is. And I am always correct." Alfred counted on the fact that Bates's native curiosity—which made him perfect for his role as the pack's hunter and gatherer of knowledge—would not let him rest until he had all his ducks in a row.

The coach trundled on, and Alfred nodded to O'Mara, who rapped the roof with her walking stick. Their pace increased to find a compromise between the hell-for-leather pace with which they had set out and the little-better-than-a-crawl that his duchess had insisted upon.

His duchess. He took a deep, exultant breath and saw O'Mara do the same, as she perceived the joy taking root in his being, the first spark of elation and security that would spread through the pack like wildfire. When his people pledged their allegiance to him as Alpha, he pledged himself in return, opening a conduit of energy, known as the *sentio*, between them. In this fashion, he stayed apprised of the robustness or otherwise of the pack, and the pack was secure in the knowledge of his presence. When his feelings for his mate began to flow, it would fall to O'Mara to regulate it, to find the balance between the much-needed hope and relief and the passion igniting within him that was private and his alone.

As the Omega of the pack, her duty was in many ways the polar opposite of his: her strength lay in her ability to soothe rather than incite and to manage the sometimes volatile reactions of a miscellaneous pack. As the Lowell clan was comprised of all species, not only wolves, her talents were routinely challenged in ways Alfred had never seen before, even in all his travels.

The role, like all those in the upper echelon, was normally held by a male, but O'Mara was unusually deft at her duties. He supposed it only made sense as females were generally considered to be less obtuse when it came to emotions. With a mere breath, with a palliative phrase, his Omega could defuse the worst temper, assuage the deepest grief, and with her signature glamour, could mesmerize even the hardest-headed human into compliance or forgetfulness. In all, her gift created a state of peace and calm that allowed a situation to be manipulated to a swift resolution.

The role of Omega often took a heavy toll on those born with its gifts, and it was no wonder that O'Mara often seemed made of stone. It never failed to flummox Alfred that she had been allowed to leave her homeplace. A pack or clowder or flock with the good fortune to contain a hereditary Omega would hardly fain let them part. Alfred suspected she held secrets, a broken betrothal, perhaps, or something odd to do with her training about which she never spoke. He kept his questions to himself and prayed she never wished to return to Ireland.

Speaking of Ireland—who the hell was Himself? Some feckless Irishman? Had Miss Templeton a betrothed? Alfred wrapped his coat around his mate and drew her closer until her head rested upon his breast. He'd see Himself in hell if that were the case. That would be for Bates to discover; it was not where his own attention was required. All that mattered was that his instincts had proven true, and after having been nothing but thwarted for the last five years, he indulged in a well-deserved wallow in the fruits of his conviction.

Five years. Five years since Miss Templeton had been orphaned and passed between London and Kent like a lost parcel; five years since he'd left the country. He would have departed just before she'd turned twenty: according to lupine lore, he would not have perceived what she was to him until that auspicious birthday. It was not for his genus, this tradition of taking child brides: a *vera amoris* must have maturity before the time came to be claimed. He comforted himself that he likely would not have known her until this very moment in time, and therefore, in truth, no time had been wasted after all.

The coach rattled away from London. Wonderful things, coaches: as well-sprung as was the ducal conveyance, the highways and byways of England were less than properly tended, and a vehicle would shudder upon myriad ruts, causing its passengers to shift about, often into or onto one another. One such rut caused the carriage to rock and thus jostled Miss Templeton even closer against his side; he tightened his arm and discovered the indentation of an unexpectedly small waist, his imagination stirred by the contrast of the luscious hips he found as his hand quested further.

"This dress is doing Her Grace's figure no favors," he whispered. "We shall summon a modiste to the Hall and provide her with new clothes."

"Indeed, Alpha?" O'Mara raised a brow. "As a woman, albeit one who does not follow fashion—"

"Feminine fashion," Bates interjected.

"—one wonders if that is the best possible course. Such an observation may cause her unhappiness."

"She is a woman of substance, and I said as much. Why do you wince?"

O'Mara looked everywhere but at Alfred. "Her Grace would,

perhaps, take that to mean you find her to be rather more robust than is fashionable, and therefore unappealing."

"That is madness. She is perfection itself."

"She is, Alpha," O'Mara soothed. "Perhaps I can be of service to you and her regarding this topic."

"Perhaps not." His eyes smiled. "Did you see how she resisted your quelling?"

"I've never seen the like," Bates said. "And she resisted yours as well."

"It was impressive," O'Mara agreed. "It presents an interesting difficulty, however."

"There are no difficulties," Alfred growled. Miss Templeton stirred, and he held his breath until she curved farther into his embrace. He lowered his voice once more. "She is mine and fit for the roles of duchess and Alpha female."

"Undoubtedly," O'Mara said. "She is strong-willed, fiery, formidable…"

Alfred gazed down on Felicity, peaceful in slumber. "All of which are qualities that may be used against me."

"Which will be used against you, almost certainly, Alpha. She will challenge you at every turn." Bates sat forward. "It will be all that O'Mara can do to keep any dissension or distrust from spreading should the pack take against the notion of a *homo plenus* as your mate."

"It will be exactly what I will do, as it is my role," O'Mara snapped.

Bates turned to her. "Between the tensions of the search and the fear that our Alpha would never find his *vera amoris* nor settle for less, you have been stretched to even your prodigious limits."

"You concern is appreciated," O'Mara said, "but this is my birthright."

"Nevertheless—"

"While you will have your work cut out for you," she said, "trying to divine what her foiled dreams entail."

Bates bristled. "That will be the work of a moment, I assure you."

"Enough." As was correct, his Beta and Omega bared their necks in submission at his stern tone, but he released them from their deference almost immediately. He saw them share a furtive look that promised a thorough discussion of such an unusual occurrence once they could be private; Alfred's temper more often than not had consequences of a much longer duration. "You both have my complete confidence. In light of this, I need your counsel. There are, of course, certain facts that Her Grace does not possess…"

"And when ought we to lay them in her lap, so to speak?" Bates sat back, and O'Mara took it in turn to lean forward.

"The delicacy of this is unlike anything I've ever encountered, Alpha," she began. "You are blazing a trail that many will follow in years, perhaps even centuries to come. You are the one who has been chosen to take the first human mate on this island, as your mate has been chosen to be the first to fulfill that role." Alfred felt a wave of thrilled trepidation course through the carriage; Miss Templeton quivered against his side. "It is a responsibility of the highest order," O'Mara continued, "one which requires patience and tact."

"But one which cannot be deferred for long." Bates rubbed his face. "We shall instruct the pack to keep quiet about their true natures, but Miss Templeton will soon notice that things are not done in the usual way in our little corner of the country. The longer it takes to apprise her, the more difficult it may be for her to accept the knowledge."

"And yet…" Alfred looked down upon his duchess, sleeping in all innocence and trust against him. How quickly would things turn sour once she awakened? A wave of remorse flowed through him, and O'Mara adjusted the atmosphere, like a harpist playing upon her strings. He raised his free hand to halt her; he would be damned if he would not feel this. "I cannot but think of Phoebe. I would not force Miss Templeton, as my sister was to have been forced. She must choose this of her own free will."

"You must woo her," O'Mara said.

"Goddess help us," Bates moaned.

"I am well able to turn the attentions of a mere human woman, Beta," Alfred growled, and Bates resumed his position of shut eyes and crossed arms.

"We shall go easily, carefully," O'Mara said, gently exuding waves of comfort. "Mrs. Birks will attend her personally, with only one maid to prevent their chatter exposing our secrets inadvertently. Mr. Coburn will take charge of the footmen—"

"Holy Venus, all those damned footmen." Bates tore at his hair, and Alfred lowered his dignity so far as to kick him in the shin.

"We shall find a balance," O'Mara continued, "one which includes choice, despite the necessity of bowing to society's dictates and our own, before the moon reaches its fullness, in eleven days time."

"We shall make haste slowly." Alfred nodded. "That's a plan."

Five

FELICITY WOKE WITH DAWNING CONFUSION. SHE TURNED over on sheets that were not the threadbare linens that adorned her bed in Templeton House, nor those of her uncle's town house in Finsbury Square, which managed to be both abrasive and clammy. The mattress she lay upon now was splendidly free of lumps, the pillowcase beneath her cheek was silk, and the quilt she pulled up to her chin was so light, it was surely stuffed with the feathers of angel's wings, with nary a one prodding her in an uncomfortable place. She sighed and cuddled the pillow close, much as in her dreams, she cuddled a warm, strong, enticingly scented male—

She awakened in full and remembered being abducted from the Livingston Ball, and under those circumstances, ought not to be wallowing in a bed in the duke's residence. She turned over onto her opposite side and decided to enjoy its luxuriousness, for someone as resourceful as she would be on her way back to London and far, far away from such decadence by nightfall. And decadent it was, the textures against her body so lush, so comprehensive, she couldn't discern why—

—until she realized she was clad only in her chemise. This momentary shock was followed by a rush of gratitude she hadn't had to sleep in her gown...followed by a flash of horror it might have been the duke who had divested her of her clothing—followed by a surge of visceral curiosity. What would it be like to have a powerful creature the likes of His Grace acting as her personal maid? To see him kneeling at her feet, unlacing her slippers, fingers dancing around her ankles as the ribbons unwound, his palm under her heel as he eased the shoe free? She could all but feel his hands lifting her dress over her head, his fingers undoing the tapes of her petticoat, unlacing her corset—

Her mind stuttered, unable to furnish the necessary imagery for what would next transpire, and instead, envisioned them at her dressing table: his hands taking down her hair, the pins yielding to his touch, the warmth of That Chest against her back as he leaned over to place the pins on the tabletop, her breathing becoming exquisitely labored, her pulse galloping, her skin quivering with awareness. She saw herself rise and turn to face him as her unruly locks tumbled about her shoulders; the Cravat of Perfection was gone, and she faced an unadorned neck and a glimpse of collarbone—

The curtains were pulled aside, and a very small maid squeaked in surprise.

"Mary Mossett!" a gravelly, countrified voice hissed. "Gently. You'll wake Her Grace."

"But—"

"You'll never rise from the grates and ashes if ye don't learn subtlety."

"But Mrs. Birks—"

"I am awake." Felicity rose and shook off the daydream; the bed hangings were so opaque, she'd slept through the sunrise, something she hadn't done for ages. "And I am not Your Grace."

"Yes, Your Grace," said Mary, bobbing three curtsies in quick succession. "That's what he said you'd say—Mr. Bates, that is. Told us you'd be right crotchety about it, he did. Not in so many words, o' course. Ma'am." She beamed, her smile revealing two front teeth so generous in size, they nipped her lower lip. Her little face was alight, her tiny eyes bright as buttons and her hair flying away from beneath her mobcap around two large, prominent ears.

"Away with you now and draw Her Grace's bath." A lean, rangy woman prowled over to the bed and hustled Mary toward a door, then bustled straight back to bob a curtsy at the side of Felicity's bed. "I am Mrs. Birks, housekeeper to His Grace and Lowell Hall," she introduced herself. She looked to be of middling years, yet hearty and fit with it, unlike her numberless colleagues who held similar roles in big houses across the nation. Her light-gray eyes shone bright and sharp, if a trifle close-set over her long nose. "You've had a lovely sleep, I must say, didn't so much as stir when Mary and I tended you upon your arrival." Felicity could have sworn that the housekeeper tipped her a wink. "Now, we've got your gown being sponged and freshened, and until it is ready, our Alph—our Alfred, Alfred, our duke, er, thought this might do." She held out a man's dressing gown.

"Well." Felicity took it, her fingers identifying silk, her nose identifying the duke. "I suppose needs must." The scent made her think of being held against That Chest, of the sensation of movement, of being laid down with care. Had the duke carried her up the stairs and put her into—into—bed? She slipped on the robe, and despite being the cast-off loungewear of a man, it was the most luxurious thing she'd ever worn. It was heavy with embroidery, with a deep lapel and long sleeves; when she cinched the belt, she was swathed in luxury.

Nevertheless: "I cannot wear this outside this room, and lovely as it is, I cannot stay in this bedchamber for the entirety of the day."

"Oh, missus." Mary appeared in the doorway. "These are the staterooms, the best chambers in the whole Hall. Why you haven't been put into the duchess's suite, I'm sure I don't know, but if you was to ask me—"

"Mary," Mrs. Birks barked. "Bath." The maid disappeared into a room that had begun to billow with steam. "That's a bathing chamber, that is, mum, and we've never seen the like of it. His Grace has been traveling away onto five years now, and he did bring back this notion from the Far East, if you can credit it."

"Five years, traveling the world?" Felicity ran a hand down the lapel of the robe, idly tracing the silken embroidery. More silk!

Her head would surely be turned. "That is a rarity, for a duke to go gallivanting 'round the globe."

The housekeeper made a sound akin to a whine. "Wouldn't be my place to pass comment, Your Grace—missus—uh, ma'am," she said as she began to whip the bedclothes about in a frenzy. "Finest view in the Hall there," Mrs. Birks said, nodding to the large windows. "Only the very best for as honored a guest as you, ma'am."

Felicity did as she was bid and wandered over to the state bed-chamber's wall of windows. Templeton House had not been in possession of such an apartment, but according to her mother, the finest visiting personages were lodged in upper rooms that faced the entryway of the domicile. Neither she nor Mama could imagine why—wouldn't the back of the house be more peaceful? Her mother thought anyone so high in the instep would wish to be apprised of the comings and goings of all under the visited roof, and they laughed themselves silly imagining a duke—or the Prince of Wales!—lurking about behind window hangings, spying on the houseguests as they jaunted to and fro.

The bedchamber was set on a corner. Felicity first chose the view of the front, to see what a king might, and saw a pristine lawn that rolled away from the front of the house, down to a grove of ancient oaks clustered like dowagers near the foot of the long drive, a drive lined by topiary, ornamentation most commonly found in formal gardens at the rear of the house. Near the front door was the expected circular drive that encompassed a swathe of grass and contained the usual fountain, which did not feature diffident nymphs or cherubs bearing pitchers but a menagerie that appeared to be capering about in the water: small beasts the like of cats and trout coexisted with a horse, several large dogs, and a bear.

"But I am not a guest. I have been carried here against my will." Dazzled by eiderdown and silken robes that smelled as enticing as the duke himself, she forced herself to remember that she had been stolen from a *ton* ball and spirited into the depths of Surrey. Why should a peer of the realm kidnap a woman to wife? Someone as stunningly attractive as he ought not need to resort to larceny to procure a duchess. Gossip had likely broken out like a riot in the Seven Dials the minute it became apparent that she and the duke were not going to reappear from behind the palms. And Rollo had surely been watching her like a hawk, ready to carry the tale to her uncle.

Well, she wasn't going to hang about like a milk-and-water miss! Never mind that she was being attended like a queen. She would write to Jemima and let her know that she was alive and well. She doubted that her friend could mount a rescue party; her movements were severely circumscribed by her draconian aunt, by whom Felicity had not been received. In the light of day, her uncle would do nothing to aid her. Rollo would be enraged by the possibility that he may be tarnished by her infamy. Dare she write to Cecil? He might be her only hope. She could call upon their childhood friendship and ask that they put the recent past behind them. All she needed was someone to come and fetch her away from this place, as she doubted the duke, having gone to absurd lengths to bring her here, would blithely turn over a coach for her disposal… But Cecil was such a ditherer, he might leave her here until she'd turned old and gray and presented the duke with heir, spare, and who knows how many children. Even if her cousin bestirred himself to liberate her from Lowell Hall, she'd still be ruined. She doubted he would wish to align himself to a scandal.

"Kidnapped. It's so romantic." Mary's enraptured voice echoed out from the bathing chamber.

Felicity turned to yet another window and found the view from the side restricted by an enormous box hedge that ranged uninterrupted toward a wood. She had expected to see an ornamental pergola, perhaps, and instead it was as though she was looking at a barrier. Located as they were at a height, despite the masses of shrubbery, she saw the sparkle of a river or brook and also spied the barn, set well away from the house.

"I'll want to visit the stables," she mused aloud. "The duke was hard on his cattle last night."

The little maid popped her head around the doorframe. "Oh, Yer Grace, O'Mara would have sorted them out right and tight—"

"Mary!" At Mrs. Birks's reprimand, back Mary popped, and the sound of rushing water ceased. Mrs. Birks gestured to the door of the bathing chamber, and Felicity went in. It was glorious, covered from floor to ceiling in colorful painted tiles, and the water smelled of—"Vanilla and rosemary," Felicity exclaimed. "My favorite scents."

"His Grace told Mr. Bates, I heard 'im say it was like to your scent—"

"Mary!" roared the housekeeper from across the suite.

"—like to the perfume you were wearing, like, and so I thought of this all myself." Mary's face flushed bright pink from the thrill of her own initiative as well as the rebuke from Mrs. Birks. "And I pinched some o' them Epsom salts from the stillroom. You'll never have such a bath in all your born days."

"Thank you, Mary, you've done so well."

Mary beamed like the sun and began to bob up and down in an endless curtsy. "My pleasure, Your Grace. Thank you, Your Grace."

"I am not Your Grace," Felicity said gently. Duchess though she may not be, there was no need to be ungracious. Mary rolled her eyes and tested the water one last time.

"There you are, mum, there you are..." Mrs. Birks set out several towels that looked to be the length and breadth of the bedsheets and fussed with soaps and hand cloths. "I'll have a root 'round the attics for an article more feminine for you to wear."

"Pity you can't wear that banyan," Mary offered. "It's only doing wonderful things for your figure. I do be wondering why the ladies go about in them dresses that cover up everything but the bosoms, not that your bosoms should be hidden away at all—"

"Mary! I apologize, mum, she's only green, and she does like having opinions."

"That is quite all right, I prefer opinions to pelisses." Felicity looked at the water, at the depth of the bath, and the spaciousness of the room and suspected she was purposefully being beguiled by luxury. She dug deep for fortitude. "Mrs. Birks, if you would be so good as to fetch me paper, pen, and ink. If I am to be imprisoned in this house, then I must insist I be given leave to tend to my correspondence."

"Eh, now, ma'am, that wouldn't be in my bailiwick, no it wouldn't," the housekeeper said. "That would fall to our butler, Mr. Coburn, and it wouldn't be proper for him to wait upon you, in your dishabille and all."

"O'Mara can bring them right along," Mary said and earned a vicious snarl from Mrs. Birks.

"How handy it is to have a female chamberlain about the place," Felicity replied and, to placate the housekeeper, added, "I must not waste the lovely bath you've both gone to such trouble to prepare for me."

"Now!" A relieved Mrs. Birks scooted Mary out the door. "That there spigot is for the hot water, and that is for the cold. We'll leave you to your privacy for there's no need for a maid laying on the water. Just pull the bell if you need anything, anything at all."

"You are most kind, Mrs. Birks, and run a flawless household."

The good lady gasped and dashed out the door with a loud sniff, as though she were about to cry.

Felicity had heard of Epsom and their famous salts; was the market town near to the duke's holdings? Closing the door behind her, she decadently let the dressing gown drop to the floor, her chemise following hard upon it, and eased herself into the tub, a full-length affair she'd never imagined could exist. She sighed as the soothing scents teased her senses, and the salts softened the water until it was as luxurious as her pillowslip. For a moment, she betrayed herself in her mind, certain she could become accustomed to such sumptuousness, but then sternly turned her thoughts to escaping.

Or tried to. Where was His Grace? Not that she wanted him walking in the door at that precise moment. She sank down in the bath, mortified. Had she been ruined without being *ruined* and then abandoned? If so, she'd find a way back to Finsbury Square, and with bowed head, she would throw herself on the mercy of Uncle Ezra until such time as the will came good and she would be free. She could face down the whole world once she had her inheritance. The niggle of worry that it all was too good to be true reared its ugly head. She must hold fast and trust, somehow, in a father who had proven so untrustworthy in the last years of his life. And write yet another letter to that law firm.

But until then, what harm was there in indulging in a heavenly bath and dreaming of an alluring, if larcenous, man? A daydream was not capitulation; it was not an acceptance of a yet-to-be-proffered proposal. Would he actually propose, like in a novel, on one knee? Why should he, when he'd simply taken her? Why had he taken *her*, of all the women on the Marriage Mart, in society—in the world? She moaned, and the sound echoed off the tiles. How could this be happening to her, she who had never acquired a suitor, or even one bouquet, in five years?

She curled up on her side, luxuriating in the warmth of the water. In the absence of the duke, his domicile was doing its part in seducing her. The length of the tub was unlike anything she'd ever thought possible, allowing her to recline fully and submerge herself. It was so deep that the water came up to her chin, uniformly hot to the absolutely perfect degree, and the salts had a calming, relaxing effect upon her person.

Her attention drifted not to the perfidy of the duke but the duke himself. And That Chest. And voice. His prowess in the waltz. The way he'd run his nose over her cheek. How could he not have kissed her then, out on the terrace? Did she still want to be kissed by him? She snorted, then laughed at the sound echoing around the room. She did want to be kissed by him, abduction or no. The very notion that he'd carried her into the Hall and up the stairs to the state bedchamber was enough to make her swoon. She rolled onto her back and ran her hands down her body, closing her eyes as though it might help her pretend she wasn't going to do what she was about to do. Her skin had never been so soft, and emboldened by the privacy, the buoyancy, the warmth, her hand found her most sensitive place. She tipped her head to the side and leaned it against the lip of the tub, her body arching, recalling the heat of the hand that stroked her back during that waltz, the tickle of breath on her cheek, the strength of the arm that carried her through the Livingstons' garden. She sighed and sank a little deeper in the water as her legs parted, moaned as the water lapped around her, adding to the sensual pleasure as she built and built toward her release—

————————

The bouquet Alfred had assembled with his own two hands trembled in his grasp. All that time wasted perusing the offerings of his conservatory when he could have been enjoying his mate enjoying her bath. Prepared to commence courting, he had arrived despite being told Miss Templeton was at her ablutions. Had he hoped that he might catch her, awash in bubbles, soaping one of her long legs? Did he imagine that she would gasp, then smile at him seductively and invite him to join her? When had he become so adept at deluding himself?

His senses had begun to quiver even before he'd crossed the threshold to the bedchamber and were now in utter disarray as he scented Miss Templeton's arousal, heard her breathy moans and the water slapping up against the sides of the tub. He leaned his forehead against the door, tempted to take himself in hand—better he do that than succumb to a Change, as his wolf fought him for primacy. His bones began to creak and crack with the impulse to cede to his wolfskin, and he growled. An agitated splash of water answered him—had Miss Templeton heard? As she settled once more to her task, he controlled his breathing as best he could, but he soon began to breathe in tandem with her as she pleasured herself. Her moans escalated, surely she was nearing *le petit mort*, and fur exploded along his neck; he snarled at his wolf louder than was prudent—

"Hello?" came a muffled query.

He snarled again, helpless to keep his wild nature in check. The sound of water surging as she rose from her bath was too much for him. He backed away, imagining her naked form, water sluicing down over the delectable curves—the stems of the flowers broke in his grasp, and petals rained down onto the carpet as he charged out of the room.

———————————

"Hello?" Blast! She'd been so close to her climax, but she'd sworn she heard a sound like an animal would make, a growl, at the door. Were there dogs let run about the house? It was no lapdog that made that noise; it was throaty and feral and deep.

Drying herself quickly, she wrapped herself in the duke's dressing gown and went out into the bedchamber. Miss O'Mara stood on the threshold, surrounded by crushed and broken flowers.

"Miss O'Mara?" Felicity gestured at the blooms at the woman's feet. "Is this some strange custom observed in these parts?"

She reckoned that the composed woman was rarely caught on the hop; she looked nonplussed now. "I will have Mary Mossett clean this up directly, Your Grace."

"I am not Your Grace!" Felicity channeled her frustrated bath play into this explosion. "I demand to see the duke." She strode over to the chamberlain, whom she saw was well more than a hair over her own great height, and O'Mara was leggy with it. Which was easy to ascertain due to the trousers. "He has not shown himself, and it is well past the noon hour. If this is ruination, Miss O'Mara, I'd as soon have stayed at home."

O'Mara took one of her mollifying breaths, as she had in the coach, and Felicity cut her off with a look. She wasn't sure what they were in aid of, but she didn't like them. O'Mara bowed her head and asked, "May I set these down for you?" She held up the writing materials Felicity had requested. The chamberlain turned in the doorway and gestured toward the sitting room. "Will this escritoire do? There is more than one in this suite, and I would be pleased to exchange this for another."

Felicity, feeling like she was being herded by a sheep dog, preceded O'Mara over to a desk that was no escritoire: it was the size of a dining table. "I cannot imagine that you would move this on your own."

"I would do my level best, Your—Miss Templeton. As all here are eager to do, in whatever fashion you require."

Felicity sat at the desk. "All but His Grace," she muttered. She pushed a pen around on the blotter—even the blotter was of the finest paper, paper she would have hoarded for special use.

O'Mara touched her chin to her shoulder. "Your Gr—Miss. I overstep even as I say this, but His Grace is…he has many…there are things…"

"Is a busy man, with many other responsibilities and there are things I don't understand? What I don't understand, *Miss* O'Mara, is what this farce is in aid of. Based on the appearance of these rooms alone, my meager legacy from my grandmother cannot be required. If the household is wanting for a woman's touch, mine is not so practiced that I would contribute anything of note. His Grace does not lack in personal appeal and could marry the Queen of Sheba did he so desire. There is no need for me at all."

O'Mara exposed her neck again and dipped into an abbreviated bow. "May I respectfully exhort you to patience? In the general run of things in high society, the whole of the day would go by before you would see His Grace."

"Were we married which we are not."

"Not yet, madam," the chamberlain muttered.

"I do believe my consent is required under such circumstances."

"It is, if you choose to consent to preserve your reputation. We are dealing with the *ton*, madam, after all. Under these circumstances, you and he would wed before the full turn of the moon."

"Even the worst rake in the *beau monde* would not hold me here against my will." *And what matter the moon made, she was sure she did not know.*

O'Mara winced but soldiered on. "I beg that you bide a while until he—until he adapts to the novelty of this situation? I have served the dukedom for several years, and you are the first—he has never—"

"Surely you jest." The duke had never—*ever*?

"Not *that*, Your Gr—he is of course a healthy male in his prime. What I mean to say is, he has never courted anyone, and it is true that his technique leaves much to be desired."

"Such as his presence. And what I assume was a floral tribute." Felicity rose and went to yet another window, blushing to think he may have heard her in the bath. Was it he who chased the animal away from the door? "Not that I have agreed to be courted."

"There is nothing you can do about it," O'Mara said. "But *how* you do nothing will make all the difference."

"What a conundrum, Miss O'Mara." And another conundrum: underneath her high dudgeon and righteous anger thrummed the paradoxical worry she would have to stay at Lowell Hall and that she would have to go. Distracted as she might be by impressive bedding and bathing chambers and determined to rebel against their charms, the realistic part of her knew what the laws of society were. A ruined miss must wed the ruining man. Would this prevent the terms of the will coming good if scandal was attached to her name? Would the duke at least let her keep her mother's horses? She could flee to Templeton House, if it wasn't far away. From her new vantage point, she could see the distant stream more clearly. "Is that by any chance Edenbrook?" Felicity asked.

"Yes," O'Mara confirmed. "But it is five miles to Edenbridge from here."

Drat. That was two hours' hard ride, if one was escaping, and she would never ask that of a horse she didn't know. "One wonders if, by some strange chance," Felicity mused, lightly sarcastic, "the duke's lands march with mine. If his holdings are so vast as all that."

"They are vast," O'Mara replied. "But any other queries must be put to him."

"Perhaps I may broach the subject over the evening meal. Will His Grace attend? I shouldn't like to assume he hasn't some other pressing business."

O'Mara nodded. "We will all be present."

Whoever "all" are, Felicity thought. "It is hard to fathom that little stream is cousin to the mighty river Eden," she said, and O'Mara did not remark the change of topic. "It ran along our northeastern border, and on the hottest days, my mother and I would spend hours on its banks, picnicking and bathing and reading and…" She would not cry. She hadn't cried in years, and she would not now, not in front of a virtual stranger. She clutched the dressing gown close to her throat and for the first time found O'Mara's silent presence to be calming. Felicity breathed and breathed, in tandem with the chamberlain, and came back to herself, strong and calm.

She turned from the window and sat at the desk. "I have several letters to write, and I insist they be delivered."

"It will be done." Miss O'Mara dipped her chin again. "Your

clothing is even now being seen to," she continued, "and if you would, please remain in these rooms until the first gong?"

Felicity smiled brightly. "Naturally. I am a captive, am I not? May I expect a serving of bread and water at some stage? Or some thin gruel?" She held up a hand, forestalling yet another appeasement. "One or two of my missives will require express delivery, if you would return in an hour? Thank you ever so much."

O'Mara bowed at this dismissal, and Felicity set to trimming a pen, adding a note to Aherne and Bailey to her list, to caution them to move Himself and the mares to the holiday field until further notice.

Six

IN EZRA PURCELL'S STUDY, A LONE LAMP AND A STINGY FIRE
were lit, resulting in a deep gloom that seemed to hold its occupants close, in secret. Cecil Purcell sat on his hands so he would not wring them, for doing so annoyed his father. How lucky that he and his brother were seated: often, they were made to stand before Father's grand desk, as though they were still mere boys, about to be scolded for some infraction or other.

Times had not changed to any great degree.

"I was bringing Waltham to waltz with her," Rollo whined. He slouched in his chair in a manner he no doubt considered cosmopolitan and devil-may-care; Cecil thought his brother looked like a drunkard slumped in a doorway. "It is Cecil's fault that Felicity was taken by that duke."

"How can that be, brother?" Cecil rocked on his hands, finding for once that they wished to curl into fists rather than flutter in confusion. It was his lot in life to play second fiddle to his older brother, to be his whipping boy and toady. Of late, after a lifetime of such a role, he found he tired of it. What if he rose up from his chair and planted Rollo a facer? Wouldn't that be shocking? And wouldn't that entertain Father, to watch while Cecil got a pasting on the carpet before the hearth? He would likely be more fearful the carpet would stain from the blood than that his youngest son would come to harm.

It was a harsh thought, but his father was a harsh man. Most of the time. Had he not bought his sons' way into high society via Eton and used Felicity's title to further that way? That would appear to be a loving, paternal deed, ensuring they had the best start in life. Unless it had been done out of spite. Father knew the *ton* despised incomers. How he and Rollo fared, thrown to the wolves, was not his concern.

"Had you been attending, you might have stopped him," Rollo sneered.

"I? The youngest son of a Cit? He would not have seen me, much less heeded me," Cecil muttered. "And why should it fall to me, when you were on the very spot when it occurred."

"It's always down to me, is it not? Find a proper partner for Felicity, escort said partner to her, proffer introductions…" Rollo slouched even further into the chair. "I have to do all the work."

"Where had you been, Cecil, if not doing your part to tend to your cousin?" His father's voice was at its most terrifying when he rendered his queries softly.

"I was squiring Miss Smythe-Watson about the ballroom." His father would be delighted to know he was close to making an alliance with a debutante who had ten thousand pounds a year—

"You will cease your pursuit."

"I had thought that securing her hand would please you," Cecil began.

"You will not offer for her. You ought to have been doing your part to ensure your cousin's failure in society, but you were not. I wonder why."

"But…I thought we were meant to bring her about so we may partake of the Marriage Mart?" Cecil assumed he and Rollo were meant to be shopping for wives. Why send them out amongst the *ton* if they were not to marry advantageously? Had he not been doing what he was told?

Cecil's nails bit into the leather cushion beneath him and found little purchase, much as he had little purchase on his day-to-day life, with the ever-changing criteria and goals of his father's oversight. He set brother against brother, ensured they had plenty to fight about, then berated them for fighting, fixed them impossible goals, and withheld promised rewards when achievements were made.

Most of all he dangled the family business before them, with the promise of following in his footsteps, thus irritating Rollo, who as eldest believed it was his inheritance and his alone, and frustrating Cecil, who in fact had an aptitude for the work. And yet, Father would not countenance they do more than sweep the floor, an indignity that he claimed was to teach them from the ground up, which made no sense. At least, not after six years of doing so.

"Alas," said Father, "your cousin's fate is all but sealed. And the thing to ensure it would be for the tale of her ruination at the hands of the Duke of Lowell to range far and wide."

"Gossip?" Rollo asked, looking intrigued.

"How odd we should look, to be telling tales on our own family member," Cecil said.

"Lament, you fool," Ezra rasped. "'How could this have happened to us,' et cetera."

"Bemoan her fate," added Rollo. "Express regret that she is nothing more than used goods at this juncture. It has been all of twenty-four hours. Quite a lot of ruin can transpire in that time."

"I fancy going about a bit myself. My friend General Smithwick has been desirous of my presence whilst out and about. I believe I will grace him with my company." Father chuckled. "I should like to see her suffer the cut direct once it is known that she will not marry the duke."

"Won't she?" What choice did she have? Cecil often thought he had as little choice as Felicity did, when it came down to it. "Has he not offered for her?"

"Oh, he has." Ezra held up a letter. "Here is his request for your cousin's hand." He trundled over to the hearth and tossed it on the low flames; it flared once, twice, and the fire consumed the proof of Lowell's intent. They watched it burn. "Who would countenance that a duke would offer for a mere honorable? One who is less than Incomparable in feature and form as is your cousin? The Quality can be as ruthless in matters of breeding as I am in business."

"Will he not expect a reply?" Cecil feared his father, but the idea of the wrath of a duke terrified him.

"He may wait until the cows come home," Father said. "Peer of the realm or no, he is naught but a man. Oh!" His voice reeked of insincerity as he made a show of picking up a letter off his blotter. "This arrived express delivery. How costly. It is addressed to you, Cecil. From Lowell Hall."

"From the duke?" Why in the world would the Duke of Lowell correspond with him?

His father looked at him as though he'd grown another head. "It is from your cousin."

"Idiot," spat Rollo, who appeared irritated to have been overlooked by the postman.

"Oh." Cecil rose and took the letter. "What has Felicity to say to me?"

"Perhaps she has always found you sympathetic to her goals?" Ah, so Father did know they had once been friends. They had not often met—Father had a hatred for Uncle Benjamin—but when they had, he remembered warm, welcoming hugs from his aunt and an ally in Felicity against Rollo's bullying. His fond memories of the few visits to Templeton House were studded with feeding carrots to horses and running through fields, poking about his cousin's hiding places in the house's park and in the barn, free and full of joy. Rollo, outnumbered, had most certainly carried tales and thus had ended a budding friendship, as they were soon banned from visiting. Father intimated that Felicity had complained about the boys. She would never have done. Would she? He should know better than to believe his father. Should he not?

"What goals could a mere woman have?" Rollo huffed.

"I know nothing of her dreams or desires," Cecil said and felt like the lowest of the low. For it was true. What sort of man was he, who neglected an orphaned cousin, who exchanged the barest of pleasantries when they did finally meet? He was no sort of man at all.

"Perhaps she is looking for an ally under this roof?" Father asked. "Seeking communication from that solicitor she's been hounding about her father's will?"

"She never spoke of the will to me." This was true; after his initial shunning of her, thanks to Father's orders to remain cold and distant, they had not spoken of anything of substance. His shame increased, and he dreaded what he would find in her letter.

"I had an arrangement with Waltham, damn it to hell, thirty percent of her portion," said Rollo. "She's ruined my chances with that Ashworth chit. I'll never be able to afford her now."

"But Felicity has no portion, so you've lost thirty percent of nothing," Cecil said.

"No, fool," said Rollo, "she's to inherit everything if she marries, but only before her birthday."

"No, *you* fool," rejoined Cecil, "she's to receive nothing if she does marry before she's to turn twenty-five. She's got nothing."

"She's got everything. A title, a fine house, those thorough-breds…" Rollo sunk further in his chair and started chewing on his nails.

"She's to lose it all, isn't that so, Father, if she doesn't marry? And that's why she won't marry the duke?" Cecil's nose twitched in honest confusion. Neither version seemed plausible, as a woman was not to own property or inherit anything of consequence. If *he* knew that, then surely his cousin did—although her ability to see the best in all things and to charge heedlessly forward when it came to goals and challenges was a hallmark of her youth. He doubted she had changed much at all.

"All that matters is that Father knows the truth of the situation," Rollo said. "Perhaps we can sell off those beasts for a tidy sum."

"About those beasts…" His father returned to his grand chair and settled behind the desk. "Something must be done about them."

"They are undisciplined and dangerous," Rollo agreed.

Cecil snorted, ever so quietly. How frightened Rollo had been of them; one of the mares in particular, with the Biblical name, had taken his brother into extreme dislike.

"Your cousin thinks I am unaware of their presence on Templeton land and of her several hiding places. They must be found. And then they must be destroyed."

Cecil protested. "But our aunt loved them."

"Never speak of her! Those damned horses killed her as surely did that imbecile she married, allowing her the means to assemble such an ungovernable group." Enraged, his father loomed over him. Cecil chose to remove his hands from hiding and wrung them with vigor, adding fuel to his father's fire.

"I believe they are called a herd. Or a band. The horses." What was he doing? This was madness! And yet, for good measure: "Felicity would know the correct terminology. She always loved them. Do you not think Aunt Anne meant for our cousin to take care of them?"

"Those animals do not deserve to live." His father had turned an alarming shade of red. "You will destroy them."

"Who?" Cecil gulped. "Us?"

"You." Father smiled at him, the callous smile that heralded no good to any who defied him. "Rollo will hire ruffians suitable to the task. You will plot the timing and the journey."

He laid out his plan, which negated anything Cecil might have conceived, something about guns and wagons and slaughterhouses. He watched as the flames fed by the duke's missive died down. This…this was not right. But if he did not carry it out, he would be disinherited. Was he even convinced he was inheriting anything? Rollo had found a series of wills, hidden not only in Father's study but also in his suite of rooms and his office at the smelting premises. Cecil suspected they were red herrings: he wouldn't put it past Father to leave a trail of false hopes for them to find and follow, to divide and thereby conquer his sons.

What if it was true, that Cecil was indeed set to inherit fifty percent of Purcell and Sons, and he risked all to side with his cousin? But she was for all intents and purposes a duchess, was she not? Felicity was so stubborn, though—leave it to her to buck convention, refuse the duke and thus embark on a life cast out from society, to become even more powerless than she already was.

Should he write to her, warn her there was a dastardly plan afoot? That would be a bold move. He could send a letter saying to hold fast, written in code! He gasped, and Rollo and Father laughed, both likely thinking they had shocked him with their cleverness. But he could be clever! To send word but disguised so his father wouldn't devise its meaning when he read it before sending it on its way? He might tell Felicity to keep the faith until he knew more. And then *she* might reply and tell him in confidence how she planned to proceed, whether she was to be elevated in her station, and thus settle his mind as to the gamble he was taking.

He wrung his hands in earnest. If only he knew what to do.

Seven

FELICITY STOOD BEFORE THE CHEVAL MIRROR, SLIGHTLY DIS-
comfited. This was the same dress she'd worn to the ball, and yet
it had been transformed in ways that were flattering, if not at all
the done thing. The neckline had been lowered and expanded so
it sat on the edges of her shoulders. This adjustment meant her
sleeves now rested on her upper arms without pinching them; the
addition of a gentle ruffle rippled to meet the tops of her gloves.
Most scandalous of all was the long sash now attached just above
her hips: when she wound it around and around, it drew attention
to her bosom above it and her hips below it in a way that made her
feel wanton and exposed.

It also made her waist look…small. She swayed in front of the
mirror, to and fro, watched the skirt billow around her toes, her
shoulders catch the light and gleam, the shadow of her cleavage
shift, mysterious. But that waistline! She couldn't take her eyes off
it. It seemed ridiculous that she would not have noticed that she
had one at all, much less how it created such stark contrast to the
curve of her bosom and her hip.

She swirled in a circle. Would the duke's eyes take on an extra
sparkle when he beheld her? Would he rise out of his chair like
a besotted gentleman, eyes on her and her alone, dazzled by her
elegance? She stepped back from the glass and curtseyed as one
ought to one of his rank, down on her back heel, all the way down
to the floor, a challenging posture she assayed ably thanks to her
fitness due to horse riding. She rose as smoothly as she descended
and regarded herself in the mirror, a thing she had more often
than not gone out of her way to avoid. Should she wear Jemima's
designs? It made less difference than ever to her reputation, and if

she was this confident in a refigured gown of her own, then would not a Coleman original lend her even greater countenance?

Mary rushed in and came to a stuttering stop. "Ohhhhhh, Your Grace! You'll shine everyone else down, down all the way to China."

"I feel rather overdressed," Felicity said.

"Oh, no, ma'am, the duke does always be dressing for dinner like Prinny himself was coming to join him." Mary took a turn around Felicity. "Now, I'd thought the sash might be that bit too long, but it is perfect."

"Did you make these alterations, Mary? They are quite seamless."

"I'm sure I don't know what that means," Mary replied, blushing. "But I did a wee bit of nipping here and tucking there. That ruffle on the sleeve, it's like a wee cloud blowing by in the summer sky." She reached out and tweaked it, just so, and bobbed a belated curtsy.

"You have a rare gift." Felicity regarded the little maid; how could she help to nurture such a talent? She'd never had to think of such a thing before, but she knew, in her heart, that it was the correct thing to do. "My dear friend, Lady Jemima Coleman, is a talented fashion artist. I must be sure to effect an introduction at some stage."

"Thank you, Your Grace, I don't know what to say, and me ma would be the first to say that is as rare as a blue moon." She checked the nearest windows were shut and fussed with the curtains. "And talking of, there's the moon, almost all the way back in the sky," she said, pointing out the waxing moon through the windowpane. "Only ten more days to the Feast of Lupercalia, Your Grace, it's very exciting."

"The feast of…that sounds rather pagan. Is it common to these parts?" While they had nothing the like in sleepy Edenbridge, many country folk held to the old ways.

Mary turned a bright red and worried her bottom lip with her large front teeth. Her nose twitched in agitation. "It is common to, eh, here, so it is. If I do say so, Your Grace, you are all the crack, and that neckline is doing wonders for your bosoms."

Felicity turned back to the glass to regard said bosoms. "It is," she said. "It is not quite the style that is popular."

"Oh, my lady, it is yourself who'll be setting the fashion, make no mistake."

"This feast, Mary—"

"May I fetch that letter down to Mr. Bates for you?" The little maid nipped over to the mantelpiece.

"Oh, thank you, but I am sure I can carry that myself." Mary's tireless activity made Felicity feel rather giddy.

A discreet knock sounded.

"That'll be a footman to show you down."

"I am happy to follow you—" But Mary had run to the door and flung it open.

The footman standing at attention on the threshold was not in the usual run of specimen fulfilling that role. Small and thin rather than large and muscular, he looked to be sinewy and fleet, and for some reason, Felicity decided he also looked...shiny. His bald head glistened, and his protuberant eyes were pale and bright. He bowed with fluid grace.

"Good evening, Your Gr—" He cut himself off at Felicity's upraised palm. "If you will follow me, I am to escort you to Mr. Coburn, the butler of Lowell Hall. He would have come to collect you himself, but he is suffering from a condition brought on by him not being a spring chicken any longer." He flashed a smile, his pointy teeth gleaming.

"How may I address you?"

"I am Shaddock, Your—ma'am."

He bowed as she passed him in the doorway and hurried to precede her down the hall. The corridor sported oaken paneling

the like to be found in a medieval manor, and everything that decorated it, from the side tables to the runner to the paintings on the
wall, spoke of age and wealth. As they made their way down one
staircase to another, Felicity noticed that an inordinate number of
the paintings featured wildlife. She paused before a wide canvas
that appeared to represent the Bible story of Noah, except the animals were neither ascending nor descending the ark but instead
were gathered before it as though posing for the artist.

"This way, miss—ma'am," Shaddock gestured down the stairs
and seemed to have broken out into a light sweat.

"An interesting treatment of the Old Testament tale," Felicity
said.

"Oh, well, don't know much about art, me." Shaddock gurgled an awkward laugh. "I'd be in deep water did I try to turn my
thoughts to culture and suchlike. Ha ha." He darted down to the
next landing, and Felicity followed decorously behind.

———————————

"Come," Alfred called, at the knock on his study door. He, who
should have been ensconced behind his desk familiarizing himself
with yet more paperwork or possibly relaxing in one of the large,
comfortable chairs by the fire, was prowling the edges of the room.
It was clear his wolf was on the brink of revolt, if Bates's expression
was any indication. His Beta had paused in the doorway as if afraid
his own creature would be set off by Alfred's.

"Another missive to be posted for Miss Templeton," he
announced, and Alfred waved him in. Bates handed the letter over;
Alfred was tempted to read it but refrained. He would not betray
Felicity's confidence in such a craven way. Its address, a solicitor
in St. Giles, was all the information he required. He franked it and
put it in a small canvas sack that had straps affixed to it.

"I'll send Brindle, if that suits," said Bates, taking the sack, and
Alfred nodded.

"He seems in need of the exercise," he said. "All are excitable because she is here."

"And due to the fact that none of us have shifted today."

"Yes, yes." Alfred resumed stalking around the room. "Devise a schedule so everyone can take it in turn. Surely the small creatures have had the opportunity?"

"It's not the small creatures who will cause concern. A bird, a mouse, a cat…if seen, they would be of no consequence…" Bates trailed off. He cleared his throat. "If I may. It occurs that this will be the way things are for the foreseeable future unless you tell Miss Templeton our secret. The longer it is left unsaid, the more difficult it will be for the pack."

"I cannot risk her rejection of the bond." Alfred's pace became more frenetic. "Nor can I lie to her. I cannot settle, I cannot decide, for better or worse…" He barked a bitter laugh. "How like the human vows they make. For better or worse…" He turned to move in an anti-clockwise direction. "The pack members are handling it well." He would have known, thanks to the *sentio*, if anyone were in difficulty.

"Far better than I thought possible," Bates allowed. "It is helpful that you have not named her, ceremonially, as your *vera amoris*. Were you to invoke the *cognominatio*, the pack would be compelled to demonstrate their loyalty in their animal forms. Even now they are eager to welcome your mate with their complete selves, no matter the risk."

Alfred paused and turned to face his Second. "You do not agree with me. On any level."

"It is not my place." Bates looked as though he were bracing himself for suppression.

"It is exactly your place, Matthias." Alfred's intense energy increased, but not to the debilitating degree his Second had clearly expected. "What am I, what is the pack, without the insight you provide, without your strength and focus?"

"I cannot argue with the facts," Bates said, hesitant. "She does not fear you, she is already inspiring adoration in your people—"

"Almost all."

"—but there is the issue of O'Mara's inability to glamour her, which I do not understand and which worries me, and she is human, which unsettles me above all things. I cannot think on what happened in France during the Revolution, what happened to our kind at the guillotine, and fail to be concerned. They were betrayed by humans, sent to their deaths by humans. We do not know what her stance is concerning those who are unlike her. We risk all."

"It is time to risk all. After years of searching, I have found my mate here, close to home. She is not one of us. If she and the pack do not accept each other, then the pack will die out. I cannot allow that to happen, not after all the work we've done to build the community my parents would have destroyed with their lies.

"Matthias, I have never..." Alfred dropped into a chair, weary. "It is my strength that is drawn upon by all here, it is my wish that this be so, it is my responsibility. I do not show weakness because I do not have weakness, or have not had, until now. I am compelled to align myself with her desires, whether or not I desire to do so. Am I explaining this clearly? I cannot progress this with brute force. She is mine, and thus she matches me, regardless of her humanity. I find that I must give her power, make myself... open to her?"

"Eh, become vulnerable?" Bates looked dubious.

"Yes, and at the same time give her sufficient incentive to wish to make herself vulnerable to me." They looked at each other, baffled.

"Is this courtship?" Matthias asked.

"Perhaps?" Alfred rose and straightened his waistcoat. "My wolf is as out of patience as you are, my friend. He is clawing at me, howling to mate, and does not understand why my humanity is at the forefront of this undertaking. He cannot be made to wait much longer, and she cannot be forced into acceptance. I will begin, perhaps, to drop hints into conversation? I need to somehow wed animal urges with honeyed speech or all will be lost."

"I will do my best to divine a solution." Matthias showed his neck, not out of compulsion but out of respect and a masculine camaraderie.

"Should you discover one," Alfred said, "the male of every species will honor your name for all eternity." He strode from the room, and Bates set off to see a man about a wolf.

"Will there be many at the meal?" Should she ask this of a footman? They'd had very few at Templeton House at the best of times, and fewer still in the worst of times following her uncle's culling of the staff. She didn't know how to behave around servants, never mind ducal attendants.

"Many, but not all," Shaddock replied and did not elaborate. For galoshes sake, had everyone in Lowell Hall been schooled in equivocation, in elusiveness of response? She wouldn't surrender, but she would choose her battles, and this was an evasion she could overlook. It was unfair to pester the servants; it wasn't their responsibility to answer her queries, and she would be doodled—*damned*—if she'd be too much of a coward to go straight to the duke.

"Your Grace." A slightly barrel-chested man with incongruously slim legs stood at attention in the foyer, unprepossessing but for the great swath of hair that erupted from his pate like a coxcomb. "I am Coburn, the butler, and I must apologize for not greeting you in private."

"Good evening, Mr. Coburn." Felicity descended the last flight. "I am sorry to hear you are unwell."

"Not at all, Your Grace." He glared at Shaddock, who beat a hasty retreat. "It is nothing to speak of, Your Grace."

What could they all be thinking, addressing her as such? "Mr. Coburn, I do not bear that title."

"As you wish, Your Grace." He bowed with several odd jerks to his head, which set the folds of flesh beneath his chin to wobbling, then lead the way down another corridor. This was lighter in aspect but was as timeworn as the rest of the house. While the walls were not paneled in heavy wood, they were hung with fabrics in desperate need of a dusting or a disposal. Another painting caught her eye. "Mr. Coburn?" He turned, and seeing where she had stopped, blanched. "Are these wolfhounds?"

"They are, ma'am," Mr. Coburn replied. Like Shaddock, his brow erupted in dew. "Of a sort."

"I see." She blinked as if to draw the image into focus. "And are they playing piquet?"

"Eh." The butler gestured, then hopped several steps down the hall. "The Duke of Lowell has whimsical ancestors. Please, if you would follow me to the Bassett Room, Your Gr—ma'am?"

Felicity followed him to a spacious drawing room. A large, Brussels weave carpet spread across the floor, and a carved white marble fireplace glittered in the candlelight. While the tones in the room tended toward brown and beige, the drapes were a rich, cream velvet. From the doorway, she saw that the duke was already standing, dither it. She fussed with her gloves and smoothed the sash at her waist. A surge of nerves made her fingers tremble and her palms dampen in her gloves. What was she doing, going down to dinner as though she were merely paying a visit? What was she doing, wearing a gown that revealed her shape for all to see?

"May I say, ma'am, that you are a vision." Coburn bowed in that jerky way of his.

"You are most kind, Mr. Coburn," Felicity replied. Her nerves settled, and she smiled at him; he blushed a painful-looking scarlet.

Coburn entered the drawing room and cleared his throat. "Her Gr—Her Ladysh—"

"Miss Templeton will do, Mr. Coburn," she whispered.

"Madam," he hissed. "I could never—it's worth my life should I disrespect you in any way."

The duke came toward them, and nothing in his manner demonstrated that he had remarked the change in her dress. He looked as magnificent as he had the night before, dressed for the meal in black evening clothes, and if it was possible, this evening's Cravat achieved even greater Perfection. She curtsied, as she had in the mirror, to please herself alone, and as she rose, she noticed the butler was holding his head at that odd angle common to all in the Hall.

"I cannot help but observe, Mr. Coburn, that there is a stiffness to many of your movements," Felicity said. "May I offer a receipt for a poultice to Mrs. Birks, on your behalf? I perceive that many in this house suffer from a similar complaint."

"See to the drinks, Coburn," the duke interrupted, leading her over to a scattering of chairs. A scattering, as it seemed each had been dragged from all corners of the room into proximity to the hearth. Added to this, none of them matched: at least three were inappropriate for a drawing room and looked better suited to the breakfast parlor. Bates and O'Mara waited, both dressed with the same degree of ceremony as was the duke.

Mr. Coburn offered her a tot of sherry. She took it and set it down straightaway. "I am afraid I do not imbibe," she said. "Apart from a small glass of wine with dinner. I hope I do not offend."

"No." The duke gestured to a chair, an oversize affair that Felicity hoped she would not fall into and disappear. She perched on the edge.

"We, too, partake only at the meal, Miss Templeton," said Bates.

She folded her hands in her lap. "Had you a pleasant day, Your Grace?"

"Pleasant?" Alfred asked, as if unfamiliar with the term.

"Busy, then? For I saw neither hide nor hair of you." It sounded as though Bates muffled a laugh, and the duke's eyes sparkled.

"Busy, yes. Estate business and such." He had taken one of the spindly chairs, and it groaned as he sat back and crossed his arms. "Pack concerns."

Pack? As in packing...for transport? Or parcels? Felicity shook her head, confused. Yet another inscrutable comment to ignore. "I am conversant with the workings of an estate, although Templeton House is nowhere near as vast as this. We were concerned with animal husbandry. Is this humorous, Mr. Bates?"

O'Mara intervened. "Mrs. Birks mentioned your wish to visit the stables to His Grace, ma'am."

"They look very impressive," Felicity said. "And also very far away."

"You may make free with the cattle," the duke said. "They are used primarily for work and get little chance to stretch their legs in a hack."

"I would be delighted. And is there a specific reason that the yard is set so far from the house?"

"There is a reason," the duke replied. "It is specific." No further explanation was forthcoming.

Silence reigned. Once again, the onus of conversation fell onto her shoulders. The duke was sitting there, sending said shoulders smoldering glances. This made up in some small way for his lack of rapture when she entered the room. It was as thrilling as it was unnerving.

"I have never seen so many paintings of animals in one household," she began. "Mr. Coburn said something about your forebears."

Bates eyed Coburn. "I hope you were not led to believe the imagery was in any way familial."

"I do apologize, Your Grace," Coburn cricked his neck. "I did not intend to mislead you."

"Of course you did not, Mr. Coburn," Felicity assured him, and by extension the duke, who looked thunderous. "You said nothing but to note that His Grace had whimsical ancestors."

"A minor confusion," O'Mara said, taking a deep breath and exhaling.

Felicity turned the duke's attention to herself. "I must ask if you have heard from my uncle. While I would be shocked if he exerted himself on behalf of my honor, he is well aware of the workings of high society and would know my reputation is hanging in the balance."

"He works in the City, if I recall?"

"He is the smelting scion of all England. Pig iron, I believe. And yet he is quite au fait with the nuances of the Quality. His devoted absorption is infused with such scorn, it makes his fascination with the doings of the *ton* all the more perplexing."

"Then he will recognize the letter of intent I sent to him at dawn is as binding as a betrothal contract."

Then she was to be seduced but not abandoned? Relief coursed through her. *No, no, Felicity*, she scolded herself. *That is not your goal! Stay the course!* "As surely as you must recognize I am unwilling to enter into a betrothal, much less a marriage."

A clatter at the drinks table drew everyone's attention. O'Mara gestured oddly, almost as though she were addressing someone across the room, although no one was there. Felicity changed the topic once more and turned to the duke's steward. "Mary Mossett offered to deliver my letter into your hands, Mr. Bates."

"It has been sent directly," said the duke.

"On a night like this? With no moon to light the way?"

Those devastating crinkles appeared at the corners of His Grace's eyes. "My messenger has excellent eyesight."

"Is he a bat?" Felicity asked, incredulous.

"No, we've none of those at present." The duke appeared amused, again, about something she could not comprehend. "Although who knows what the future might bring." He changed the subject. "I noticed that the direction was that of a solicitor's office in St. Giles."

"It was," Felicity replied, deciding it was her turn to evade. "It appears we share a waterway, Your Grace. I wonder as to the distance between our family homes. Miss O'Mara was unable to inform me as to whether or not our borders march upon one another. It would be rather curious if they did so."

"Curious?"

"Or enlightening. In that my lands might be found to be very attractive. And substantial."

"Ah." The room became rather airless, in an instant, as it had in the coach. Felicity merely wished for a fan, but the others appeared to be severely affected: Mr. Coburn was doubled over the decanters, and both O'Mara and Bates froze in place, their faces etched with tension. "I have no need for your lands, Miss Templeton. Perhaps I can show you the extent of mine. What I want from you is rather different."

"A threat, Your Grace?"

"A promise, my dear."

"Which will be rendered meaningless, as it will not be honored." She could not, would not risk honoring it at the expense of her dream, though it would bring her name into disrepute and infamy.

His Grace stood. Bowing respectfully, which was unexpected given the tartness of her reply, he held out his arm. "If I may escort you in to the dining room."

"Should we not wait for the bell—" and Mr. Coburn rang the bell, with energy and not a small degree of desperate relief.

Eight

THE ROOM DESIGNATED FOR FORMAL DINING WAS VAST, AS WAS the custom in an antiquated hall, and yet was made cozy by the scores of candles burning and two enormous hearths blazing with roaring fires. Equally passé were the multitude of tables that, should there be a need, could assemble into one great length if the company was large. Tonight, a table that suited four sat at the center of the great room, which was sensible, being the number of those who were to dine. However, there were rather more than four present.

The floor was ringed by the inhabitants of Lowell Hall. Every servant, from Mr. Coburn to the boot boys, from Mrs. Birks to the scullery maids, stood at attention along the walls. And were those faces at the windows? Mary Mossett gave a little wave as the duke seated Felicity at the top of the table. Footmen took their places behind each of the diners, and Mr. Coburn pulled a bell rope.

Felicity smoothed the napkin the footman had placed in her lap, glancing around at the many faces looking at her with such welcome and joy. It was rather overwhelming, and she shifted her attention to the table settings, an ostentation of fine crystal and china, with a gleaming, silver bowl in the center holding clusters of sweet william. She looked up and saw the duke watching her, waiting for the moment she recognized the blooms, and gooseflesh coursed over her person. As ever, his eyes twinkled without the rest of his face showing any emotion. The company sighed as though they were privy to her feelings. She blushed and looked away.

Four more footmen strode into the room, each holding a covered bowl, which they placed with solemnity before the diners. They removed the covers, and a rich broth of beef was revealed.

Felicity, grateful that her mother had tutored her in the proper procession of cutlery, took up the correct spoon. The serving footmen retreated, and the original quartet replaced them, filling the wine glasses with a ruby-red vintage. She took a sip of soup and then a sip of wine.

"My compliments to the cook and the vintner," she said, and if it were possible, the smiles around the room widened.

"Mrs. Birks is responsible for the elder wine," said Mr. Coburn. "Our cook is French." This last was said with an absence of joy.

"He must, therefore, prefer to be addressed as chef?" Felicity asked and was answered with a pruney grimace and a violent wattling of the flesh beneath the butler's chin.

"Monsieur Louveteau has been a welcome addition to Lowell Hall," O'Mara said, and Coburn's expression softened.

"It would appear that the entire staff is here," Felicity said, smiling around at all, who appeared delighted to be standing in a circle around their table.

"Ours is an informal household," said the duke, as the serving footmen removed the first course.

"I beg to differ. All these footmen…" she said. "I doubt the prince regent himself has as many attending at table."

"This is not an ordinary occurrence, Miss Templeton, but one appropriate to the occasion," said Bates. Four different footmen appeared and presented each diner with a filet of beef.

"Would your own family have adhered to such high style, Mr. Bates?" Felicity cut into her portion, which gave like butter to her knife.

"Somewhat, Miss Templeton," the steward replied. "My father is the Earl of Rendall of Lincolnshire. I am the ninth of my family."

"What a lively home that must have been," Felicity said, with a wistful smile.

"It was," said the duke. "I fostered with Mr. Bates's family from the age of seven."

"Fostering? That is an old-fashioned practice. And Miss O'Mara?" Felicity inquired. "Is your family as large?"

"It is." O'Mara took rather a large draught of wine, earning a stern glance from the duke.

"Mine was not," Felicity said. "I was the only child and was not close to our extended families for the majority of my life. My father and my mother's brother were not on terms." Felicity was never this familiar with her story and found it strange that she had no compunction in sharing, and before such a crowd. In fact, it was as though a wave of something wafted over her, something like sympathy and comfort. "And by your accent, I conclude you are not from these parts?"

"I am from Ireland."

Felicity kept a look of interest on her face and waited for elaboration. There was none.

"Well." She looked up at the duke, who had devoured his course with speed. "Your Grace? What of your family?"

Tension rippled through the group standing witness, and Felicity held the duke's gaze as if it was the most important thing she'd ever done in life.

"I am the eldest. I have a sister." The footmen who had served the current course cleared the places. "My parents are…my father passed the dukedom on."

"I am sorry for your loss."

The duke hesitated, then elucidated, "He deferred it during his lifetime."

"Truly?" Felicity took another sip of the delicious wine. "I am by no means an expert on the laws of peerage, but is that permitted? I have never heard of such a thing."

"We are a special case."

"Interesting. May I ask, did the transfer require the services of a solicitor, Your Grace? I find I am in need of someone well-versed in unconventional procedures as regarding legacies—"

"You will have no need of the law going forward." His voice dropped, low and rough, and Felicity bristled even as the cohort tensed.

O'Mara took a deep breath; this was the usual cue for Felicity to interrupt the intervention, but as everyone around her relaxed, she allowed it. It was unfair to the staff to involve them in concerns private to her and His Grace.

The original footmen—at least they appeared to be taking turns, rather than expanding to an infinite number of attendants—set down a breast of fowl, fragrant with rosemary. Had this meal been designed expressly to her preferences? Felicity glanced at the duke, who was watching her again.

"You mentioned your family seat," he said.

"Yes. Templeton House, in Kent."

"Do you not reside there? I would have known—I would have paid a call. Had I known."

"I have been under my uncle's care since the death of my parents. Once it was decided that I would debut, I spent more time in Town than I did at home." She allowed the footman to replenish her wine but chose not to drink. "I find it difficult to fathom a duke calling upon a baron."

"I do not stand upon ceremony. In certain cases." The duke lifted his wine glass and touched the rim to his lips but did not drink.

"How enlightening. And what is the criteria for relaxing your standards?" She could feel the gazes of the servants following the conversation.

"When it suits me and all those under my aegis."

"How wonderful for those under you." What was so amusing about that, she'd like to know. She'd swear the duke came close to laughter.

"How did your parents die?" he asked. O'Mara coughed, and Bates winced.

"My mother was an avid horsewoman and fell in the hunt," Felicity said. "And my father later perished from the lack of her."

"They were a love match." The duke looked satisfied, and the room sighed as one.

"They were." Perhaps one more sip of wine would not go amiss.

"To be loved like that," said the duke, his voice hitting new depths of resonance. "It is a powerful thing, rare in any stratum of society. To be unable to bear being left behind."

Felicity carefully set down her wine glass. "Never mind that there was a daughter left to mourn them both, alone."

A ringing silence resounded, except for the audible breath that O'Mara took. Felicity thought the rush of grief and rage that coursed through her, even after all this time, would explode out of her like a ball from a cannon and decimate the gathering. She breathed in tandem with the chamberlain and calmed.

"The support of community is without price," the duke said.

Thinking of her herd, she agreed. "One cannot take for granted the benefits and joys of such."

"Nor the challenges," the duke supplied, and she smiled fully; the atmosphere lightened as though every window had been opened and a warm, spring breeze flowed in.

"Oh, the challenges," she agreed. "Your Grace, as regards community, Mary Mossett mentioned a feast, or a fete? A country fete? Something with a Latin name." A squeak sounded in the corner.

His Grace waved a hand. "It is like to Saint Valentine's Day, which is growing in popularity."

"Ah." Felicity blushed. "The fourteenth of February is in fact my birthday." A communal gasp resounded through the air; Bates looked at her in surprise, and O'Mara—of all things, the taciturn chamberlain threw her head back and laughed. "Miss O'Mara?"

"Many, many happy returns, Your Grace, in advance." She raised her wine glass in a toast.

"I don't understand the fuss that has sprung up around this single day," Bates grumbled, and the females in the room exchanged rueful, arch glances.

"It is a scheme on the parts of the confectioners and the printing industry," the duke groused. "I pay no mind to it."

Despite the roaring fires, the temperature in the room plummeted to freezing.

"In the past," O'Mara said, in her palliative voice, "our Alph—Alf, Alfred, Duke of Lowell, had no reason to honor the day, but the present is altogether changed."

The room seemed to hang on Felicity's next utterance. She waved away the wine footman and allowed the serving footman to take her plate and leave another course, which ought to have been fish but appeared to be venison; this was not the only curious thing she'd noticed about the meal. She sliced a portion, raised it to her lips, chewed, and swallowed. Only then did she respond. "One must often make allowances for the wishes of others, is that not so, Your Grace?"

"Possibly," he growled.

"It is often when one is at his most stubborn that it is necessary to compromise."

"Compromise." The duke made it sound like the foulest of epithets.

"I would argue that it is at such a juncture it is most necessary to do so."

"Is it."

"It is. I believe it provides one with the opportunity to build character."

"Such an undertaking requires change."

"It does." Felicity beamed.

"Do these notions apply only to contrived holidays? Or might they apply to fashion, for instance?"

Felicity paused with her fork halfway to her mouth. "Fashion?"

A rustle moved through those attending, and Bates took it in turn to clear his throat. "As in clothing?"

"As in following fashion, the ways in which the ladies of the *beau monde* are devoted to its dictates." The duke gestured in her general direction, and the crowd muttered amongst itself.

"I do not find myself unnecessarily following fashion and have my reasons for doing so when I do, which have nothing to do with blind devotion," she babbled. Did she not appear improved in this gown? Was that what he was implying?

"What reason could anyone have in following styles and modes that do not celebrate a particular form to its fullest expression?"

"You sound quite like my dear friend, Lady Jemima Coleman," Felicity said. She would not infer the worst in this line of conversation; she would not assume he referred to her shape—she would not. "Her Ladyship is a clandestine dressmaker, sub rosa due to her station in life, but more than that, she is an artist with fabric and texture. She is forever exhorting me to break away from the standard and claims to have designed and sewn an entire wardrobe for me."

The duke nodded at Bates, who rose and headed for the door.

"Informal, indeed." When she had become such a stickler for manners, she had no idea.

"Bates." The duke's tone stopped him in his tracks.

"I take my leave of you, Miss Templeton, and will return anon." Bates bowed and waited upon Felicity's nod before he once again made for the door. A heavy silence followed his departure. Her little dream of the duke's response to her new clothing disintegrated, and she found that this made her not a little bit furious.

She cleared her throat. "I find myself thinking to follow in Miss O'Mara's footsteps. Trousers look to be a comfortable way of going about."

"No." The duke's fingers flexed around the stem of his all but untouched wine glass.

"I would very much like to investigate this mode of dress."

"I repeat, no."

"You are not in a position to dictate to me."

"There are trunks of well-kept clothes in the attics, many never having been worn."

"You are apprised of the contents of ladies' trunks in the attics, Your Grace? How astonishing."

"They are at your disposal."

"I doubt they will suit me as my figure is not what is considered fashionable."

"Any one of the females in this house is nimble enough with a needle to do whatever it is needs doing, should there be a need for letting them out to make them larger—"

A piercing wail rang out from the one of the witnesses, accompanied by the explosive upset of O'Mara's wine glass and the rush of Mrs. Birks and Mr. Coburn to the table. Thanks to the chaos, the duke ceased his disquisition on the size of clothing she might require. A swarm of footmen cleared, and Mrs. Birks fussed, and Mr. Coburn ordered, and the servants rushed hither and yon, and Felicity was a still, calm center in the tumult, staring down the duke, daring him to pass another comment regarding her figure. She raised her eyebrows.

He shook his head and raised his brows in return.

She tilted her head at the crowd; he threw up his hands, bewildered. "I wonder," she said, changing the subject, "that there are no vegetables to accompany these delicious courses."

A small, wiry man burst into the room. "What is this mess that these louche footmen have brought into my kitchen? What has become of my *glacée du venaison*?"

"Out, Louveteau," hissed Mr. Coburn, flapping his arms. "Back to your spits and your pans."

"Louveteau," the duke said, "Her Grace was just commenting on the lack of vegetables in the meal."

"The wonderful meal," Felicity assured him. "The most extraordinary meal I have ever eaten. What a glorious way you have with a sauce, Monsieur."

"Madam." He bowed. "At last, a true palate shows itself in this blighted hall."

"If it's not too much trouble," Felicity continued, once all had calmed, "might a few greens accompany the courses? I have no thoughts as to such beyond a lowly bean or two. I fear such are far beneath the talents of a man of your experience, but perhaps a carrot dish or beets?"

"Whatever your heart desires, Your Grace," the chef bowed again, with greater pomp and circumstance. "I am your servant, your humble servant, in all things. I will produce only the most delicious, most healthful accompaniments of *les haricots vertes almondaise, les petits pois au buerre, gratin au—*"

"That will be all, Louveteau." The duke stood, against all protocol, which dictated the presiding lady at the table signal the end of the meal; O'Mara reached out and yanked him down into his seat. They exchanged volatile looks, and Lowell shrugged and slid down in his seat like a crotchety child.

As she was the only female of rank in the room, Felicity supposed it fell to her to decide the meal was concluded. She rose, a footman at her back in a heartbeat to slide her chair away. "Mrs. Birks, we will take tea in the drawing room, please. If you would be good enough to serve the dessert with it, Monsieur?"

The assemblage descended into curtsies and bows, like a field of wheat blowing in the wind. She stood and waited at her place. The duke rose, and wonder of wonders, his lips (Those Lips!) parted in the merest impression of a smile, revealing a hint of attractive teeth (teeth, attractive?), and the servants seemed to sway as one, to sigh as one, as His Grace approached her and held out his arm, as Felicity took it, and as they processed out of the room.

Alfred accepted Coburn's obeisance as he closed the door behind them.

"Will Miss O'Mara not be joining us?" Miss Templeton fussed with the tea things and rearranged the plates of tart and custard.

"She is off on an errand." Glamouring the poor, unfortunate animal Alfred would be riding in the next day or so as he escorted Miss Templeton around his grounds.

She set down the teapot with a testy thump. "This is improper. It's all improper, of course, but this compounds it. Your staff marches to the beat of their own drum, disappearing here, running off there."

"I allow them to obey their instincts."

"What ails their necks? Not only Mr. Coburn and Mr. Bates, but all down to the laundry girls persist in bending their heads at odd angles. It cannot be comfortable."

"May I have a cup of tea?" He put on what he thought was a humble mien.

"Are you unwell? You look bilious. I cannot be surprised, given the excess of meat at table." She poured a cup, without the usual flair found in ladies—not that he'd say so. "Lemon? Cream?" She put both in without waiting for his preference and all but thrust the cup and saucer into his hands. She moved away.

He set the concoction down on the tea cart and let her peruse and handle the china dogs decorating the mantle. "We are a carnivorous lot," he allowed. "But I believe Monsieur le Chef will bow to your dictates."

She mumbled something, and he was at her side. "Do excuse me, I didn't quite catch that." Which he had, naturally. Something about her dictates not being here to be bowed to for long…

"Never mind." Miss Templeton went back to the teapot and poured herself a cup. He rearranged the china dogs.

"There is only one outcome," he said. "You have been in Lowell Hall, unchaperoned, overnight, and into this day. You know the ways of our world."

"There must be some compensation made for a maiden who has been taken against her will."

"You are a maiden." He had never thought otherwise, but to hear her say it...

A blush not so much rose as exploded across her face. He watched it spread down to her décolletage. "Be that as it may," she said, "I cannot fathom why you, of all people, found it necessary to abduct a female in order to force her into matrimony."

He subtly scented the air. Still no fear, to his amazement; there was frustration to a great degree and curiosity tinged with something he could not put a finger on. "I, of all people?"

"One of the highest in the land, superseded only by the royal family." She looked at him, incredulous. "How is it that you have not been betrothed from the cradle, to one such as you?"

"None such as I suited me. You," he purred, "suit me."

"I do not understand how you know this, as you know nothing about me." She crossed her arms beneath her bosom, and he came over somewhat light-headed.

"Then do tell me about yourself, Miss Templeton." He gestured to the sofa behind the tea cart, and they both sat. "I assume you are accomplished as all young ladies are?"

"I am not so young. As Mr. Bates's précis demonstrated."

"It matters little in my world." A *vera amoris* would ever be fertile until such time as the need for progeny abated. "Are you fond of embroidery?"

"I am not. Nor am I at my best on the dance floor, as you well know."

He made to stretch an arm along the back of the sofa and subsided at her aggrieved look. "I know nothing of the sort. I have never had such a thrilling partner."

"You would be the first to claim such." She would tear that sash did she not desist in worrying it.

"I will throttle any and all who would have you believe the contrary."

Miss Templeton laughed, or tried to. "You would find no sport in taking on my cousins Rollo and Cecil, who would break into tears did you challenge them."

"They sound revolting."

"They are Odious and Querulous, respectively."

A shared smile. "I shall vouch for your dancing. Do you sing? Play the pianoforte?"

"Music to soothe the savage breast—beast—uh?" She leapt up and fled to a window, the cart teetering in her wake.

"Just that." He rose, as she had risen, but held his place.

"I have no talents in either direction." She fiddled once more with the sash that showed off her delectable waist. "I sketch," she allowed. "I am fond of drawing animals."

"Animals?" He pretended to scoff. "A lowly subject."

"I disagree. I find there is nothing nobler than the beasts of the field, the birds of the air. I admire their freedom to be themselves, despite many species having been domesticated by humans. I commend the way they take care of one another in their groups or herds." She peeped at him, hesitant. "I speak of horses, in the main."

"There is little that is natural regarding man's treatment of the horse."

"I do not disagree. Man owes civilization to horses and often repays them with mistreatment. I believe we can show true gratitude to the horse with conscientious husbandry. I believe our diligence in this matter will make the whole world a better place."

"A bleeding heart." He was baiting her, of course, and her defense of creatures both great and small thrilled him to the core.

"A beating heart, a heart that acknowledges the dignity of all sentient beings." Her hazel eyes glowed like topaz with her passion.

"Had they any will of their own, they would not allow themselves to become subjugated by us."

"I do not deny that there are many who would seek to subjugate so-called inferior creatures," Felicity allowed, "but those who are sensitive will garner only the best from the animals in their care. If only we would learn from them."

"A radical, bleeding heart."

"Better a radical than one who stands by and does nothing. Better a bleeding heart than one that has turned to stone." Miss Templeton scowled at him. "I know your kind, looking down on all around you, full of your position in life that was nothing more than an accident of breeding. Little separates you from the animals, Your Grace."

"Oh, very little indeed," he agreed, struggling to keep his composure. "But come, such a fuss over mere animals."

"Mere animals?" She very nearly shrieked.

He went to meet her fury. "For why would we, who have speech and independence, care for beasts of burden or common house pets?"

"If it is speech that elevates us, only recall the numberless times that words have caused ill. Only think what is being said about me at this precise moment and tell me that language is something to be proud of." Miss Templeton forgot herself so far as to fist her hands on her hips. "And as for free will? Those such as you, Your Grace," she spat, imbuing a world of spite in his title, "those in the upper echelons of society may consider free will their birthright, but the majority do not have that luxury. Why must one species be found superior to the other? Why can we not live in harmony? Why must our own baser instincts cause our animals to be abused? How simple it would be to change our behavior, to make a difference."

"It is all well and good my dear, but one woman? Make a difference? In the larger world?" By the Goddess, whatever she wanted, he would ensure she achieved it.

"Yes, one woman. One woman, who has the knowledge and the will. Knowledge and will are not the sole provinces of men."

"And what do you speak of, then?" he challenged. "Training house cats? Bringing dogs indoors?"

"Well," she hesitated. "Just for the sake of argument, mind. Horse breeding."

"A gentleman's time-honored pursuit—"

"A pursuit that has resulted in inbred mounts that, more often than not, do not live up to expectation and must be destroyed. Or result in unreliable beasts that end up hurting their riders or themselves." Miss Templeton stood near enough to him to bite him on the chin. "All it would take is the cross of stock in such a way that would guarantee the best of both will out."

"But, madam, how then would our equine friends acquire their mates?" Alfred inquired. "Do the studs apply to the fathers of the mares for the hands, or rather the hooves, of their intended?" He snuck a breath, inhaling her dudgeon, her ardency, her ferocity, and his wolf was like to howling at the full moon.

"Do not be ridiculous."

"Or do they see, and scent, and take?" He leaned in, all but whispering in her ear. "Do they follow instincts unknown to anyone but the stallion and mare involved? Is it the stallion's pursuit that inspires the mare or the mare's willingness to be covered that inflames the stallion?"

"You seek to discompose me." She blushed but held his gaze. "You are mocking my beliefs. You are mocking me." She turned to leave, and he stopped her with a hand on the slice of bare arm below her puffed sleeve and above her glove. "You mock me by keeping me here, as if the whole world would believe that you wanted me above all others. I will find a way to leave here and put this sham behind me."

He gripped her arm. "You will not leave me." The *dominatum* rushed through him and once again had no effect on her whatsoever. "We will marry, and not only because it is what society will demand."

"You may force me to the altar." Miss Templeton stuck out her chin in defiance. "But you cannot make me respond to the vows."

"What might you respond to?" He leaned in and ran his nose down her cheek, around her jaw. "This?" She shivered. "Ah, I do know something about you, after all—that a stroke on the cheek makes you tremble." He breathed in her scent and breathed out, gently, against her neck. "I was merely playing devil's advocate," he crooned as he let his lips touch her earlobe. "It was not my intention to mock you. I find your passion quite…stimulating." He felt her quiver, said, "Do pardon me," and kissed her.

———

Here was The Kiss Felicity thought was in store on the terrace last night, but to call it a kiss would be to call the Himalayas a hillock. The few she had received previously had been of the stolen variety whilst the thief was in his cups; even someone as untried as she comprehended the gulf between that pathetic past and his present prowess.

Lips that were firm yet inexplicably soft brushed hers, once, twice, then hovered, a mere breath between them. With an inhalation of expectation, she swayed, arrested, waiting. A hard, strong hand cupped her jaw, and she followed its direction to tilt her head just so. Those lips returned, brushing hers with greater intent, stroking them, beguiling them, coaxing her toward a great unknown. As Felicity parted her lips to take a needed breath, his tongue stroked hers and withdrew. Far from freezing in shock—well, in fairness, she was shocked, but it was the stimulating sort—Felicity discovered that the loss of his touch was insupportable.

When her tongue lightly touched his lower lip, a rumble rolled through That Chest—how had she gotten so close to it? Her bosom was crushed against it, and she could not recall experiencing a headier sensation. She also became aware that one of his hands was caressing her hair at the back of head, and the other was gripping her hip, his fingers stroking it, stroking the side of it, directly over her backside, very nearly stroking her bum.

He had answered her audacious sally and was now plying her mouth with his tongue, teasing it, and she somehow knew how to respond, to riposte, and as impossible as it seemed, she sank even further against his body. She shifted her hips and heard him groan, so she did it again and then slid a thigh in between his. Her mind reeled at the hardness she found there; in fact, her entire body reeled. Her arms—which she discovered had wound themselves around his neck—tightened, and she sank her fingers into his lustrous hair, then scraped her nails on his scalp, doing it again when he growled.

Gently, gently, he explored her mouth and encouraged her own explorations through moans and growls. As their breath became ragged, as his hand slipped to curve around her bottom, his other hand slipped down her back, slid up her ribs, ventured forward, and curved around her breast. It hovered, as though waiting for permission, which she granted by leaning into his grasp.

The arm around her waist was as though fashioned from steel, and she dangled on tiptoe as he ran his fingers over the skin above her gown's neckline, skin that was hot and flushed and needy. His fingers delved and caressed the top of her breast and edged closer to…closer to a part of her that had never felt a man's touch. She held her breath, her teeth biting his lower lip, and he plumped her breast, his thumb stroking her nipple, and the sound she made— she nearly sobbed from the effect it had upon her. A telltale dampness surged between her thighs, and she trembled, wanting, fearful, lustful. She trembled again and moved away from his touch.

As she did so, the duke did something altogether unexpected. He dropped his forehead to hers and stood there, both arms around her now, holding her, breathing as rapidly as she. She took a leaf from his tome and inhaled, scenting fresh linen, vetiver, the elder wine, and something else, something raw, something primeval and intoxicating.

"How I yearn to see this glory unclothed," he murmured. Any retort was lost in a sensual haze; while an appropriate rejoinder might run along the lines of, *How dare you, you shall never regard my unclothed self*, instead she thought, *Does he think me glorious? Glorious, not "substantial," not in need of outdated gowns that require letting out?* The hand that should slap his face was in fact cradling it while the other had moved to hang on to the Cravat of Perfection for dear life. The eyes that should have been shooting outraged glares fluttered closed as he reached up and traced a finger around her ear.

"There is no glory," she whispered.

"You are wrong." He squeezed her waist and wrapped his arm around it, lifting her off the floor. "I must beg your forgiveness if I have given you the impression I am not utterly intoxicated by your figure."

"Oh." Intoxicated? "Well, that's fine, then. But I must insist that you unhand me," she said, not even convincing herself that it was what she wanted.

He inhaled and set her down. His gaze, once more, burned like blue ice. "I will not lie to you by saying this won't happen again, but I concede that I was too hasty—"

"You will do nothing I do not wish to do, regardless of speed." Felicity found her outrage. She swept toward the door. "If anything is to happen, which it won't, you won't be in charge or at least not the only one setting the pace." With that incoherent rant, she swept from the room, past Mr. Coburn and at least seven footmen, and made it to the first landing before it became necessary to ask for directions.

Nine

THE IMAGE IN THE GLASS MADE FELICITY BEAM WITH EUPHORIC defiance. She had taken breakfast in her rooms, not out of cowardice but with the view of giving Mary Mossett time to work her magic on yet more garments. Felicity's comment over last night's meal had been taken to heart, and the little maid had altered a suit of clothes for her quite literally overnight. A white, muslin shirt had been tailored to fit her bosom without being too tight, and its collar had been lightly starched to complement her feminine neck and jaw, and a waistcoat framed her breasts in a most spectacular way. Over the top of it all sat a jacket that emphasized and flattered her hourglass figure. The fabric was warm without being heavy, a luxurious wool that hugged Felicity's shoulders and draped into shortened tails that suited the shape of her bum, which looked voluptuous and rather enticing. She hopped up and down in the half boots Mrs. Birks had unearthed; they were the only ladylike accoutrement on her entire person, and yet she'd never felt more womanly in all her life, even if she was garbed in trousers.

The trousers! The falls were strange against her most sensitive parts, as were the smalls: ladies of refinement did not wear undergarments apart from their chemises. Her legs did not lack for muscle, having ridden since she took her first steps, but seeing them out in the open gave her perspective as to the rest of her figure. In contrast, her bosom no longer looked unwieldy, and her waist created such a dainty distinction between breasts and hips, it was astonishing. All her parts looked to be in balance, making her figure appear healthy and alluring.

Nevertheless, she was only willing to go so far in defiance of the duke.

"Do try the cravat, Your Grace, do," Mary begged. "It's nothing but a scrap o' lace, why, it's only a ladies' cravat, so it is."

"Let us compromise," Felicity said. "We will plait my hair and secure it with the lace."

She sat at the vanity—how easy it was to sit in trousers—and Mary applied a brush to her unruly locks. "Oh, Your Grace, what a head of hair you have. Your lovely mum must have had the dyspepsia, that's what the biddies do say. 'Keep nothin' down, a feathery crown,' they do be saying that." Her methodical strokes almost sent Felicity off into a snooze, as she'd gotten little sleep the night before.

Small wonder, because she could not stop reliving That Kiss.

Not just the touch of lip to lip and tongue to tongue, but the stroke of hands, the variety of textures, the roughness of his jaw, the softness of his hair, the solidity of That Chest, the heat of his person, the…firmness against her thigh. She knew what *that* was due to secondhand information via several of Jemima's novels, and, naturally, from her own animal husbandry experience, but she couldn't—how would she look him in the eye? It was too personal, and yet she yearned to feel it, all of it, again.

Would he kiss her again, trousers and all?

Mary was braiding her hair. "I do be wondering why the Quality bind their hair up like a baby in swaddling. Yours should be flinging about your shoulders like the goddess you are."

"Goddess? Hardly," Felicity said. "But thank you, Mary, you are too kind."

"Oh, no, missus," Mary cried. "You do be only the image of the mate—eh, the lady that was promised and sought and, er, wedded by Romulus himself. Or was it Remus? Either. Both are the princes of the tale that tells the story of, uh, how…people be falling in love." She used the lace to tie off the braid and dashed to tidy the bedclothes.

"Were they not brothers in a Roman myth? My classical

education is virtually nonexistent. But then, so few women in the *ton* have any education at all."

"Wellllll." Mary paused. "They were brothers, but I'm thinking it's maybe not the same tale as most heard." She plumped the last pillow and set it just so on the counterpane.

"Has it anything to do with that feast of yours?" Had she landed in a den of paganism, so near to the Sussex border?

"Wellllll," Mary repeated, edging toward the door. "I suppose you'll know soon enough, as we're coming on to the full moon."

"I've never encountered a household so concerned with lunar matters."

"Ye've seen nothing yet, Your Grace," Mary muttered and hastened out of the room.

Choosing not to wait for another of the duke's numberless footmen to fetch her, Felicity descended. Sitting was nothing like to walking, nay, *striding*, in trousers. A part of her was hoping she'd meet the duke in the corridor, in her men's clothing, even though he'd forbidden she wear them and would no doubt turn up cross. If he became infuriated enough, could she soothe the savage, er, beast, not with music but with a kiss? In fact, she entertained anew a notion that had taken root sometime before the dawn: she was ruined in name, therefore why should she not be ruined in fact and deed? If she and the duke were to kiss again, who was to say it might not go further?

Mr. Coburn was at his usual place at the foot of the stairs. Only by the infinitesimal fluttering of his extraordinary hair did he betray a reaction to her costume.

"Your Grace," he said, and Felicity sighed. "I hope your morning meal was to your liking?"

"Very much so, Mr. Coburn," she replied. "My compliments to the chef. Although I perceive that he is no friend of yours."

Mr. Coburn quivered so with outrage, the skin beneath his chin wobbled. "I would not like to complain," he said—and then did so. "Monsieur Louveteau has a Continental approach to the meals belowstairs. He is far too egalitarian and refuses to prepare victuals that differ for the upper servants and the lower and expects us all to dine as one. It is not in order, Your Grace, not in order by a long chalk."

"I see." Compromise would seem to be the sticking place of this household. "I cannot think of a solution at this moment, but I shall think on it." Would she? Why would she? The machinations belowstairs, abovestairs, or on any stairs in Lowell Hall were none of her concern. "Both of you give exemplary service, and each of you is the king of your own domain. I comprehend the challenge and ask that you leave it with me." It seemed she was making it her concern.

This decision was underscored by the gratitude glowing in the butler's eyes. "I cannot convey my gratitude more sincerely, Your Grace, I cannot." He bowed and inevitably contorted his neck.

"Oh, madam." Mrs. Birks hurried into the foyer. "I do be begging your pardon for coming upon you on your way out, but I had no end of this and that all morning. Here be the menu for this evening, if you would approve it."

Felicity took the card and nodded at the artichoke terrine and the haricot hollandaise. "Still rather a lot of meat," she commented, "but the additions are perfect; do thank the chef for me. I did have a query that may fall in your and Mr. Coburn's domains? The…disposition of the furniture in the drawing room we used last night. There are several chairs that are unsuited for use in such a room, and I suspect that His Grace would be the last person to notice." It was not the fault of the staff that the furnishings had gone awry.

"He would at that, madam." Mrs. Birks laughed and laughed. And Mr. Coburn joined in. It was rather farcical, that a man of such masculinity would worry about where spindle-backed chairs belonged in a house.

"I shall see to removing the offending appointments from the

Bassett Room," Mr. Coburn said. "May I impose upon you to resolve any issues that may occur during the adjustment of the room?" They both looked at her, hope shining in their eyes.

"You may," she promised, confusing herself no end. She hesitated. "And His Grace? Is he about this morning? As I intend to visit his stables, I thought he might like to accompany me, or…?"

The retainers exchanged a glance, and Mrs. Birks said, "He's attending to estate matters and will be doing for the guts of the day, ma'am."

"Ah, of course. A busy, busy man." Felicity tugged on her waistcoat. "I'll be off then, if you would be so kind as to direct me."

"He has left you a token, to occupy your time." Mr. Coburn hopped over to a panel in the wall that revealed a shallow cupboard. "With his compliments."

They beamed as she opened the satchel he'd handed her to reveal a sketchbook and pencils. Her heart pounded with excitement and joy, and the two exchanged a delighted glance.

"How thoughtful." She was certain her calm voice did not betray her rioting emotions. "I look forward to thanking the duke when next we meet."

"I will leave Mrs. Birks to take you through the Hall at some stage," said Mr. Coburn, "but if I may conduct a brief tour of the grounds on the way to the stables? It would be my honor."

The sounds of a busy household followed them through a sitting room and out a set of French doors, one pair of the many that ran the length of at least half the house. An equally long terrace gave out onto a series of shallow steps leading to a parterre, which was not unusual, except that this one was. The hedge she'd seen from the staterooms was indeed a concealment device, for the land it hid was untamed in the extreme.

Oh, there was the usual kitchen garden and rose arbor, but any attempt to create a manicured, meticulously designed park had been abandoned, had it been attempted in the first instance.

Shrubbery sprung up willy-nilly, there was not a decorative flower bed in sight, the wood marched toward the house as opposed to receding away from it, and all the paths as far as she could see disappeared into tangled groves. There was one clear path, and onto this she was lead.

"A unique approach to landscaping."

"Indeed, indeed." Coburn cleared his throat with something like a squawk, and his arms crooked oddly at the elbows, flapping like wings. "His Grace's family has always preferred a more, er, naturalistic design. You will find a bridle path, Your Grace, that has been cleared for your enjoyment, should you care to ride."

"Overnight?"

Another squawk. "We seek only to serve." He moved in quick-step beside her. "Nearly there, ma'am—ah! Here we are."

Most country gentlemen looked to their stables as an adjunct of their display of wealth and constructed buildings along the lines of the great manse itself. The Duke of Lowell was not of that ilk. A plain, stone building loomed over a small forecourt comprised of the expected water troughs and mounting blocks, but there was a decided lack of flair; the cobblestone drive, which led to the coach house around back, was pristine yet without pretension, and like the rest of the land, the softening use of cultivated flower beds had been eschewed.

The stable master sauntered out of the wide door that presumably led from the barn, followed by a band of energetic stable lads. Forelocks were tugged as Coburn said, "Marshall will be more than happy to conduct you 'round the yard, ma'am."

"Thank you, Mr. Coburn." She turned to accompany Marshall, his lads cavorting around her as if they had no control over their exuberance. "My own—the stables at my family home are like to this size, I would guess."

"Hold your proverbials, missus." Marshall bowed rather grandly and swept his arm to lead her over the threshold—

Into the yard of her dreams.

It was as if the massive courtyard went on for miles, with loose boxes lining three sides. She walked to the center and turned slowly around, noting the large tack room to one side of the entrance and what she guessed was the feed room on the other. The tiled floor angled to the middle where water was even now draining after morning stables wash down. The doors to each stall were wide, hinting at large accommodations for each animal; the paint was bright and sparkling clean; and each equine head that hung over their half doors shone with health, ears flicking in her direction as she moved from door to door. "Wonderful!" Felicity stood with her hands on her hips, a posture made easier by her jacket and trousers. "I doubt that even the royal yard is anything like to this."

"Oh, well," Marshall replied. "They'd have one of two things in common, I suppose. Will we sort you out with a mount? His Grace sent word you're to have a hack if you like."

One of the lads led a stunning, dark bay gelding, at least seventeen hands high, over to a mounting block. The horse had been groomed to a shine, and he turned a spirited eye to her as she approached.

"Here's Jupiter," Marshall said, tugging down the offside stirrup as Felicity did the same to the near side. "He loves a gallop, but he'll ease up the second you ask."

She took to the saddle and adjusted the stirrups. "I am very much looking forward to this outing."

"You'll enjoy yourself with this one," Marshall said. "He's not one for the roads now, missus. There's no meanness or madness in him at all, but he does tend to go spooky when he's on unfamiliar ground, if you take my meaning."

"I am an accomplished horsewoman, Mr. Marshall," Felicity replied. "There is nowhere I cannot go on a horse." She tapped her heels on Jupiter's side and was away.

"We have received word from our holdings in the Fens, and Lambe is hopeful as regards the state of the drainage works, which are at last begun after much protest. The frontage will be substantial..."

Alfred slouched in the chair behind his massive oaken desk, turned toward the window with his eyes on the park while Bates droned on and on. *Unfair*, he thought to himself. Bates's voice was renowned, as was his own, for its mellifluousness, its timbre, its ability to melt the chemise off any willing female. His steward was known far and wide throughout their own brand of society for his magic touch with the ladies.

Had Alfred lost his own touch? He had gotten a good sense of Miss Templeton's frontage, and it was all he could do last night not to toss her over his shoulder—hell, he wouldn't have even made it to the ducal suite. He'd have taken her there on the floor, beneath the gaze of those damned china mutts in the Bassett Room, would it not have been the height of disrespect no matter what her essence did to him.

Ah, Goddess, the scent of her. It was well and truly embedded in his being, much less in his aristocratic nostrils, and added to everything—the freshness of her skin, the tartness of her tongue, the lushness of her vanilla and rosemary and sweet william scent—he now knew the fragrance of her arousal, and the sweet yet savory perfume had wound its way into his essential self until he could not tell where he ended and she began.

"...in reference to the tin mines in Cornwall, a new vein has been discovered, and Trevelyan wishes to be apprised of our thoughts regarding carrying on..."

Ha! He knew what his wolf thought regarding carrying on and had kept Alfred up the entire night whining and howling to take her, to mate her, to end any ridiculous excuse for a courtship ere it even began. This tentative approach was not the way of the Alpha. He thought of the rough-and-ready crowd from North

America behind that revolution in the late 1700s—as if they would loll about on their haunches waiting to be accepted. His Russian forebears, the *versipelles* of the Steppes, would sooner rip out their own throats than hang about waiting for the favors of a mere human.

He rubbed his eyes. His kind needed little sleep, but he was weary to his soul. Forcing, taking, violence—these were the very things he was attempting to purge from his pack, his beloved miscellany. Even the mice had barbarous tendencies when their backs were to the wall; even the lowest predator would turn if pushed too far. When it became clear that he would not find one of his own kind and must needs take a human to mate, he had consoled himself that the blend of their species would go some way toward taming the dark sides of their natures. Now he feared that he would be sent feral by his lust for his *vera amoris*. He had thought achieving the bond would unfold in an elegant process, as elegant as the name itself. Instead, he was more like his beast than he had been in his entire existence. He was less than pleased.

"My brother…" Alfred heard the catch in Matthias's voice, the combination of rue and impatience, of nostalgia and vexation that colored the relationship of the Bates twins. Alfred knew taking Matthias as his Second was the least of it, but he felt a measure of regret as regarded the way it exacerbated the siblings' discord.

"Your brother?" Best to get whatever it was out of the way.

"Is insisting that as his heir, I join him for the foreseeable future learning about the management of the Rendall holdings."

Well, that was ridiculous. Matthias had forgotten more about stewardship than Nathaniel would ever know. His Beta was charged to the Lowell Pack and would be for the length of his life. Nathaniel knew it, and yet he would continue to prod the sore spot until—until what? The human version of the tale of Romulus and Remus sprung to mind.

"I shall write to him myself," Alfred said, "and to your father, since Nat is behaving like a child, and remind them of the impossibility of that thoughtless request."

How he regretted his thoughtless question about Miss Templeton's parents. The wave of grief she exuded was as fierce as if it were only yesterday she lost them. He knew he was rather rough around the edges, but one of his breeding knew better, was better, than that. No stranger to such regret himself—he thought of his sister, how he had failed her, and was heartsick with remorse—his gauche query had resulted in pain for his mate.

"...our man in Kircudbright says that the aging of the malt continues apace, and this year the yield was, in his typically reserved terms, phenomenal..."

It would be phenomenal if she would yield, and then he could tell her everything. Let her have a glimpse of the phenomenal sexual union they would enjoy, the extraordinary power of their joining, and then say, "By the way, my one and only, I am a man who turns into a wolf. And vice versa." But no. And as unlikely as it was, it was his wolf that would not allow the deception. Despite his animal's eagerness and excitability, he would not lie to his mate. Alfred's inner creature growled with desire and something that transcended desire, something larger, something pure he'd never thought could go hand in glove with raging lust.

"She eschews spirits." He turned and saw that at some stage during his reverie, O'Mara had joined them. "There is no need to take delivery of any of it here at the Hall."

Bates made a note. O'Mara looked a little unsteady and red in the face.

"The intensity of my feelings affects you, O'Mara," he said, and if possible, she turned a deeper shade of scarlet. "I would apologize, but..." and he offered one of his rare grins.

"The intensity of your feelings proves the truth of the bond," she said, "and will normalize once their power, eh, fuses with the source of their inspiration."

Alfred looked at Bates, who appeared absorbed in his note-taking. "Your colleague has his doubts."

"I believe his doubts stem from his rejection of the concept of life mates," O'Mara said. "And the possibility of him having met his."

"Desist, O'Mara." Bates threw the paperwork down and shot out of his chair. "Your responsibilities do not include divination." He stalked over to the decanters, and Alfred sent his Omega an arch look. Had Bates come across his true mate? When had he the chance to do so?

Alfred set that aside to work out later. "Perhaps we can progress beyond this epistolary morass and determine why Miss Templeton is so intent on contacting or securing a solicitor?"

Bates sniffed the brandy, set out for the rare occasions when humans engaged on business visited the room, and returned the stopper to the bottle. "Brindle reports that there is no law office at the address Miss Templeton provided. It is a slaughterhouse in the stews, specializing in equines."

"That uncle of hers must be behind the confusion, the bastard. I have received no response from my letter of intent."

"Brindle remained and questioned the workers," Bates continued. "There have never been solicitors there, nor did they know of any such in the locality."

"There must be a firm attached to the family or to the uncle." The plot thickened, Alfred thought. "Find someone, for the love of the Goddess. And thus, discover why she is so keen to secure legal representation."

"It is being done even as we speak." Bates returned to his seat but gave O'Mara the cold shoulder; rather than being dismayed at this, she appeared amused. As amused as the aloof Omega could manage. Her laughter last night was the first time Alfred had heard any such sound emit from her person.

"The meal went well." He said this almost defiantly.

He was met with a beat of silence that went on a touch too long.

"Indeed, Alpha," said Bates.

"Oh, yes," agreed O'Mara. "Very well."

"Do not humor me." Alfred leaned his elbows on the desk. "I allow that there was a disruption or two."

Bates and O'Mara hummed deep in their throats.

"We are well-acquainted with the fact that I have no pattern upon which to design my addresses," he growled. "This courtship nonsense is not our way. Unless either of you have suggestions?" Bates hunched his shoulders to his ears; O'Mara regarded the ceiling. "Precisely." Alfred ran his fingers through his hair. "I begged her forgiveness had I given the impression I did not find her figure pleasing."

"Pleasing?" O'Mara pushed.

"Intoxicating, if you must know."

"Oh, well done, Alpha." She almost smiled. What was the world coming to?

"And I kissed her."

O'Mara regained her blush. "Yes, I am aware."

Bates picked up the paperwork again and sorted through it, for all intents and purposes nonchalant. "And your wolf? How did he handle the event?"

"With the barest civility." Alfred's essential self rose into his aura, and his Beta and Omega braced themselves and their own creatures. "I will not be able—I must let him have his head or I dread what will happen."

O'Mara offered, "Let us distract Her Grace with the friend she spoke of, the titled mantua-maker, Lady…?"

"Lady Jemima Coleman, late of Berwick-Upon-Tweed in Northumberland, resident in London since 1814," Bates recited. "Daughter of the Earl of Crawford and the Countess Margaret, née Lauder, of the Marches. The lady's arrival in Town, without fanfare, hints at obloquy, but my usual sources are coming up with nothing. She resides in Grosvenor Square with an aunt of similar breeding who does not often go about in society. Thus the lady and Miss Templeton were well met at entertainments, both all but abandoned by their families. Her aunt's garden is of the usual Mayfair standard, spacious and ample, and Lady Coleman has a workshop tucked away at the bottom. No one knows it is there. Well, I found it," he finished, cheeks tinted the faintest of pinks. "The lady was absent when I ran to Town. I left a note." He hunched his shoulders and found something of interest on the carpet at his feet.

Alfred regarded him beneath lowered lids. "I believe you have the right of it, O'Mara." They exchanged a look, buoyant and merry. "Do fetch the lady, and her creations, with the usual precautions taken."

"As you wish, Alpha." O'Mara uncrossed and recrossed her legs. "Your Grace," she began. Both Alfred and his wolf sat up at that. She rarely, if ever, used his honorific. "I beg that you enlighten Her Gr—Miss Templeton—as to our situation here. She is of such fierce constitution and has such fortitude, I would not be surprised if she fought this to the last because she does not know what she is fighting against. You disagree"—she turned to Bates—"but it is your own prejudice that is informing your opinions."

"*My* prejudice?" Bates surged to his feet, and Alfred followed, prepared to intervene. "You speak of my prejudice against the race that seeks to annihilate anything and anyone that differs from them in the slightest regard? That is outrageous, O'Mara, even coming from you."

"Even coming from me?" Icy cold, O'Mara joined them on her feet. "Do you refer to my Goddess-given talents with regards to emotion and their management within the pack?"

"Anyone's emotions but your own," Bates spat.

"Tread with caution, wolf." O'Mara's voice took on a low-pitched, wuffling tone, and her nostrils flared.

"With all due respect," he retorted, "I suggest you do the same—"

"Silence!" Alfred tore off his jacket and dispensed with his waistcoat. His steward and chamberlain assumed full obeisance, necks aslant, bowed down on one knee. "I will leave you to sort out your differences, but know this: I have chosen. Nothing will alter that fact. My wolf has chosen. That is inviolate." Bates and O'Mara nodded to one another, which was all it took to regain equilibrium. They rose, and their Alpha accepted their unspoken apologies.

"I must Change. I cannot wait." He shrugged out of his shirt. "I am for the meadow."

"Her Gr—Miss Temple—I wish to resolve this if only to settle on her address," O'Mara said. "She is out on the land this hour."

"Marshall has been instructed to recommend she remain on the bridle route," Bates said.

"I exhort you to caution, Alpha," O'Mara began.

"It must be now." He threw open a window, the remainder of his garments shredding as he Changed and was away.

Ten

AFTER A THOROUGH SEARCH OF THE PARK'S NEAREST BORDERS, Felicity took one look at the bridle path, winding decorously on its way, and chose instead to make for the meadow.

She galloped off the frustration of not finding a way safely through the thickets and brambles to freedom. She would not risk Jupiter's well-being by crashing through underbrush that might conceal any manner of ditches or drops. She doubted she would get three strides down the drive before someone came to prevent her departure. She galloped off the relief that she was here for at least another day…or night…and galloped off her incredulity at herself for not fighting her fate with greater fervor.

She spurred the hearty gelding on, thrilled to ride astride as she hadn't since she was a girl, thrilled that she had been offered a proper saddle. Was it to do with the trousers? Did they convey authority in her as they did in a man? Or was it her status as presumptive duchess? She'd been greeted with deference at every turn, even from those irrepressible stable lads. She did not discern even the most subtle of sly looks from any of the duke's staff; the farther up the heraldic chain they served, many domestics became as high in the instep as their employers, and she was amazed to be accepted in such a heartfelt fashion. No one treated her as a fallen woman, as a trollop, as though she were ruined. They embraced her, and she found herself willing to be embraced.

Was this how life would unfold, were she Duchess of Lowell? Even when Mama had been making up fantastical stories of her debut, even she had not reached so high. Despite being an honorable and having expected to make some class of aristocratic marriage, she would never have dared to aspire to a duke. She would have been happy enough with a viscount or even their village's gentle vicar. Her mother had always thought anything was possible and used to wax eloquent on all the lovely choices her daughter would have.

What were her choices now? A little voice in her head told her she was fooling herself in her obstinacy: if she did not marry the duke, she could never appear in society again. As much as that did not pain her, it was still daunting, to think of being shunned by the *beau monde*, though her welcome had bordered upon glacial. What difference would marriage to the duke make? She was a nobody, and it was doubtful she would make much of a duchess; from what she had seen, Lowell was not much of a duke, with his growling and his odd retainers and his…his kissing.

She sat back, and Jupiter transitioned down into a trot, then a walk. She gave him a loose rein and let him pick his way toward a grove of willows that swayed over Edenbrook. As she moved in perfect time with the horse's gait, she remembered the duke's face lowering to hers, that first light touch of his mouth upon hers, his tongue touching hers so gently, too gently, and she reddened at the memory of how she'd grabbed his face and, and *licked* his lip—*oh, help*!

Dismounting, she stretched. "It has been ages, Jupiter, since I've had a run of so high a standard. My sincere thanks. Thank you, good boy, oh, you are such a good boy." She fed him slices of apple from her pockets. Pockets were the most glorious things!

Up to now, kisses had been nowhere near as glorious as pockets. Despite not having taken, like any young lady out in the world, she'd suffered through her fair share of stolen, sweaty embraces, had the teeth of more than one callow lad scraping her lips, the hands of said lads roaming far too close to her bodice, or worse, her bum, but the sensations she experienced at the hands of the duke were incomparable. She had nothing to truly compare them to, and as such, suspected she might be exaggerating his charms.

"No," she scolded herself aloud. Jupiter looked over his shoulder. "Not you, darling, I'm talking to myself. Which is only somewhat madder than talking to a horse. Well, my fine fellow, given your namesake, I wonder if you can help me?" She stroked the gelding's neck. He reached down and rubbed his nose on her knee. "I'd thought I'd been kissed before, but I find that I have not. Am I making a mountain out of a molehill, or was that something extraordinary?"

She loosened his girth a notch and rested her cheek against his shoulder. "Come, you would know. Jupiter was rather a rake, was he not?" She ran a hand down his mane. "What if I took the duke as a, a lover? What think you of that, my fine friend?" Jupiter looked dubious. "My reputation is already in shreds, the whole world likely thinks it is a foregone conclusion, so what matter if I took on His Grace as a… What is the masculine version of a bit o' muslin? Bit o' trousers?" She laughed, and Jupiter shook off a fly, as he wasn't shaking his head in disagreement. Was he?

"Jemima's novels say a lady is permitted to 'investigate the mysterious matters of the flesh' only with her husband, but…" But? She kept the rest of her thoughts to herself as they were too bold to speak aloud, even to a horse. She was not so sheltered, not after five years amongst the *ton*; did any of the men of Quality learn of the audacious chitchat indulged by the fairer sex, even those behind the palms, they would likely collapse in shock. Women took lovers every day—every night, more like. If she chose Lowell as a lover, she'd be in excellent hands. She sighed, remembering his tongue tangling with hers, the heavy weight of his hand on her breast, and oh, when he squeezed that part of her near her hip, right above her fundament. It had been glorious.

"Those books fail to instruct as regard *amours*, as you can well imagine." Jupiter lowered his head to crop at the grass that grew near the brook. Felicity ran her hand up and down his neck. One needed emotional distance, she reckoned, when conducting a clandestine coupling, and since His Grace was occupied by his own concerns, she would have ample opportunity to keep herself at a remove. But how, when in his company, would she guard her heart? If she were to fall in love with anyone, let herself be quite honest, there was no one better—or was it worse—than Alfred, Duke of Lowell. "In truth, Jupiter, what female is safe from his charms?" She said this as a joke but feared she meant it. One lusty kiss and she was ready to tip head over heels. She could not take him as a lover and wave him off with aplomb.

She turned to retrieve the satchel she'd hooked to the cantle; all at once, Jupiter stiffened and bunched; as she reached for the reins, he reared and spun and galloped away. She turned to see what he saw: a massive creature emerged from the willow fronds near the bank. His coat was pitch-black, from snout to tail, without relief. His ears pricked, and despite his clear dominance over her frail femininity, he looked hesitant, his bright-blue eyes wary. It could not be, but he looked like—he looked like a wolf.

She opened her mouth and drew a deep breath—

He tensed—

"Blast! And damn. That horse—my sketchbook. Don't move!"

He froze, apart from an inquisitive flick of an ear.

"Oh, double damn." The beast blinked. "I do hope my language doesn't offend, kind sir."

He stood, frozen, watching her, and she comforted herself that she would have been his midmorning snack by now if he was a…a wolf. He *looked* like a wolf. His snout was long, the ruff of fur around his neck bristled with tension, and fangs appeared beneath his upper lip. She took a deep breath as she sought to quell any trepidation and fear that would translate to the animal. With another breath, she concentrated on releasing her tense muscles and kept her hands loose at her sides. As with horses, the more confident one was around them, the more relaxed the animals were, but a creature less likely to be as skittish as a horse she had yet to see. Moments passed, and when he did not attack, she became less convinced he was a wild animal. Another breath, then another, and her confidence increased. She would befriend this creature—she would be damned were she to fall prey to yet another enormous beast.

She moved toward him, and he tensed again. "No, no, stay… staaaaay… Good boy, goooood boy. Are you a boy? Are you? I suppose you must be, good Lord, look at the size of you. Look at you! Look at you!" He slowly sat and then lay down, never taking his eyes off her.

As she cooed at him, her mind ran riot. Who in their right mind expected a wolf in the middle of England? Hadn't the Scots reeved them all away? Or was it the Irish? His legs were long and muscular, his coat thick and wild, his paws were massive, paws which he now placed over his muzzle, his eyes gleaming at her as if…"Are you laughing at me? Are you? Am I silly? Oh, how handsome you are, so very handsome," and on and on until she moved as near to him as she dared and sat down on the ground.

"You're like a cross between a Great Dane and a wolfhound. I'm sure I've seen Welsh cobs smaller than you are. What must you eat?" He edged forward; she pretended not to notice and looked out over the meadow. "I am so unhappy with Jupiter for bolting, how I would love to sketch you. Although if I did, I doubt anyone would believe you were real, you are five feet tall at the shoulder, for the love of God—galoshes."

He crept closer still. "I'm no artist, but I am good at animals. Or people who look like animals, like my cousins. Rollo looks like a stork and Cecil like a hedgehog, and my uncle their father like a boar, B-O-A-R not B-O-R-E." She ran her hand back and forth over the grass, to allow the creature to get her scent. "I am also able to draw my dear friend Jemima—the Lady Jemima Coleman to you, my friend, as you've not got an acquaintance with her. She is lovely, so small and delicate, not like me, not a great strapping girl who should eat a husband out of house and home at this stage rather than her uncle… I may find such a future in the duke's household, whether I like it or not. If only I can persist until my birthday without being forced to marry…" The dog reared back, ears at attention. "Well, you should recoil, my friend. What lady in her right mind would reject the hand of a duke? Oh, what is your name, and to whom do you belong?" He nuzzled her, and she cautiously patted him on the head.

"I will call you Your Grace, I believe. You are the nearest thing to wolfish peerage, aren't you, handsome? Aren't you, Duke Alfred? Oh, no—you are Alfie." The dog's ears perked up, and he smiled, his teeth showing to alarming effect, but she laughed as his tongue lolled out of one side of his mouth. "Oh, Alfie, Alfie, yes! That will be your name when we are private with one another."

He laid his head near her thigh and chewed at her trousers. "Are you admiring my rig-out? His Grace the Duke of Doom and Gloom seeks to dictate my dress, and I will continue to defy him. Lady Coleman would be beside herself did she know I was wearing something this scandalous that wasn't one of her creations. She designed a cunning habit for me, split skirts so I might walk around the grounds with dignity and yet ride astride. I'm afraid I hurt her feelings when I declined them, but it was only that I was too afraid to wear it.

"I am tired of being afraid, Alfie. Afraid that I will be cast out of society should they discover I've been building my own breeding stock." The dog's mouth gaped open. "Yes. It is scandalous. A lady in trade, much less a man's trade. But I know I can bring my mother's mares bloodlines into sound union with my stud. Yes, I have a stud." She giggled, and the dog growled. "I'm having no luck with him; he's refusing to do his duty, but I insist he be the one to found my line. He is so big and strong, and the mares so volatile, I am certain I can develop the perfect, safest ladies' mounts…"

A tear trickled down her cheek, and the dog came near to

tackling her in his effort to lick it away. "Silly me. I am a grown lady and should be beyond tears. But sometimes I miss my mother so much. She was so beautiful and fine, and her love for my father was like a fairy tale. Like so: Once upon a time, there was a daughter of a wealthy Cit. Her much older brother, who adored her no end, bought her a fine palfrey—she loved horses, you see, and it was as though she'd been born to the saddle. She would ever sneak into the throng during the fashionable hour in Hyde Park, and there my father—I mean, the handsome baron, saw her, fell in love with her, made her his lady, and gave her everything her heart desired…

"My father's heart broke when she died, as did mine, watching him pass away by inches. Drowning his sorrows in the bottle, losing vast sums every night at the gaming tables. I can't imagine how there is anything left for me to inherit. Yes, me, a female, to inherit my father's fortune." She tapped the beast on the nose. "I know what you're thinking, but my uncle said if I remained unmarried until this birthday, then…" The dog nudged her arm as if encouraging her to go on and barked to emphasize the request.

"No." She curled up on her side, and the dog lay down as well. "I tire of worrying, tire of waiting. I did not imagine my life to be this way. Nor did Mama. She dreamt my whole life for me, and none of it has come to pass. And now I try to dream it for myself, and it is nothing like to hers. Oh, Alfie, what am I to do?

"I wish you were a wolf." She yawned, blinked, let her hand rest on the beast's paw. "How safe I would feel, with a friend who was a wolf…"

———

Alfred watched her, unblinking, and thus caught the moment when she abandoned herself to sleep.

He was stunned by how unafraid of him she was, how easily she took him into her confidence. How clever she was not to have fled from what was clearly a predator; how confident she became once she understood he meant her no harm.

Shifting shape had its drawbacks; here was a notable advantage. He regretted not having thought of this before. He'd learned more in his wolfskin in a handful of moments than he had as a man. While he was able to respond in a limited manner, she seemed more than adept at reading his intentions.

He ran his muzzle all over her face, her hair, tickled her neck. Perhaps his wolf could win her heart, and his human could woo her body? Perhaps they might meet in the middle—if they *compromised*—and achieve the all-important bond?

What was this nonsense about inheriting a fortune? He leaned into her side, and she curled closer, resting her head on his shoulder. He was no solicitor, but even he knew the laws of primogeniture were ironclad. More information for Bates; now he understood why she sought legal advice.

And horse breeding! He'd surmised she was thinking along those lines, given their discussion last night. He snorted. She could do what she liked as far as that was concerned. They had the land and the facilities for it; O'Mara might try glamouring the stud into doing his job. It was the work of a moment to make this dream come true, and he would see it done.

Thought she'd take him as a lover, did she? Thought he was charming? He grinned, all lupine toothiness, as he considered ways in which he could charm her. Oh, yes, he would be her friend and so much more.

The salty taste of her tear was still on his tongue, and he let out a low, mournful howl. The notion that she had been alone, grieving, made him want to tear the world apart.

Over the rise came his Beta and his Omega, leading a pacified Jupiter. They both gasped when they saw him curled up next to his mate.

"Alpha!" Bates looked apoplectic. "She was meant to stay away from the meadow."

"Shall I see if I may glamour her in her sleep?" O'Mara offered.

Alfred rose and shook himself, then growled.

"But this is a catastrophe," Bates insisted. "She must not become curious about you."

The wolf bared his teeth, and Felicity stirred. His Beta and Omega looked aghast—was she about to awake? With one last sniff, Alfred bounded away.

_____

Felicity stretched and patted her hands around her. She blinked and stared at Bates, O'Mara, and Jupiter looming over her.

"His Grace, has he gone?"

"His Grace?" croaked Bates.

"The gigantic dog."

"Dog?" O'Mara whispered. "A dog, Your Grace? All the dogs we have at the Hall have jobs and belong to the tenant farmers and shepherds, so it is possible you are mistaken or it was a dream, perhaps, only a dream—"

"Miss O'Mara, desist." O'Mara desisted. "He must have gone. The large dog? Looks to be only slightly smaller than Jupiter here? I named him Your Grace. Well, Alfie. I prefer Alfie."

"Alfie?" O'Mara squeaked.

Felicity rose, and Bates belatedly moved to lend her a hand. "I cannot imagine who had his breeding. Mr. Bates, I am shocked that you allow such a noble creature to roam willy-nilly over the duke's lands. What if harm should befall him? The dog, not the duke? I am concerned, should he come across someone intimidated by his size, he will be shot. And if he is unknown to you, then who has his care? He cannot be expected to look after his own needs, not a beast of his size. And when I say beast, I cast no aspersions, his shoulder was well-nigh up to my shoulder. I cannot allow that any living being go unattended, for their own safety and welfare. Well, Mr. Bates?" She crossed her arms and stared him down.

"Your Grace." He went down on one knee before her. "I will do my utmost to ensure the welfare of this creature, and all our creatures. It is my joy and my duty to do so, at your command."

"Ah. Excellent." Felicity glanced at O'Mara, whose head was also bowed, and whose eyes seemed to shine with unshed tears. "Well. That's sorted. If you would give me a leg up, Mr. Bates?"

Mounted once more, she looked down at His Grace's closest associates. "Shall I send a groom with mounts for you?"

"No, Your Grace," said Bates. "We will make our way back on, er, foot."

"Well, then." She nodded her thanks, turned her horse, and galloped back across the meadow. Something had passed between the three of them; she didn't know what it was, but she felt it deeply, deeply, in the very center of her heart.

Eleven

EARLY THE NEXT MORNING, FELICITY JOGGED DOWN THE stairs in her gentleman's attire. She greeted Mr. Coburn in passing and headed for the main part of the house.

"Your Grace...?" Coburn called.

"Off to beard the lion in his den, Mr. Coburn," she called back.

"His Grace is breaking his fast," the butler said, scampering after her. "He asks that you join him, if you will."

"Oh." She stopped. "Thank you. If you would show me the way?"

The breakfast parlor was all one hoped for in such a room: sunny, thanks to yet more French doors, decorated with bright yet tasteful appointments, and featuring a sideboard full of a variety of delicious offerings. His Grace rose and scowled at her trousers. "Good morning, Miss Templeton."

"Your Grace." She fought the instinctive urge to curtsy; it was not a gesture to be performed in men's clothing.

He had been absent from the meal last night and therefore not available for kissing over cups of tea. Even in less formal clothing—a simple hacking jacket, breeches, and high boots—the duke was still devastatingly handsome; she thrust her hands in her pockets, as if to prevent herself from reaching for him. He stopped frowning at her garments and sent her a lambent look, as if he could read her mind. Which she wished he would, and dismiss the servants, and, and...kiss her over these tea cups. She lowered her gaze and glanced up at him through her lashes, picturing him sweeping the contents of the breakfast table to the floor, hauling her up against him, pushing her down onto the tabletop, his hands touching her in places she'd only touched herself. She squirmed as she dampened behind her falls, and he let out a long, low sound, much like the one she'd thought she heard during her bath the first day. His eyes flared, and he took a step forward, and she—she must not let her fanciful thoughts run away with her.

She made to seat herself, but Mr. Coburn did not allow it. The chair the butler drew out for her was from the Bassett Room, and this observance was accompanied by a little pulse of satisfaction that her edict had been fulfilled.

Footmen ringed the room; Felicity counted nine. They stood at attention, stiff and staring straight ahead, but all were smiling, not the done thing in a footman. Nor did any of them adhere to the tall, muscular, handsome pattern: they ranged in height and varied in coloring—two were gingers!—and were as unalike one another as fish were to fowl. She sat and accepted a napkin from one of them; as she reached for the teapot, Coburn fussed until she allowed him to pour.

"Shall I make you a plate, ma'am?" Coburn asked.

"I'll do it." The duke rose and went to the sideboard. "May I tempt you with eggs and ham, toasted bread, scones, kippers, or beefsteak?"

"Eggs, please, and two slices of toast, thank you." She smiled up at the attendants. "His Grace would leave you idle."

"A more idle lot is unknown to man," said the duke, "or beast." The lads laughed.

"You may like to take on some of the ducal duties, perhaps," Felicity joked.

"Oh, no, madam," said one of the gingers. "We know our places."

"Your places?" The duke turned from the sideboard. "Holding up the wall? Looking decorative? Vexing Mr. Coburn?"

"Eating you out of house and home," said one.

"Growing out of our livery at a rate of knots," added another.

"Brawling like wild animals," chimed one more; they all creased themselves laughing at this.

"And to think I drew you here from far and wide"—the duke glowered—"only to have you take advantage of my good will."

"That's us, Alph—Your Grace. Taking advantage, we are." The second ginger was as cheeky as the first.

"From far and wide?" Felicity stirred her tea.

All the footmen made to answer, but Mr. Coburn prevailed. "His Grace is ever on the prowl—on the alert, to those who are in need of gainful employment. At the ducal seat, it is preferable that the lads have the opportunity to benefit from the duke's presence, that they may settle into themselves until such time as they are prepared to venture forth."

"That is quite extraordinary." Felicity was moved by this generosity of spirit, this evidence of nurture and care. "And how are you discovered?" A plate hit the table with a thump before Felicity, laden with enough eggs to feed an army and four pieces of bread loaded with butter and jam. "Your Grace, I cannot eat all this."

"I'll finish what you do not."

"Your Grace," Felicity repeated, "I have only the manners my mother managed to convey, which she herself had to intuit on many levels, as not one born to the gentry—"

"I know," the duke said.

"You know what?"

The duke's cheeks reddened as though put to the blush, which was patently ridiculous. "That your mother was, eh, not born to the purple, so to speak."

"Mr. Bates at work, again? He should seek employment in Bow Street."

"He is kept well occupied by the needs of this estate."

"As I was saying, one does not eat from another's plate." Felicity poured herself more tea and held up the pot. At his nod, she refilled his cup. "I am keen to ride your lands, as you promised."

"Ah. Yes. Today will suit."

"I had intended to remind you at the meal last evening, but you did not join us."

"I was detained." He cleared his throat and looked away. "On the land. Farthest boundary. Miles away."

"I experienced something of your lands yesterday, on my hack." Felicity ate some delicious eggs. "How in the world did you get about? For I doubt a horse would make its way safely over most of the underbrush, and I would scold you soundly had you attempted such."

"Scold me, would you?" The duke leaned toward her. "Soundly?"

"And another thing," she said, longing to touch his face and see if was it as warm as it had felt two nights previous, "I came across an animal near Edenbrook. I am supposing it was a very large dog, black as night—"

"Ma'am, forgive me, if I may interrupt." Coburn drew her attention from the inexplicably sniggering footmen. "You have received post." He set a silver salver at her elbow.

Would it be bad manners to read it before all? She had not broken her fast in company for years, and her mother had received little post. *Bedamned with rules*, she thought. *Rules have done little for me.* The first note was from Aherne: the horses were safely hidden, and he and Bailey had taken it upon themselves to use their second hiding place, the western paddock that lay even farther away from the house than the holiday field. Her heart could rest easy in that regard, at least.

She opened the second missive; it was from Cousin Cecil.

There was no salutation.

How surprised I was to hear from you, cousin.
Of course, the word of your ruination has spread far and wide.
La! That you would think to write to me.
Do not believe that there is recourse to be found here in Finsbury
*   Square!*

Felicity, you must know that my father would look upon this with apathy.

As ever, he holds the Quality in scorn and is disinclined to save your reputation.

Sincerely,

Thine cousin, Cecil

Post Script: I await your confirmation of receipt of this missive and any enlightenment regarding your marital status you may see fit to impart.

"What news?" the duke asked.

"Nothing to speak of." Her hands shook as she folded up the note and thrust it into a pocket in her jacket.

"If your uncle has written you ill…" His Grace's tone promised death and destruction.

"It is from my cousin Cecil, informing me that all is as I expected it to be from that quarter."

"And what is to be expected?" The duke's voice was mild, and yet Felicity sensed the pressurized disturbance in the air that was becoming familiar.

"That I have no recourse to family." She took a shaky sip of cooling tea. "That I am left to my own devices."

Out of the corner of her eye, she saw the duke straighten in his chair. His hands clenched into fists. The footmen quivered, chins aslant, and Mr. Coburn stood as though carved from marble next to the sideboard.

"You are not left to your own devices." His voice sounded calm, but its very stillness made Felicity's hair stand on end. His face was set in mild lines, but his eyes were like ice. "You are not alone. You are here. You are under my protection. You are mine."

"I," said Felicity, "am not yours." A thrill had run through her at the word *mine*, something heady and grounding, a paradoxical mélange of giddiness and stability.

"May I read the letter? Perhaps in your upset you have misread it."

"You may not. It is quite clear. All the world knows of my abduction, and my uncle cares not for the shame brought upon the Templeton name. This is, of course, all your fault."

She calmly held his gaze, watched as he struggled to keep his composure before his servants, perceived his need to demand she allow him read her letter, to take action, to do something— watched him fight for control as she defied him. The footmen were agog, and Mr. Coburn seemed oddly rapturous. When the duke sat back and nearly smiled, she turned to the butler. "May I trouble you for a fresh pot of tea? Gentlemen," she said, addressing the footmen, "if one of you could fetch me a scone? I would hate to see them go to waste, as delicious as they must be."

"Allow me." The duke rose to fetch her a scone from the sideboard, still piping hot. "I would tailor our tour to your interests." He leaned over her shoulder as he placed it before her, his voice deep and low, close to her ear. "What is your pleasure?"

"The, em, tenants?" There might be something in this smelling of a person. She took a breath and swore she would recognize him from his scent alone, of sun-washed, laundered linen, the way he smelled of earth and fresh air. "And the animals. I'd like to see the situations the rest of your animals enjoy."

"Then let us finish our meal and kill two birds with one stone."

They were still arguing over his phrasing as they descended the terrace at the front of the Hall to mount up. Felicity stopped short on the final stair.

"Jupiter?" The gelding, so fiery the day before, flicked an ear half-heartedly. "Are you well, my friend? You look somnambulant." She turned to regard the horse that stood on Jupiter's offside. "And you, sir," she said, running a hand down the large, enervated cob's neck, "I doubt very much that you are able for an outing."

"He'll be fine," said the duke. "He's always like this." He pulled down Jupiter's stirrups, then the cob's.

"This is your mount?" A less lordly equine could not be envisioned. He was hairy and piebald, with hooves like serving platters and a back like a hay wagon.

"He is." The duke patted the horse on the flank; it shivered as though it might bolt but stayed in place.

"The poor creature looks to have been mesmerized."

"That has to do with animal magnetism, does it not?" He came up next to her; Jupiter twitched. "Perhaps it is my fault he is so torpid. Perhaps I have an excess of such a quality."

She lowered her lids and smiled, sultry. "That practice is said to promote unseemly behavior in ladies."

"What does unseemliness entail, I wonder?" The duke led her around to Jupiter's near side, his fingers stroking her palm.

"If you have to ask..." Felicity murmured then laughed at her own cheekiness.

"I would inquire, but I think my mouth can be put to better use." He leaned in, and Felicity sighed, in relief. More kissing, thank Go—galoshes.

Marshall bounded around the corner, and they leapt apart, Felicity knocking into the cob.

"I'm only half-asleep looking at this feller," he said. "Poor auld Juventus. Not so young any more, are you?" He held Jupiter's offside stirrup and said, "Up you get, missus."

"Her Grace." The duke glowered.

"Thank you, Marshall," Felicity said, looking pointedly at the duke. "May I have a leg, please?"

"You may have all of me," the duke whispered in her ear, and as he lifted her with her own impetus, he nipped her on the knee. "I find these trousers to be appealing, of a sudden."

Marshall held the cob for form's sake, as it would have been amazing had the animal moved of its own initiative. She applied her leg to Jupiter's sides and had to squeeze with far greater strength than she had only the day before.

"Off you go, you two," Marshall called as he headed away. "Home in time for supper!"

"Insubordination," the duke growled; Felicity was certain this was for form's sake as well. In fact, she was beginning to believe much of his apparent truculence was a blind for his true nature.

"Poor Juventus," Felicity cried, as they crept down the drive. "Not quite the ducal mount I imagined."

"Have you imagined my mounting?"

"One envisions a destrier, along the lines of Bucephalus, or Wellington's own Copenhagen." She ignored his inflammatory comment and turned in a circle round the duke; even lethargic, Jupiter's gait covered more ground than did that of the heavy cob. "One more suited to the impression that your manse conveys." She looked up at the facade, a rich concoction of redbrick, numerous windows, of terraces climbing and winding around both sides before fetching up against the hedges.

"And how are you finding it here?" The duke applied a little more leg, which resulted in a dozy flick of an ear.

"I cannot imagine a more welcoming estate on which to be held captive." She looked at the house as she made another circuit around him. "It is impressive, and luxurious, as well as old-fashioned and somewhat helter-skelter."

"I have not the time for domestic issues."

"It is not within your remit to tend to them yourself," she replied. "It is, however, your duty to provide the framework within which your butler and housekeeper may make decisions for themselves."

"Have they registered a complaint?"

How lethal he sounded. "They have not. Yet, anyone with eyes in their head could see that those extraneous footmen ought to be given the opportunity to learn other jobs of work on your estate, that the kitchen is feuding with the butlery, which is not ideal for the well-being of the lower servants, that the decoration of the house is languishing somewhere in the last century—" None of this was any of her concern.

"What you are saying, madam, is that the house needs a woman's touch." Juventus quivered at the duke's sonorous tone.

As did she. "And yet there is much that is unique to recommend Lowell Hall. Is that amusing, Your Grace? This topiary, for example." She once again rode tandem with the duke, although rode was overstating it. "Most often, one finds such treatments of shrubbery at the back of a great house, and here, it marches along your drive. Quite a charming…welcome." She trailed off as they reached the end of the lane, over which two topiaries ranged, shaped as lunging beasts that looked to be ambushing the unsuspecting visitor. "Is that—those are—are they wolves? Or some crossbreed perhaps, something similar to the Irish wolfhound?"

"They are common in these parts."

"Will you ever answer me without equivocating?"

"We shall sally forth to the right, if you please," the duke said. "There is much to see, and at this rate, we will see almost nothing."

"I take that as a no." Felicity looked about as they curved 'round the bend. Unlike the wild hedge shielding the park, well-manicured, low-lying shrubbery bordered the road. From her vantage point on Jupiter's back, she saw fields, both fallow and fertilized, rolling away in every direction. As they ambled along, the workers looked up and saluted as they passed; how they heard them or even saw them was impossible to fathom. The Edenbrook soon made an appearance and veered off to the left even as they turned to the right.

Did the big dog live in the wood by the meadow? She hoped he didn't venture out into these fields, as they seemed well-attended. Was he the only one of his kind? She hated to think of him alone, with no others like him. How a creature that size could see to his own feeding without decimating the park and village of its smaller beasts was beyond her. His presence must be known by the land's inhabitants. She looked at the duke, who, in all unlikelihood, was struggling with his reins. "O'Mara mentioned that all the dogs on the estate are working beasts?"

"They are. They have their places and know it, madam."

"And I begin to understand that you are taunting me. You allow your people the run of the place, you take in all and sundry as is necessary, and you seem to have a sense of humor I would not have credited. I cannot believe you would allow even the humblest creature within your bounds to suffer or lack in any way."

A large hand reached out and grabbed Jupiter's reins; that same hand shifted to her elbow, pulling her toward the owner of that hand, who kissed her on the lips. As quickly as the kiss was stolen, the thief resumed his saddle but kept his hand on her arm. "You may call me Alfred when we are in private together," he said. "Is that amusing, Felicity?"

"Come, Jupiter, hup, hup!" Shaking off his hold, Felicity transitioned upward into a less turgid trot and headed away from the farms and down the road. Let him think he'd offended her, perhaps; perhaps next time, she thought, her heart pounding, she might steal a kiss from him.

"...thirty-thousand hectares. Not as vast as Northumberland's holdings, but respectable." Was he droning on and on? Alfred had never needed to talk so much in his life. "There are several tenant farms, in addition to the ones we've passed, scattered over the acreage on the opposite side of Edenbrook, ten in number, of one thousand hectares per share. We have sheep and cows and goats and crops. Despite rumors to the contrary, this is a working estate."

Good Goddess, she hadn't said a thing for miles. All he wanted was that she'd see how much would soon be at her feet, how much he had to offer her. All his wolf wanted him to do was to get off this ridiculous beast, take her into the woods, and lose himself in her, body, mind, and soul.

She had been scanning their surroundings, and Alfred reckoned she was keeping an eye out for the big doggy. Big doggy! Bates had told him of Her Grace's vociferous defense of his wolf, so she was not searching out of fear. The notion she thought the beast couldn't take care of himself made his heart ache—but pleasurably, in a way he'd never known was possible. She posed a few questions here and there, but he couldn't tell from outward signs what she was thinking. He scented interest, concern for the "dog," and her lingering arousal from his stolen kiss—and distress, likely due to that damned letter from her damned cousin.

"Is that building inhabited?" She pointed with her crop to a small holding tucked back from the road.

"It is in use." He received her irritated look with equanimity. Explaining an odd little shack was not high on the List of Things That Required Explanation; there was plenty to distract her. "Here is the village."

Several dwellings lined the road, which debouched onto a square. These he would be more than happy to explain. "As you can see, Edenbrook widens here, thus the mill. The blacksmith is beyond that, and the baker is down the square. We hold market day on Saturday and small market on Wednesday, as is common in rural parts." As they processed down the road, the villagers flocked to the sides, offering their deference and beaming with joy at the sight of them. "We are largely self-sufficient. Each holding produces its own dairy via cows and chickens, and the wealth of the overall harvest is shared out."

"It seems as though each house is a shop," Felicity observed. "Or a guild?" Elaborate signage hung from the eaves of the majority of the buildings and were nothing like anything she'd seen before.

"Our villagers are, in the main, artisans and craftsmen," Alfred said. "Weavers and potters, carpenters and masons, blacksmiths and goldsmiths—we even have a resident composer."

"How remarkable," Felicity said, smiling around at the villagers who had gathered in front of the village green. "I have never heard of such."

"Our people enjoy expertise not in the usual run of things." Alfred drew Juventus to a halt and sprung out of the saddle. He was over to Jupiter's side in a heartbeat, reaching up without ceremony and lifting Felicity out of the saddle and slowly down the length of his body. "I am keen to encourage their talents, no matter how outlandish their dreams."

"Then they are fortunate." She held his gaze, her hazel eyes gone a brilliant green in the sunlight.

"Far be it from me to thwart natural talent and the ambition to make good of it."

A throat cleared, long and loud, and Alfred turned to the source. "Miss Felicity Templeton, if I may introduce Mr. Sebastian Gambon, the, eh, mayor of Lowell Close." The large and bristly-looking man had a long, sober face, and his eyes, though smallish, twinkled with welcome.

"Your Grace. Ma'am." The Gamma of the pack bowed to Miss Templeton. "Welcome to Lowell Close," he went on, turning and offering his arm. "If I may continue the introductions?"

"Thank you, Mr. Gambon, I would be honored." Felicity accepted his escort, and they moved through the crowd; Alfred watched, accepting the reverences made to him by those who were not enraptured by his mate. His artisans brought out their goods to show off, and Miss Templeton displayed true interest in all that came to her. As he shook hands, kissed elderly cheeks, and listened to his people, he kept an equal part of his attention on the reception of his mate. All were enthralled, and he saw more than one eye glisten with a tear.

When Gambon and she rejoined him, a small group of senior pack members gathered around, and the publican offered them all the last of the winter ale. Felicity sipped at the hearty brew with reluctance, and Alfred refrained from offering to finish it for her. He'd learned his lesson there.

"How fares your sister, Alf, Alfred—Your Grace? asked one of the women. "We do miss her about the place."

"All is well," he replied. "And I assure you she holds you all in her thoughts."

"Any sign of a pup or two?" asked one of the villagers.

"Did he say pup?" Felicity asked.

"I am sure you misheard, ma'am." Gambon didn't miss a beat.

"It's a term of endearment," said Alfred, "specific to the locality." Everyone nodded, and the unfortunate interlocutor turned tail and ran.

"Speaking of pups," said Felicity, "I was near to the meadow only yesterday and came upon a rather large dog—"

"More beer, my dear?" Alfred asked. He turned to the man beside him. "I apologize, Harper, I am treading on your patch. Harper is our resident bard." Everyone laughed and laughed. "Come, let us walk around the green before we turn for home."

The duke offered his arm and led her around, Gambon on her other side. As they circled the green and Gambon gestured toward ginnels and larger streets that fed away from the square, Alfred wondered if she would pass comment on the breadth and wildness of the village green, a smaller sibling of the untamed park of Lowell Hall. Her forehead wrinkled, but she said nothing, looking about with interest, but he sensed that there was growing consternation underneath the courtesy and tact.

"How do you find the village?" he asked.

"It is as unique as to be expected. It is as though something's missing, however…"

"Well, we've no church," Gambon offered. "We had a chapel; we're more chapel-going folk."

"Had?"

"It burned down. Sadly." This was said rather cheerfully, truth be told. "Torched nearly that whole line there, but we reacted with speed. We are considering setting up a public house once permission comes down from on high." He winked.

"And the vicar?"

"The man who had the living died. Not in the fire," Gambon assured her. "No, old age, Goddes—God rest him."

Alfred took control. "Will you help me decide how to disburse the role?"

"You would have greater knowledge in that regard than I would," Miss Templeton said with some asperity. "Finding a man of the cloth who would disregard your upcoming pagan festivities may be easier said than done."

They had come full circle. Gambon pulled his forelock and legged it away. Good man, Gambon, always knew when to make himself scarce.

"Things are different down the country," Alfred said, preparing their horses for mounting. Good Goddess, how people enjoyed this pursuit was beyond him. Up and down, up and down, the livelong day.

"I am from down the country, very near to your part of the country," Felicity said. "And I daresay we did not go about worshipping idols and suchlike."

"Is that where your imagination has taken you?" Alfred leaned in and tickled her ear with his nose. "Idolatry and revelry and vice?"

"And bonfires," she replied, fluttering her lashes at him. "And salacious dancing and, and stolen kisses."

"Magnificent things, kisses," he murmured. "So satisfying at the moment, and yet the more one shares, the more one yearns for…" He lowered his head even as she raised hers, watched her mouth soften. He slipped his hands around her midriff—never mind the scandalousness of her gentleman's costume, he could get well used to laying his hands on that gorgeous waist—and without waiting to be given her leg, he flung her up in the saddle, and almost laughed at her peeved expression as she turned up her nose, turned her horse, and cantered away.

———

It wasn't much of a canter. Felicity was back down to a walk in less than twenty strides and slowed even further to allow the duke and poor, old Juventus to catch up.

She needed what little time she had to herself to settle. The letter from Cecil played upon her mind. Why was it written so oddly? Granted, she had never exchanged correspondence with him, but the stilted tone and the strange use of outdated language could not be his common style. And she had yet to hear anything from Jemima, nor had her uncle responded to the duke. She thought Alfred would tell her if he had. No, she knew he would. He had been more than forthcoming about his holdings and his wealth—the ladies' magazines said that wives never worried their pretty little heads about the solvency of their husbands and not to quiz them indiscriminately about the state of their finances. He had not, apparently, read that article.

From all she had seen, the Lowell family coffers were in rude, good health. What was one to do when faced with such prosperity and fecundity? Who would say no to all this? What would it be like to be the lady of all that she'd surveyed that day? And for all the duke's formidability, his people adored him. It was as close to utopia as she'd ever thought to see, but something was not right; it had been troubling her as they'd ridden the farms, but once in the village, the notion that something was amiss had taken root.

"You are pensive."

Felicity turned to him with a weak smile. "I am overwhelmed. By the robustness of your holdings and the warmth of your people."

"Our people."

"They are so kind and so easy with you," she continued. She was excelling at ignoring his statements. "And they asked so graciously after your sister."

"They are all that is kind. And gracious."

"Alfred." Enough was enough. "Tell me about her."

"She is in America, in the state of New York, on the island of Manhattan. By her account, it is quite sophisticated, considering. Very civilized."

"Is she married?"

"She has yet to experience that joy." Juventus skittered, and the duke took him in hand.

"You must miss her."

"Yes."

"How adventurous of her, to go off to the wilds of North America. Alone?"

"Yes." She saw his hands clench the reins. "We have acquaintances there through whom she was introduced into American society. She is well received and goes about often. I expect she is once again the diamond of this season and is much in demand, as my latest letter has been long in answering."

"I did not intend to cause distress by asking about your sister." Jupiter started to jig, as though he were awakening from a long sleep, and the duke was silent as they turned up the drive.

They halted at the foot of the terrace. "I would know were she unwell or unhappy," the duke said suddenly. "When we were children and I was fostered away, she used to sneak me letters, in the most ingenious ways…" He looked over at her, his expression bittersweet. "I was happy in Matthias's homeplace, and for the first year, was delighted to have shaken off my silly little sister. But as the years passed, I realized she was the only sibling I would ever have…so I sent her a letter and got a proper ladylike reply contained in my mother's correspondence, then received Phoebe's true missive, by clever subterfuge. Thus, we…we became friends and…she was the only reason I came home at all. And then, when it became necessary that she leave England, under a cloud, my heart…my heart…"

He hopped down, and Juventus shook himself from nose to tail. Felicity took her feet out of the stirrups and was halfway through swinging down when the duke's hands fell on her waist; between her impetus and his abnormal strength, she all but flew through the air, landing backward onto That Chest. She went to move away, but he turned her to face him, swifter than thought, and his arms banded around her, and she felt—she felt like he needed her embrace, so she gave it, without reservation. She squeezed his bulk as best she could, sighed when he sighed, and tilted her head up when his thumb, under her chin, urged her to do so.

"This was not home, for almost all my life," he said. "I was born here but not reared here. I was nothing but a role to be fulfilled, a figurehead—never a son to be cherished, a boy to be indulged. It was a place to escape and then return to reluctantly. But now that you are here…it is a home, as never before. There is life and joy and hope. There is vibrancy and promise and heart. This becomes home, for all of us, now that you are here, beneath its roof."

On tiptoe, Felicity reached out to stroke a fingertip down his cheek. His eyelids drooped, and as his head lowered, she moistened her lips with her tongue, heard him groan, felt his growing arousal against her belly, and—

Two of the stable lads whooped as they raced one another around the corner of the Hall. Felicity leapt out of Alfred's arms, Jupiter squealed and turned to bolt, and even Juventus made as if to hare off. The boys had them in hand soon enough, and Felicity blushed, chagrined. Would they ever be left alone?

"Good lads." The duke waved them off, and they trotted the horses away.

Lads. That was it! Felicity laid her hand on the duke's forearm and ignored the flare of desire in his eye. "Alfred," she said, "where are the children?"

Twelve

THE STATEROOMS WERE OPULENT, AND EACH CHAMBER WAS appointed to the highest degree. The chandelier in the withdrawing room was the most majestic Felicity had ever seen, hung with thousands of faceted crystals that would blaze like the sun were the candles lit. She was sure she could have the candles lit did she but ask, but that was wasteful and ridiculous. She was not so far gone in notions of her own consequence, despite all the encouragement to the contrary, to act as one to the highest manner born.

As she wandered from the anteroom through to the withdrawing room, around her bedroom, and into the dressing room, she noted furnishings here and there that could use freshening, draperies that would benefit from turning, and carpets from beating. The paintings were of the standard she now understood as the style of the Hall, and she paused before an image of two small dogs that adorned a wall in the dressing room. Dark as night, the larger dog loomed over the smaller one, who was a honeyed brown. There was a purple bow around the bigger dog's neck—perhaps that's what made him look so disgruntled—while the little one sat on a red, velvet cushion, smiling, tail aloft. Felicity was certain it was a she; there was something about the bright-blue eyes and relative daintiness that was feminine. Was this what that man had meant by pups? Did the duke's sister have the raising of hunting dogs, perhaps?

Felicity regarded her gown, hanging freshly sponged on the door of the nearby wardrobe. She herself was freshly sponged, as she could not get enough of that bathing room, but the thought of donning the same dress for yet another evening was less than exhilarating. She'd prefer not to go down in the latest set of trousers that Mary Mossett had tailored for her; even though Alfred had been taken with her in them, she wished to be ladylike tonight.

Would there be more kissing? She wondered that she wanted to kiss a man who deflected every inquiry and fled when she asked about the Hall's children. This was on the one hand; on the other was the man who held her like she was a precious being and vowed that her presence here was making Lowell Hall a home.

If that solicitor was ever going to respond, it had best be now. How she hated the notion of marrying because of some ridiculous societal edicts; how she hated the notion of leaving Lowell Hall, which was beginning to feel like home to her as well. She hadn't realized how alone she'd become in the last five years, how one by one—from her father all the way down to her personal maid—she'd been stripped of company in her life. If not for Jemima and her horses, what would she have done?

Perhaps she could sneak the mares onto Lowell land. Marshall seemed a likely enough fellow—but she would not endanger someone else's livelihood, for her own ends. What if she *said* what she wanted? What if she made the freedom to establish her stud a condition of the marriage? She must have some bargaining power since he was so determined that she wed him.

I will not sneak about, she thought. *I do not require permission. I am not a child.*

She thought again of Jemima, how she wished for her counsel, when a cursory knock on the door sounded before it flew open. In bounded Mrs. Birks, directing a stream of footmen burdened by trunks and bandboxes and hatboxes. Behind them came O'Mara and—"Jem—Lady Coleman! I was only just wishing for you!" Felicity ran and embraced her friend. "Are you well? However did you get here, and bearing such abundance?"

"His Grace sent for me," she answered. "Mr. Bates left me a note about bringing your clothes, and O'Mara came to fetch me from Town. I am in alt to kit you out, finally, in garments that will truly reflect your beauty and the fineness of your figure."

"Please, at the very least, let us offer you a cup of tea."

"The hour grows late and the first gong approaches," Jemima said. "I would not have your toilette rushed."

"Nevertheless. Mrs. Birks, tea, please, and perhaps something else to fortify Lady Coleman after her journey." The housekeeper went to pull the bell, and Mary Mossett ran into the room. "Your Grace, wait till you see—" She spotted Jemima and stopped abruptly, her mouth agape.

"Lady Jemima Coleman, may I introduce Miss Mary Mossett?" Felicity asked. "Lady Coleman is my dearest friend, Mary, I believe I mentioned her to you? Lady Coleman, Mary is adept with a needle, I am sure you two have much to discuss."

Mary snorted. "And a thing or two in common, to be sure—"

"Mary!" Mrs. Birks tweaked the little maid's earlobe. "Make your curtsy."

She did so, never taking her eyes off Jemima.

"Mary," O'Mara said in her soothing tones, "this is Her Grace's dear friend, a fine lady from high society who honors us with her visit to Lowell Hall. It is no surprise that you are so taken with her appearance, is she not wearing a lovely gown? She has brought a beautiful new wardrobe for Her Grace, do help Lady Coleman organize it, do."

"Aye, Ome—O'Mara," Mary said, with a tiny yawn.

"Good evening, Mary," Jemima said. "I would be delighted to no end to discuss the art of fashion with you. Perhaps you might help me unpack?" She gestured to the nearest case, and Mary joined her there.

It was as though the Pantheon Bazaar had come to Sussex. Mrs. Birks supervised the decanting of the two largest trunks, and they yielded a wealth of dresses: day dresses, walking dresses, evening gowns, ball gowns… Felicity spotted at least three of the split-skirt riding habits that Jemima had devised with her in mind. Jemima and Mary unpacked a profusion of shawls, stockings, ribbons, as well as reticules and fans and gloves. The footmen lined up hatboxes along the top shelves of the wardrobes, and underneath, set the sort of containers that held slippers and half boots. Felicity felt as breathless as when the duke had kissed her, and she blushed.

"Are you well, ma'am?" Mrs. Birks hung up the last of the ball gowns. "That bathing room! I hope ye didn't do the water too hot. These newfangled things, they be dangerous, why, a maid knows just how much hot to lay on, and then how much cold, and so on." She took a tray from a goggling servant and poured out cups of tea.

"I am well," Felicity assured her. "I am stunned by this finery. When you said you'd made me clothes, Lady Coleman, I did not imagine it was an entire wardrobe."

"From the skin out," Jemima crowed as she set a smaller case on one of the chairs that ranged around the vanity. "Now, Mary, may I ask you to do Miss Templeton's hair? Very good." Felicity took the seat in front of the vanity table, and Mary brushed out her drying tresses.

"What is this about a bathing room?" Jemima asked while she reviewed the settling of the clothes in the cupboards and presses and moved boxes about.

"An innovation of His Grace's," said O'Mara. "Lowell Hall will soon contain one in every wing, if not every suite."

"It is a room in which hot water pipes through the wall and into a large receptacle, rather like a horse trough." Felicity smiled at the analogy, and Mary giggled. "It is an invention the duke discovered whilst on his travels these past five years. I am astonished that the dukedom could spare him."

"Lucky old duke," Jemima said. "I understand that you have made a tour of the estate."

"I rode about on my own, and today His Grace took me 'round to see as much as we could see. Miss O'Mara, I believe Juventus and Jupiter are off their feed. Both were not at their best today, they were all but asleep."

"You wouldna want 'em otherwise, Your Grace," said Mary, who winced before anyone could shout her name.

"Such fine Roman names," Jemima said and then winced as well.

Felicity slapped a hand on the vanity. "Have you heard of such a thing as Lupercalia, Lady Coleman? Would it be observed up in Northumberland?"

"How quaint that sounds. Oh!" Jemima threw her hands in the air rather dramatically. "I must not neglect to gift you with an innovation of my own." Jemima presented Felicity with a piece of graphite, around which had been fashioned a sleeve made of tin.

"Oh! This is clever." Felicity inspected Jemima's offering; even in something as small as this, it had a certain flair, the metal embossed with imagery that looked like—like pawprints? "Have you pockets in that skirt? Everything should have pockets. Even ball gowns."

"I will take that under advisement." Jemima turned to the little maid. "Oh, Mary, that is a lovely chignon, so full and flattering. And how fortunate that you did not need the hot tongs, as Miss Templeton's hair has a natural curl all its own. I have brought a hair ornament…" She went off muttering and chattering and unearthed from a bandbox a ribbon studded with sparkling crystals. "This is a perfect match to what I have in mind." She handed the ribbon to Mary, who took it without demur.

The little maid dressed Felicity's hair so its natural wave showed to the utmost advantage and carefully wove the spangled ribbon around her crown. Felicity turned her head to and fro. "It looks like stars have been caught in my hair."

"Just the impression I wished it to give. But before we carry on…" Jemima opened the small case beside her and withdrew several books, holding them to her chest. "I know you struggled to make time for reading in the past, but I have brought several new novels. I so wish you would read them. I have no one to discuss them with!"

"Oh, Jem—Lady Coleman." Felicity scowled at the titles and read them aloud. *"The Castle of Lupenbach…The Beastly Baron Bardolph…*and *The Mysteries of Woldolpho.* Oh dear."

"Ooh!" Mary said. "I like the sound of that. If only I had me letters."

Felicity frowned. "I can lend any and all to the servants' hall, if there is someone to read aloud. I would also be happy to organize a tutor."

"We used to have a tutor," Mary piped up, "but he's long gone."

"Not gone the way of the vicar, I hope?"

Mrs. Birks cleared her throat and cast a glance at O'Mara. "His Grace had ideas about education and suchlike for the lower orders, and that old tutor didn't agree and took himself off."

"I thought the children in the village might be in school. It would have explained their absence."

Mary tucked in the end of the ribbon and secured it with a pin. "Oh, we've no need for no school, as there ain't no—"

"Mary!" Mrs. Birks, O'Mara, *and* Jemima hushed the maid.

"If I may be left to help Miss Templeton dress?" Jemima asked. "Mary, you've done so well with Her Grace's hair." Mary pulled a few more curls to dangle around Felicity's neck. "Mrs. Birks, if you would ask Mr. Coburn to send up a footman on the half of the hour?" She turned to the chamberlain and simply said, "O'Mara." Jemima led them to the door of the dressing room. Mary rushed ahead, Mrs. Birks dropped her chin to her shoulder, and O'Mara turned in the hallway.

"How did you get those books past me?" Felicity heard the chamberlain hiss.

"I am skilled at hiding what needs concealment," Jemima replied and closed the door in O'Mara's face.

"What news from Town?" Felicity asked. "Have the gossip rags bequeathed me with a sobriquet?"

Jemima joined Felicity and fussed with a few curls upon taking a stool at her side. "I have not been sociable these last few days, nor taken the papers. This is nothing but a nine days' wonder, as the phrase goes, although of course only four have passed—"

"Jem. Do not cozen me."

"You are known as Fallen Felicity," Jemima said, "and Lowell as the Dastardly Duke. Or the Duped Duke, if they are of the view that you worked nefarious wiles to entice him to carry you away. And you have fled to the Arctic Circle or, worse, America. Where you are even now preparing to present him with a love child."

"Nine days' wonder, indeed."

"Society waits with bated breath for the announcement of a betrothal or a marriage forged over the anvil in Gretna Green."

"And they will wait for as long as I can hold fast," Felicity said. "Has no one else committed a social crime?"

"Well, Miss Miranda Ashworth is betrothed to the Viscount of Walbershire."

"He is seventy if he is a day!"

"According to the *on-dits*, one of your cousins, Odious, I believe, had thought to court her."

"Unlikely. Not that he thought it, but that her family would have wanted a smelting scion for their daughter. Despite her own humble origins." Felicity aped a dowagerish tone, and they both laughed.

"A title makes all good." Jemima leaned forward and grasped her hand. "And here at Lowell Hall, it cannot be all bad."

"It is not. It is that…" Felicity turned to look in the glass and gestured to her coiffure. "My hair is lovely, but it is not at all the done thing, and I hesitate to go below where few will see me, for fear of being thought original or forward. And yet I think I can foster a stud and hold up my head? Neither fear the scuttlebutt, nor let it affect me? Leave here without having wed the duke and expect to be left in peace? I cannot carry on in business if I cannot carry off an unusual coiffure."

"O'Mara mentioned you've been going about the place kitted out in men's clothing," Jemima said.

"Is that progress?"

"It is dead shockin', as we would say in the Northeast." Jemima rose and laid out a chemise, a set of stays, and silken stockings. "But it is also thumbing your nose at convention. I wonder you do not tell the duke about Himself and the mares."

"I did mention it, the first evening. I got on my high horse and delivered my conscientious husbandry speech. He mocked me."

"Mocked you?"

Felicity shrugged. "Perhaps he was teasing. As I begin know him better, I perceive he is all bark and no bite."

"I wouldn't go that far," Jemima muttered.

Felicity looked at herself in the glass. "And then…"

"And then?"

She cast her eyes down. "The subject turned."

"Did it." Jemima folded her arms. "How did it do so?"

"Well, he kissed me."

"Was it unpleasant?"

"Oh, no. Not unpleasant."

"Unwelcome?"

"No…"

"If it was unwelcome, then we shall leave here this instant. You will not be left to receive his advances against your will."

"No, Jem, I do not fear them. In fact, I may like to take them further."

"How far?"

Felicity covered her face with her hands. "I cannot speak of it, not even with you. And if I cannot speak of it, however shall I do it?" She shook her head. "In any case, I have kept the secret of my mares for so long, I am not accustomed to the idea of speaking of that, either." Felicity rose and took the chemise behind a dressing screen. "He is determined to marry me. Me, of all women. It occurred that if he is so intent, I would make my stud a condition of the union."

"How?"

"I thought to draw up my own marriage contracts."

Jemima laughed. "My friend, only you would conceive of such. That is a spectacular notion." She regarded the chemise Felicity now wore. Its thin straps hung off her shoulders and looked rather precarious, but if Jemima made them, they would stay in place. "Yes, that suits you perfectly. Turn, and I'll lace you." She set the corset around Felicity's torso, and pulling the ties, emphasized her tiny waist, lifting her bosom just so.

"There appear to be no children in the village," Felicity said. "I asked him where they were, and he all but ran from me."

"Perhaps it is a sore point."

"I presume so, but how am I to know, if he cannot answer a simple question? How am I to know him if he is evasive and elusive?"

"How is he to know you...?" Jemima mused and tied off the laces.

"To think I had been so happy to see you walk through the door," Felicity grumbled.

"The duke is known far and wide amongst many of our class as the strongest of us all. He is perhaps the strongest man you have ever known, may your father rest in peace." Jemima fussed with the straps of Felicity's chemise. "A consequence of preserving that strength for all to draw upon, to take refuge in, is a lack of acquaintance with the softer things in life. And yet without a balance of both, he is incomplete. You are strong, too, but the feminine mysteries make the softness in life easier for you."

Felicity put a hand on her heart as though it ached. "And yet I have had no pattern of wifely softness since my mother passed and have felt that lack so."

Jemima drew them to the side of the bed to sit. "Is it impossible to believe he may have a lack in his life?"

"He misses his sister. She left England in scandalous circumstances, as far as I could divine. He has not heard from her and is concerned."

"There, that is something."

"My mother…" Felicity took a deep breath. "She flung herself into a life she had no preparation to live, and if not for her blind love of my father, she would have been crushed by every snub and slight. I have been flung into a life I have little preparation for, and know what will come, and dread it. I, to be a duchess, in no time at all."

"It is not uncommon amongst our set for the interval between betrothal and wedding to be no time at all. And I must speak truly—when there is scandal attached, the quicker the better."

"Things are so odd here, it does not seem as though our usual rules should apply. I have longed to be lost to convention, but find I cannot abide the strangeness of it."

"This from one who wishes to devise her own marriage contracts?"

They burst into laughter, and Felicity rose to stand in front of the mirror, admiring her new silhouette. "I will act as though I am the great lady they believe me to be, the one who controls every utterance in the drawing room," she said, "and thus with great subtlety I shall divine what His Grace believes as regards unconventional approaches to life."

"If there is one thing I have learned on my own way, it is that a dream is a Destination, and one must remain flexible upon the Path." Jemima held out a pair of gossamer silken stockings.

"Will I find such sentiments in those novels you brought me?" Felicity took them and drew them up her legs, then tied off adorable little garters that had the image of a feather sewn on at the ends of the ribbons.

"You will find what you need to find," Jemima replied, lifting the evening's chosen creation over Felicity's head.

"Do not speak to me in riddles!" Her protest was muffled by the heavy velvet. Her head emerged, her countenance annoyed. "Every statement made under this roof is three-quarters enigma. It must be contagious."

"I shall strive for plainspokenness," Jemima said. "As best I can. Come, a few finishing touches, and the duke will sign any contract you put before him."

———

A speechless Coburn opened the doors to the Bassett Room and allowed Felicity to pause alone on the threshold. The duke turned in his chair and rose, an arrested look on his face. She waited.

His reaction was as exhilarating as she had envisioned. He came toward her, his eyes glittering, almost ferocious in their regard as he took in her raiment. Rich, cobalt-blue velvet wrapped around her shoulders like a shawl, but no shawl ever looked so enticing; it framed her bosom, lifted and displayed by Jemima's cunning corset. The luxurious fabric hugged her waist and flowed over her hips and outward to the floor, down into a train. The ribbon sparkled in her hair, which was not a tight knob on the top of her head but gathered up behind. Her gloves were a darker blue, almost black, and yet their satiny finish caught the light to match the ribbon and shone in the light. She wafted the air around with her fan, a glittery concoction of crystals and silk in a stunning, bright white, as pure as the burgeoning moon.

Alfred held out a hand. She took it. He drew her closer to him, as close as she could get to That Chest while in company, and he raised her hand to his lips.

"Magnificent," he murmured, and the heat of his lips through the silk of her glove scorched her fingers.

"Magnificent things, clothes that do not heedlessly follow fashion?" she asked.

"Utterly magnificent without qualification." He escorted her over to chairs arranged pleasingly before the hearth.

Felicity nodded to O'Mara, who was once more dressed as though by royal command. Jemima had fluttered in her wake and sat herself nearest to the fire. Her own gown was subdued at first glance, a silvery gray that complemented her coloring but was not the most vibrant of hues. However, its texture was as though thousands of tiny indentations had been stamped on the cloth, giving it depth and movement.

"As you know, Lady Coleman, I do not take spirits, but please do, as the duke no doubt has only the finest on offer."

"I am not enamoured of sherry," Jemima said. "I would prove myself to be lowly bred did I avail of anything else."

"Your refinement cannot be taken into question, my lady," said the duke, who nodded at his butler.

Mr. Coburn offered the lady a short glass, which she sniffed with interest. "It is whisky, my lady," he told her.

Jemima sipped. "It is rather like my great-great-uncle's own brew, yielded by his estate since the eleventh century. It was due to his superior malt that the family was elevated."

"Such is often the way," the duke concurred.

"And how did your title come into being?" Felicity inquired.

"The usual favors done to the Crown," he replied. He was having difficulty keeping his gaze above her chin. "Well before the eleventh century, however, if it is no insult to Lady Coleman."

"Oh, heavens, no." The lady took another delicate sip. "This would be from just over the border, I suspect. It's the heathery midtones that give it away."

"Well spotted. Or tasted," he commended her. Felicity and Jemima exchanged a glance; the duke was positively ebullient this evening. "It derives from our distillery in Kircudbright and can be vouched for by Mr. Bates."

"Will he join us this evening?" Felicity inquired.

"He is away, on matters of ducal importance."

"It cannot be right, having him to and fro at all hours."

"This is a special case."

"Lowell Hall is a repository of special cases, Lady Coleman. Has that gone down the wrong way?" Felicity asked, concerned as Jem choked on her drink.

"It has, but I am well now," her friend assured her. "I understand you enjoyed a tour of the estate, Miss Templeton."

"I did. I thank you again, Your Grace, for the outing this day," Felicity said to the duke. "I did wonder if you have neighbors who are of the gentry?"

"Keen to mix with the better sorts, as you did at home, perhaps?"

"I have no love lost for the inhabitants of Edenbridge. My mother did her best to inspire them to warm to her, and they were ever cold and distant. And when she died, they made no pretense about cutting us directly."

"Humans—humanity is at its worst when it assumes that one's birth conveys special treatment."

"Who is the radical now, Alf—Your Grace?" Felicity teased.

Jemima said, "I believe that speaks to the duke's integrity, Miss Templeton, that he would believe so. And an admirable degree of tolerance."

"Oh, indeed, Lady Coleman," she replied. "One learns more from the way a man treats his so-called inferiors than from his dealings with his peers."

"So-called peers." The duke began to slouch but pulled himself up at Felicity's wide-eyed glance of opprobrium.

"We cared not so much for class in Ireland," O'Mara, all out of character, chimed in with a personal observation. "But it was perhaps more insidious for feigning its lack of import, when in fact, all were aware of where they stood."

"Well said, Miss O'Mara." Felicity was warming to the topic. "If

only one was accepted despite one's status or the perceived societal role to which they have been born, beyond false limitations and
outdated notions of what is acceptable. As regards the sexes, for
example. I can think of no one more nurturing than a vicar, and yet
women are not permitted to serve in that way, despite being natu-
rals in that role. Or, as another example, the strength of a woman
in the instance of childbirth. And yet many would not deem this to
be strength, merely an animalistic instinct."

"I am all that is admiration for your wide world view, Miss
Templeton," said Alfred. "I do not believe in reducing anyone
to the perceived societal role they have been born to and in fact
refuse to allow any in my care to fail to achieve their goals."

"Hence, Lowell Close," O'Mara said.

"Oh, Jem—Lady Coleman, I did not tell you about the village!"
Felicity cried. "It is a hive of industry, of fine art and trade. It is in
want of a vicar, though."

"My brother is in holy orders," Jemima offered and then looked
as though she wished she hadn't.

"Has he a living?" Felicity tilted her head at the duke, and his
eyes laughed at her. "Perhaps I shall see to that disbursement after
all. As well as that of a schoolteacher. I understand that your servants do not have their letters?"

"Good Godde—God, woman, will you foment the revolution
under my very roof?"

"The education of every man and woman is something to
be striven for, and it would be a great leader who would allow
such."

"It is not I who will lead, my dear," he said. He rose and nodded
to Coburn, who moved to ring the bell.

He helped Felicity up from her chair and leaned down to
whisper in her ear. "Your passion is almost as intoxicating as your
person. Perhaps we shall forego tea this evening?"

She looked up at him. "But our—your guests..."

"*Our* guests can entertain themselves for the mere hour or two before…bed."

She licked her lips and considered her answer, when Bates came thundering over the threshold.

"Forgive me, Your Graces. Lady Coleman." He appeared befuddled by the latter's presence, and his usual eloquence seemed to have deserted him. O'Mara cleared her throat. "Ah, yes, and O'Mara. Alph—Your Grace, if I might have a word?"

"I take it your news affects Miss Templeton?" Bates nodded. "Then proceed. Unless she wishes otherwise?"

"As I have no idea what this could pertain to…" Unless it was to do with the will, but how?

"It is to do with your father's solicitors. Which were not in fact solicitors, I am afraid," said Bates. "Your father most assuredly dealt with men of law. One assumes, his being a baron. But the address to which you wrote…and the truth of the document…" He appealed to the duke. "Your Grace, if I could speak with you in private before I disclose my findings."

A bitter chill flowed through Felicity's veins. "Mr. Bates," she said, "as this concerns me, I insist you tell all."

"It is terrible news, madam." For a moment, it looked as though his eyes changed color to a bright gold, but she was surely mistaken. Mr. Bates glared at Alfred before continuing, "My man delivered your letter to the law office to whom you addressed your letter, but it was not a solicitor's office to which that address applied. Miss Templeton, it is a slaughterhouse."

"But when I went through my uncle's desk—" She took a moment to look abashed. "I discovered correspondence from that address, from the firm dealing with my father's estate."

"I would hazard a guess he knew you were searching, Felicity," Jemima said, all need for formality gone.

"I do not understand. Why go to such lengths to deceive me?"

"To prevent you from discovering that your uncle told you

lies. Your father made no provision for an independent legacy should you fail to marry by this year's birthday—it is entirely of your uncle's own invention. I am so sorry to bring you this news, ma'am." Bates dipped his head, as did O'Mara, in that now familiar tic.

"But how can you know *that*? About the legacy?" Felicity left off hanging on to the duke's arm and stepped away. She would take this horrendous news standing on her own two feet. The will was false, her dreams were dust, and the choices she had thought she had were null and void. It was over. She had no means, nothing to count upon, nothing.

Bates looked angrily at Alfred again, and his teeth—Felicity thought his teeth looked transformed, long and sharp, but that could not be possible. "My men are very clever at winkling out information, by whatever means are most expedient. They located your uncle's solicitors and appealed to their, er, higher natures for information. Your uncle's solicitor confirmed that the whereabouts of your father's true will remains a mystery to all who deal with the family's holdings. It is why, despite numerous attempts, your uncle could not sell Templeton House."

"Sell? My home?" A curious buzz filled her head, and Felicity took hold of the back of a chair.

"It is illegal to sell any chattels and appurtenances of a peer without directives from that peer or from the executor of his estate." The duke's voice was little more than a snarl. "Purcell is a fool, but he must not know where the true will is if he is trying to disburse the barony's holdings."

"My sources think this may be a double blind, that he must be the executor, as the only living adult relation, even by marriage, that he is publicly abiding by the law, but in secret has another plan. Forgive me, madam, how I wish I could spare you this."

"Mr. Bates, I thank you, but I am a grown woman and must face facts."

"Felicity." Jemima's delicate hand touched her arm. "Shall we go up? Perhaps this is enough for one night."

"Is there any will at all?" she asked, patting her friend's hand. She would see this through.

"It is impossible to believe Purcell does not have the baron's testament, as it is the linchpin upon which this whole scheme turns. To risk the wrath of the law without having it in his possession is foolish." Bates turned to the duke, who remained silent. "I've sent the magpies to Finsbury Square—"

"Magpies?" Felicity swayed at that.

"One for sorrow, two for mirth," Jemima sang, "three for a wedding, four for a...search."

"I—I hadn't heard that particular version. How interesting."

"Your Grace." There was O'Mara, standing before her, taking her hand with fierce strength. "Believe me when I say His Grace and Bates will do everything in their power, in their considerable power, with mine added to it, to clarify this matter. Know, please know, none of us would ever abandon you. We will see this put right."

"Miss O'Mara, I am honored." She squeezed the chamberlain's hand in return.

Felicity closed her eyes, and even before she opened them, Alfred had taken the place before her. His hands, those warm, strong hands, cupped her face, and made her look into his eyes, his ferocious, brilliant, blue eyes.

"I have resources you cannot imagine," he said. "I have might to call upon that you know nothing of. But know that in whatever way necessary, I will secure for you the promise you believe your father made."

"I thought I had everything, but I have nothing at all." As near as she was to the hearth, she was cold, so cold. "And no longer any reputation to treat cavalierly." She moved away from the vigor of his hold and from the seduction of his scent.

"If you could trust in us, Your Grace," Bates urged. "If for only a little while longer, you would carry on—"

"I have done nothing but carry on," she said. "Never mind that I have been persisting since the age of twenty. That I put my faith in one I knew had no love lost for me or my father. That my uncle would disgrace the memory of his sister so..." She moved to the door, the train of her glorious gown feeling like nothing more than deadweight. "I believed him. How he must have laughed. I don't mind his spite, but I cannot abide his lies."

She stood on the threshold once more. "I accept your petition for my hand, Your Grace." Her voice was composed, and frosty with it, but the hand she pledged trembled. "It seems you have won, for I have lost everything." She blinked and swayed, and the duke was at her side before she took another breath. "I shall see myself up."

"You look to be about to faint."

"I do not faint," she declared, as her eyes rolled back in her head, and she swooned into his waiting arms.

Felicity felt the duke lift her into his arms and hold her fast against his chest. There was a pause, a tightening of his embrace, and she heard him say, "We will destroy them. Utterly, completely, comprehensively—destroy them" before she gave herself up to darkness.

———

In the darkest hour, before the dawn, a mouse scurried out of a shrub and sat on its haunches, looking up at the state bedchamber's window. She was soon joined by more of her own kind who had raced up the long drive. This nest of mice kept well away from the clowder of cats who had slunk down from the stables, and close behind them, solemn for once, a herd of colts followed suit and took up sentry. Soon, it seemed that any animal that one might find in the English countryside was represented: a colony of beavers, a knob of wildfowl, even a caravan of stoats appeared. A dove floated above the assemblage and joined the clattering of jackdaws perched in the topiary. They bowed their heads and bared their necks as one as the leading members of their eclectic pack joined them, the largest of them bristling with the kind of power that inspired fear or safety, depending upon one's loyalty. All here were loyal to him and to his *vera amoris*, whose heart was broken. They gathered their own powers, as small as the mouse's, as eager as the colt's, as fierce as the wolf's, gathered and spread them like a blanket over their grieving lady, sent to her in sleep so she might heal, and yearned for her to know them, complete in their dual natures, with her whole heart and soul.

Thirteen

AFTER TWO DAYS OF HIDING AWAY IN THE STATEROOMS, Felicity decided she'd had enough of her own company and made her way below. As she reached the foyer, she found it bereft of Mr. Coburn and the halls curiously unpopulated by footmen. Immediately, when Mr. Bates had brought his news, she had been listless and bewildered but in short order had become impatient with herself for indulging in such maidenish behavior. Slipping behind the green baize door, she followed her nose to the kitchens.

She would not be a maiden for much longer. Her choice had been made for her. She was not an heiress; she was not to be independent and a woman of means and of business. She would marry the duke, be a wife and a duchess, thriving under the care of the staff of the house and doing all in her power to improve their lots in life.

She paused before a painting of a horse whose rider was occluded by shadow. There would be kissing and the other carrying-on…and if that carrying-on was anything like the kissing, she would have babies. As many babies as her advanced age allowed. "Or pups," she said to the horse in the picture. "When in Rome, as they say." How fiercely he had promised to champion her cause, as he appeared to champion all in his care, with brusque kindness and dry good humor. How fiercely he would defend his child, love his child. He would be stern, no doubt, but as playful as he was with his miscellany of footmen. An image came into her mind of His Grace rolling around on the carpet with squealing children crawling all over him, pretending he was at their mercy. His hair was terribly mussed, and he laughed and looked up at her, so handsome and relaxed and joyous, it took her breath away.

The power of the fantasy stunned her, her heart so full of love and contentment, she felt disloyal to her herd. She ran a finger down the painted muzzle and worried for her mares. Aherne had assured her they were safe, but she feared that her uncle knew everything about her horses; it would not surprise her to discover he was aware of her hiding place for the band. She would insist they be brought here and that she be permitted to cultivate them. Would His Grace allow such a thing? She could see in his relations with his staff that while he was gruff and abrupt, he was not an autocrat. He took in anyone from anywhere and gave them employment under his roof, and his fostering of the talents in the village alone were unheard of—yet she sensed that an uncivilized aspect to this character was very near the surface. His notions of marriage could be as old-fashioned as Lowell Hall itself. They must compromise or…or else she knew not what.

As she approached the kitchen, voices rose in a dull roar. She heard Mary Mossett shout, "It's time for the *cognominatio*." Whatever could that mean? She stood before the door, tempted to eavesdrop, but no, she would not betray the staff in any way. She knocked briskly and opened the door. "Excuse me." She smiled and accepted the bared necks, curtsies, and bows.

"Your Grace!" Coburn dispelled the crowd, flapping his arms about as he was prone to do.

"Here, now, Your Grace, will I get you a nice cup o' tea and a bitta toast?" Mrs. Birks gestured her toward the door.

"No, thank you," Felicity said. "I wish to take exercise in the park and wondered if Lady Coleman was still in residence and she would join me."

"Here I am." Jemima appeared from the corridor and handed a length of fabric to Mary. "If you would finish this off for me, Mary? It is well within your capabilities."

"Oh, milady, I will, of course, and whatever else you ask." Mary skittered away.

"I was working on a new piece with Miss Mossett," Jemima

explained. "You were correct, Miss Templeton, she is very gifted. I may steal her away from you, er, from the duke."

"His Grace is in his study," Coburn offered. "If I may bring you to him?"

"No, thank you," Felicity said again. "I would not dare interrupt his day. Shall we, Lady Coleman?"

"I must fetch my cloak," Jemima began, and a whirlwind of activity commenced: Jemima's cloak and bonnet were fetched, and Felicity was handed a small picnic in a sack; they were led through to the kitchen and out a side door and exhorted to enjoy the fresh air.

As they made their way through the park, a pattern to the apparent unbridled wildness asserted itself. While the acreage was vast, there seemed to be a series of groves, dells, and nooks laid out in a clockwise procession. It was a robust and challenging walk, with embankments, fallen logs, and a variety of gradients that required adeptness of foot to manage them. What was likely a tributary of Edenbrook wound its way amongst the groves and obstacles. The weather was brisk, the sky gray, and a light wind at their back helped the ladies in their exertions.

"You are far more fit than I," huffed Jemima, as she leaned against the bole of an enormous oak. "I do not walk often."

Felicity stopped and let her friend rest. "I used to walk with my father throughout the whole of our park at Templeton House. While it was much smaller, at least it was navigable. Where are we?" She walked around the small clearing in which they had paused. Not a folly or a bench for resting in sight, and only a hampered view of the Hall itself. "And of course, I rode with my mother. Every day and nearly into the night. My father." She laughed, a memory rising up to counter those from the last, difficult years she'd had with him. "He hated to ride, but once he mounted Delilah, of all the mares he could have chosen, and came to fetch us as we were working late into the night devising even more challenging obstacles for the hunt." She ran her hand down the trunk of an ash tree, remembering how cross she was to be taken away from their course-building, how her mother laughed and teased until her father, who was also cross, mellowed and helped them move a heavy log into place. "At least Uncle Ezra was prevented from getting rid of my home. Although whether it is mine at all is in doubt."

How Mr. Bates was going unravel her tangled affairs defied her imagination. Had it to do with being a man in the world? She doubted even her trousers would get her as far as the duke's steward had gone. As she slowly came out of her fog of fear and disbelief, the number of questions that came to mind were staggering, and not only in relation to her uncle's perfidy. How had Mr. Bates and the duke known, on the strength of one letter, to initiate an investigation? Had the duke read her post? How infuriating that would be, but how like a man. What was within their abilities to aid her? For, duke notwithstanding, Alfred was not the King, nor the Prince of Wales—even his power must have limits. They all seemed very confident that they would meet with no resistance and sort out in a few days what had been flummoxing her for years.

"I am sorry, Felicity, for all that has come to pass," said Jemima. They resumed their walk, taking care as the terrain steepened.

Picking her way over the large boulders in the way, Felicity led them up to the top of a slight rise. "Look." She pointed: Was that Alfie? No, just before it leapt from sight, she saw that while large, this creature was lighter in color, a golden blond, and much leaner than His Grace. "Did you see that?"

Jemima huffed her way up to the crest. "I can't say I did. Good Goddess—God. Or galoshes. How steep that was."

"What is this doing here?" Felicity led the way toward a well-kept stone building. Its thatched roof was in excellent repair, and its exterior glowed with whitewash, but who would live in the middle of Lowell Hall's park? "It is much like another such building I saw...four days ago? Five? I have lost track of time. It is seven days since the Livingston ball. It is like a mere moment on the one hand, and an eternity on the other."

Felicity knocked as she pushed open the door. "Hello?" she called. Shelves lined the walls of the single room and were piled with clothing that upon inspection proved to be of all sizes for men, women, and children. Apart from a few chairs and a low table, there was nothing else in the hut. "What is this in aid of?"

Jemima rested against the doorway. "One never knows when the weather might change?" she hazarded.

"Perhaps it is for those who are in need and do not wish the stigma of charity. They come and take what is required?" Felicity rummaged through a pile of men's shirts and refolded what she'd set askew. "I've seen no want in these lands since I've been here, however."

"A mystery," Jemima chirped and took a seat.

Felicity laughed. "All that sewing and drawing has left you in poor condition, my friend."

"This is not my usual mode of transportation," Jemima said. "And this landscape is not designed for such as I."

Opening the sack that Mrs. Birks had thrust upon her, Felicity removed a small flask of lemonade and passed it over. Jemima took dainty sips in quick succession.

Felicity moved around the little one-roomed house, restless.

"Have you slept at all?" Jemima asked.

"Yes, to my surprise. The first night was as though I had been struck over the head. The second night was the same. I apologize for neglecting you—"

"Felicity. Don't be ridiculous." Jemima's bosom puffed up in offense. "If the duke had not asked that we leave you in peace, I should have made quite a nuisance of myself."

"I did not want to see anyone," she admitted, wondering how Alfred could have known.

"Not even your betrothed?"

Felicity picked up a shawl that had been mixed in with the

men's waistcoats. "My betrothed. I remember accepting him, for what it is worth."

"It is worth all, as he intends to wed you."

"Now his goal is achieved, he seems strangely absent."

Jemima threw her hands in the air. "He was there in his study for you to call upon."

"Jem, I am in such a state." Felicity twisted the shawl in her grasp. "I have never had a suitor, much less a betrothed. My mother simply made up stories about balls and gentlemen and bouquets and calling cards. She never had a Season, so how could she have advised me? I don't know how to go on."

"How do you wish to go on?" Jemima rose and tidied the garments as she checked them for wear.

"I wish that all that has been exposed were lies. That I had a fortune to do with as I pleased. So I needn't work out how to go on." Felicity's face crumpled, and she buried her face in the shawl she was near to rending in two. "There is no going back, of course," she muttered into the cloth.

"One can never go back," Jemima said. "I am curious as to what your dreams were before your ambitions blossomed?"

"Oh. A quiet marriage with a loving, steady man, and a houseful of children so no one would ever be alone. A union blessed by the accord of both sides of the family. Peace and joy."

"While I doubt your union with His Grace will be entirely peaceful, I think he is capable of love, and it is clear that his pack—his people—his pack of people loves you, and you bring them joy, which they will return to you beyond measure."

"I am an Antidote," Felicity whispered. "I have not taken. I do not understand his passion for me."

"That is the fault of your perception, my friend, because it is clear to all around you," Jemima said, a touch of bitterness creeping into her tone. "Believe me when I tell you that one such as he cannot dissemble."

"If only I had a sign," she insisted. "An incontrovertible sign..."

Jemima took the shawl from her. Shaking out the wrinkles as best she could, with her back to the room, Jemima said, "All are working toward sorting out your father's will. The sheer number of people devoting their energy to finding you a solution is quite an honor. Not all can count on such support in their time of need. If only all women had such a clan, willing to put all else aside for them." She left the building and walked off.

Felicity followed and caught up to her friend. "I had already given up on the dream of a family, Jemima, after Mama died and Father lost his will to live. I had no one to speak for me, no dowry, no beauty. And after I had resigned myself to a lonely life of nothing, of emptiness, the hope roused by the terms of that will inspired me to take my talent with the horses and do something useful. And now I discover that the means to bringing my vision to fruition was a lie, a vicious lie." She sobbed, once, and it echoed around the clearing they had stumbled into. She covered her mouth, and Jemima turned to embrace her.

"*I* am sorry, I am so sorry," Jemima whispered, tearing up. "In your words I heard only my own sad tale, and I was selfish and unkind, I am so sorry."

"I am sorry, because while it appears I have everything now, how can I trust it? I cannot lose everything all over again, I cannot. I cannot."

The women embraced, and Felicity wept, wept for everything, for her parents, for her lost dreams, for her unpredictable future. The wind soughed through the trees, moaning as branches scratched one upon the other; what leaves remained after a long, cold winter rustled mournfully, as though joining in with her grief. As their tears diminished, Jemima naturally had two exquisite hankies for them to dry their eyes upon. "It is a crime to use such beautiful examples of embroidery to blow my nose," Felicity scolded.

"Mere scraps," Jemima replied and then honked.

Felicity looked about them; as she did so, the clouds parted, and a beam of light filled the clearing, illuminating it as if by design. They were in a circle that played host to a flat stone set alone in the center. The area was cleared of all the wild underbrush that was a fixture of the park and appeared large enough to hold a multi-tude. Off in the distance, she could see the roof of Lowell Hall and smoke coming from its myriad chimneys; a path led out of the circle opposite to where they entered to a footbridge that bowed over a brook, and another little house stood atop yet another hill.

"This looks positively pagan." She put her hands on her hips. "Is this where they perform their rites of Lupercalia or who knows what?"

"Felicity. I have been less than forthcoming with you, and whether it angers your betrothed or not, I must tell you I am a—" Jemima began but stopped when Felicity grabbed her elbow and pointed into the trees.

"Is that a rooster? Why in the world would a rooster be in a wood? Oh! I had the oddest dream last night, as though Noah's ark had come to rest beneath my window rather than on Mount Ararat. And have you seen the paintings in that house? I have never seen so many renderings of animals, not lapdogs and the like, but actual wild animals, rhinoceroses and elephants—and fish. If I didn't know better, I would think they were posing." She shook her head. "Please, go on, Jemima, you were speaking. It's only that I have had no one with whom to share my thoughts."

"No, no, this is not the time to burden you with my secrets and woes," Jemima said. "I do believe the duke will do all in his power to right every wrong done to you."

"Has he said anything, in my absence?"

"He would hardly confide in me," Jemima scoffed.

"What about Mr. Bates? He looked befuddled with ardor when his gaze fell upon you in the drawing room."

"Which speaks to a lack of wit that cannot be appealing." Jemima blushed.

"How did he know of my father's will and my ambitions? I told no one. Well, no human."

Jemima's eyes widened. "I cannot think what you mean?"

"I told the big dog about my parents and the stud," Felicity said. "I doubt he carried tales to Mr. Bates."

"Big dog?" Jemima whispered.

"How pale you look!" Felicity exclaimed. "I came across a very large dog on my ride out, my first day in trousers. If I wasn't sure of being called mad, I would have said he was a wolf."

"Holy Godde—God."

"I was perfectly safe; of course it was not a wolf. How could it be? It would not have let me near it, were it a wild animal. And yet he really was too large to be a dog. His shoulder was well above my waist. That sounds rather large for a wolf as well, does it not?" Felicity sighed. "But I admit my perceptions are muddled. I am a maelstrom of confusion, betrayal, desire…"

"Desire?" asked Jemima.

"I must not give in to this, this madness I feel for him, this need that has built and built in no time at all," Felicity said. "That night, before Mr. Bates came in—that night, I was going to take the duke as a lover, Jem. I was going to give him everything. And I know he, and Mr. Bates, and Miss O'Mara are intent upon standing by me, but how do they know what they know? What is he not telling me?"

Jemima reached for her hand. "Once I made a choice I considered to be correct, based on propriety and society's dictates, and now, could I do it over again, I would follow my heart. I think that once you follow your heart, it will become more whole than you could ever have imagined."

"It is all I have to rely upon. I have no family to stand for me. Cecil wrote and has abandoned me to my fate." She removed her cousin's letter from one of her many pockets and handed it to her friend. "And he did so in the strangest fashion. Look, I cannot stop puzzling over it."

Jemima scanned it quickly. "Strange, indeed. 'Thine' cousin?"

"And 'la'! And what could the postscript mean? As though I should overlook his refusal to come to my aid and send him a chatty reply?"

"The very way he scribed his lines is bizarre." Jemima handed it back. "Line by line, as though it were one of your lists."

Felicity stared at it. "What a sharp eye you have. I was so dismayed by the content, I paid no mind to the form. I shall give it further attention." She sighed. "Shall we scramble our way back home—back? Back to the Hall?"

"The time grows late, and I fear I must leave you," Jemima said. "My aunt will be most cross to have spared me even this long, and the coach has been prepared for me to leave upon the hour."

"Thank you for walking with me," said Felicity as she embraced her friend. They began to pick their way out of the park. "I shall return to the staterooms and summon the duke. It is past time I demanded some answers."

Dressed in his most ducal attire, down to his ceremonial sash, Alfred made his way to the staterooms. He had received word that Miss Templeton desired his company, in no uncertain terms.

Your Grace, I require your presence in the staterooms no later than the first gong. F

The imperious quality of Felicity's request intoxicated him. The power that he exuded expanded, and rather than oppressing the footmen he passed on the way to answer his summons, it invigorated them. Never lackadaisical, always keen to please, they went about their work with increased energy, with pleasure—and, dare Alfred say, joy.

His mate's command was not a challenge to his authority but an assertion of her own. Would she take him to task? He listed his transgressions for his own benefit: kidnapping, general obfuscation, turning tail and running from her query about the children… He did not think he would be reprimanded for leaving her alone the last two days. *Alone*, in a manner of speaking: he had lain across the doorway in his wolfskin and prevented any and all from disturbing her but for the delivery of trays, which she only lightly touched. He had intuited her need to take in all that had transpired and respected it. Surely that counted for something— perhaps not for the kidnapping, but even so. He would listen to her complaints and then present her with what was tucked in his pocket and escort her to dinner to celebrate their first meal as an officially betrothed couple, and that would be that.

He would champion her and punish her uncle and keep her safe… His most painful memory intruded, reminding him of the last female he had promised to champion and keep safe, all of two years ago, and whom he had failed…

He had arrived at speed from Dover, and nevertheless just made the gong, his lateness exacerbated by the Lowell Hall custom of formally dressing for dinner. Coburn announced him, and his parents' latest assemblage of sycophants bowed and curtseyed as he entered the Bassett Room. He received a nod from his father and a reserved smile from his mother and could consider that his warm familial welcome after an absence of a year. While the *ton* assumed he was doing an endless and indulgent grand tour, sowing his wild oats abroad, he was on the hunt for his *vera amoris*, and he would still be on his quest had Phoebe's letters not become urgent.

He wandered the perimeter of the room, giving the impression he was greeting his parents and exchanging pleasantries with the knots of flatterers who surged forward, but in fact he was reading the mantelpiece.

It had started as a silly game between himself and his sister. She had proclaimed a passion for china dogs, and so he'd commenced sending her the ugliest, most preposterous figurines he could find. As his travel broadened, the variety of statues grew, and in their letters, they had assigned personalities to the little beasts. From the tableaux Phoebe devised over the years, Alfred was able to discern the mood of the Hall.

Looking at the grouping on the mantle, none but he would understand that there was trouble afoot.

The large mastiff that designated their father and the pampered poodle that was the representation of their mother clustered with a foul, hoary hound so grotesque, it seemed to have drool hanging from its frowning mouth. All three had backed an adorable little lapdog into a corner. He spied his own figurine—a cross-eyed, grinning springer spaniel—hidden on a far-off windowsill. He fetched it and joined Phoebe at the hearth.

"Ulrich." His sister smiled coolly and curtsied; their mother had insisted she do so from the age of twelve, as well as address him by his title. Her honey-colored hair was arranged in the latest style, and her evening attire reflected the latest trends; her light-blue eyes, a match to his, conveyed distress.

"Sister." They clasped hands. He held up the cocker spaniel. "Your collection has dispersed, hither and yon."

"Do aid me then, brother, in setting it to rights."

"It does look ill," he agreed, and he shielded her from his parents' gaze as they turned to the hearth. "Who is this loathsome chap?"

"The Marquess of Castleton," Phoebe moaned through a playful, society smile.

"Damnation." Alfred squeezed her elbow as if teasing her, but his touch conveyed his alarm. "He has gone through four mates at last count."

"Behold the prospective fifth."

"As if I would ever desert you to that." He set the mastiff and poodle at the opposite end of the mantle, and they both considered the hound. "I will talk to Father and insist that you must wait to wed until I do."

"Brother," Phoebe said, laughing gaily. He answered it, long and loud, as she whispered, "You are not the duke; you have no say in my fate. Your search infuriates them, and selling me off to the highest bidder is within their remit."

He swept the hound from the mantle, and it smashed to smithereens upon the hearthstone. "Clumsy," he said when the crowd murmured in dismay. As they regarded the shards at their feet, he whispered, "I shall divine a solution. Trust me."

She nodded and then shone a bright smile up at him, for all to see. "And how goes your quest?"

"Poorly." He settled his parents' china dogs even farther away from himself and his sister. "India is next, although I wonder if I am able for a tigress."

"I confess myself surprised that one of our American friends did not suit. I would find New York quite congenial, myself."

He raised his brows, and she lowered her lashes. "That is the last resort." The bell for dinner rang.

"Indeed," Phoebe agreed as she curtsied again. "But I, for one, would embrace it with my entire being."

"I will do whatever is necessary to protect you," he said as Phoebe's escort into dinner made his way toward them. He crushed the fragments of the bulldog under his boot heel.

"No." Her smile never flagged, and she took Alfred's arm as he led her to meet her dinner companion halfway. Her eyes flashed up at Alfred. "Do not throw over your search. Our people rely on you. You must put them first." She squeezed his hand as she left him for her dinner partner, and he vowed he would see her safe and sound…

———————

He had not. Arriving at his destination, he adjusted his sash and entered the parlor, which was bereft of his mate. He went through to the bedchamber. Not there. His heart began to race; he fought his uncharacteristic panic and paused to breathe and scent, and there she was, not in her dressing room as he assumed, but sitting at the desk in a smallish study, reading. She started when she saw him in the doorway.

"Your Grace. How stealthy you are." She composed her face into cool, calm lines. She was not dressed for dinner but was wearing another of Lady Coleman's unconventional creations. This one looked like a modification of his dressing gown: richly embroidered and fashioned from satin, it buttoned casually up the front as though the lady could, of all things, dress herself. Or as though a gentleman could divest the lady of the garment in a trice, without the bother of laces and stays. He found himself distracted by the vee that plunged between her breasts, which revealed just enough cleavage to send his senses mad.

"My apologies. I received your note."

"As I see." She closed the book with a letter. Was it the one from that useless cousin of hers?

"What do you read?"

"Jem—Lady Coleman brought me some of her horrid novels. I find them quite enthralling, if ridiculous. This is *The Mysteries of Woldolpho*. I am not certain yet, but there is something passing strange about the behavior of the Count Woldolpho."

That cheeky goose—he'd have a word with her ladyship soon enough. "You are in good looks," he said. "Your gown is rather casual for tonight's meal."

"Anything would appear casual against your plumage." She regarded his regalia from head to toe. "I have not decided whether I will come down." She rose, clutching the book to her bosom. As she swept across in front of the desk and her skirts billowed around her ankles, he saw she wore some odd sort of slipper that left her toes bare.

"If there is any way I can influence your decision…" He allowed his desire for her to fill his aura, to show in his eyes; she did not rise to the bait.

"Your Grace." She took a breath and lifted her chin. "I would like to be apprised of the situation concerning my uncle and the fraudulent will."

Blast. He should have known, of course. "I have nothing to report on that matter at this time."

"I find that impossible to believe."

"Believe we are doing all in our power to address the situation."

"I am asking what that situation is. Mr. Bates did not appear to be secure in his facts. Is there or is there not a will that is the true testament to the wishes of my father?"

"All is yet to be revealed."

She regarded him for a long, silent moment, and for the first time since he was a very, very young pup, he squirmed under the gaze of another.

"I do not find these answers satisfactory." She set the book down as though to stop herself from throwing it at his head.

"There is much we do not know—"

"There is far more I do not know. I do not know how Mr. Bates had the inkling to begin his quest. Unless you or he read my post?"

"I ordered him to investigate the address. We did not read your post."

She nodded, all condescension. "A mark in your favor."

"I am relieved." He could not help the bite of sarcasm.

"As you should be, Your Grace. Unless you desire a wife who will bow down to your every dictate, meek and mild." Felicity lofted her chin, as she was wont to do. "I fear I may have given you the impression I will be such a wife. I will not. You may like to reconsider your proposal."

"I will never reconsider my proposal."

"I insist you explain why."

"I cannot, at this juncture."

"How is it that you have focused on me with such insistence? Can you tell me what it is about me that enraptures you so?"

"I will, I swear this to you, on my life and soul, when the time is right."

"When will the time be right?"

"Soon."

Her face fell, and he saw her, Felicity, behind the aloof mask she had donned. He came as near as he dared but did not touch her. "Trust me, Felicity, please." He dipped his head to catch her eye, and she turned her head. "Bates and his men are scouring Town for clues that will lead to the truth."

"It no longer matters," she whispered. He yearned to lift her chin, to see her eyes, to let her see his, and see his wolf's, but he must not risk it, he must follow their laws, he must wait to name her before all, and have her accepted by all, before he shared their secrets.

"It matters, because you have been misled, in a most egregious manner," he said. "I will take steps to ensure your uncle will never have the opportunity to cause you pain in the future."

"I object to violence and do not permit you to harm his person."

"I will do what I think is right in this instance."

The frost descended once more. "Against my wishes? Marriage to you becomes increasingly inauspicious."

"It is inauspicious to begin with such calumny going unpunished." He could not stop the growl of his wolf bleeding into his response. "I will avenge you as I see fit."

"What good is vengeance? Lying to me was vengeful, and yet my uncle remains an unhappy, cruel man. If it was his goal to ruin my life, he did not achieve this ambition, for in you swept on your white charger and gave me an advantage he never would have reckoned."

"Your pain is my pain." He inhaled her distress, her grief, his wolf going mad with him to *get on with it, get on with it!* "It is my duty to exact the recompense that is yours for this betrayal. Else it will eat away at you, at your gorgeous, open nature, and make you bitter and small."

Felicity pushed past him and went to stand at the window. "Nothing I say will dissuade you. I shall take my dinner on a tray and perhaps meet you again at our wedding, Your Grace. Or shall I call you Lowell? How like a *ton* marriage this already is."

Alfred stood behind her, vibrating with revolt. A ruff of fur emerged around his wrists, his visage strained to devolve into the face of his wolf, and he fought against the Change. "Oh, no. Not one of those white marriages for us, my dear, not one of those society unions that are nothing more than business arrangements. You will come to understand that this is a fated meeting of minds and hearts. And that I mean every word when I say we will be true to one another. Forever. Look."

She turned to him. He withdrew his hand from his pocket and thrust out a ring. "Here. This is a family custom, one that has been observed throughout centuries. Each of the Lowell wives receives them."

"A betrothal ring? I believe the practice is in the midst of a renaissance. And that the bestowal of them is often an occasion of some ceremony." Felicity clutched the neckline of her gown close to her throat. As much as he'd wished for another glimpse of her décolletage, he found himself captivated by her feet. She had the tiniest toes. "Your Grace." He looked up, and her visage was frostier than ever. "I had begun to hope in the possibility we would suit, that we might forge a manageable, fulfilling future. An action such as this convinces me I must be mad to envision such an outcome."

He held out the ring again. It was an heirloom, for Goddess's sake. "If you will do me the favor of accepting this, then we may officially consider ourselves promised to one another."

She stared him down and did not even glance at the enormous diamond that glittered in the candlelight. No one in his life had ever held his gaze like this. No one had ever faced him down in

such a manner. If only he could tell her what he was, and why
that made them what they were—he had to tell her. Enough was
enough. He would do so, without waiting for his pack's approval,
now, this instant—

A coterie of footmen led by Mrs. Birks collected in the doorway. "There you are, Your Graces. We saw the open door. Will you
go below, ma'am, or will you be joining Her Grace, Your Grace? It's
the work of a moment to fetch up two trays."

"I shall be dining alone," Felicity replied. "If the footmen will
prepare the sitting room, Mrs. Birks? Thank you. Good evening,
Lowell." She lofted her brows, and he considered himself routed.

One last try. "Will you take this…?" His hand holding the ring
hovered between them.

"I will not." She turned and walked out of the room.

───────

Alfred burst into his study, dispensing with his clothing. It would
not do to allow his wolf to tear through his sash and garters. He
tossed the ring onto his desk and growled when Bates and Coburn
appeared. His butler remained trembling in the corridor, but his
Beta strode forward, all satisfaction.

"Here is everything. Well, almost," he said, brandishing a worn
leather portfolio. "I have a flock of magpies combing the offices
of Purcell and Sons, as nothing was found in the uncle's residence
regarding the baron's true will. I cannot think that Purcell did not
turn Miss Templeton's home inside out, but it would be sensible to
let the birds loose on the property—"

"Well done, Matthias. Coburn, I entrust those to you." He dared
not take the portfolio to consult the documents: they reeked of
the scent of Purcell, a putrefying blend of duplicity, venality, and
spite. "They are of the utmost importance. Take the utmost care."

Coburn collected the portfolio and hopped away down the
corridor.

Alfred took one breath, took another. "What else? Quickly."

"We have alerted the King's justiciar and sent along copies of the uncle's fake document. I anticipate you will be called to Town to shed light on the drama."

Alfred, down to his shirtsleeves and breeches, pushed past his Beta and made for the door. "We must discuss our next move, Alpha," Bates pleaded, following behind.

"It must wait. If I do not Change immediately, I cannot promise that our secrets will not be exposed in the worst possible light."

"Did you not convince Miss Templeton to come down to sup? She has been far too withdrawn these last days." No one would call his Beta a coward. "It cannot be a wise idea to leave Her Grace all alone abovestairs."

"And now you're an expert on females?" He and his wolf huffed out a mutual laugh. Almost there, almost free, they entered the foyer.

"I took it to heart when you said I ought to figure out this courting lark." Matthias ran a hand though his golden hair. "I read one of those courtship books. When a gentleman woos a lady—"

Alfred leaned against a newel post. "Oh, my friend, thank you for behaving in a ridiculous fashion, that I may not seem such a fool."

His Beta crossed his arms. "With all due respect, this is a terrible way to court a woman, running off in her time of need."

"I am dealing with her need," Alfred growled, "and I will court her all my days. Every single day of this life, she will know she is my one and only." He took another breath. He would not hold his manskin for much longer. "I will name her tomorrow. Tell Gambon to alert the pack."

"Alpha—"

"Go!" He roared and then leapt, with preternatural speed and grace, toward the front door; two footmen, born with excellent reflexes, opened the door before he went straight through it.

His wolf burst from his human skin, leaving scraps of torn clothing all along the front terrace. He paused to stretch, to exult in his animal self, then bunched and exploded into motion around the corner of the Hall, leaping over the grand hedge as though it were nothing. Giving himself up to the speed of his beast, he flew through the park.

With the strength and speed common to his kind, he flew over the obstacles in his path, his sight sharpening in the dark, not needful of the light of the waxing moon to light his way. The *animalis purum* that dwelled in the park ran as fast as their mundane legs could carry them, but it was not Alfie's intention to hunt. Alfie? He snorted, and the wolf chuffed. He was in charge now, and as his wolf shared his mind when in his manskin, so he did when his wolf took precedence. *My name*, Alfie growled. *Mine.*

Alfie crashed through underbrush, bounded over logs and boulders, and headed for the highest hill. He would soon explain the wildness of the park to his mate as the only way the pack could keep their instincts sharp and their *versipellian* identities fit and strong. Human progress had encroached upon the natural world, and their freedom to roam had become severely circumscribed. How good it was to be duke and able to provide and sustain so much land for his people to range upon.

He crested the hill, nowhere near winded, and howled, in the age-old manner of his kind. Was it Alfie who howled or the duke? Alfred knew, in the part of the wild mind of his wolf that nevertheless remained his, that he was bemoaning the mess he'd made of things—again. From the depths of his lupine heart, he was calling to his mate, giving voice to his intention to have her, to bond her, once and for all.

In the distance, he could see the house, saw Felicity's silhouette framed in a window. She could not see him, but he no longer feared exposure; he cared not that she may have heard his plaintive cry. It was past time to take her into his confidence and that of his pack. *Human ways*, snarled Alfie, *have gotten us nowhere.* And Alfred finally agreed.

Fourteen

ONE BY ONE, IN THEIR HUMAN FORMS, THE PACK GATHERED AT the conclave rock. It was said to have been placed there by the goddess Diana, she who ruled the moon, and she who saved Romulus and Remus from the war between their father, Mars, and his wife, Venus, caused by his love for the wolf Laurentia. As their foster children, the wolves were loyal to her, and those loyal to the wolves considered her, and this sacred place, their own.

This was one of four gathering places, but the only one that contained a piece of lupine history. At each of the moon's four festive seasons in the year, its journey tracked around the wild park. It was here the most important rite was held, that of mating, and the stone was said to draw down the moon and bless—without reservation—every union forged on Lupercalia.

All from the house and all from the village came, and as they congregated to wait for their Alpha, it was only natural that talk would ensue. After years of waiting, with the end in sight, all the Shifters were desperate to embrace their promising futures with their whole hearts. Their *homo plenus* compatriots, those who were only human, had a better grasp of what was behind the delay and did their best to explain the vagaries of their ways.

"Look, it's simple," Marshall said. "Us humans ain't instinctual like you shifties."

"Don't call us shifties," growled a sheep dog. "*Homie.*"

"Ver-si-pell-es." Marshall rocked back on his heels. "The human ladies, it's overwhelming for 'em, all this scenting and chasing and declaring. It's kinda desperate-like, and I'd say Her Grace is thinking, 'Hang on there, old son, it's been a wet week since ye clapped eyes on me.'"

"But she'll be sensing the bond by now, won't she?" An owl looked affronted by the notion that this might not be the case.

"Her own senses will have begun to expand, won't they?" asked a mule.

"But it ain't instant, all right?" Marshall replied. "The ladies like to be made much of, given little gifts and being read poems, and getting bouquets, like. They call it 'courting.'"

"If I never hear that word again, Marshall, it will be too soon." Their Alpha strode into the clearing, behind Bates and Gambon, with O'Mara at his back.

All present exposed their necks to their Alpha—their way of showing submission in their human forms, akin to the manner in which they showed their vulnerable undersides when in their animal skins. As they each looked up, Alfred made eye contact with every single member of the pack, acknowledging every soul in his care, reaching out along the *sentio*, so much stronger when they stood in his presence, and he searched for grievances, for unmet or unconfessed needs, for unrest or unhappiness, so he could do all in his power to make things right. With all the hope in the world, the process would lengthen as they added to their numbers, when he and Felicity pledged themselves in this very place.

He nodded to Gambon.

"Alpha." Gambon repeated his submissive gesture. "I speak for all when I say we are honored you have called us to meet."

"The honor is mine, and it was indeed my desire. We gather here in the dawning light of our lady's brother, Apollo, so I may illuminate you all." The words were formal; whilst he preferred plain speaking, this moment deserved its due, and his people deserved the respect that ceremonies such as these paid them. They, who had supported his quest, deserved to exercise their right to have their voices heard.

"Have you found your *vera amoris*, Alpha?" Gambon asked.

"I have found her."

"And will you name her before all?"

"She is Miss Felicity Templeton." He paused. "And she is *homo plenus*. It is deemed in the old ways that I should reject her."

A rousing chorus of "nooooooooooo" rang out. Gambon waited until the dissension died down. "We all know this, the greatest of our laws," he said. "Do you seek to contravene this, Alpha?"

"*Versipelles* were forbidden to reveal their true natures under any circumstances to those unlike ourselves. We observed this law to preserve our myriad species. And yet…" Silence reigned, breath was held, hands were wrung. "We have chosen to adapt to modern times. Our species will die out unless we continue to join with humans. Our friends in France fell due to prejudice and too strong an adherence to such laws." Alfred saw someone clap Louveteau on the shoulder. "Our friends in America are prospering because they are taking human mates. I will not reject my bond with Miss Templeton because of her status, merely because we have never known a human to suit the role of Alpha female. If we allow prejudice and hatred to prevent us growing and thriving, then we are no better than the humans."

Alfred took a breath, one that was echoed by O'Mara. "And so I ask you, humbly, if you will trust my judgment and allow Miss Templeton into our fold." He looked around the circle and spoke from his heart. "I would tell her of us, my friends. I cannot do so if you do not wish it. There is a grace period of a turn of the moon for all of you to think upon it—"

A wave of denial rocked the clearing, and yet several voices aired their concerns.

"What if she fears us?"

"What if she cannot love us as we are?"

"Will she flee?"

"What will happen if she rejects *us*?"

Alfred raised his hands, and all quieted. "I acknowledge your worries. I have them as well." A communal gasp answered their leader's honesty. "I would call upon one of you who is perhaps the best fixed of us all to tell us what Miss Templeton might do. Mary Mossett? If you please?"

Someone shoved the little maid forward. She sent a glare over her shoulder, and on tiny feet, crept into the center of the circle. She made a full reverence, shaking like a leaf, baring her neck, and taking both knees.

"Here." Alfred sat down on the stone and helped her stand.

"Oh, Alpha," Mary gasped, "that's the holy stone, that is, it's not for sitting on like it was nothing special."

"But it is nothing special, my girl," he said, "until Miss Templeton stands before it with me." Alfred leaned his elbows on his knees. "Our pack is afraid that she won't be able to accept her role."

"Oh, never. Her Grace, even when she didn't want to be called that, she was like, the lady of the house soon as she set foot in the Hall. Well, you carried her in, 'cos she was sleeping and that was only like right out of a fairy tale. But she knows how a big house works, and she's making little changes without rufflin' Mr. Coburn's feathers or rubbin' Mrs. Birks the wrong way."

"Then Miss Templeton is a natural in the role."

"And she always knows the right way to say something, even something that might be a scoldin'. And the way she says it, it makes you feel good about yourself and how you want to be better, because of the feelin' that lands up in your heart."

"She is nurturing, and kind to all."

"And"—Mary cast aside her shyness—"she says she don't know what she's doing, but she does, Alpha, she does. She's got all the furniture in the right rooms and the vegetables at the meal, which I think are delicious even if the cats don't like 'em." A jeer from the back of the crowd greeted this, and she lifted her chin, Alfred noticed, as Felicity herself did. "And even though that terrible thing happened, about her money and all, she isn't after taking it out on anyone who may be lower than her."

"She possesses good instincts and is conscientious."

"She does, and she is." Mary nodded again. "I don't think anybody needs to be worryin' about Her Grace not loving us. She already does."

"You sound very sure of that, Mary Mossett." Alfred reached out and tapped her on the chin.

"Well, I am." She smiled. "And she loves you, too, I am sure of it," she whispered, which made no difference, as all had the acute hearing that came with their animal natures. "So don't you be worrying either."

Alfred leaned his forehead against hers and let her inhale his essence to her heart's content. And then he hugged her gently, mindful of her delicate bones, and she hugged him back as hard as she was able. When he released her, Mary blushed a deep scarlet and ran back into the crowd, and a scatter of applause made her squeak with mortified joy.

Alfred stood. "I invoke the *cognominatio*. My mate is found." His voice rang out, amplified by his power as Alpha. "We shall celebrate the feast as it was set down, those many generations ago. And by this joining, we all shall be one."

"Hope there's to be a proper wedding," Marshall called out over the general mayhem.

"The human ceremonies will be observed as well, a small affair," Alfred said and ignored Marshall's dubious expression.

"Don't forget the flowers, Your Grace, for the love of all yer gods." The stable master shook his head and led the way out of the space.

"He has a point, Alpha," Bates said.

"Our new expert on male and female relations," Alfred said to O'Mara and Gambon as the pack filed out, chattering amongst themselves.

"Who better than a human to be expert on human ways?"
Bates retorted.

"Gambon, see to the proper decoration of the stone and the
circle," Alfred said and headed for the Hall. "And I've plans for that
cottage up on the rise."

"The women have been cogitating since they met your lady,
Alpha," Gambon replied. "It's well in hand."

"O'Mara? You outdo the Oracle of Delphi in dispassion."

"All is well, Alpha," she said, refusing to be drawn. "The euphoria that is about to surge requires strength and silence for me to
hold it."

"Bates? Any useful *bon mots* to convey?"

"I thought to bring word to Lady Coleman." Alfred winked at
O'Mara as Bates fell into step beside his Alpha. "It's the least we
can do, seeing as how she is a good friend. To Miss Templeton—
Her Grace. And as there is no family to stand for her, it would be
too cruel not to invite her friend. I am happy to run into Town.
Straightaway."

"Do, Bates. Do run." Alfred stopped at the edge of the park. "I,
myself," he sighed, "must once again consult with the gardener."

━━━━━━━━━━

After another strange dream, this one set at the rock she had come
upon in the park, Felicity chose to go down to breakfast. She was
well rested, and for no good reason at all, optimistic; it may have
something to do with the joy and excitement that came with the
strange images in her sleep, of all of Lowell Hall gathered, cheering
and smiling. As obstreperous as the duke was, and as unyielding
as he had been last night, in the cool light of day, she would begin
again. She would not allow him to harm her uncle, no matter how
foully her relation had behaved, nor begin to dwell upon his dreadful presentation of that enormous ring. It was as though he had no
notion of how to go on with a lady, as if their common customs

were strange to him. What man of breeding did not know how to propose in a proper fashion? It beggared belief.

She smiled at the two small, ginger footmen flanking the breakfast parlor's doors, who bowed with the utmost grace and opened the doors in concert. As ever, the room boasted five more attendants than were absolutely necessary. The butler guarded the sideboard as she was sure he had done every morning, whether she had descended or not. "My apologies, Mr. Coburn," she said as he pulled out her chair. "I neglected to tell you my plans regarding breaking my fast. I hope I have not inconvenienced you or your staff."

"Madam." Coburn's mouth trembled, and the footmen dropped their chins to their shoulders. "You do us too great an honor, when it is our duty and pleasure to see to your comfort in all things."

"Courtesy never goes amiss," she said, accepting the cup of tea he poured her. "Let us begin as we intend to go on. Where is His Grace this morning?"

"He was out and about quite early, and I believe even now he is in the conservatory consulting about a bouquet." The footmen grinned and elbowed each other until the power of the butler's implacable gaze inspired them to resume their stoic stances.

As Mr. Coburn poured her tea and prepared her a plate, Shaddock rushed in with a note. "Express delivery, Mr. Coburn, for Her Grace!"

A silver salver was fetched, the letter taken from the footman and placed upon it, and only then was it delivered into Felicity's possession. "My thanks." She bit the inside of her cheek, amused by the ceremony and realizing she'd best become accustomed to it.

Another letter from Cecil? This was a surprise, as she had not replied to the last. The paper was very wrinkled and had been sloppily closed with a cursory blob of sealing wax.

As before, there was no salutation.

So, dear cousin, I wonder what news there is but
Alas! Surely it is too late for you.
Verily, you have been taken off by A Duke of The Realm.
Everyone in the world knows that you have no recourse.

Marriage is the only solution.
Alack! My father is not moved by your dilemma.
Rollo, neither.
Egad, it all looks as though you have no choice.
Sincerely, your devoted cousin, Cecil

Felicity gasped, standing so abruptly, her chair tipped over onto the floor. She scanned the letter again, fingers tracing along the beginnings of the sentences, threw it down on the table, and ran out the French doors and away.

A mere breath behind her, Alfred entered the parlor, accompanied by his Second and armed with an enormous bouquet.

"Your Grace!" Coburn cried. "Her Grace has run off, I believe in reaction to the contents of her post." He gestured to the missive on the tabletop. Alfred read it, found it to be nonsense, and thrust it at his steward.

"This was not the plan," he growled. Petals once more rained upon the floor as the blossoms shook in his grasp. "Today is the day, damn it all to Hades, for wooing and such, not for chasing and Goddess knows what—"

"'Save mares,'" said Bates.

"I *beg* your pardon?" Alfred bellowed.

"This letter, from her cousin. A rudimentary code at best, one we ourselves dispensed with well before we'd donned our long trousers—"

"Mares?" Another bouquet met a terrible fate.

"Miss Templeton's, one assumes," Bates said. "It is an acrostic.

See? The initial capitals of each sentence form a message." Alfred snatched the letter out of his hand, read it, and then crushed it in the fist that had strangled the poor flowers.

"What do you require, Alpha?"

Alfred drew up the *dominatum* from the well of strength within him, deeper than he ever had drawn before, and in so doing, realized he had only ever been dipping shallowly into the depths of his power. It crystallized into a form he had never experienced, not as a mode of suppression or oppression but as a force for unity. He sent it along the *sentio*, and the strength he exuded wedded with that of his people, down those invisible connections, became infinite in its capabilities. Before his eyes, as Bates, Coburn, even the footmen, incorporated the benefits of their Alpha's puissance and made it their own, their creatures showed in their eyes, fervid yet obedient, ready to do whatever was required for their Alpha and for his newly named *vera amoris*.

He went to the French doors, scented his mate, discerned she was headed for the stables, and turned to the room. "It is fortunate that she will never make Templeton House before we will. She must not engage with whatever transpires. Her safety is paramount. Felix, Leo, wait until she has ridden away, then tell Marshall to gather the colts and that I will be there directly." They cricked their necks and headed out the doors. A disturbance in the air met with a pair of yowls, and two abnormally large, ginger cats tore across the lawn.

He turned to the footmen in the breakfast room. "Shaddock, take those here and ensure that Her Grace stays safe on her way. Coburn," he turned to his faithful butler, who was quivering with the need to provide service in some fashion. "Send word to Gambon and tell him he is needed and to bring as many men and women from the Close as can be spared. Bates." His Second was grinning like a loon. "I cannot see the enjoyment in this, Beta."

"If you do nothing else for your betrothed but as the letter bids

and what you have in train in the Close, then you are minted."
Bates kicked some of the broken blossoms out of his way.

"Alpha, what news?" O'Mara ran into the room. She picked up
the letter from the floor and read it.

"'Save mares,'" Bates said and filled her in on the plan in his
usual succinct fashion.

"I can prove useful in my Changed form," O'Mara offered.

"We'll give the colts an outing," Alfred said. "It will do them
good to be heroes."

"There is the chance that Her Grace may make good time,"
O'Mara said. "It would not do for her to wonder at an assemblage
of creatures who would not normally mix."

"It matters not," Alfred replied. "I can wait no longer. She has
been named and accepted. I will foil whatever dastardly plot is
afoot, and then I will show her my true nature."

"That will require the utmost care," said O'Mara. "Try to bring
the thought into her mind gently, what our history is, what we
strive to achieve as a species. Nothing too abrupt or dramatic."

"Sweet, blessed Venus." Bates shook his head and headed away
to prepare for his Change.

"Shall I join you, Alpha?" O'Mara asked. "Only in order to
begin the conversation. If you think she would talk to me?"

Alfred's eyes gleamed. "Oh, I know to whom she'll speak."

Fifteen

ALL WAS GOING TO PLAN: CECIL HAD LED HIS BROTHER AND HIS
father's hired guns on a wild goose chase to Templeton House,
delaying their arrival in hopes that his express delivery post would
arrive at Lowell Hall in good time. It had been decided by his
father that the slaughtering of the mares would take place under
cover of night, which was all well and good in the pages of a Gothic
novel but another thing entirely when ferrying hired help beyond
the bounds of London Town. Never mind that the two mammoth
wagons, one reserved for the corpses of the beasts, were not the
most subtle of conveyances. Added to this, of the seven thugs, only
two had ever been as far south as the Seven Dials; the five who
were not as well traveled had begun grousing after the first hour.
As it was, between changing horses and a providentially shattered
axle, it was noon before they reached their goal.

They had not decided upon this day—or rather, Father had
not—until they were very nearly on the road itself. He had been
correct in the location of the animals: the first field had been bereft
of beasts and the second, farther from the house and well hidden
if one did not know what to look for, had proven to be the correct
paddock. It seemed there was nothing beneath his father's notice.

Cecil fretted. Had Felicity received his letter? She hadn't
responded to his first, even though he had hinted he was waiting
for her reply. Surely she had discerned his clever little construction? His secret message? He had spent a good deal of his pocket
money on that daybreak express delivery, which he hoped the
duke would be glad enough to reimburse. How awful it was to be
a grown man dependent upon a quarterly allowance! In throwing in his lot with Felicity, let him be utterly honest, he was not

in fully altruistic mode. He wanted a reward, perhaps enough for him to set off in trade on his own, perhaps enough even to go into competition with Purcell and Sons. He laughed, and his brother sneered at him.

"When Father discovers you brought us here so late, you will not be chuckling to yourself, I do declare."

"What matter the time we arrived?" Cecil scanned the field, the horses' ears swiveling to and fro as they began to sense a threat. "Once the deed is done, its timing will make no difference. And the work of shooting a horse requires sunlight, no matter what Father thinks."

"I say we ought to take these horses and sell them on." Rollo adjusted the floppy brim of his foppish hat—*What all the young bucks wear whilst about to commit equicide,* Cecil scoffed.

"To whom would you seek to sell them? We have no papers, no proof they are ours to offer." Cecil shot a look over his shoulder at the thugs. "We would not gain enough to pay these good gents the worth of their time, not in the way our father will."

"Ha!" Rollo sneered. "As if *he* is ever punctual in paying the trades."

The thugs started muttering to themselves, and Cecil widened his eyes at his brother, as though in alarm. *What an ass,* he exulted. *Perhaps he will do all the work for me.* "This is a special case, brother. Father would never renege on remunerating such an arduous mission."

Rollo stood and began to remonstrate unconvincingly with the gunmen. Once they arrived, the ruffians lay about, drinking from jugs and scratching and pissing as though they were on a picnic. Cecil listened as his brother repeated the plan: one man would be responsible for one mare. A shot to the head and down they would go. The wagon for the horses would be taken directly to an abattoir in St. Giles so that all evidence of their existence could be destroyed.

This plan seemed shoddy to Cecil. Would it not be sensible to herd the horses onto the wagon rather than slay them on the ground upon which they stood? Moving live creatures as opposed to dead ones was less likely to be strenuous and would take less time. It was possible that there was a deeper layer to this plot: Father may have hoped that he, Cecil, had warned Felicity and she would come upon the dead mares strewn throughout the paddock. Or was he imagining shadows where there were none, as usual? A rustling whispered from the northern end of the field. Cecil jumped, and Rollo and the ruffians sneered at him as one.

The sun was well up the sky, and the men had waited long enough. One jerked his chin at him and Rollo and directed his fellows to follow him into the clearing.

"I say!" Rollo hissed, leaping to his feet. "You will take direction from me or not at all."

"There are only six." Cecil stood as well, gesturing with a finger as he counted again.

"They's meant to be seven," growled one of the thugs. "We's gettin' paid for seven."

"…four, five, six. There's one missing." Did this mean that Felicity was here to save the day? He thought he heard something at the southern end of the enclosure but saw nothing. His imagination was running riot.

"What have you done with it?" Rollo demanded, grabbing Cecil by his neckcloth and brandishing the cudgel he carried.

"I?" For once in his life, there was no need to feign distress. Cecil wheezed as Rollo took a surprisingly strong grip on him. "Why in the world would I have done anything? How would I have done anything?"

"I don't know." Rollo released him, and he stumbled backward. "I shouldn't be surprised if you hadn't mucked this up to make me look bad."

"You are well able to do that for yourself." Cecil had had

enough. "Think you that this will elevate you in Father's eyes? You are nothing but a puppet, a fool. Putting on airs as though you were a fine gentleman, even knowing how greatly Father despises them. Idiot! You do not even command respect from these lower-class hoodlums, look, they're paying no mind to you at all."

As the ruffians entered the field, the mares clustered, hind to hind, their eyes rolling in their heads as they braced themselves against this obvious aggression. The men took their time coming upon the horses, savvy enough to keep silent, as they primed their double-barreled shotguns. Rollo pushed Cecil aside again and took the lead, confident thanks to the wealth of firepower before him.

Until the mares' ears perked up, and they turned away from the human predators. A distant sound of pounding drew the attention of all, of hooves pummeling the earth, coming closer and closer. The six in the paddock parted to reveal the seventh of their number galloping through, sliding to a halt a mere twenty yards from Rollo. This mare was not abject with fear: her nostrils flared, and her eyes—her eyes promised death to any who dared approach her.

Rollo dared. Cecil covered his eyes then uncovered them at the mare's furious whinny. He covered his ears and debated concealing his eyes once more as she reared, hooves pawing the air in warning as Rollo flapped his arms about, the cudgel he held slipping from his hand. She snorted once more, in fair warning, and leapt for him. His brother turned and ran, as if he could outpace the beast; as Cecil watched, it was as if she were toying with Rollo, never catching him up but keeping him on the run until they were near a stream. Only then did she move closer, showing him her hind and kicking out with her hooves until Rollo stumbled and fell into the water, where he thrashed about, wailing.

Then, a horde of creatures burst from the underbrush: Cecil counted several horses that looked to be much larger than the mares, a pack of gigantic...dogs? They could not be wolves. Could they? And if he wasn't mistaken, there was a wild boar, whose tusks lowered as he made for the gunmen. That lot, no fools, had dropped their weapons and turned to run. Two of the big dogs gave chase, as did the boar and several gigantic house cats.

The newly arrived horses danced around the mares, shunting them into a cluster in the center of the field. Rollo, meanwhile, was flailing about in the stream as that diabolical beast stood over him, teeth bared, preparatory to take a chunk out of him. "Cecil!" he called, and the demon mare snapped at Rollo. "Cecil, help me, call off this creature!"

Cecil edged over to three men, who had also appeared as though from the thin air.

"Careful, lads." One of the men called to the horses that had calmed the mares, and if Cecil wasn't losing his reason, they appeared to be flirting with one another. "Keep them nice and close, but not too close, if you take my meaning. Colts!" He turned to Cecil and crossed his arms over his chest.

"Mr. Cecil Purcell, at your service," he managed and sketched an awkward bow. He heard movement behind him that proved to be the two biggest dogs, one with light fur, one black as pitch. The boar lingered near Rollo and was snorting at the intimidating mare, who turned her hind to him and kicked. Good God! It was as though the Tower Zoo had run amok.

Cecil turned back to the men. "Do I have the pleasure of meeting the Duke of Lowell?"

"Do I look like a duke, you numpty?" The man waved his arms, and the colts started herding the mares away, following the boar. Meanwhile, the seventh mare refused to allow Rollo escape from what was surely freezing-cold water.

"I beg your pardon?" Cecil's vision was starting to flicker around the edges.

"I said," the head man replied, "was it you that sent the letter to Her Grace?"

"Has Felicity married him, then?" Oh, joy! Perhaps his life was not on the slagheap after all. "I mean, yes, I am her cousin, her beloved cousin, well, not so beloved, not lately, but I am in hopes that she will look kindly upon me in relation to the saving of her horses."

"I'm Marshall, stable master at Lowell Hall. These two be Aherne and Bailey, of Templeton House." He pulled a piece of paper out of his pocket. "I've a few questions here from His Grace." The big dogs crowded closer, and Cecil cleared his throat nervously. The blond pounced forward and back aggressively until the black one batted him hard enough that he rolled away. He took it with equanimity, and he smiled. The blond dog…smiled.

"For the love of all that's holy, man, will ye attend me?" The stable master shouted. "I asked if ye knew where the stud is? Big lad, chestnut, meant to be seeing to those fine ladies."

"I am afraid I do not," Cecil said. "Only six of the mares were present, and then that one came and attacked my brother." They turned to look at the mare, who bared her teeth at them.

"Know anything about that will of her father's? The duke's people will be going over the estate and are looking for any ideas to aid the search."

"Eh, no." Cecil cringed as both dogs snarled. "I spent little time here as a child. When I did, Felicity and I were the best of friends, I must say, the larks we had! She was even then quite attached to the horses and had many hidey holes in the barn—"

The black dog let out a series of howls and barks, and several magpies, who had been lurking about in the trees, took flight toward Templeton House.

"Is that all you know?"

He explained his father's plan to kill the horses and his suspicions that Felicity was meant to find them dead in the paddock. The black dog snarled unceasingly throughout his account, and Cecil ensured that the part he played in the success of this rescue scheme was not understated. He concluded: "And if there is anything else I can do to help my cousin, I am happy to do it." And he meant it. This satisfied the big, black dog. How he knew this he did not know.

Marshall turned to the big dogs. "Will we take him back with us?"

The black one made a sound that gave even the diabolical mare pause; her ears perked up, and she bobbed her head at him respectfully. The blond one barked, and the two began to argue—Cecil was certain that Bedlam might be a lovely release from these flights of fancy. Finally, the blond one howled but rolled and exposed his belly to the black one. The latter caught Cecil's eye and held it; not daring to breathe, Cecil lowered his gaze and, for some ridiculous reason, bowed to the beast.

Who then chuffed and bounded away after the magpies. The blond one glared at Cecil, and after a rush of air and the sound of cracking bones, the youngest Purcell, who'd had more than enough shocks for one day, looked upon what stood before him and fell flat on his back in a faint.

―――――――――――

"That clearly runs in the family." As any Shifter, Bates was comfortable in his naked skin.

"What'll we do with that one?" Marshall gestured to Rollo, who was curled in a ball and shivering beneath the mare's belly.

"Alpha has plans for him that involve a long sea voyage." Bates used his hands to scrub through his hair, as if he had not entirely left the wolf behind. "Ensure that the villagers keep the gunmen under guard, and take this one," he nudged Cecil with his foot, "and tell O'Mara only her finest glamour will do."

"What about these two?" Marshall looked at Aherne and Bailey, who had been rather blasé about the whole thing.

They cricked their necks at Bates, and Marshall made a show of throwing his hands in the air. "Is there a human being left in

England? I'd like to know." He laughed and chucked the two lads on the shoulders. "Don't tell me that mare...?"

"Nah," said Bailey, and left it at that.

"Delilah's awful canny for an *animalis purum*," said Aherne. "I'll take her on down to the Hall, and if it's all the same to you, we'll be staying to mind them mares."

"Her Grace would have it no other way." Bates let out a deep breath. "His Grace has gone to meet her at Templeton House, but I daresay one of you might at least impart the knowledge the horses are safe?"

"Yah," said Bailey, who then slunk away.

"A man of few words," Marshall commented.

"Only around the big bads," Aherne replied.

"Sure, and that's only what I call them myself," said Marshall, tossing a companionable arm around the man's shoulders as they made their way over to Delilah. "Now, I know the law an' all, but I'm guessing you're not as mangy as our Beta there?"

Bates snarled, Changed, and headed off to see if the magpies had any news.

Sixteen

FELICITY GALLOPED JUPITER AS SHE HAD IN THE MEADOW, this time with intent rather than for pleasure. As the miles sped by, only her superior abilities as an equestrienne allowed her to ride full tilt over unfamiliar roads and fields. Marshall's warning about keeping the gelding off the roads was nonsense, and she pushed him as she had never pushed a horse before, leaping intemperately over stiles and walls along the way; thankfully he was well able for it and enjoyed being given his head. Her mind turned her cousin's message over and over, *SAVE MARES*, its brevity causing her thoughts to run riot. Her band was in mortal danger, for what but the direst of schemes could require such a terse message?

She charged into the stable yard at Templeton House and found it deserted, as deserted as the western paddock, where Aherne had been meant to hide the mares. Swinging down from Jupiter, she stood, unsure what to do next, fearing the worst. She rolled up the stirrups and tied up Jupiter's reins, then a shout called her attention.

"Miss!"

Felicity turned: it was Bailey, the second head lad. She never quite understood the point of the distinction, but first head lad Aherne had insisted. Bailey was long of leg and broad of shoulder, and looked powerful yet lithe with it. His great mane of sandy hair flopped around sharp, amber-colored eyes lined with thick, black lashes.

"How are ye, miss?" He stopped well short of her and tugged his forelock like to tear it off his skull.

"Bailey, you're on your best manners, stop that this instant." He shrugged, looking uncomfortable, but at least stopped trying to snatch himself bald. "Where are the mares? And Aherne? I got a note this morning from my cousin—"

"They're grand," he assured her. "There was some toughs from London came down, sent by yer uncle, and meant to kill the poor things, but some lads showed up, from that duke over the border, and took care o' them, right and tight."

"Kill the mares?" Felicity's fingers tightened on Jupiter's reins, and he shook his head in annoyance. She stroked his neck, more to calm herself than him. "He sent men down to destroy my mother's band?"

Bailey scratched his ear. "Them lads from Lowell Hall was there before we showed up with their fodder, so's the girls were never in danger, missus."

"I would never have gotten there in time," Felicity said. Unnerved, she led the gelding to a paddock near the courtyard.

"Nor had a chance before seven armed men, nor even that pigeonhearted cousin of yours, the skinny one. Delilah nearly knocked the stuffing outta him, Rolly, or something."

"Rollo," Felicity corrected. "And Cecil? Was he there as well?"

"The roundy one? I heard him say he was the one as sent you a warning. Yeah, and then he fainted." Bailey clapped a hand over his mouth.

"Fainted?"

"Scared for his brother, mebbe." Bailey busied himself with taking off Jupiter's saddle and setting it on the fence. "Delilah," he shrugged. "You know how she is."

He opened the gate, and Felicity let in Jupiter, who trotted away and commenced kicking up his heels. How he had the energy after their mad dash, she did not know.

"They are safe, you are absolutely certain?" She closed the gate herself, and her hands trembled as she closed the latch.

"Safe as houses, mum," her second head lad asserted. "They was trotting away, not a bother on 'em. Off to the duke's place, I reckon."

"That is excellent news." How had anyone from the Hall preceded her to the paddock? She had had a head start. She turned to Bailey. "And His Grace? Was he present?"

"Eh…it was right confusing, hard to say," Bailey said. "Sure I wouldn't know a duke if he nipped me on the arse."

Felicity tried not to laugh at that. "Present yourselves to Marshall, the stable master at the Hall. I will insist on keeping my mares at Lowell Hall and that you and Aherne oversee them."

"Sure, that won't set the cats amongst the pigeons," Bailey scoffed, and Felicity shook her finger at him.

"That's more like it, you cheeky fellow. Off with you, and see to it that Himself gets his usual private paddock."

"Eh…" Bailey grabbed his forelock once more for good measure and backed away. "Off I go, miss, off to the Hall, it'll all settle in sure enough." And with more speed than she'd thought possible, he nipped around the side of the stable and away.

"Bailey? Is all well with Himself?" Her only answer was the decreasing sound of running steps. "Bailey?"

Giving up, she turned toward the house. The Templeton ancestral pile was fashioned of cream-colored stone; it was a two-storied structure that lacked wings and an impressive forecourt, but whose portico lent grace to the facade. Modest flower beds flanked the shallow staircase that led to the unprepossessing door, and everything about it was not in the least bit imposing, something of a failure as the seat of a ranking peer. But it was her family home, and that was all that mattered.

She entered through the servants' hall, where she once would have expected to see Cook preparing luncheon, or at least one of the tweenies trying to nick a heel of bread from the bakehouse. Felicity thought to nick a heel of bread herself, but as she roamed around, she found that the cupboards were bare, the larders were bereft, and the fire in the washroom had long been cold.

It appeared Uncle had closed the house with a view, as Mr. Bates had said, to selling it. She made her way into the ground floor parlor, where the shutters had not been drawn, for there was little to no furniture to protect from the ruination of the sun. Odd pieces were scattered about, but the bulk of the appointments were gone. "I doubt the neighbors would have stopped the servants robbing us blind," she said, then winced. It was one thing talking to the horses, or even paintings of horses, another to be caught talking to herself. How dare Uncle Ezra do this to her inheritance? "If it is even my inheritance." Blast it! She'd talk aloud if she desired. It wasn't as though she'd be heard. She was alone.

"I am alone." The state to which she had aspired since she debuted. She'd imagined she'd be kicking up her heels, much like Jupiter had, but instead she felt as barren as the vegetable store. The silence was not the silence of peace but of desolation. Templeton House was an empty shell, one too large to fill, even with her dreams and her autonomy. It was as unlike to Lowell Hall as it was possible to be.

Looking around, she saw that her father's golden snuff boxes were no longer in the display case across from the hearth; the rosewood games table was not under the window where it should have been, and over half the pictures on the walls had disappeared. She doubted any of the paintings had been worth anything. That thought had her fleeing down the corridor, rushing into her father's study—and it was gone, the portrait of herself and her parents, gone, taken, worth nothing to anyone but herself.

She leaned against her father's desk, its drawers missing, and stared at the blank space on the wall. Who would have stolen the portrait? Had her uncle come himself and taken it? She looked around the room, dizzy from this loss. She regarded the divested desk. The odds of finding her father's true will were slim to none, and sitting about like a woebegone partridge would do her no good. "If partridges do in fact have feelings, which I am certain they do, but 'woebegone' is rather a sophisticated sentiment."

As she returned to wander around the public rooms, little appealed to her, in the end. She did think that Mrs. Birks would have use for the old chatelaine that had somehow ended up in the curiosity cabinet, and wouldn't Coburn adore that carriage clock, the one with the ormolu and porcelain facing, even if it was French? She collected them to bring back to the Hall.

Perhaps the poor servants hadn't been the ones to steal the art—perhaps the walls had always been that way, but had they been stripped over time, she'd never noticed, had not wanted to notice. How often had she dreamed of her future but dreaded it, too? Dreamed of making a splash in order to be free of the genteel struggle that was the result of her father's sorrowful decline? Dreamed of being wanted for herself and not because her family was titled or in spite of being odd and willful and badly dressed. Hoped to be courted for herself and for her own qualities—yes, both good and ill.

Courted. Not kidnapped. Not ruined! *Imagine* being handed a ring, a gorgeous, probably ancestral ring, but handed it, diffidently, as though it were a glove she'd dropped. She deserved to be courted like the lady she was, because she was in fact a lady, even if her birth was not as high as the duke's. She deserved a proper proposal. Even if it was a foregone conclusion, she deserved to be asked for her hand with decorum and honor.

"Enough." Piling her booty on the piecrust table near the main staircase, she ascended, determined to keep her mind off the duke and on her quest to garner mementos. Mary would love one of the china bud vases Felicity had scattered around her childhood rooms. She'd also seek out the silver-chased hand mirror she herself had often mooned in front of, when she dreamt of being snatched up by the most eligible male of the season—

"Oh, no." Felicity paused, mid-stair, aghast. "Bloody hell and the devil!"

It couldn't be true. Could it? Had she been snatched up by the most eligible male of the season? She wandered up to the landing and braced herself against the marble-topped side table that stood there. Her mother had forever been putting furniture every which

where, which made her father laugh and her mother blush, smiling
yet adamant. Felicity thought it was a lovely quality, that smiling,
blushing adamance, and decided to scatter little tables and lounge
chairs in unlikely places in Lowell Hall to make it more like a
home. Would it be a good home, a good life? Was it enough to go
on, a few dizzying kisses and the adoration of the staff? And would
she ever stop torturing herself with unanswerable questions?

"Buggery!" she bellowed. "Arsy bollocking bedamned
devilment!"

A gurgling growl shocked her out of her foul-mouthed spree;
she grabbed a candlestick from the side table and spun to see the
big doggy glaring at her from the top of the stairs.

"Your Grace!" Felicity lowered the candlestick. "However did
you find me here? Aren't you a good boy? Aren't you? But did I
leave the door ajar? Come, we'll shut it and then—" But the beast
had barreled down the stairs and all but bowled her over in his
eagerness to sniff at her trousers. "Are you glad to see me? Good
boy, good boy…" and on and on, relieved at not being solitary any-
more. "Come, let me show you something." She turned to the next
flight of stairs, and he followed close to her side.

"I grew up here," she explained, "and lived here until my
father…well, I told you all about my father." The dog rubbed
against her waist, offering comfort as they moved in sync up the
stairs to the second floor. "I have discovered that the will he left
was false, and all the plans I made could never have come good."
She paused at the top, and the dog whined. "I cannot dwell upon
it, or I'll go mad. I feel all aswirl inside, as if I would faint, which I
never do, but even so. I have no notion as to what I will do, I have
no one and nothing and—"

The dog started barking, howling in fact, and Felicity sat in the
bergère that her mother had placed in the hall. "Hush, easy, hush,
Your Grace. Be still!" The dog settled down somewhat, and she
stroked his face. "I suppose I have you. Shall I hitch you to a pony

cart and drive off into the sunset?" He snarled, and she laughed. "I agree, that is far beneath your dignity."

She slumped back in the chair, and he laid his head in her lap. "Speaking of dignity, your namesake made less than an appropriate fist of asking me to marry him. Ha!" The beast winced, and were it possible, his expression was both incredulous and disgruntled. "He barked at me about *ton* marriages and held out a ring as though he were handing me a handkerchief and was astonished when I refused to accept it!" The dog tilted his head as though confused. "Oh, you're all the same, you male creatures. Surely you can see my point of view, silly boy, silly boy." She leaned down and kissed him on the forehead. "Come, enough about His Gracelessness. I've something in my rooms for Mary Mossett. And then...I'll leave."

She turned left at the head of the hall, the dog grumbling and growling all the way. The door to her suite was ajar, and she pushed it open.

"Oh." Like the rest of the house, her suite of rooms had been pillaged. The bedding, the bedclothes, the curtains, all gone. The few paintings that had adorned the walls, the smaller bits of furniture, the bed tables: purloined. All that remained was the bed frame—which, listing to one side, looked as if an attempt was made upon it—and the two-seat divan, host to a lone ornamental cushion, that faced her hearth. The drawers of her dressing table hung out at drunken angles, and the doors of her wardrobe gaped open, revealing one lone slipper and a shawl she remembered had torn fringe. "It is just as well I did not escape on Jupiter that first day, Alfie. There is nothing for me here."

She moved to stand at the bare window and looked out over the kitchen garden, which had been ravaged. "I expect the servants took whatever they could carry when they got their notice. I cannot begrudge them, though they were my uncle's staff. I'm sure they were poorly paid and overworked." The low growl from the center of the room made her smile. At least she had an ally. "Ah, well. I have a keepsake box hidden in the hayloft," she said, "a few remembrances of my parents, so all is not lost. They are only silly things, as my uncle told me all my mother's jewelry is gone." The equanimity of her speech was ruined by the quiver in her voice at its conclusion. Alfie snarled, long and low. "If only I'd thought to fetch away that picture…" The big doggy cocked his head and huffed. "A painting of myself as a young child, little more than an infant, with my mother and father." She tried to smile, failed. "All is not lost, Alfie. I shall call upon the Lowell influence to find it. Perhaps the duke will come in useful for something."

His Grace let off a flurry of barks that most would find intimidating, if not terrifying, but Felicity was comforted. He bounded to her side and herded her over to stand by the mantelpiece. "There is no one to spy me at the window," she laughed and made to move to the wardrobe to see if that shawl was redeemable. He cut her off and pawed at her feet, making her skip back into place. "I'll stand here then, shall I? Very well, if you so desire. Have you something to bring me? Have you something to show me?"

He leapt over the divan and disappeared behind it. His head popped up once, and she raised her hands to signal her compliance.

Later, when she thought about what happened next, she would attempt to separate the myriad sounds and sensations that followed. There was great oppression of air, like the coming of a storm, then a swirling of energy like a driving wind, but how could there be a wind in her plundered rooms? It was a rush, like a hurricane, and yet nothing fluttered, not her hair nor her jacket; it was a gathering, as though everything flew together toward a center she could not identify, and all in a matter of seconds. The rush was accompanied by a growl, followed by a crack!—sudden, like the collapse of a burning log, and then—

And then His Grace—the duke, not the dog—rose from behind the divan, his nakedness shielded less than adequately by the small sofa.

Seventeen

"DO NOT FAINT," HE ORDERED, SNATCHING UP THE CUSHION TO cover his nether parts.

Felicity's first thought was: *Thank Go—galoshes they left a cushion.* Not: The beast has transformed into a man. Not: His Grace is His Grace! No, simple gratitude that the desperate servants hadn't denuded her suite in its entirety. *Denuded*? She'd never used that word in her life! She blushed.

"You will recall, I do not faint," she said, belatedly.

"I beg to differ."

"Beg all you wish, Your Grace, but as you see, I am standing." *Although I am weaving about inside.*

Silence followed her pronouncement. Must it be she who was meant to initiate whatever conversation was to follow this extraordinary event? She looked at him expectantly, and if she said so herself, with an inordinate amount of aplomb. If she was not mistaken, a large beast had just transformed into...another large beast. On top of all of that, she was mesmerized by all the ducal flesh on display. To see That Chest bared was enough, but the arms, the shoulders, the dark mat of hair that dwindled down in a line that lead—to his—*oh, help, help!*

The duke cleared his throat, sounding quite like the big doggy. "There is an explanation," he began.

Felicity exploded. "Wonderful! Finally!" She flung her hands about like a lunatic. "How unlike other men I thought you, Your Grace, as you eschewed explanations left, right, and center. How surprised I was, as there is always some godforsaken reason for every outrage when it comes to men, much more so for titled men."

"I am more than a titled man—"

"Evidently." She breathed in deeply, once, twice. "In Jemima's novel, the Count Woldolpho was a were…were…werewolf." *A ravenous horror whose only goal was to bite helpless young women and turn them into monsters*, she added to herself, taking a step away. And then another step. Her vision came over all in sparkles around the edges, and she wobbled on her feet. Before she even thought to right herself, he was there, grasping her shoulders, squeezing them…with both hands? She shut her eyes tight, and she was certain she heard him chuckle.

"Do not chuckle," she managed. "How dare you laugh at my distress. This could be considered the shock of a lifetime for Go— for galoshes' sake." Even to herself she sounded peevish. Peevish? Was that the strongest emotion she called to the fore? Should she not be insensible with terror? How was it she was not in a state of nervous collapse? How could she even summon such dispassionate thoughts?

"Breathe," he instructed. "Lean." He propped her up against the wall by the window. He opened it, and a cool breeze soon wafted over her face. She sensed him rush away again to retrieve his cushion. He returned and gripped her with only one hand. She breathed and leaned, and as her eyes closed, her other senses opened. She perceived a hint of fur in the air, a blast of heat emanating from his body, as warm as a hearth fire, and it wrapped around her, soothing what little distress she was experiencing. So calming in fact, she had the desire to demand he transform again, so she would know for sure it had occurred.

She stood, and that hand stroked down to her elbow, a sensation of peace following in its wake. Eyes still shut, she said, "Please return to the divan."

He started to chuckle and swallowed it. She intuited when it was safe to open her eyes. She met his, and he looked—he looked proud of her.

"So." Where to begin? Scold him further for withholding salient details, or insist he reveal the details themselves? She folded her arms and chose the latter. "Werewolves."

"That is an old name that indirectly applies to what I am," the duke replied, in palliative tones, as though he were Miss O'Mara. "Keep breathing, my dear. Your heart is beating precipitously, which is only understandable, and I would seek to assuage—"

"I am not afraid."

"—your concerns. I am aware that you are not afraid."

"How? How are you aware of such a thing?" Felicity took refuge, as ever, in facts.

"I am all that is eager to tell you, but I am at rather a disadvantage," he said, glancing down. Felicity blushed again. "I took precautions and would clothe myself, and then I will expla—I will share all you need to know."

Felicity nodded. The duke gestured to his cushion. She closed her eyes.

She sensed his movements as he passed by the sofa, passed her, and entered her dressing room. Between one breath and the next, he was standing at her shoulder, and she was once more in proximity to That Chest and…everything else.

"Please?" he said.

Her eyes flew open. That was a first: a gentle exhortation as opposed to the usual brusque orders or canny evasions. Despite being garbed in nothing but a dressing gown, he was all ducal graciousness and gestured to the divan. She sat. He stood before her, hands behind his back, and began.

"The werewolves of horrible novels are vicious, intent only upon corrupting humanity. The legends are based on my ancestors, who had gone so far down the path of ensuring our bloodlines remained pure that the inevitable effects of inbreeding occurred, in a barbarous direction. Steps have been taken over the last eight generations to diversify the lines of those similar to us, in order to reinvigorate all species.

"We have striven to become peaceful beings who happen to have an unusual biology, one that does not in any way, shape, or form inspire them to violence or inability to live in accord with mankind. Whilst we are supernaturally adept at things that humans are not, and though we may heal, for example, with a speed unknown to humanity, we do bleed, we do yearn, we do love, we seek to protect our young and care for our old, we want only the same right to inhabit this world, for the whole of our lives, in peace—I apologize."

Felicity's brows rose in disbelief. Pleases, apologies—whatever next?

"I have never found it necessary to explain myself to a *homo plenus*, a full human, before," he said. "In fact, it is frowned upon as our very existence demands secrecy."

"What do you call yourselves if not fully human?"

"*Versipellis*. Latin for 'turn skin.' In the vernacular, we refer to ourselves as Shapeshifters. A race of humans who contain the energy and essence of a certain beast within them. If you can name a creature, of the air, of the earth, of the sea, you will find they manifest as *versipelles*," he replied. "Well, not quite. We have heard tell of unicorn Shapeshifters, but we believe this is only wishful thinking."

"We?" Felicity asked, much calmer than might be appropriate under the circumstances. As though they were discussing the weather or the disbursement of the living in Lowell Close.

Casual attire notwithstanding, Alfred exuded power. "My pack, for whom I am pleased to serve as Alpha. My people, who are my responsibility. The majority of souls at Lowell Hall are as I am."

"Wolves?"

"Not all wolves. All species of Shapeshifters are in decline, and as such, we have allied one with the other for protection, in hopes of our continuance, if not in purebreds then in hybrids."

"Would a wolf marry a, a fish?"

The duke's eyes smiled. "They would be compatible in their human forms."

"And what class of cross would result?" Was she initiating this discussion?

"As you know from your own experience, dominant characteristics will out, but over time, the lupine progeny will find themselves siblings to a little trout or a salmon."

"And what of…" No, even she could not go so far.

"And when a wolf mates a human…" That voice hit a register so low, so seductive, that she wasn't certain she hadn't been impregnated by its resonance alone. "Both races are exalted. The *homo plenus* gains powers and abilities unheard of in their species, and the *versipelles* are ensured of continuance and are secure for posterity."

"Ah." Felicity rose and started closing the drawers on her vanity.

"Ah…?" If nothing else, hearing uncertainty in the voice of a peer of the realm might be worth the heartbreak.

"*Ah*, as in, any human will do, but why not guarantee the outcome by destroying the hopes and dreams of a nobody who would be grateful enough to have a litter got on her?"

Again, faster than a beat of her heart, he was at her back. "You are not *any* human. And it would be I who would be grateful, beyond thought, beyond words."

She felt his breath in her ear and sensed that indescribable pressure attempting to force her to submit to him. "Explain this, please, this attempt to control me by, what? Your will? Explain the speed. And the smelling. And where that robe came from."

She spun around and headed back to the sofa, flipping out the tails of her coat. He dipped his head to the space beside her, and she nodded. They sat side by side, his heat enveloping her once more.

"My wolf has yearned to be honest with you," he began. "It

went against his instincts to withhold the truth, and he knew, with his superior instincts, that you would be receptive to our history."

"You speak of him as being separate, but that cannot be."

"We are… It is as though we walk within each other always, no matter which skin we wear. When you saw us in the meadow, I was still aware of who you were, and he was very aware that, for once, he would lead the way."

"But you cannot speak in your wolf form. Not in your human voice."

"No. It is not possible. I can think human thoughts but not express them when I am in my wolfskin, as my wolf can think lupine thoughts and not express them when I am a man." He looked down at his hands, and his ears turned red. "There are limitations and also taboos…"

"I take your meaning, say nothing more." She turned scarlet and avoided his gaze strenuously. "I assume you read my cousin's note and knew to come here?"

"Bates deserves the credit for discerning the code." He explained what had transpired. "Marshall and the colts are taking your horses to Lowell Hall. We were all able to outpace you with our superior speed. And with excellent planning." His tone betrayed the satisfaction that it was he who had planned excellently. He gestured to his dressing gown. "I was able to send this along with Marshall and bring it in with me."

"You move with speed as a man as well. How is this so?"

The duke relaxed back into the curve of the divan and stretched an arm along the back of it. The sofa was so small that his fingers landed on several of the curls that had escaped Felicity's windblown coiffure. They stroked so lightly, yet it thrilled her to her marrow. "It is primarily through our bodies that my wolf and I connect. Therefore, I have the speed and agility of the beast, along with myriad sensual amplifications."

"Sensual?" She tipped her head back, and his fingers traced the back of her neck to her collar and back again.

"As pertains to the senses, of course." It was unbelievable that his voice could go any lower; as it did, she perceived Alfie's presence beneath his human skin. "My sight is impeccable. I can see great distances and clearly in the blackest of night. My hearing is beyond human comprehension—I can hear Jupiter grazing in the paddock, your heart beating, your blood racing through your veins. I require excessive amounts of touch, due to my wolf's natural propensity for affection. My sense of smell is highly attuned, far exceeding human ability." He leaned in and ran his nose briefly over her cheek, as he had done the night of the ball.

"Why did you inhale so deeply of my person at the ball?"

"My nose led me to you," he said, his fingers moving to trace the shape of her jaw, the lobe of her ear. "I had been searching for five years, across the globe, for the fragrance that would reveal my *vera amoris* to me."

"Your…"

"My true mate." The timbre of his voice crashed through her, made her skin tingle, and she swore she heard her own heart beat despite her less-than-acute hearing.

"But I am not *versipellis*—it cannot be true."

His hand rested fully on the side of her neck. "It would not have been imaginable until we willingly sought human mates. Those of us who honored the old ways had to compromise—your favorite word—because we saw that the bloodlines were corrupting. We had to do something to survive. The more we integrated with humanity, the more connected we became. As well, our foundation myth had a human element to it."

"Mary Mossett said something about Romulus and Remus?"

"Mary Mossett is a fount of knowledge."

"Mary Mossett is the only one who even came near to telling me the truth."

The duke—Alfred—lightly squeezed her neck. This was another apology, she sensed. "In the human myth, the twin brothers were royalty whose existence threatened the current king. They were abandoned by the river Tiber but saved by a she-wolf who took them to the cave Lupercal and suckled them to health."

"Lupercalia."

"One of our highest feast days. It was also said Romulus would one day kill Remus and become the founder of Rome. This is not the true story, for the twins were a threat not only due to their high birth but also because they were *versipelles*. What we celebrate on the day of Lupercalia is that they both found their *vera amorum*, and thus assured the continuance of our race. They set the course for true mating, from the heart and soul, that all good-thinking Alphas follow."

"And if this course is not followed?"

"Then, if you are my parents, for example, you marry for position and wealth and out of prejudice. They were not sympathetic to what they perceived as the dilution of the race and did not allow the mixing of human and wolf. They were not true mates, yet they chose to present themselves as *vera amorum*. The lie angered the Goddess, who laid a curse upon the fruitfulness of the Lowell Pack. This trickled down to the rest of the species that served us, and as a result, my sister was the last child born to this pack."

"That is why there are no children."

"Once their lie was discovered, the curse took hold for the first time in the long history of lupine affairs and decreed that, until there is a true mating of the Alpha, then none of the matings that had gone before would bear fruit, and those who have not mated, cannot." He turned her face to his. She saw Alfie shining through his gaze, his irises so icy a blue as to be bright white. "Unless I bond with my *vera amoris*, the pack will die out over time, never to grace the earth again. It will be as though we never existed. Unless you take me to mate."

Felicity gasped. "That is far too much responsibility, Alfred."

"Oh, Goddess," he moaned. "Hearing you speak my name… It sounds in my heart like the clearest bell…" And his lips descended on hers.

This was nothing like to the stolen kiss, nor even the kiss in the Bassett Room. Any restrictions or barriers between them, of hesitation or of manners, were utterly obliterated. His fingers tore out the few pins impeding him and ran through her hair, as hers did his, and their tongues clashed for dominance before agreeing to share the wealth. She broke off to rid herself of her jacket and slung her leg over his lap, situating herself against That Chest, her sensitive female parts settling down onto his masculine gifts.

"Magnificent things, trousers," she whispered as she slid a hand under the lapel of his dressing gown and over his shoulder.

"Magnificent," he agreed as he slipped his hands over her hips and onto her bum and then squeezed.

He captured her mouth once more, and her senses enflamed. She smelled the delicious, dry, vetiver earthiness of his soap, the musk of his skin, and yes, fur. That Chest heaved against hers as they held each other closer. There was a rumble within him that was doubtless Alfie, and she found that it made her want to laugh more than anything else. She heard the sounds they were making, her sighs, his groans, the rustle of their clothing, the sound her tailored shirt made as he yanked it out of her trousers, dragged it up to her shoulders, nearly tearing it off her body, the scrape of the hair on his chest against hers—

"My shirt," she began, having no idea what she intended to say next.

"I neglected to mention my sense of taste," he said as he ran his open mouth up and down her throat. "I have a very fussy palate."

"You'd never know from those meals." She sat up, her nearly naked breast very close to his mouth. "What about all that meat you eat? As one with an animal essence, you must be averse to such."

"I am a predator." His eyes had chilled to his usual icy blue, and yet they smiled at her right before he leaned in to nip where her neck met her shoulder. "You taste delicious. I seek to know the flavor of all of you, head to toe."

She hated her toes. "I don't think—"

"Excellent." He untied her soft-wrap corset and pulled it off. "Don't."

She thought she might die. The roughness of his flesh against her breasts made them feel all the softer, and his moan told her he felt the same. His hands joined his mouth in worshipping that part of her that had always made her feel so ungainly, so much, too much. She had a new appreciation for that aspect of her anatomy as he demonstrated his wholehearted admiration. He squeezed, coaxing a variety of sounds out of her that had no name but for passion. He licked, closer and closer to her nipples, and she held her breath, wary and impatient. He licked one, and she squeaked. He smiled and licked the other while he pinched the first, lightly then with more force as her back arched. Her hands came up to grip his hair, pull him closer. She lowered her forehead to the top of his head, her fingers wound in his thick locks, then roamed down to his shoulders and pushed the banyan off.

He snapped his head up, eyes slumberous, his tongue licking his lips. She ran her hands over his unclothed shoulders, around and down, and found his nipples. "I wonder…" she whispered and slid down to lick one, felt it harden under her tongue. She pinched it as she licked the other, looking up at him, his head thrown back, his hands gripping her hips enough to cause pain—but of an exquisite sort. Her hands roamed down that tantalizing line of hair that lead to his *masculinity*, his *family jewels* as she heard a groom call them once when he didn't know she was in earshot, his *reproductive organ*—"The words for this are not very nice," she said as she ran a finger down the hot, steely, silky length.

"Words?" He looked at her, dazed. "No words, madam." He

unbuttoned her modified falls and yanked her trousers down around her knees and nestled her against his chest. Oh, holy night, he was throbbing against her—her…if there were no good words for his part, the ones for hers were patently ridiculous. *Mount of Venus, pincushion, fancy bit*, all so silly. He squeezed her bum as if he heard her thoughts wandering, and she leaned against him more fully, her own bits throbbing, bit him on the jaw even as he nipped her on the earlobe. They kissed again, licking, holding still as their tongues played, as if they had all the time in the world before they joined. Were they going to join? Here and now?

"Alfred," she said and felt his dismayed reaction throughout her entire being. "Stop. Alfred. I cannot."

"We so very nearly are," he coaxed, running his fingers alongside her honeypot. That was another, *honeypot*! She found the strength, somehow, to kneel and pull up her trousers. He rubbed his chin along the tops of her breasts, eyes closed, inhaling all the while. "I cannot even begin to describe what the scent of your arousal does to me."

"I can feel what it's doing to you," she quipped and regretted it as he pulled her back against him. "No, stop, please."

"Let us bond now." His voice was a guttural plea. "I swear, on my life, on the lives of all in my pack, that this is true and meant and that all will become clear once we have made love."

"No." She climbed off him, leaving him exposed, about which he did nothing. She yanked up her trousers again, and pulled down her shirt, and moved to the end of the divan. "That is clearly the version of *versipellian* rakery. I said no."

A flash of the oppressive feeling tried to take hold of her, brief and almost reluctant. She buttoned her shirt with unsteady fingers. "You did not explain this breathlessness, this impulse to give in to you."

"It is known as the *dominatum*, the power of the Alpha. It is employed to prevent poor decisions at best, and insurrection at worst. And to get my way when my way is what is needed…or what I desire." He belatedly pulled his banyan closed and retied the sash. "It is yet another indication you are meant for me. There is no one else in my life who can resist the compulsion of my power, only you."

"But I am no one—"

"You are *yourself*, and you are *mine*."

It was as if he leapt atop her but gently. She lay beneath him, without fear, nor was there force. His fingers cradled her jaw, caressing it, and she couldn't help herself—she parted her legs so he might sink down against her.

"Your hair," he murmured, "I had no idea how beautiful it was until you let it down. I had no idea how pleasing your figure was until I held you in my arms while you slept in the coach. I had no notion of how perfectly you would fit in my arms until I embraced you that first night after the meal. How brave you were until you met my wolf in the meadow, how kind until I saw you with my people in the village." He buried his face in her hair; she licked his neck; he huffed, in a way she was beginning to understand meant both he and his wolf were well pleased. "I knew none of this, yet I knew you and wanted you."

He leaned up on his elbows. "Do you understand? I would have taken anyone, would just anyone do. Any one of those dreadful debutantes with their repugnant parents, who would run screaming from me did they know the truth of my nature. As you did not. As you never will. It means nothing to me where you stand on the social ladder, what the world perceives as your fitness for this role." He held her face in his hands, held her gaze as if to make her see the truth of it. "I would make you mine in truth, now." He rolled his hips against hers, and Felicity embraced a moment of surrender before she came to her senses.

"Up, up." She pushed against his chest, and he sat, pulling her along with him. "You cannot turn from a wolf into a man before my eyes and expect I shall follow your will without question."

"I am at your service." His tone was gentlemanly enough, but she heard the undertone of animal frustration.

"You think little of society and its mores, and yet such a whirlwind courtship is in fact how *ton* business proceeds." These questions were important, her mind assured her, as her body wailed in reproof.

"This is nothing," he growled. "We'd have had you bedded and mated that first evening."

"How can you be so sure about…us?"

"Because it is known in the soul."

"Of the Shifter, but not the human."

"I take your point," he said, to her shock, "but your instinctual nature has begun to accept this match. You were anticipating my actions and emotions as early as our waltz, and if you release and let go of your inhibitions, you will know what I know, despite your lack of Shifter nature." He drew her against his side, and she went willingly. He kissed her on the forehead. "We have our own traditions and nothing need be done in the conventional fashion. When we join, we will be connected in ways beyond any human ceremony. If you wish to forego traditional practice, we needn't marry if you do not wish it."

She elbowed her way out of his embrace and stood. "I will not be your mistress."

He lay on the divan and displayed himself before her like a tray of delicious macaroons. "What of being the mistress of all you survey?"

"Do not play with words with me." She thought of her uncle and his lies. "Words hold nothing for me."

"I offer you everything." He rose, and she could not move away.

"My independence is the natural casualty of this."

"I wonder if you are confusing independence with authority." He reached out and touched her face, tucked a lock of hair behind her ear. "Only the queen enjoys greater authority than a duchess, only she has longer reach and greater influence. Were not these the very things you sought when you conceived the idea of establishing your stud?"

"Yes, but the responsibility of being a duchess, under these circumstances—"

"You would be responsible for all those horses. Why not add a few species to the list?"

She moved again, restless, and looked around the room that was bare of everything, of possessions, of even the simplest comforts. She shut the window; no need to let the elements have their way with the place, even if in all likelihood it was no longer hers.

"Having had such brief acquaintance with you—" A growl sounded behind her. "Alfie! Hush!" The hush that ensued was profound. "I cannot take what you have revealed lightly and must have…must have proof that my role here is all that you say." *I must have proof that I am not hallucinating, that this is not all in my mind,* she thought. *Proof that everything—everything—he says is true.*

"Felicity." Oh, galoshes, the sound of his voice speaking her name nearly had her falling all over him, crying, *Yes, yes, yes, anything, anything at all!* "We shall talk to my people. Tomorrow, together, you may ask questions to your heart's content. From now on, you will receive answers." He rose. "A carriage from Lowell Hall will have arrived. I shall make my way back in my wolfskin if that meets with your approval."

"Yes, thank you." It was far too late to make the journey back on Jupiter, and some time alone with her thoughts would not go amiss.

"Then until tomorrow." He stood before the divan, handsome and virile and imposing, and yet for all that, vulnerable. "I assure you, without doubt, you are my *vera amoris.* I will choose no other. Ever. I ask that you choose me in return, of your own free will, out of your own desire. I await your decision." He gave her his leg in a full court bow, as though she were the queen herself, turned, and left.

Eighteen

"So. The mum of Romulus and Remus was Laurentia. She was a wolf that was beloved by the Roman God Ares. He was all about the fighting, and his wife, Venus, she was all about the loving. But Ares changed Laurentia into a woman so's he could love her, love her, and Venus changed her nature and was vengeful"—Mary Mossett bared her little teeth—"and she cursed the offspring of their union forevermore to be *versipelles*, to be caught between the fighting and the loving, the human and the wolf."

Felicity began her investigation into the life and times of a ducal Shapeshifting pack with her little maid. "What a stirring tale, Mary. I wonder how this explains other species?"

"Oh, mum, sure there's only all kinds of gods getting up to all kinds of shenanigans." Mary looked happy enough for this to be so, without need for further proof. "We mice have no stories such as this, but I do adore it."

"It seems unfair to punish the boys so."

"Wellll…if they hadn't got transformed, they'd not have the power and the heart to know their one and only mate. If Ares never woulda mated Laurentia, Venus wouldn'ta been so vengeful." She bared her little teeth again. "But if they hadn't a mated, then there never woulda been no Shifters…"

"I begin to comprehend the excess of conundrums in this world."

"What it all comes down to, Your Grace," Mary continued, "is that Ares was all the one thing, the strength, and Venus was all the other, the heart. And they didn't meet in the middle. Maybe if they'd met in the middle, they'd have got some of what the other had? And he wouldn't a needed ol' Laurentia to make him feel soft and sweet."

"Were the boys the first wolves who were also men?"

"Yes, madam, and then what happened was"—Mary perched on the edge of a stool—"the moon goddess, Diana, looked down upon the strife and took the boys away from that big mountain they was on and brought them to Rome, where she watched over 'em all their days. And when they did be needing wives, sure she only made sure they was both, woman and wolf, by such means a goddess could make anything she wanted to happen."

"And must all human women who would wed a Shapeshifter become a, a wolf?"

Mrs. Birks came in carrying a tea tray. "Mary Mossett, are you sitting in Her Grace's presence? Have you seen to changing them bed linens?" The little mouse jumped up and went to work. "Here you are, ma'am, here you are." Setting down the tray nearby, the housekeeper poured Felicity a cup of tea. She took the seat Felicity indicated and fussed with the breakfast things.

"Now then." Mrs Birks smoothed her apron over her lap. "I, myself, am a wolf and well placed to answer any questions you may have as to being mated to one of us, and also to, er, add to any knowledge your dear mother had time to impart before she left this earth."

"I am aware of the...mechanics of the wedding night." She thought back to what had almost happened in her old room in Templeton House and turned a bright scarlet. "Is it different for Shapeshifters? Do your kind change skins in, um, this regard?"

"No indeed, mum," Mrs. Birks said. "There's laws and all, and you and His Grace meet only in human form." Her briskness was a much-needed antidote to mortification.

Felicity downed her tea. "Mary mentioned the goddess Diana turning the wives into wolves?"

"She does love that story." The housekeeper sighed. "You will never become a Shifter, as the ability to turn a human has been bred out of us, but you will only give birth to those able to Change."

"Mrs. B, I did forget to say about how the babby won't be a wee pup when it's born." Mary bundled up the sheets. "None of us can Change until we be seven years of age," Mary added.

"It is considered the age of reason for both humans and Shifters," Mrs. Birks added. She flipped her hands at the little maid to send her on her way, which Felicity forestalled.

"And you can have as many as you like for as long as you like!" Mary hopped up on the bed and kicked her feet.

"My mother…" Felicity began and took a tremulous sip of tea. "I had no brothers or sisters. When I was old enough to understand, I realized my mother had been unable to carry another child to term."

"You will receive more than one boon as the *vera amoris* of one of our kind," Mrs. Birks assured her. "The strength of the Alpha is yours now, ma'am, and will extend to your growing offspring. We are long-lived and hearty, and you will become so yourself—"

"You won't be getting much older, not in looks, which I am thinking more than one of them fancy society ladies would spit nails if they only knew." Mary bounced on the bed. "And then Alpha's aging will quicken, and you'll both match up at the end."

"But he has reached one score and ten, at most?" How much she did not know about him, much less his people!

Mary laughed so hard, she was like to fall onto the floor, and Mrs. Birks huffed, sounding rather like Alfie. "He has more than one thing to tell you, I see. That's not my place now, but it's only a small thing. When all is said and done, we age well, so we do. As will you." The housekeeper held up a plate of buttered bread, and the appetite Felicity lost the past few days returned. "Now, as to the bonding ceremony," she said, and Mary squealed. "On the night of the full moon, we shall meet and Change to show ourselves to you in our native skins—"

"Naked?" Felicity nearly spat out a mouthful of tea.

"Best get used to it, Your Grace," Mary muttered.

The housekeeper passed Felicity a fresh serviette. "Words are spoken, and not too long-winded, as His Grace has little patience for the formalities. We honor you, then you accept His Grace and all of us."

"And then! You run, just a wee way, mind, so that our Alpha can chase you as his wolf and then catch you. And then…" Mary trailed off, her eyes shining, hands clasped to her lips.

"And then?" Felicity's heartbeat thundered, Mary's excitement contagious.

"And then there's the bite!" The mouse looked to be in raptures.

"A wee bite, a small one, now, don't you be thinking he'll be having your arm off, mum." Mrs. Birks chuckled, but it sounded more akin to a nervous whine.

Felicity did not consider this humorous in the least. A bite? As in a…bite? "Where?"

"Oh, there's a cottage up the way from the clearing," Mrs. Birks assured her, "we'll have it readied right and tight."

Felicity found she was able to laugh after all. "Where on my person, Mrs. Birks?"

"That's up to the wolf, Your Grace," Mrs. Birks said. She and Mary beamed as if there was nothing to be afraid of and everything to anticipate with joy.

A cursory knock sounded, and Alfred appeared on the threshold. A new awareness thrilled through her, not merely because she knew his secret. *He is mine if I so choose*, she thought. She took in his hacking jacket, its looseness unable to disguise the robustness of his physique; skipped up to his hair, which her fingers had disarranged to great effect only the day before; and slid down That Chest to regard the placket of his breeches, a regard that was protracted as he playfully bent down to meet her eyes.

"Good day." His eyes twinkled, and those crinkles appeared. Now that she was to spend the entirety of the day in his company, she wondered if she had the sangfroid to keep her hands to herself. And knowing what he was, and the trust he had placed in her... It was breathtaking.

"Good day," she replied as Mrs. Birks and Mary Mossett sank into curtsies. She gestured to the women to stand. "I have begun my education almost immediately upon rising."

"I would expect nothing less from one as curious and open in mind as yourself," Alfred said, "my dear."

Mary squeaked, "My deeeeeeear," and was rushed out of the room by an apologetic Mrs. Birks.

"Well." Felicity stuffed her hands in the pockets of her skirt.

"Well." Alfred tilted his head, much like Alfie did when he first appraised her. "Have I mentioned how beautiful you look in that...that..."

"It is a walking habit." Felicity strode toward him, the split skirt alternatively revealing and concealing the breeches beneath. She stopped before him. "It is very practical."

"My mind is even now furnishing scenarios in which it may prove its usefulness."

She found herself spun around with her back against the wall beside the door, and a ducal thigh nudged its way between her own. His mouth hovered about hers, tantalizing; his hips leaned into hers, titillating; his fingers tickled her neck, teasing. She rubbed her cheek against his, rubbed her nose along his jawline and whispered, "Have I thanked you properly for rescuing my band?"

"Properly?" He brushed his lips over hers, and they dipped down, like a bee lighting upon a flower. "Would you be averse to expressing your thanks improperly?"

She shifted her hips so her honeypot rubbed against the hard muscles beneath it. His whole body shook with the contact, and she smiled against his mouth. He slowly, inexorably raised his leg until she quite lost her breath. "We will not take the horses today," he said throatily, "but you may avail of your daily ride after all."

"I…" Felicity's toes were all but off the floor. The sensations were as unlike the sort she conjured for herself as night was from day. She wriggled, and he groaned, and she was as intrigued as she was inflamed. It should work under these circumstances, should it not? She moaned and heard a door slam down the hall, and footsteps approached. "No. Alfred, we are not entirely private."

"I will eviscerate anyone who dares disturb us."

"Charming." She dismounted and fluttered her lashes at him. "Come, Alfie, we have a busy day ahead."

As they made their way through Lowell Hall, Felicity appreciated the paintings with new eyes. Alfred pointed at one of the more lurid images of a wolf with his prey. "Old Granduncle Adolphus. Something of a brute, but my grandmother would not see him banished to the attics."

"Oh, ma'am," called a footman from below—Leo, she remembered. "Ye'd not like to see what all that lot did to get banished!"

"They's right gruesome," added his compatriot Felix.

"Gentlemen." Like any good butler, Mr. Coburn possessed the ability to materialize out of the ether.

The lads, only slightly penitent, went back to their tasks. "I apologize, madam," said the butler. "The footmen are in my remit, and as such, their behavior reflects upon me."

"I am sure that their natures will out, Mr. Coburn, no matter the strictures of the roles they fill."

"It is my pleasure to see that all in the house act in dignity to service of the duchy," he rebuked her gently. "It is a privilege to ensure that civility reigns. We walk a fine line, madam, of wishing to be allowed to live free in our essences and also accepted as part of humanity." He directed them down the corridor, and they processed to the back of the house. "I am well placed to see to preserving this balance in the Hall, while it is the duty of Mr. Gambon specific to the village. And I am used to ruling the roost. Eh? Roost?" He shook his head and tapped the side of his nose, his impressive coif waving, and the skin beneath his neck wattling.

"I believe I nearly met you in the park, Mr. Coburn." Amusement welled up within her.

"That you did, ma'am, that you did." He opened a door leading down to the kitchens and Mrs. Birks's domain. "I will always do all in my power to keep this house and all in it safe in both their natures."

"I expect nothing less, because you have shown me it is a foregone conclusion."

———————

Alfred let her take the lead. Down at the paddock in which her mares had been installed, he stood well away, unwilling to spook them as they had only been settled after the excitement. He watched Felicity and Marshall observe the mares as they followed their mysterious instincts to crop grass, move along, crop again, move again.

Delilah lifted her head and looked directly at him. Prepared for the worst should she react badly to his Shifter nature, he was stunned to see her gallop over to stop in front of him. Not entirely confident that she wouldn't take it off at the wrist, he extended a hand for her to inspect. She sniffed it with delicacy and then touched his knuckles lightly with her tongue.

"I will take excellent care of your mistress," he said, "and I give you leave to kick me senseless should I fail in that vow."

She switched her tail and bared her teeth, as if to say, *Your permission is not required,* but then she bobbed her head twice before blinking her limpid eyes at him, sweetly. She turned as Felicity approached, allowed her mistress to bestow a good scratch upon her withers, and wandered back to her sisters.

"That was extraordinary." Felicity gaped at him.

"I believe I handled that very well," he began.

"Not you. I have never seen her so well-behaved. Good girl," Felicity cooed to the mare, who turned her head and whinnied. "What a good, good girl!" She smiled up at him. "Lowell Hall must meet her standards."

"My relief at this conclusion is profound." In truth, it was. "What news of your stud?"

"Marshall tells me Mr. Bates can't find Himself," Felicity said. "He disappeared well before those wretched thugs descended upon my mares."

"I shall put more of my people on the hunt," Alfred assured her.

"Sure he'll turn up if he's got the scent of the band in his nostrils," said Marshall. "And if he wants his proper fodder as well."

"And Aherne and Bailey? Are they well and settling in?"

"Them two." The stable master rolled his eyes. "It's overrun, I am."

"Are they…?" She wasn't sure she was meant to ask.

"So ye've copped on, have ya?" Marshall rubbed his hands together, and they headed back to the barn. "Welcome to the menagerie."

Alfred growled, and Felicity hushed him with a touch. She smiled at the stable master and withdrew a small journal, and a piece of graphite that looked to be wrapped in metal, from her pocket.

"How did you come to be here, Mr. Marshall?"

The stable master rocked on his heels. "Fell in love with a lady with a difference, didn't know it at the time. Wanted to leave off working at a posting house in the arse end of Yorkshire, followed her here, had a rude little awakening when I chatted with her da." He stopped to laugh. "Lordy, that was something shocking, I'm telling you. Agreed to abide by their ways and was recognized by the pack as one of them and got the keeping of this equine palace. Nothing bad to be had, all round."

"I wonder at your equanimity, as I find I have it, too."

"It's part of their way, nothing sinister-like, but once they choose you, they make it easier for you to believe, somehow." He shrugged. "Listen, there's nowt so queer as folk. But if the choice was never to have met my beloved, well…"

"Then it was no choice at all." Felicity watched the stable lads trot around the place like a herd themselves. She raised a brow at the stable master, who made a show of inspecting his fingernails as he nodded. Felicity asked Alfred, "Is it not odd for them to live amongst creatures who are like them, but not?"

"It is difficult for prey animals such as they to be in proximity to predators such as I," Alfred said. "It is good to keep them gainfully occupied."

"They can live amongst the smallies, like the cats and the dogs and the birds. But the big bads? No indeed," added Marshall. "And they'll grow up appreciating their gifts."

"Is it a gift, Mr. Marshall?"

"Anything's what you make of it, Your Grace."

O'Mara awaited them at the end of the drive. They turned toward Lowell Close and walked for a time in silence. Felicity discerned a wave of whatever O'Mara manifested and said, "I do not require soothing, Miss O'Mara, if you would be so good."

"You ought not to be able to resist my glamour," O'Mara said. "No one can, not even—if not most especially—humans."

"I do not understand your powers." Felicity reveled in the swish of her skirts and the freedom of the breeches beneath. A magnificent thing, this walking habit.

"She is the Omega, the opposite of the Alpha," Alfred said. "I, who compel through strength, and when necessary, force, am balanced through the peace and equanimity that O'Mara can summon and disperse."

"In order that a calm state be kept within the pack," O'Mara added, "as far as is necessary."

"Or wanted." Felicity paused on the road, made a new heading in her journal, and wrote a new note. "I cannot imagine that a mesmerized household or village is the plan."

"No, indeed. But," O'Mara said, and Felicity rolled her eyes, "there is always a but, ma'am. We are an array of excitable creatures, and there must be a subtle way of keeping equilibrium. I am that way."

"And how does this affect your own emotions, Miss O'Mara?"

"If you will excuse me," Alfred said, "I have something to see to in the village before we arrive."

They watched him stride down the road and disappear around a bend. "Even our Alpha sometimes finds the finer points of what I do to be cause for discomfort." The women resumed their walk. "My own emotions are to be acknowledged and released, as it should be. But often with a speed which is…onerous. And often it is better do I not indulge them at all."

"It must be a great challenge." Felicity now understood what she had perceived as coldness was monumental control.

"No greater than that of our Alpha, who holds us all safe and as one."

"Such power," Felicity said.

"Such discipline," O'Mara retorted. "Such temperance. He is as a spider, weaving a web that is strong and subtle, often unseen by the naked eye, and yet a vital presence that is not a trap but a source of safety. It is his gift and his obligation to hold us together for as long as he lives."

And I myself must play some part in that. It was as thrilling as it was daunting. She consulted her notes. "Please explain these terms to me? Alpha, Omega? Are they Italian as the myth seems to be?"

"They are Greek terms. The myth is Roman in nature, I believe."

"It is the foundation story of you wolves, is it not? Would you not have heard it growing up? Should your titles not be Italian, then?"

"I would not know, madam," O'Mara replied. "As a female, my education was not what it ought to be."

"Tutor!" Felicity stopped and wrote for a length of time. "Would you like one?" She looked up at O'Mara, who shrugged. "I want one. And one for the servants who wish to better themselves. And any of the humans here who wish it. Can we all learn together? Is there a *versipellian* law against that? And how will I discern who is who?"

"You will know us soon enough, on sight," the chamberlain said. "But you must not inquire as to individual species. It is seen as the height of rudeness, and that courtesy is among one of our greatest laws. Another such a one is the *cognominatio*, the sacred ceremony in which Alpha named you as his mate and you were accepted by all."

Felicity heart swelled. "And no one thought it too hasty?"

"Oh, no. Many thought he tarried too long. And he himself is eager to secure your hand, and the wolf his bite." Felicity grimaced as they came upon the entrance to the Close. O'Mara grinned. "Sure you'll be grand, it's only a wee nip." She sobered. "It is vital that you accept all of him as he is, ma'am. He sought you, only you, for years and years. It was the very thought of you, if I may not mince words, that caused the terrible but necessary upheaval in the Lowell Pack."

"He does not speak of this upheaval. I presume it has to do with his family," Felicity said.

"Ask him of them, and you will learn all you need to trust him with your life and your heart."

They soon reached Alfred, who stood waiting with Mr. Bates and Mr. Gambon. O'Mara remained behind, and the quartet moved on. Felicity looked back and saw the chamberlain watching them walk away, and her heart ached for the lonely picture she made, standing there as though she were the last woman on earth. Would she as duchess be able to lighten the Omega's load?

"Well, gentlemen," Felicity said, "I feel we must make proper introductions."

Bates began. "I am the Beta of the pack, the Alpha's right-hand man, no different from a human steward. I am also a wolf," he said, his eyes glinting with a smile, "although not as dark in appearance as His Grace."

"It was you I saw in the park." Felicity considered his hair, as golden a yellow as the wolf she'd seen. She hadn't even thought to ask about distinguishing characteristics between animal and human selves. She stopped to make another note.

"It was the best way to keep an eye on things," he said, "and not a complete contravention of our laws."

"And we were only getting that desperate, madam," said Mr. Gambon. "The few glimpses you caught of us in animal form were done in the hopes it would make the knowledge that much easier to bear."

She quite liked this blunt, genial man and wondered if he was in fact a bear.

"And how did you acquire your roles? Is there a, a registry office for *versipelles*?"

"As wolves, we thrive on community," Alfred explained. "Whilst the dukedom makes us the highest in our order, in Bates's case, the earldom of Rendall was near enough the top to be a suitable place for me to foster."

"It soon became apparent that I was His Grace's match as Second," said Bates, "and so I was raised to be such."

"And his brother was not happy, not the tiniest bit." Gambon's eyes glinted with mischief.

"My brother, who is my twin, will someday hold the family title of earl." Bates refused to rise to the bait. "Being placed at the Hall allowed me to move up in the world, in the hopes that my sisters would benefit from my elevated state. They have but are living in suspension as we are, as regards the young."

"Because of your connection to Alfr—to the Alpha?"

Bates nodded and then hesitated. "I have not been an advocate of mixing the races," he admitted. "We keep our secrets close, but often not close enough, and Shapeshifters have suffered from pogroms and annihilation. And yet, if we are to survive, we must amalgamate the benefits of our makeup with the camouflage of the human race."

"Camouflage?"

Gambon took up the explanation. "When we mix with humans, we look less like our animals and blend to a greater degree. We have not been at it long, only a century or two."

Felicity made yet another note, but the notion she would forget any of this was remote. She took a deep breath and looked around her. How many communities across England, across the world, harbored such souls as these? How many had she met and not known? Did her natural affinity for animals make this all easier to comprehend and accept?

"O'Mara could not tell me why the titles of your roles are Greek when your stories are Roman."

Bates grumbled low in his throat. "Those bloody—pardon me, ma'am. Those stories! Credulous tales for children, and I wouldn't put any store in them."

"Despite every indication to the contrary that the *vera amoris* myth is true," Alfred mumbled.

"If it is true, then it is not, by its very nature, a myth." Bates looked irritated beyond measure. "The hierarchical terms are common across all species of Shapeshifter and do not derive from our Roman roots, roots which may be as mythological as the time-worn tales that nevertheless continue to thrive."

"Mr. Bates, how cross you sound." She resumed their stroll, and she came out all over in gooseflesh when Alfred took her hand and twined his fingers with hers. "And what are your responsibilities, Mr. Gambon?"

"Well, madam, I am the liaison between the souls on this land and the holy trinity." He laughed and dodged a good-natured blow

236   SUSANNA ALLEN

from Bates. "I handle what I can. What I can't, I take to Bates or O'Mara, as needed. If there is need of greater recourse, then we take it to the Alpha himself."

"Surely you would like to know all that is occurring in your domain?" She raised her brows at the duke.

"I needn't be bothered because the dogs and cats are brawling again or the magpies have gone on a spree," Alfred replied. "Or that the mourning doves are in bits over Goddess knows what. The former would be under Bates's remit, and the latter O'Mara's."

"He needs to be free to attend to greater matters," Gambon added. "Our Alpha is our strongest member, but also our greatest servant."

"Yes, O'Mara implied as much."

"As only she can imply." They shared a smile over that. "It is a place of beauty here, Your Grace," Gambon continued, as they paused before coming upon the village green. "In its aspect and in its heart. The wolves and I are natural enemies, and yet here we bide in as much harmony as different beings can, and with a greater hope for the future now you are among us. And not only for ourselves, but also for our duke." She looked over at Alfred, who, for the first time in their acquaintance, looked discommoded. "He is a good man and a splendid wolf, and his integrity has been a challenge and an inspiration for us all."

"I understand you are to offer knowledge of your inner self only of your own volition." Felicity peeked up at him, and he roared with laughter.

"And I understand that Alfred has met his match." He bowed and said, "I am a boar, madam. B-O-A-R, not B-O-R-E. It is my lot to be solitary as a male in a matriarchal society such as my kind live in, and I found it not to my liking. I heard tell of an aristocratic wolf that sought a way forward for those who wished to mix and left my sounder. It was the work of the Goddess that he required a Gamma, the third in his personal coterie, and that I fit the bill. So here I am, expanding my nature by leaps and bounds."

"Your Grace." Bates smiled down at her. She'd never met so many tall men in all her days. "If you would follow us, you will find a gift from His Grace." His Grace went from discomfited to tense in the beat of a heart.

The villagers looked even happier to see her than they had before, and she blushed to wonder what exactly was communicated along that web of Alfred's. As she greeted the artisans and the crafts folk she had met previously, she noticed hammering and shouting drifting from the square.

"Has that empty acreage been put to use, so soon?"

"We have been given permission for the construction of that public house I mentioned," said Gambon, "and another building with a very special purpose."

They paused before said structure, the scent of sawdust and fresh paint in the air. It was extraordinary how speedily the workers were moving, smiling as they went, their bucked teeth gleaming as they flung a wall into place. *Beavers*, Felicity guessed. They'd be well able to build a sturdy property, if so.

"And what shall it be?" The sign for the shop was obscured by a length of canvas.

"Beresford," Mr. Bates shouted, "let us see the name of this fine establishment."

"We've only just put up that there cloth," the stocky little man huffed.

"Beresford," said Alfred, and nothing more; the builder and an equally thickset colleague scurried up ladders with greater ease than might have been expected. They released the cords that held the canvas in place and let it fall to the ground.

Very much opposite to the way Felicity's heart soared into the boughs. "That…that is a magnificent sign."

It was hewn from finest oak and simply read: *Templeton Stud*.

Nineteen

ALFRED'S BREATH LEFT HIS BODY AS HE WAITED FOR HIS MATE'S response. His heart pounded, and it was as if his blood had frozen in his veins. His muscles trembled with tension, and his palms—his palms, the palms of the Alpha of the greatest pack in the British Isles—sweat like a pup's. Was this what was experienced when he exercised the *dominatum*? It was not comfortable, to say the least.

"These are your premises," Gambon explained, a hand hovering at Felicity's elbow. "There will be a show paddock behind. We think. We're not sure yet as to how your stock will respond to our natures, and frankly you'll not shift much cattle if they're glamoured into submission."

"It is my hope you will look upon this gift with pleasure," Alfred said.

Felicity nodded, her hands gripping her skirt.

"The sign meets with your approval? You did say it was magnificent, did you not?" She left his side and approached the entrance. He rushed to follow her, his Beta and Gamma close behind. "And should the interior not be up to your standards, then we shall set the beavers to work at once."

He saw Bates exchange a concerned look with Gambon, who said, "Perhaps if we showed you 'round and explained our Alpha's thoughts—"

"No." Felicity looked at Alfred and only at Alfred. "His Grace will take me through. Thank you for your patience with my questions and for your honest answers. That will be all."

She took his hand and led him into the building.

"A very duchessy dismissal, my dear," Alfred joked.

Felicity turned to stand before him. There would be time to investigate her premises—her premises!—but there would never be this moment, in which he presented her dream on a silver platter, or more like, in the shape of a building she had never dared conceive of. Speechless, she ran her hands over his arms, over his shoulders, and down to his heart. She held her hands there, feeling the rapid beat of it, and leaned her head against That Chest. She embraced him, held him, beyond words. Upon reaching up, she cupped his face in her hands, stroked her thumbs over his lips, and then kissed him, a new kiss, a sweet one, one of thanks and appreciation and purity of heart.

"I take it you are pleased."

She smiled at the uncertainty in his voice. "I never thought to reach this high. I would have been happy enough with a satchel full of papers and a sturdy pair of boots."

"All the world will come to you," he said, his hands caressing her waist. "There will no finer equines in all of England."

She raised her lips to his, melted against him, and the sweetness, the purity, transformed to fire and wantonness. Everywhere he touched her burned with desire. She slid her hands down around his back, laughed against his mouth as she grabbed his posterior, and whooped as he hoisted her up onto the reception room's countertop and once again insinuated himself between her thighs.

"Alfred, there are no curtains in the windows."

"We need not remove our clothing for you to be pleasured. I know you know to what I refer. Do you often pleasure yourself, Felicity?" She mumbled and he—it wasn't a chuckle, but it wasn't a proper laugh either. "I did tell you about my exceptional hearing, did I not? 'Never so much as you've done since your arrival at Lowell Hall'? I wonder why?"

"That bath." Even to her own ears, her voice sounded sultry and abandoned. "One can recline at full length in that bath. One can relax in the warmth and the scents, and if one had asked Mary Mossett to secure the exact blend of vetiver and bay as used by a certain duke of one's acquaintance, then the entire experience is rather more…"

"Rather more…" He wrapped his arms around her.

"Rather more invigorating that usual," she said. "Rather more sensual."

"And are you aware," he asked, as he parted her thighs with his hips and ran his hands over her belly, "that there are a variety of ways to invigorate yourself?"

"Earlier, in fact, it had occurred, when your—your leg was underneath my sensitive place—"

She gasped as his hands parted her thighs even further, and he dipped his head, leaning it against her thigh and kissing her very near her honeypot. "Oh, yes, many ways." His hands squeezed, and then his fingers ran over her falls, and his tongue peeped out. His eyes on hers, he lowered his head toward her—

"Alfred! You cannot think to—"

An almighty clatter from above on the roof gave even the duke pause, and Felicity did not hesitate to sit up. After a quick buss on his lips, she braced her hands on his shoulders and hopped off the counter. "That is quite enough for now, Your Grace. I would acquaint myself with my office. For despite his dastardly schemes, my uncle has not succeeded in thwarting me." She wrapped her arms around herself. "How he could think to murder his sister's beloved band? And Himself is nowhere to be found…"

"Felicity." Would she ever tire of hearing her name spoken with that voice? "I must deal with him. It is to do with my second nature as much as my first that I must. Vengeance need not be bloody to be satisfying, I assure you."

"What has become of Rollo?"

"He is even now reposing in the belly of a hulk bound for the Antipodes. I would ensure that Purcell join him."

"I have known nothing but spite from both," Felicity said. "It pains me that we have come to this pass, but I will abide by your solution." She sighed. "I understand that Cecil, in his way, did much to help. He deserves a reward."

"He does indeed," he said. "It is down to him that we found your father's true will. He revealed several hiding places about the property and our magpies made quick work of it."

"How he remembered after all these years…" After all these years, she thought, the truth would come out. Thousands of questions ran through her mind, not only regarding her father's wishes, but also how Cecil had known to contact her, how the plan to kill her animals had been devised—how her uncle could have known her so well as to have divined her very soul and used it against her. Alfred waited, watched her, and likely sensed her every emotion, his desire to come to her aid almost palpable, there for the asking, and she felt…she felt as though, after all these years, the answers would wait another day.

And yet: "Did my father elevate me above all females through his legacy? Am I to receive a fortune, or no?"

Alfred looked regretful. "Somewhat, and not precisely."

"Then it matters not," she said. "Nothing matters, as I look around me."

"There is indeed a legacy," he began.

"I am only interested in the future," she countered.

"It is quite a…" He was lost for words. "It is significant."

Felicity shrugged. "Then I will read the will myself, at my leisure."

"And we will marry in two days."

"Will we? I have yet to be asked. In a manner indicative of my position in life." She swanned out of the front office and inspected the stalls that ran along the left side of the structure.

"I will sort out the special license and then propose in a style due your consequence. Thus, I must to Town."

"I am certain the proposal comes before the license."

"I have a plan. It is a secret."

"Another surprise? How I have grown to enjoy them. Away with you, then." She made her way over to the right side of the building, peering over dividing walls, opening cupboards, beaming like the sun. "Perhaps on the way you may like to think on a proper application for my hand."

"Or an improper one, perhaps?" he called, but she ignored him as she set about going over her new offices with a fine-tooth comb.

———

The nearly full moon hung overhead, a beacon in the night. As Alfred entered the Hall, after a day spent in London setting certain events in train, it was as if the whole estate had woken from a long sleep. He made his way through his ancestral birthplace—very nearly doomed by his parents' calumny—went up and down the stairs, and through the corridors, taking in the vitality of the servants, the chatter and laughter, the joy with which he was greeted, and his heart filled with exultation. The Hall was becoming a home before his eyes.

He saw this joy reflected in his Beta's expression as he entered his steward's office. "Matthias. All is well?"

"Alpha." Bates handed Alfred a sheaf of foolscap. "It is. Depending upon that."

Arthur raised a brow, and his steward fought to keep a straight face. He glanced at the opening lines set down in a feminine hand. "Is this a marriage contract?"

Matthias gave in to the grin and followed Alfred out of the room. Alfred read aloud: "*Your Grace. Herewith I present to you the articles of our marriage, an event that will inevitably unfold, despite the fact that you have yet to ask it of me with anything like the approximation of a maiden's dream.*"

Matthias's wolf snorted with delight. Alfred elbowed him in the

side, to the amusement of Felix and Leo, who had been chunter-
ing at each other in the corridor. "You two. Fetch Mr. Coburn, if
you would." The footmen raced away; he continued reading. "*I set
before you my terms for this union, embracing not only the marriage,
but the welfare of all in Lowell Hall.*" He stopped, overwhelmed,
and his friend's hand gripped his shoulder. Alfred's wolf was like
to howl his joy for all to hear. "*My mares are settled in the southern meadow, and in concert with Mr. Marshall, I have agreed that my
head lads, Aherne and Bailey, late of Templeton House, are responsible
for their care. I will require a steward or chamberlain of my own to aid
me in bringing Templeton Stud to its fullest potential.*

"All staff are to be given pay rises. Is this your work, Beta?" he
teased. "*Mary Mossett is to be encouraged in her gifts as a seam-
stress and a mantua-maker in her own right through an apprentice-
ship to Lady Jemima Coleman. We will secure a tutor for any staff
who desire, as does Miss Mossett, to further their education. Mrs.
Birks may have someone in mind to attend me as my personal maid.
I do not wish to be served by a fraudulent French maid found in a
servants' registry. Unless the one Mrs. Birks has in mind is, in fact,
French.*" The men headed for the green baize door. "*Monsieur
Louveteau is in need of an apprentice in order that such a person
take charge of the lower servants' meals. This will appease a complaint rendered by Mr. Coburn.* What has Coburn been com-
plaining about? Never mind, she's got it sorted..." He mumbled
through the rest of her directives. "There's nothing here about
her own jointure."

Bates pointed to the next page. "Ah. *As regards my portion
should you predecease me...I cannot write of this, it is too difficult. I
see now why such documents are drawn up by unfeeling parties. It is my
intention that Templeton House, which would fall under your remit as
my husband, be returned to me in a settlement of trust that it may be
used as a home for business-minded women with no family or whose
relations are hostile to their ambitions.* That's moot, or will be once

she learns of her father's true bequest." He paused at the door to his suite and tapped the papers on his thigh.

"Once she learns of it?" Bates looked at him as though he were a lunatic. "Did you not tell her we found the will?"

"She is weary of the entire business and chooses to leave off reading it for now. I told her of it and that the legacy was not as she expected. It was not as if I set out to hold back the knowledge."

"Wives dislike being left in the dark."

"I bow to your infinitely greater experience. All those wives you've had." Alfred resisted the desire to shift and let their wolves loose on each other. Just for a lark. "I will tell her when I deem the time is right."

"I bow to your infinitely greater desire to live dangerously." Matthias rolled his eyes.

"In any case, it would be poor form did I not strive to negotiate," he said, turning back around to head for the staterooms.

"She is not here, Alpha."

"Had she thought to meet me in Town?" Bates turned over the last paper in Alfred's hands. "Oh. *I have repaired to London and am making use of the Lowell town house in St. James's Square to collect my thoughts as I prepare to reenter society as an imminent duchess and face down the* ton. *Like it or not, our children…*" Emotion swamped him, and he had to take a breath. "*Our children will have to mix with these people and do the pretty, and so we must begin our rehabilitation sooner rather than later. I shall attend the Montague ball tomorrow evening. Invitations are unexpectedly easy to obtain when one is as notorious as I. You may stay at your club and turn yourself out in full ducal vesture, as you seem wont to do, to join me there. As I mentioned earlier, an improved approach to proposing marriage would not go amiss. Yours, et cetera.* Hers, et cetera, indeed."

"Your Grace." Coburn stood at the end of the corridor, pretending he hadn't heard a thing. Alfred looked between his friend and his faithful retainer, and for the first time, perhaps since he'd been a young man, perhaps since he'd been a very small boy, he fully, completely, and unabashedly smiled. Coburn cleared his throat, and Bates's eyes glistened even as he grinned in return. "We have our orders, gentlemen. Let us prepare a run to London, posthaste."

Twenty

IT WAS A VERITABLE CRUSH.

The utter squeeze that packed the ballroom of the minor Viscount Montague sent his viscountess into alt. Servants ran hither and yon like chickens with their heads cut off in search of more ice, more ratafia, more wine, more flowers, for it was not until almost the very last moment that Fallen Felicity chose this ball to reemerge into society. Had she even been invited? It was of no consequence: word had spread like wildfire, and simply everyone was there. Including the Duke of Lowell himself. The event was set to go down in history—or in infamy.

It was all of eleven days since the fall of Felicity Templeton. The orchestra played, the dancers danced, and the gossipers gossiped, as they had at the Ball At Which It All Happened, and if the *on-dits* were to be given credence, something would transpire tonight to put that in the shade.

"If he hasn't wed her by now, he never will." A dowager nodded to Sally Jersey across the room. Only an incipient scandal of this caliber would induce such a lady to enter the ballroom of a lord of middling repute. "Should they find themselves in this room together, I assure you he will give her the cut direct."

"She intends to cut him," said an old fellow. "She has fallen under the care of the prince regent himself."

"Under the care or under *him*?" said a silly buck, whose company guffawed.

"I heard she threw herself in his carriage and accompanied Lowell to Somerset." This season's diamond of the first water looked scandalized.

"The estate is in Westbury," corrected her less luminous friend.

"It never is! It's in Shaftesbury!" claimed a lady who fell somewhere between them on the scale of glister.

"Her marriage contracts are all that is beneficial to His Grace," said a widow.

"She drew them up herself." Her attending beau looked very sure of himself.

"Don't be ridiculous." The widow glared at him. "I've never heard such nonsense. I wonder that you would even think to repeat it."

"I believe her uncle is in the card room," said a chaperone. "He has been bewailing her lost virtue."

"That is her cousin," added her charge, gesturing to a spot across the ballroom with her fan. "The youngest one, lurking behind the Dowager Countess of Covington."

Alfred prowled the edges of the dance floor and, as ever, eavesdropped without giving the appearance of doing so. Bates joined him, well nigh brushing debutantes off his coattails as he came. "How did they find out about the contracts?" Alfred asked.

Bates grinned, and several ladies fluttered their fans with ferocity. "I let it drop in the cloakroom. No one believes it."

A brief burst of noise at the head of the ballroom's shallow staircase caused the dancers to stop dancing, the gossipers to stop gossiping, and the orchestra to cease playing with the discordant whine of a dying violin. Alfred felt his entire being expand, from his heart outward, to fill his entire body. His wolf, sulking at attending yet another ball, surged to life as Alfred turned to face the disturbance.

The viscountess's butler appeared. The room went as silent as the tomb. "Miss Felicity Templeton."

Alfred turned, and after a beat, a heartbeat, he bowed in perfect time to Felicity's appearance at the head of the stairs.

A gasp ricocheted around the room. Felicity stood, as she had stood in her long-ago dream of her debut, and lifted her chin. She was no longer the Antidote the *ton* had become inured to snubbing. Her dress had short sleeves, and she carried a fan, but from there her ensemble parted company with the fashion of the day. Her shoulders were exposed in their entirety, calling attention to a décolletage that put lesser-endowed maidens to shame. The gown was a watered silk in leaf green, which ought to have been a travesty for a redhead; it flattered her dewy complexion no end. Rather than fall in a straight column from beneath a sash tied high, the skirt dropped from a fitted waist; and rather than descend into a ruffle or two, layers of fabric spread around her ankles. Her gloves were the palest ivory and lacked cover for her fingers. It was all too unusual and original, and yet she stood as a goddess in the porch of her temple—fearless, composed, magnificent.

She looked only at Alfred. The dancers and the watchers, the mamas and the dowagers, the young bucks and the old had cleared a path on the floor between the two, agog. She waited, and he took one step, another, and another until he reached the stairs. Only then did she go down to him, oblivious of the gawkers.

"Good evening, Miss Templeton," Alfred said, as he bowed over her hand. His eyes gleamed with humor as he gave her knuckles a good sniff.

"Your Grace." Felicity executed a flawless curtsy. "I find myself bereft of a partner for the next dance—"

"And well you might, trollop that you are." The crowd parted at the back of the room, and Ezra Purcell came forward. Alfred moved to stand between her and her perfidious relation, but she stopped him, much as she would have stopped Himself, with a hand on his chest. She would do this, not alone, but with his support of her own authority.

"I am astonished you have the cheek to present yourself here."

Her uncle's small eyes shifted from her to the duke, splendid in the array due his rank. "And you, Lowell, how low you have gone."

"I am astonished you think to address me in such a fashion," Alfred growled, proof positive that Alfie was very near the surface. That would not do: Felicity looked up at her duke, arching a brow. Both wolf and man looked displeased but deferred to her wishes.

"I am astonished," Felicity replied, "that you are present at a *ton* gathering, you who despise them so heartily. That you have made no attempt to liberate me from the duke. That you did not respond to his solicitation for my hand in marriage." She heard the news rustle throughout the gathering; here was new grist for the mill. "I am astonished you have the gall to accuse anyone else of perfidy, much less accuse them of such before all the world."

"As to perfidy…" Her uncle gloated. "With tomorrow your birthday, I suspect you are in expectation of your inheritance coming good. What an unhappy surprise that will be. Oh dear, I have all but ruined it, have I not?"

"You refer to my father's will, which left me dowerless but paradoxically offered me a fortune should I remain unwed," Felicity said, confirming that rumor once and for all.

"It did strike me as odd," he mused, "and it preyed upon my conscience, so in your best interests, I took it upon myself to investigate."

"Much as I did myself. As you well know, since it was you who posted letters for me, to the solicitor in St. Giles."

Ezra nodded, all beneficence. "But as your guardian, I was able to go where you could not. Oh, dear Felicity, imagine my dismay when I discovered the document is false."

"Is it?"

"It is. There is nothing at all. As you well know, your poor father went into rather a dramatic decline and gambled away his funds, in a drunken stupor, one supposes. You have no recourse to the house or the land, such as it is, and as there is no male heir, the entirety will revert to the Crown."

"How distressing." Felicity held her uncle's dolorous gaze, which became less tragic the longer she held it. "This is all moot if a true will exists."

"Alas, the baron appears to have been remiss in attending to such legalities."

"And I must assume you searched for it?"

"Far and wide, niece, far and wide. It does not exist."

"You are behind the times, Father." Cousin Cecil stepped from his hiding place behind the dowager countess. "The true testament was found." His voice wavered, but he carried on. "Thanks to me."

He glared at his youngest son. "You dared betray me?"

"You dared betray me." Felicity stood tall, and Alfred stood at her back, as strong as a fortress, as immovable as a rock face. The *dominatum* gathered around him, not at its fullest power, but she perceived it was well able to burst forth should the need arise. She took some of its force for herself, and through it, through their growing connection, knew his pride in her, his admiration of her strength and poise, and it flooded her being. "You lied to me, an orphaned young woman, and attempted to sell my family home out from under me. You sought to slaughter my horses, my only remembrance of my mother. And you knew, somehow, of my scheme with them—"

"As if I'd no idea of what you were up to." Uncle tucked his fingers in his waistcoat pockets, to all appearances enjoying the reactions of the *ton*, uncaring that his family's dirty linen was airing before all. "As if I'd not had spies in every corner and behind every door. A woman, breeding horses. Foolish creature! Chasing a mad ambition you had no prayer in carrying off with those wretched creatures that were the death of my sister." The listeners, who had been as still as though a pin were to drop, reacted with shock at the thought of an honorable miss embarking upon a life in trade.

Felicity looked at him with sadness. "You loved my mother, and my mother adored you, even though you ever held my father in low regard. How despicable your behavior is, how foul a person you are to devise this plan, to ruin my life. For I lost her as well, and you wished to ensure that I lost all."

"There is nothing to prove I have done anything untoward." Her uncle had the audacity to chuckle. "If a will has been unearthed, by the churl whom I no longer recognize as my son, there is nothing to show I have been plotting against my own niece. You will struggle to place the blame at my door."

"Father does like to burn things," Cecil said. "He threw the duke's offer for my cousin's hand into the fire."

"As luck would have it, Cecil," the duke rumbled, "your brother Rollo liked to hoard things. Just as he was taking ship to the Antipodes, he revealed that he kept several copies of a variety of wills in your father's hand, and strangely, several versions that are attributed to Baron Templeton—also in your father's hand."

"You resorted to forgery to thwart my family? Was it greed, Uncle?" Felicity asked. "Have you not earned enough of your own wealth?"

"Money?" Ezra scoffed, as only a Cit could. "Money is nothing to one who knows how to cultivate it, manipulate it. It was never about money." He clenched his fingers, knuckles turning white. "It was about the line. The lure of the aristocracy that led my sister to abandon the bosom of her loving family for the embrace of that titled, useless man. It was about that line dying, that minor, insignificant branch of the peerage that meant nothing to anyone of importance, about it disappearing from the face of the earth." Another gasp exploded. Felicity imagined their reaction had less to do with the Templetons and more to do with a mere Cit conspiring to bring down the Quality.

"It was all for naught, Purcell," Alfred thundered. "I am delighted to inform you that Miss Templeton's true endowment was far more than mere guineas or land. Her father, despite his humble rank, was a great favorite of the King's. Because the baron had not produced a son, the title of Templeton will instead endure through his daughter, and all his earthly possessions are hers."

Felicity turned a shoulder to her uncle and laid a hand on Alfred's arm, its trembling betraying her apparent composure. Alfred's eyes were the only still point in her suddenly tilting world, and she felt as dizzy as she had when she first heard the will was false. "I—I do not understand."

"No matter what choice you made, to marry or no, the baron ensured that the power of the title would rest in you." Alfred slipped an arm around her waist; Felicity leaned into his embrace, and Alfie roared with joy.

"My mother was forever telling me I would be exalted above all the other debutantes." Felicity shook her head. "Mama would have thought saving the title was all that was wonderful, but it seems to have been nothing but a source of pain and trouble. I do not know that it means anything to me, in truth."

"Perhaps you honor your mother, then, by allowing it. Perhaps somewhere down your father's line was a relation such as you, a woman of purpose who was fierce, protective, nurturing, and bright," Alfred said. "In continuing the title, you do so for her. Only think, your firstborn son will carry on this legacy from your line."

"No." Felicity turned to face her uncle and the onlookers. "My daughter. My firstborn daughter will be the Baroness Templeton. The title in my gift will continue only in the female line from this day forward."

"It will be as you say," Alfred said before one and all, before whispering for her ears only, "and in actual fact, she will be our daughter."

"That cannot be legal," Ezra blustered.

"As a soon-to-be peeress of the realm, I would say my cousin's word was beyond law," Cecil piped up.

"None of us are above the law," Purcell protested.

"As to that…" Alfred nodded to the guards, who then swarmed through the room. The King's guard entered the ballroom without fanfare and laid hands on Ezra Purcell. "You'll find the punishment for fraud is quite heavy, but not less than the crime of seeking to ruin a young lady's life and her bloodline through her." A smattering of applause accompanied a snarling and shouting Purcell on his way to justice as the guards dragged him away.

Alfred turned to her. "Before we were so rudely interrupted, you mentioned something about the next dance?"

"I believe it is a waltz. Would you do me the honor?"

"Would you do me an even greater honor?" He dropped to one knee before her, and yet another gasp flew through the gathering. Felicity saw the Viscountess Montague swooning with joy; the dowagers, as one, raised their lorgnettes. She hoped the wallflowers gained a heroine; the debutantes, a new dream; and the suitors, a new nightmare.

Alfred looked up at her, her whole future laid before her in his loving gaze. "Long ago, I swore to leave my heart to fate. I swore none would do but my own true love. Far and wide I traveled, and all the while, the one whom fate decreed would take my heart into the finest, most loving care was here, at home, in England." Whisperers informed the room at large that their lands marched at the Surrey border. "I have searched for you everywhere, Felicity." Tuts met the evidence they were on familiar terms. "I hope I am to be found. Found in your heart, found in your soul, by you, my one and only. The only one for me." He opened his palm; on it rested a beautiful ring, with four stones set in a silver band. "I offer this as a symbol of my pledge to revere you above all others, as a symbol that our joined lives will shine as brightly as these gems. Do tell me you accept my troth and consent to be my wife."

In a heartbeat, all her doubts dissipated, and all her dreams were fulfilled. In her imminent acquiescence, she found power and possibility and the surety of promises that would be honored for a lifetime. "I accept," Felicity said. "Alfred."

He rose and slipped the ring over the fourth finger of her left hand, held that hand in both of his, closed his eyes, and kissed the back of it; and then, known only to her, he nipped her knuckles. He offered her his arm, and the watchers fell away as they made their way to the dance floor. Alfred led her into the center, nodded to Bates, who nodded to the orchestra, who began to play. They took their positions as was proper, and on the downbeat, Alfred swept her into a great swirl around the floor. The dress that had looked so odd came to life, its skirt opening and closing with the movements of the dance like petals, revealing a pale-ivory lining, and Felicity looked like a lily as the duke spun her 'round the floor.

"I called upon you today." Alfred indulged in a great inhalation, and Felicity snuck a sniff of her own.

"How kind of you to leave your card," she said. "Sadly, I was not receiving."

"Vixen."

She attempted to remain impassive, as was proper, but failed and smiled up at him. "The floral tribute was all that was glorious."

"Marshall recommended posies."

"Taking courting advice from a stable master?"

"Was it effective?" He squeezed her hand.

She squeezed his in return. "It was."

"Well, then."

They swirled down the side of the floor, and all at once she became aware of her surroundings, of the susurrations of gowns and the murmur of voices around the room as innuendo was sown hither and yon. Rather than feel self-consciousness descend upon her like a heavy cloak, she found it was the simplest thing in the world to ignore when her new life held her in his arms.

Alfred, however, able to discern their every comment, snarled at the spectators.

"Alfie! Pay them no mind." Felicity smiled. "Let us relive your proposal."

"It was magnificent, was it not?"

"It more than atoned for the first two attempts."

"Third time is the charm," he whispered in her ear. "May I say how charming you look in that exquisite gown? But indeed, the gown is a very minor enhancement of your grace. Your Grace."

They swept down the side of the ballroom where Cecil stood in the company of a petite debutante who gazed upon him in admiration.

"That is Miss Smythe-Watson," Felicity said. "She has ten thousand a year."

"Your cousin's eligibility will increase, should he desire her hand," Alfred responded, "when it becomes known he is the sole proprietor of Purcell and Sons."

"But would my uncle's possessions not fall under the remit of the law?"

"They would, under normal circumstances, which would not generally include O'Mara glamouring a solicitor into conveying all to your cousin."

"If I never hear of another solicitor…"

Alfred essayed a particularly exuberant turn through a corner, and the candlelight from the chandeliers sparked off the gemstones that adorned the hand resting on his shoulder. "This is not the ring you first presented me with."

"I am impressed you noticed, as you gave that offering the barest glance." Alfred's smile was wry. "I determined that a new token was in order."

"This is rather more than a token." The diamonds that circled the band were small but bright, and the four precious gems that marched in a row across the top of the ring were large and varied. The first was rich green, the second a sparkling violet, the third a vibrant yellow, and the last—"I recognize the emerald, but the first three are unknown to me."

"They are malachite, iris, and nephrite," Alfred said. "I hope it pleases you."

"It is unique and stunning," She smiled up at up him. "The perfect symbol for my new life."

"Comprised from the best of the old." He drew back and held her gaze. "They are from your mother's own collection. When the magpies discovered where your father's will was hidden, they uncovered a cache of jewels and gemstones as well."

Was it the waltz that made her dizzy or the relief of knowing her father had not been utterly lost to his grief—that he had not forgotten her after all? "Uncle told me…" She blinked. It would not do to weep in the arms of her fiancé in the midst of a waltz at a society ball. "He told me they were all gone, that my father had wagered them away."

"Your father had hidden them away," Alfred said, "and thus the horses are not your only remembrance of your mother."

"Oh, Alfred," Felicity murmured, and once again, faster than thought, she was off the dance floor…spirited down the back of yet another high society garden, out through a mews, and into the ducal conveyance.

"Apparently you threw yourself into my coach and ruined yourself." He rapped on the roof and found himself with an armful of incipient duchess. "Felicity?"

She shook her head even as she nestled it against his shoulder, wrapping her arms around him as she buried her nose beneath his jaw and inhaled, once, twice, thrice. His arms lifted her into better position on his lap, and he returned the favor, running his nose along the curve of her shoulder, up her neck, behind her ear, taking a breath of his own, once, twice, thrice.

She wiggled closer and ran her fingers through his hair, down around his ears, and tugged at this evening's Cravat of Perfection. She tore out the pin holding it all in place, an emerald the equal of the one in her ring, and he took it from her, sticking it into the wall of the coach. She laughed but said nothing, unwound the stock, undid his collar, and set her cheek against the base of his throat and breathed.

She reached up to touch his face, to run a finger down the side of his neck, all the time breathing him in, until that hand strayed under his shirt and over his chest, and her lips lightly, lightly touched his collarbone—

"Felicity. Love." He set her away from him. "We are very near the Lowell town house, and I do not wish to be hasty."

"I want to know what would have happened did I not stop you at Templeton House. Or even in my new premises." Her voice was little more than a whisper, and yet she looked him straight in the eye, her provocative gaze set to undo his conviction. "I want to touch you; I want you to touch me. "

"You want your wedding night, which is tomorrow."

"Tomorrow, tonight, this minute, what matter?" Felicity tried to open his waistcoat, but Alfred's tailor favored the tiniest buttons to be found in Europe. She stopped and looked at him, aghast. "You have done this before, have you not? O'Mara said as much, but she may have only been placating me."

"Yes, I have done this." Alfred gripped her arms and then shook his head. "Which is not a conversation I wish to have with my mate, if you don't mind."

"When you asked me to marry you, in front of all those mean-spirited, small-minded people…" Her face was a mixture of awe and incredulity. "When you asked me and you meant it, when you said I was your one and only, I…I knew it to be true, unlike anything else I've known my whole life. When you spoke those words, I thought, yes, now, now we can live. Now we can love. We can love right now. Alfred," she breathed, leaning against him, her lush breasts doing their best to undo his good intentions. "You have given me both my dreams, the one I lost, and the one I sought. Neither would be anything without you."

"I have given you nothing that you did not create, or inspire, yourself."

Her eyes glistened, but still she did not weep. She nipped him on his earlobe, and he gurgled in an undignified manner, his hands sliding down to her glorious bottom and—

"No, no, no," he said, setting her on the opposite bench. "This is not how I will make you my mate, in truth and bond. Not in a carriage rattling around London where anyone could see."

"The curtains are drawn."

"No." Alfred filled the coach with the *dominatum*, to the degree that his coachman started singing the horses down to walk as they fought against their traces. He expanded it as much as he dared, and yet Felicity was as ever unaffected; she crossed her arms and leaned back, annoyed.

"Are you certain you have done this before?" She scowled at him and then burst into laughter. "Your expression. It is the image of Alfie's when I complained about your first proposal." She roared with laughter, and the tears came, happy tears, yes, but tears nonetheless.

He pulled her back to sit beside him. "No, not on my lap, minx." He put his arm around her, allowed her to set her head on his shoulder. "I shall see you to St. James Square and go on to my lonely club—no." He set her hands off his falls. "And tomorrow, bright and early, we shall wed."

"Tomorrow, we shall wed," she repeated. "Tomorrow it will all begin."

They sat in silent accord as the coach drew to a halt in St. James Square. Alfred opened the door and leapt out, holding out a hand to his almost-mated mate. "O'Mara said I'd never done it before?"

Had any denizens of the fashionable square been at home at such an unfashionably early hour, they would have enjoyed the sound of a lady's laugh ring out, a laugh full of joy and life and love…and it would have done them well to hear it.

Twenty-one

FOR A DUCAL RESIDENCE, THE LOWELL TOWN HOUSE WAS small but perfectly formed. The duchess's suite was one delightfully appointed little room after the other, and the dressing room, while intimate, was airy and light. The morning following the Montague ball, the bottle of birthday champagne she had promised to share with Jemima was open and had been poured out, and Lady Coleman took personal charge of her toilette—and what a toilette it was. Felicity's wedding clothes, which had been executed with breathtaking speed, would be the envy of an empress.

"Hold still…Your Grace," Jemima said.

"I will have well and truly gained the title in a matter of hours." Felicity played with the long, fat curl that lay on her shoulder. Her hair was as down as it could be without looking debauched and was showing to its best advantage, lush and thick and in all its auburn glory. Half was piled up on the top of her head, swirling in curls around her crown and the other half had been coaxed into that lush, sensuous curl. Jemima had firm notions as to how she was going to be presented on this day.

"And it's grateful we are for having that sorted." O'Mara lounged in a chair near one of the floor to ceiling windows. With her new ease in Felicity's presence, her Irish accent had become more pronounced.

"It's grateful I would be did I get you out of those trousers," Jemima huffed.

"You wouldn't be the first to try." O'Mara shot her cuffs.

"Do you prefer women as bedmates?" Jemima twirled the last curl around Felicity's head, as she herself gaped.

"I do not," O'Mara said, throwing an arm over the top of her chair. "Aren't you sophisticated."

"I get about," Jemima said, laying down the hairpins. "And your reply to my sally implied as much."

"Miss O'Mara's choice of lover is up to her, of course," Felicity placated.

"As is my choice of trousers."

Jemima lifted garments out of boxes. "But if only you would allow me to fit you for one of those split skirts?"

"I choose not to, thank you," O'Mara continued, polite and calm. "I am comfortable as I am."

"And I unreservedly vouch for trousers," said Felicity.

"But not today." Jemima smiled.

"No, not today." She turned and regarded the *habillements* draping every surface in the dressing room. "I cannot comprehend how you managed to produce all this in so little time."

"I have yet to see Lady Coleman quail from a challenge." O'Mara smirked.

"When needs must, I am quite swift," Jemima added, and the two of them roared with laughter.

"I feel rather left out of the joke," Felicity admitted once they had subsided.

Jemima and O'Mara exchanged a portentous look. The former set her jaw, and the latter made a sound not unlike Delilah when she was irritated. The stalemate drew out until O'Mara shrugged and said, "It is your affair. Her Grace has been apprised of the laws of our kind."

"Your kind?" Felicity gaped at her friend, who appeared chagrined.

"I am a dove, Felicity," she admitted.

"A dove?" Did *versipelles* comprise the majority of the English population?

"Hence the avian puns," O'Mara said.

"It is not my intention to take the shine off your day," Jemima began.

"Do not be ridiculous," Felicity scolded. "I am grateful you shared this knowledge with me, as I am aware *versipelles* hold it dear. Now I need not censor myself in your presence, and for that, I am also grateful." Jemima allowed a very careful embrace in deference to her coiffure, and a tear or two was shed.

"Now." Jemima sniffled into one of her ever-present but well-concealed hankies and went to fetch the bridal gown. "There is no bonnet as I believe His Grace wishes you to be crowned with your tiara once the vows are taken."

Felicity opened her mouth to protest, but why should she bother at this late stage? "What will the officiant think?"

"I wouldn't worry about him." O'Mara rose to help Jemima with the dress.

Oh, the dress. It boasted the off-the-shoulder neckline that suited her so well; made of heavy satin, it glowed like the interior of a shell, sometimes showing pink, sometimes showing silver, sometimes showing cream tones that glistened in the sunshine. As it settled down around her body and Jemima fussed it into place, Felicity saw thousands of glittering beads sewn around the waist, which decreased as they drifted to the hem. The skirt was form-fitting, hugging her hips and curving in toward her knees and out again at her feet to reveal a froth of organza. Behind, a bell-shaped overskirt spread around her, the lining of it a darker silver, with a few layers of organza tucked in for good measure.

"You are as Venus rising from the scallop shell," O'Mara said.

"A fitting propitiation," Jemima muttered as she fluffed out the overskirt.

Felicity regarded herself in the pier glass. She doubted she had ever missed her mother more—and her father as well, for the first time having an inkling of how dreadful the loss of his beloved wife had been for him. Her hands shook as she smoothed them over the soft satin at her décolletage. O'Mara touched her on the elbow.

"They are both here with you today," she said. "I promise this is true. They could not be happier for you, nor prouder, nor could they imagine any woman in the world more fit for the part you are about to play in this world."

"Miss O'Mara, if I am to set the tone, then I am Felicity, and I would be honored did you call me thus when we are private."

"I am O'Mara, Your Grace," she said, shaking her head. "And that is how it shall be unless I desire my throat torn from my neck by His Grace."

"My thanks for such pleasant imagery." She looked over her shoulder to admire the back of her gown and saw Jemima had a familiar jewelry box in her hands. Felicity's breath caught, and she could almost hear her mother's voice in her ear as she showed her the beautiful parure that her father had gifted his bride on their wedding day. She nodded, and Jemima revealed the very set, a delicate tracery of diamonds set in pale gold, the necklace as light as a spider's web, the earrings clusters of diamonds from which hung perfect pearls.

"Mr. Bates said this will be an astonishing match to the Lowell tiara," Jemima said, blushing.

"Mr. Bates knows everything," Felicity said, as Jemima fastened the necklace and handed her the earrings.

"Almost everything," O'Mara murmured, shooting a look at Jemima the lady chose not to meet.

"I am sorry that you cannot join us at Lowell Hall, Jemima, after the ceremony," Felicity said. "I imagine we will make for Sussex as soon as all is said and done."

"I am delighted to witness your wedding, but then I must be seen—see my aunt, for I have neglected her these several days."

"Does she guard you jealously as treasure, Lady Coleman?" O'Mara inquired.

"Something very like," Jemima returned.

"You must come as soon as you may," Felicity said.

"As soon as your duke releases you, which will not be in one hour or two hours. I hope you are at ease with thoughts of the marriage bed?" Jemima looked slyly at the duke's chamberlain. "O'Mara can answer any questions you may have, I am sure."

"It will not be necessary."

"Won't it?" Jemima and O'Mara chorused.

"Not entirely," Felicity said. "Have I a cloak to go with this gloriousness?"

Jemima laid a Cloak of Equal Gloriousness over her shoulders, and as Felicity smoothed on her gloves, she took in her entire ensemble. "Jemima, your genius makes the luckiest bride in Christendom."

"The loveliest," Jemima retorted and nodded with satisfaction. "You'll do. Ma'am."

She curtseyed, and O'Mara made her deepest reverence. A light knock on the door signaled the readiness of the coach, and Felicity took a deep breath, filled to surfeit with hope and joy. It would appear that her twenty-fifth birthday was turning out rather auspicious after all.

"Do I need a reticule?" she asked. Jemima shook her head and pointed, hopping up and down and letting out one of her characteristic laughs as Felicity ran her hands down her hips and slipped them into the pockets of her wedding gown.

———————

The coach rolled a very short distance to the district's signature edifice. "We are to be wed here?" Felicity stopped short of pressing her face against the window to gape at Carlton House.

"His Highness is a very dear friend of Lowell Hall," O'Mara replied.

"Are you joking?" The door opened, the steps were let down, and Jemima exited. Felicity turned to O'Mara and hissed, "Is he…?"

"Remember the law, Your Grace." O'Mara gestured; Felicity took the footman's hand and stepped down.

A crowd had gathered as word spread that Fallen Felicity had been caught after all. A raucous cheer grew in strength and followed them through the front doors as a voice boomed down from the landing of the grand staircase. "His Grace is in a desperate state. I've never seen a man so eager for the leg shackle." George Augustus Frederick, Duke of Cornwall, Duke of Rothesay, Earl of Chester, and most notably, Prince of Wales, stood with his fists on his sturdy hips. Turned out in full, majestic regalia, his lush head of hair coiffed in great waves, he was impressive in height and girth, and yet there was something warm and endearing about his personage. The women made their way up the stairs, and he smiled toothily as they made their curtsies upon joining him. "How finely feathered you are, soon-to-be-erstwhile Miss Templeton," he said, raising her to stand. "Doubtless your work, Lady Coleman?"

"Stuff it, Georgie." Jemima unclasped one of the medals on his sash and re-pinned it one millimeter to the left of its original placement. The Regent giggled and leaned down to whisper in her ear. Felicity, agape at this familiarity, glanced over at O'Mara, who was occupied with studying the sculptures in the recesses around the gallery.

"Your groom awaits," Prinny said, offering his arm to Felicity as a servant took the ladies' cloaks. "It is my honor to bring you to him."

Carlton House put the Lowell Hall staterooms to shame. As they processed from the Ante Room, the Lesser Drawing Room, and into the Lesser Throne Room, Felicity noted an excess of footmen, serving to put the Hall's ranks in perspective.

"This, madam, is in all likelihood the last grand event to be held in this tedious pile," the prince said, slowing his lumbering gait to accommodate her smaller strides. "What think you, is Carlton House not too…too tedious?"

"Your Highness," Felicity replied. "I think you are an artist, and each room has been your canvas. Having achieved your masterpiece, it is time to create elsewhere."

Prinny tapped her on the nose as Jemima rolled her eyes. "Very good," he said. "You'll do. Unlike your bosom friend, you appear to be a good egg. Do you agree, O'Mara? Yay or nay?"

"You are all that is perceptive and fair in judgment, Your Highness," the duke's chamberlain replied.

"An equivocation such as only you can utter." He nodded to the footmen who flanked the doors to their destination. "In we go, madam. Welcome to the family." He winked and led her through.

The Blue Velvet Room had been cleared of all unnecessary furniture; Alfred gazed with some dismay upon the massive chandelier that hung, in his estimation, far too close to the floor. Otherwise, it was a fine place to get married and private without looking as though they were ashamed of the event. They had the royal imprimatur and would receive a joyous sendoff from a partisan crowd, assembled by his Second, as they drove away.

He paced around the edges of the room, his wolf very near the surface, delirious with the knowledge that soon, soon, this would be done. Alfred sensed, through his beast, and even from the great distance, that the entire pack was gathered at the Hall, their love and support ready to flow without reservation through the bond.

"I have the ring," Bates said, before he asked again. "The etiquette book said only the lady receives one."

"It is the human custom."

"Just as well, you would find such ornamentation awkward during a Change," Bates said.

"Just as well," Alfred agreed and turned to pace in the opposite direction to keep—Goddess help him—Alfie distracted.

"It does present an interesting problem," Bates mused. "You might start a fashion for wearing one on a chain 'round your neck, perhaps." He laughed as Alfred turned on him and bared teeth that had transformed into Alfie's.

"You are playful of late, my friend." Alfred shot his cuffs, and speaking of rings—but then he remembered he kept asking Matthias did he have it.

"I am, of late, remembering you are my friend," Bates said. "These last years of waiting and worrying…"

"…have robbed us of our ease with one another," Alfred continued. "That it has returned is yet one more boon that has been visited upon us."

Were they in their wolfskins, they would rush and play, tumble and roll; as men, the best they could do was embrace, thumping one another on the shoulders, and back away, mumbling sheepishly. It did not aid their expression of emotion that an observer was present.

"To what do we owe the pleasure, Osborn?" Alfred asked.

"His Highness's decree." Arthur Humphries, Duke of Osborn, stood near the window like a mighty oak planted there for a thousand years, and despite the royal invitation, was dressed to his usual commonplace standard. Known to be asocial at best, in a state of hibernation at worst, his presence in London was enough to raise eyebrows, much more his attendance at Alfred's wedding.

"You were never one to adhere to George's directives too closely." As a royal cousin, Arthur had taken the relentless piss out of Georgie during their childhood in Court. All the young Alphas and their retinue were called into the royal presence to meet often, but once childhood was left behind, so was such enforced frivolity. Alfred doubted George's impulse was a nursery reunion.

"Times change." If so, Osborn did not look well pleased by this fact. His response was little better than a snarl, and he threw back his shoulders as though preparatory to a brawl, which was antithetical to his nature; he famously refused to engage in the violence of their kind.

Matthias cleared his throat. "Perhaps His Highness wishes His Grace to see what joy is in store when it is his time to mate and bond." Alfred turned away to hide a smile; Matthias and Osborn had ever been in competition regarding who knew what and who had known it first. That notion was worth considering if it was indeed George's intent: Osborn's looks and lineage attracted the attention of the Marriage Mart, but for so large a creature, he evaded their machinations with all the slipperiness of an eel.

"Perhaps the Lowell second is behind the times, as usual." Osborn relaxed his posture and glared at them both. "Even as his Alpha looks to outshine the bride with his toilette."

"One would accuse those of the ursine persuasion of being sartorially unsophisticated," Matthias returned, "were it not for the example your cousin makes."

"Ah, now, Matthias," Alfred admonished, "diamonds do emerge from the rough."

"'Sweet are the uses of adversity which, like the toad, ugly and venomous, wears yet a precious jewel in its head,'" quoted Osborn to the ringing groans of both men.

"Holy Venus, still at it with the Bard, are you?" Matthias loathed the theatre to the same degree as Osborn adored it, and the latter knew a well-placed quote was enough to send Alfred's Beta round the bend.

"Matthias, you risk maligning His Grace, for a 'good name in man and woman is the immediate jewel of their souls,' is it not?" Alfred only just got that phrase out before he dissolved in laughter.

Matthias muttered about boils and plague sores, betraying his own Shakespearean knowledge, and Osborn smirked. "Not as nervy as you were, eh, Lowell?"

Calling attention to the levity had the opposite effect on both dukes: Osborn went back to brooding out the window, and Alfred recommenced pacing. He completed another circuit of the room, then paused. His wolf heard the footsteps, the laughter, the heartbeats well before the wedding party appeared. He nodded to the prelate Georgie had laid on, some bishop or other, and turned to face the doors.

They opened, and despite the royal presence, he had eyes only for his bride, his mate. She sparkled, and not due to the jewels that adorned her, nor the dress that shimmered like the dawn. Her hair, ah, Goddess how he wanted his hands on that hair again, on her lush figure so gloriously displayed in Lady Coleman's creation. All of her was his. He had succeeded, he had found his *vera amoris*, and all would thrive, all were safe. And yet, he had achieved something greater, something he had not expected: he had gained a true partner, a woman whose open heart and mind had given him and his pack far more than he had ever thought possible. Beyond hope, beyond peace, beyond the satisfaction of a responsibility met, he found joy, such joy.

"Off we go," said George, ruining his flights of fancy. "Come along, Cornelius, we've a man in need of a wife."

He brought Felicity to Alfred's side, and before he released her, he said, "Know that I am less than a mother and father to you, my dear soon-to-be Duchess of Lowell, but I will be all they would be, should you need to call on me for aught." He waggled a finger at Alfred, kissed her cheek, and stepped back.

Cornelius, the resplendent prelate, cleared his throat. "Dearly beloved," he intoned thunderously, as if reaching for the gallery in St. Paul's. He cleared his throat again and adjusted his volume. "We are gathered together here in the sight of God, and in the face of this congregation, to join together this man and this woman in holy matrimony..."

Full names were spoken, hands were taken and released, exhortations were delivered, vows were exchanged, the ring was placed on Felicity's finger, more blessings were said, Prinny sighed loudly and theatrically, and—"I pronounce that they be man and wife together, for as long as they both shall live." A cross was drawn over their heads, and it was almost done.

Alfred turned to Bates, who was holding a weathered, wooden case chased with fading silver and gold. The duke opened it and removed a glorious tiara, as delicate as her parure, studded with diamonds and pearls, and wrought of pale gold. "It's almost as though it were meant to be," he whispered to her as he set it on her head. "Ah, see? It fits," he growled.

"Hush, Alfie," she whispered, and it was all he could do not to set the bishop on his ear and kiss her before all the world.

"And thus falls another fine lord," the prince sighed. "It is almost too, too much to be borne. Is it not, Jemmikins? Unbearable?"

"Stuff it, Georgie." Jemima looked piqued beyond measure. The prince reached out and pinched her side, causing her to flap about like a mad thing.

"Shall we, my dear?" Alfred consulted his wife—his mate. "I thought to forego a wedding breakfast and make for the Hall. I intend that we make Sussex well before moonrise."

"I would prefer to celebrate there." Felicity looked down and exuded shyness and trepidation and eagerness. The tiara sparkled but was no match for the radiance of her aspect.

"I do hope you've a bottle of something nice in the coach, Lowell," said the prince. "How very beastly of you, should you have nothing to hand to while away the miles to Sussex. Whatever shall you do otherwise?" And with that cheeky *bon mot*, he turned to leave, then paused. "Osborn, Bates, if you would." Matthias left them with a bow to his new duchess and an arched brow for Alfred. Osborn followed without so much as a word of congratulations as Georgie bellowed for his secretaries and his valet, the wedding party bowing and curtseying in his wake.

———

"'Having achieved your masterpiece, it is time to create elsewhere.' If I could embroider with any expertise, I'd stitch that on a cushion," Felicity said.

Alfred lifted her hand to his lips. "Your body shall be my

canvas," he said and bit her knuckles, "a masterpiece from which I shall never move on."

"Oh, goodness." She blushed.

"You seem rather…" Alfred tilted his head and let Alfie show in his eyes. "You are shy."

"It all went so fast." Felicity turned to look out the window of the coach; Alfred grabbed her chin to prevent it. "I have never been to a wedding before, and I supposed it would take longer."

"Thank the Godd—thank goodness it did not."

"You needn't censor yourself any longer."

"It will take time," he replied. "Nor should you. Censor yourself."

"To what do you refer?"

"Felicity." He growled, low and long, and ran a finger along the top of her dress.

She batted it away. "O'Mara said His Highness is a very close friend of the family."

"I do not wish to speak of Wales at this precise moment."

"I am nervous," she blurted.

"This from the hoyden who would have relieved me of my virtue in Portman Square?"

"Alfred!" Goddess, how that thrilled him. "I…I *am* feeling shy."

"Then let me be gentle with you," he whispered and pulled her onto his lap. "Let me take my time."

He removed the tiara and tossed it onto the opposite bench and ignored her gasp of dismay. "Trappings," he said, "when all you need to be a duchess is to be yourself. Your gracious, warm, welcoming self."

"I thought St. George's would be daunting, but to be married in Carlton House…" She sighed as he removed a glove and massaged her palm before placing a kiss on it.

"That tedious pile? Not the slightest bit intimidating." He slid the other glove down her arm, kissed that palm, kissed the rings on her finger, pressed his open mouth against the pulse throbbing in her wrist. He heard her heartbeat stutter and scented her blossoming arousal. What was it with themselves and coaches? It was a long way to Sussex, and several bottles of champagne notwithstanding, he had no desire to go too far.

Perhaps halfway would do?

Felicity fussed with the dress. "Do take care, I love this garment and would not have it ruined," she said. "It has pockets."

"How shocking." His eyes smiled, then heated as he took in her coiffure. "I believe there is something I shall ruin," he murmured and removed the first pin from her hair.

"Oh," she breathed. "That first morning—" She blushed again.

"How delicious you looked, pink and abashed. That first morning…" Alfred prompted as he slid another pin out of a tress, and a long, luscious curl fell free.

Felicity peeked up at him. "That first morning in Lowell Hall, I wondered what it would be like, did you take down my hair, and, and remove my slippers. I imagined you standing behind me and pulling out my pins, and…well, that is as far as I got."

"Let us improve upon this scenario, then." In a trice, all the pins were gone, scattered on the floor, and he ran his fingers through her hair, teasing out the curls, playing with its length, draping it across her breasts, teasing them with it until her breath caught. He massaged her scalp until she let out a little moan.

"You can do better than that, Your Grace," he teased, increasing the pressure, and pulled her close until she lay across his chest; his mouth skated along the side of her face, across her brow, everywhere but her lips until she growled and gripped his hair and took his mouth with hers. He heard her heart pounding throughout her body, scented her arousal. The grip she had on his hips with her thighs, oh, how he imagined she would ride him when the time came. Speaking of… He set her on the bench, slid down to his knees, and grinned up at her.

That smile. She had only become accustomed to the way he smiled with his eyes and the devastating crinkles created when he did so, but this was almost too much.

"Whatever do you intend, Duke?"

"I intend to make another of your dreams come true, Duchess." He slipped a hand under the organza ruffle, and his eyebrows lifted. "What have we here?" He withdrew a spangled shoe that had an adorable little heel. "This is very like the sort of shoe a French lady wears."

"I am not interested in learning the extent of your knowledge regarding women's slippers." She drew back her foot, annoyed and worried. How would she compare to a French lady?

"My own sister had a thousand pairs." He grabbed her foot back and stroked strong fingers down the arch to the tips of her toes.

"A thousand." How could this touch on her heel manifest in her most sensitive places?

"Give or take two hundred." He removed the other shoe and lifted her feet into his lap. Oh, dear. He was experiencing this in his most sensitive place as well. He blinked up at her as she wiggled her toes, trying to investigate his interest. "Such tiny little toes."

"They are silly, and odd."

"I adore them." He leaned down and kissed to the tops of her feet and then tickled them—to no avail.

Felicity shook her head. "I do not suffer from that affliction. Do you?"

A hesitation. "I do not."

"Don't you?" As she leaned forward and reached for his ribs, he ran his hands up her ankles, to her calves, to her knees, to her honeypot, knocking her back with desire.

His strong hands slid around her thighs, all the while disturbing her gown not in the least. "So soft," he whispered.

"Mrs. Birks said—" she gasped, as his hands teased her thighs apart, and his fingers traced little nonsense designs very near her lady parts.

"I absolutely do not wish to speak of Mrs. Birks at this precise moment." He reached down and raised her hem, exposing her calves, her knees, and the tops of her thighs to his kisses.

"She said the wolf, Alfie, is to take a bite, and I, she didn't say where, you see, and I wondered..."

"It is not for her to know where the Alpha will bite you." He nipped her left knee and kissed the place, then nipped her right knee and laved it with his tongue. "It is only between mates that the place be known and ever seen."

"So it is on a...sensitive place?"

"Not *the* sensitive place." He set a hand over her mound, and she moaned like a wanton. He kissed the thigh near that hand and moved his fingers, petting her, stroking her. "It could be very near to it, however." He nipped her belly, then her hip, then licked her belly, rubbing his face against her thighs until fire streaked through her veins, and her entire body turned to gooseflesh. "Or it might fall on the back," he said as he ran a hand up her spine. "Or..." His hand squeezed her bottom, and she gasped, "Alfred!" and he squeezed harder, with both hands, and lifted her honeypot to his mouth.

Reason fled as he touched her in a place she had never thought to be teased by a man's tongue. Her entire body gave itself up to his touch as it explored her, with haste, then with idleness, with a touch as light as feather, then with strength, licking up one side and down the other, his fingers teasing her opening, skating close to the bud and then away. The deeper he lapped, the further she sank against the velvet, the sound of her breathing filling the coach.

He teased, teased around that little bud until she grabbed his hair and held him to it. He laughed, oh, against her, and she writhed against his mouth as he parted her legs as far as they could go. The familiar sensations began to build, but in such an unfamiliar fashion, with a ferocity and focus that Felicity had never known. She heard herself moan, and heard Alfred answer, and as the tension within her gathered, and his mouth feasted upon her, she gave herself up to it, her body writhing against her husband's mouth, her mate's tongue, reaching, until the pinnacle exploded within her, and she cried his name, over and over and over.

———

Later that evening, she marveled at wearing yet another beautiful gown. Her dress for the pack ceremony seemed little better than a night rail, a diaphanous series of layers that fell from the edges of her shoulders, wrapped around her newly appreciated waist, and fluttered to the ground like a cloud crossing the moon. The cape paired with it was equally translucent and would give no warmth at all. She had protested, but Mary Mossett proved to be rather intransigent for a mouse, and even though Jemima was not present, Mary would not contravene the lady's vision.

The little maid had run off, but not without strict instructions for her mistress: at the next chime of the parlor's eight-day clock, she was to go to the window of her bedroom and look out. Then, she was to wait for the very next bell before she left the Hall. Mary refused to depart until Felicity had repeated the directives—twice.

She sat, tiara back on her head, her hair loose around her shoulders and curling down her back. As little as she had known what to expect from the human ceremony, she knew even less what to expect regarding *versipellian* customs, apart from the running after the words had been spoken—and the bite. The thought of seeing everyone unclothed as they Changed from their creatures into their human skins was worse than the thought of being bitten. But she would prevail. She would honor the tradition and carry on. It would pass in a finger snap. She who had thought she'd lost everything had been given more than she'd ever imagined, and if this small thing had to be done to honor her husband's ways, then do it she would.

Felicity fussed with the skirts of the white gown; it was virginal, and yet it implied a maturity she hoped to live up to. How bold she'd been in the coach! Clearly, that luxurious conveyance had some effect on her virtue in that it made her want to throw it out the moving window. How gentle Alfred had been, and yet how determined. Was this what married life might be like? If so, those novels of Jemima's were in desperate need of amendment. For example, there had been no mention of such an intimate kiss as he had bestowed on her, but would she have credited it, had it been in front of her, in writing? She would not.

The clock chimed, and she made her way to the window; when she parted the curtains, she gasped. It was so like the dream she'd had, that awful night when Mr. Bates had imparted his terrible news. A flock—herd—pack? An assemblage of any animal she might imagine congregated on the lawn: mice, dogs, oh, the colts! There were cats and wolves, a paucity of birds, which was odd; there were beavers and stoats and small woodland creatures she'd never seen before. She put a hand on the glass and the other on her heart, and in their fashion, they bowed to her. The second chime of the clock told her they had spent a quarter hour looking upon one another. She stepped back, and the animals—beings—*versipelles*, all turned as one and made for the park. They reached the edge of the wood and began their transformation to their human selves; she let the curtain drop. Surely Alfred had organized this, an opportunity to accept his charges as her own, without bringing anyone to the blush.

It was, she thought, a wonderful compromise.

Felicity made her way through the silent house, its quiet unlike that of Templeton House's desolation; while empty, it was not bereft of life. And yet, she experienced a pang of loneliness. It was too strange that she found herself to be the only creature within its walls, and she all but ran out of doors.

Small, flickering lanterns lined a path to illuminate her way to the clearing, where she paused. Light spilled from torches all around the edge of the circle, and the fullest moon she'd ever seen rode high in the sky and shone its light down like a benediction. Heaps of flowers were piled on the flat stone and hung in garlands from the trees. Marshall and several other humans in their Sunday best stood back from the edge, and they were soon joined by the souls of Lowell Hall, dressed in clean but simple clothing, very like those she'd discovered in the cottage with Jemima.

Mr. Bates, Miss O'Mara, and Mr. Gambon joined her at the entrance. She held a hand out to Mr. Bates, who grinned and slipped something into her palm.

Then Alfred stepped alone from the shadows on the opposite side of the circle and moved to stand before the stone.

"Felicity Blakesley, née Templeton," he said, his voice taking on a power that leapt through the glade. "Do you come to this holy place of your own free will?"

"I do." She lifted her chin. "I am humbled by the trust you and your pack have put in me. I swear to return this honor"—her voice broke—"to return it every day I live."

"There was a script to be followed," he grumbled and held out a hand. "Come." She arched her brows. "Please."

All present laughed as she walked into his embrace.

He addressed the crowd. "There were words to be said, in tribute of Lupercalia and the great debt we owe to Mars and Laurentia despite the strife they caused." He looked down at her. "And et cetera. But as ever, my duchess cuts to the quick and wastes no time."

"Are we not wasting time now?" She whispered this, she was sure she did, and yet everyone laughed again.

"Felicity, Duchess of Lowell," Alfred intoned, stepping away. "Do you declare me your mate, before all my people, in this holy place, on this night of the most sacred moon of all our year?"

"Wait! I have something for you. I wasn't sure, I didn't know what to do, but it was in my mother's jewel case, and you'll have to wear it…differently." She held out a chain from which suspended a ring. "This was my great-grandfather's," she said, her hand trembling. "I know convention has it that only ladies receive rings, but I did not think it fair, and I suspect we shall start a fashion."

All in the clearing held their collective breath. He lowered his head. She slipped the chain over his head, and he lifted the ring to hold it against his heart. "I thank you most sincerely," he breathed, and she saw, in his eyes, Alfie fighting to be free.

"I couldn't think what to do and so consulted with Mr. Bates." She lay her hand over his, over his heart. "He thought of the chain." She patted his chest where it lay.

"Isn't he clever," Alfred growled, and she heard his Second snort. "I still need you to say the words, love."

Love! "I declare you my mate, Alfred, Duke of Lowell, before all our people, in this holy place, in this beloved place, in our home. On this most special night of the year."

She tipped up on her toes to kiss him and heard a squeak. "Wait."

They turned to see Mary, Mrs. Birks, and Mr. Coburn move into the inner circle. Mary carried a flat package arrayed in bright, colored paper and held it out to her. "It's your birthday, Your Grace. And Valentine's Day. And Lupercalia! Ooh, you'll get some bride's gift for certain."

"Is this what it is?" Felicity took the parcel, and Alfred shook his head.

"It's from us." Mary Mossett was like to fly up into the boughs, she was so excited. "Many happy returns, mum!"

Felicity struggled to remain composed. "This is the finest day I've ever had, I can assure you."

"Open it." Mary bounced up and down until Mrs. Birks hissed her name. "It's not like we made it or nothing, but we did find it. Well, a few of the wolves that be doing Mr. Bates's bidding in Town did come across it when some terrible bad people tried to sell it.

And then the Alpha said, he said, why don't we be making it a gift to you, like? Because he could just give it to you, but if it came from us, it would be even more special. I don't know that anything from the likes of us is better than a gift from the *Alpha*—"

"Mary." Felicity laughed. "Here, hold this while I remove the paper. It is rather large, isn't it? I can make out something like a frame… Oh, I am awful for trying to guess at a gift when all I need do is—"

Her parents' faces smiled out at her. Her own little face, rosy-cheeked and bright-eyed, looked happier to be seen than anything in this world. She remembered this image almost before she remembered anything; she remembered being held in her father's arms, her mother beside him, as he pointed to each figure and asked her who they were. "Mama, Papa, me!" she would cry, and they would laugh as though she were the cleverest creature ever born. She touched her mother's face, and her father's, and her own, that child who had known love and knew it again.

"This is the greatest gift I could be given on this night. You have returned my first family to me even as I so happily join my second." She looked around, tears in her eyes. "I cannot thank you sufficiently for such kindness. I can only promise I will always return such kindness, a thousandfold, to all of you, forever."

Alfred tapped her on the shoulder. "Now?" she asked.

"Now," he said, Alfie swirling in his eyes, his body already changing, not frightening but fascinating. Tucking her gift under her arm, she turned toward a lighted cottage, up the hill from the clearing and her new pack, and ran.

Twenty-two

FELICITY RAN AS BEST AS SHE WAS ABLE WHILE CLUTCHING HER family portrait and dressed in a full-length cape and a dress that billowed and threatened to wrap itself around her legs. She heard his paws hitting the ground, under the cheering and revelry from the glade; he had to be faster than she, but he stayed behind, huffing and howling as she giggled with nerves.

She dashed to the cottage at the top of the hill, its windows glowing with candlelight, a welcoming stream of smoke puffing out of its chimney. She fell against the door, and Alfie bunched behind her as though to pounce; her hand found the door latch and pushed it open. She watched him sweep around her, once, twice, thrice, magnificent, lethal, beastly, and yet there was no fear, only the now-familiar push and pull of air, which resulted in Alfred standing behind her in his human skin.

"Do not turn." He shut the door. "Close your eyes." She did so. He removed the portrait from her arms, and she heard him set it down nearby. He moved to stand behind her back, his essence surrounding her, his head near to hers as he reached around and undid the ties of her cloak, hands warm as they drew it off her shoulders.

She turned her head. "Don't," he said. "I am mindful of your nerves."

"I'm not…" She was, a little. Less afraid of the wolf than of the marital act.

"You are." Lifting the tiara from her hair, this time he set it aside with care. Running his hands down to her waist, then up her back, then around to her belly, his gestures seemed to be less about seduction than—"Where are the bloody laces on this garment?" He pulled at the layers of veils, and she batted his hands away.

"I do not know how Jemima did this," she said, as she, too, began rummaging for buttons, or some other sort of closure. "I wasn't paying attention when Mary was helping me dress."

"Distracted, were you?"

"I was in rather a languid state," she said, tilting her head to nuzzle his shoulder. "Especially after my bath…"

"Another bath?" His hands squeezed her waist and left off trying to disrobe her for a moment. "I cannot imagine you had the energy for bathing after our journey."

"It was merely a bath," she sighed. "I believe they are ruined for me forever. Alfred. Let me turn around."

"Pardon me," he said. "I know this dress has pockets." That quiver vibrated in the air, and something hard and sharp and cool tickled the base of her neck. Then there was a tug, and fabric rended, and her ensemble was at her feet, sliced clean through from back to bum, through dress, chemise, stays and all. Then, in the place of what had surely been a claw, a finger traced all the way down her exposed spine.

His hands ran down her shoulders to her palms, where his fingers entwined hers, and his mouth caressed the tops of her shoulders. His hands moved to run down her sides, over her hips, her belly, skating down below, and then back up again, over her ribs; then one arm wrapped around her waist, as the other hand lifted one breast, caressing, then the other, fingers straying over her nipples until she nestled, insensate, against him.

The feel of his body against her back was so strong, so warm, so large, it made her writhe; her bum nestled against steely thighs; the heat of his cock made her squirm against it. A growl—he spun her to face him, his arms banding about her waist, her arms twined 'round his neck; his hands caressed her everywhere, stroking, stoking her passion, passion of an intensity she had no notion she possessed. His hands notched under her bum; she lifted her legs and wrapped them around his waist, and he, stronger than any man, didn't move an inch.

"I will not let you call this tune, Your Grace." In a trice, she found herself flat on her back on an enormous bed. "You would have us bowing ere we have enjoyed our dance."

She lay before him, reveling in the perfection of that moment. Where she might have once cringed in dismay at the thought of being beheld naked before anyone, perhaps most of all a husband, she saw in his expression he thought her as beautiful as she felt. The candles whose light had warmed the windows were set about with abandon, and the fire that sent smoke up the chimney burned in the small grate. The lavishly appointed bed was almost as large as the cottage itself, its length and breadth such to support a man of size.

Oh, help. Size. She tried not to stare, but there it was, laid bare before her, and she didn't know what to do next. Confidence lost, she reached for one of the many layers draping the bed with a view to covering herself and got no further than a cursory scrabble.

"No." He lay down alongside her and pulled her close. "Trust me?"

"Yes." She rolled to face him. His face above hers, his expression was unlike anything she'd ever imagined, a mixture of self-control and yearning, tenderness, a fervent desire. His thick, black hair hung in his eyes, so she reached up and brushed it back. She ran her hand over That Chest, down his belly to… "May I?"

"Oh, yes, you may," he growled, his eyes firing, his nostrils flaring, his body tensing.

She kept her gaze on his as she ran a tentative finger around the top of his member, down along the side, back up. His eyes never wavered, but his entire body strained to her touch, and she knew from the tenor of his breath, she was affecting him as he did her. She used her palm, stroked up and down, down and up, around; his jaw flexed, and yet he did not move so much as an eyelash. She gripped, harder, her reward a deep inhalation of breath, and she smiled. She slid her fingers around, it quivered; she felt a drop of moisture at the head; she gripped it again, released, gripped, released—

And was set firmly on her back, her hands over her head, breathless with his power. "Enough," he said, setting himself between her thighs. "I'll not explode like a pup, not on my bonding night."

She drew her legs up, drew him closer. She wanted nothing more than to join with him, all trepidation gone.

"When we join," he growled, "we will bond. There will be no going back from this, Felicity."

"I have made vows," she said with some asperity, which, under the circumstances, was a miracle. "They may be human, but they are meaningful to me."

"This means everything to me." He dropped kisses where he would. "You mean everything to me."

He released her hands, and she ran them up his arms, then down his ribs, and he nearly jerked out of her arms. She burst into laughter and went for his ribs again, resulting in a wrestle for dominance she lost straightaway. "This will not work if I cannot touch you."

"I am less—" He twitched as her hands found his back. "I will become accustomed to your touch."

She stroked her hands up and down his back, down to his bottom, which was not ticklish, and thought about all the women who had touched this body. Well, they had had their chance, those women, and wouldn't get another. She looked up at him, fierce, and he growled in return.

"Mine," she said.

He took her left hand in his. "Malachite," he recited as he rubbed his thumb over the first stone in her betrothal ring and proceeded. "Iris. Nephrite. Emerald. It is an acrostic."

"Oh, Alfred." Felicity's eyes sparkled brighter than the diamonds that surrounded his bold claim.

"Mine," he repeated. "Mine."

He fit his hands beneath her head and slanted his mouth against hers, his tongue taking hers hostage, licking, biting her lips, her neck, her throat. She arched into his body, returning kiss for kiss, biting his shoulder as he inched into her, stretching her, until she gasped against his shoulder.

"I would be gentle," he breathed, and she wrapped her legs even more closely around his hips.

"It feels..." she said, unsure how to explain that everything she'd overheard or read had left her in expectation of being rent asunder, with the accompaniment of lashings of pain; yet in reality, something gave, and it was followed by an expansion and a fullness throughout her body, much more so in her delicate parts, without the agony the aging wallflowers whispered about behind the palms. Those delicate parts no longer seemed so delicate, and so she thrust herself forward until he was flush against her body.

"Bloody hell, woman," he groaned, and she gasped out little puffs of air as she became accustomed to his shape. "Are you in distress?" He made to move away, and she clenched him with muscles she didn't even know she had. His forehead lowered to her shoulder. "You are going to kill me."

"You are no use to me dead." She bit him on the bicep.

"My toothsome bride, in more ways than one." He moved slowly, and she let him, then moved up against him as he returned.

"This is very nice," she sighed as they did it again.

"Nice." He wrapped one arm around the small of her back and somehow brought himself even closer. "Let us do better than nice." He tilted his hips and touched her within in a way that had her legs scrambling to keep him in that exact position. Every nerve in her body was afire, and she rubbed against him, the abrasion of his rougher skin against hers stimulating beyond sanity. He lifted himself up on his knees and shifted deeper within her, then he leaned down to suckle her breasts; she drove her fingers into his hair and welcomed the building sensation that meant she was close, so close.

"So close," she managed. "Please, please, Alfred—"

He growled in her ear, burying his face in her neck. "Now, my love, my love..."

And it burst within her, the chaos of love that shook her from head to tiny toes. With it came a gathering much in the way the air pulled in on itself during one of Alfred's Changes, a compression that connected them, wrapped around them, and flowed between them, such that she experienced the tension of his release as well as hers as it moved up his spine from a well of fire in his lower back. Her own release built, in no way resembling the way it always had: this was a conflagration that took each one of her senses, magnified them beyond bearing, and turned them in stunning disarray, until all—sight, smell, touch, taste, and hearing coalesced and burst within her. In the midst of it all, she heard his roar as he reached his summit, their bodies trembling as one until they trembled no more.

Neither moved. Neither could. Their labored breaths evened, their hearts slowed, their eyes opened, each into the other's; he rubbed his face against hers, then she stroked down the center of his back, along his spine, down to his bum. They murmured and breathed, breathed and caressed, until both lay still in one another's arms.

"You called me your love," she whispered in his ear.

"You are." He held her close. "My one and only. My beloved. My love."

"I love you," she said. "My beloved, my unexpected, extraordinary love."

"I love you," he replied. "My mate, my true heart, my one and only." He pulled up a sheet and wrapped it around them, breathing nonsense words into the nape of her neck as he tucked himself against her back. She threaded her fingers through his as they came to rest underneath her breasts, and her thoughts drifted.

Here was her husband, a husband the like of which she'd never imagined for herself. A peer of the realm, for the love of galoshes, virile and influential and impressive... She remembered the passion she'd had for the vicar and giggled into Alfred's forearm, shook her head when he nudged her inquiringly. The vicar, who had been slight and gentle and wispy, bless his heart, whom she reckoned, since he had a living, would ensure her security for all her days.

She was secure now, but no quotidian, pastoral security for her. Her safety was invigorated by the strangeness of her new people, by the unlikelihood of their existence, by the notion that her dreams would become reality, by the reality that the man holding her chose her above all others and made her dreams come true.

Would she have been an able match for him had she not been so independent for the last few years? It seemed hard to think any good had come from her terrible losses, but she might not have been who she was now had she not needed to grieve and resolve to thrive. Might she have met him at some function at the Hall had he determined years ago that she was his? Would he have been his same self, untempered by his own losses? Would they have met then, in all their innocence, and had the same quality of bond? It made her wonder.

Here they were, now, and that was all that mattered. She doubted he was game for philosophical debate at this moment, as his, his—willy stirred against her. She giggled again and found herself turned, in a heartbeat, in his arms.

"I would know what amuses you, my love." His hands lifted her up, and he turned once more, settling her atop him.

"I had not thought you would revive with such swiftness. That never happens in novels." She raised herself on her hands and lowered her breasts onto That Chest, and exulted in the resultant resolve of his member.

"Yet another benefit of being such as I," he said. "No, do not," he cautioned as she rubbed her sensitive parts on his belly. "It will be too soon for you."

"It is not," she said as she moved to lie beneath him.

"If it is not, there is no need to change position." He slid her down and onto him.

"Ah!" She laughed. "I have skills in this area." His deep intake of breath proved her right. "Let us see how they translate in this situation, shall we?"

Twenty-three

Bedclothes rustled, a glass touched her cheek, and she opened her eyes. She had dozed, sated and spent, as the evening closed in. Her duke, her husband, her mate held out a glass of spring water.

"Why are you wearing that dressing gown?" She accepted the refreshment with pleasure.

"I cannot think what came over me." He slid it off his shoulders and left it where it fell. He pulled down the covers, and she lay there, wanton. "Only fair," he said as he set a tray of dainties down between them. He fed her part of a buttered scone. Then the rest. Then a slice of cheese and bread.

"We shall be rather rustic," he said. "There is no bathing chamber here, I am afraid, only a copper tub. Food and drink will be left us over the next few days."

"Whatever shall the footmen do in our absence?"

"About the footmen." Alfred took extreme care in preparing another scone with butter and jam. "It is not from excessive pride that Lowell Hall is attended by so many. In many packs or clowders or flocks, the weakest of the litters are often not allowed a chance to…"

"To thrive?"

"To live. It is the males of the Shifter species, the so-called stronger sex, who are the likeliest to be the runts. Did I not take them in, due to their perceived lack in strength or hardiness, they would be put down. We cannot afford to lose even one Shapeshifting soul, and so…"

"And so you have created a place for them to find their way." Felicity's eyes welled with tears, and her duke looked chagrined, as he did when he was caught out in a good deed. "However do you find them to bring them—oh, allow me to hazard a guess. Mr. Bates."

Alfred nodded. "He has many connections that surveil many things. This is one of them. And thus the myriad footmen of Lowell Hall. Despite taking in the weakest, the Lowell Pack is the strongest in the British Isles. And possibly Europe."

"I believe that several may find employment in the newest business concern in Lowell Close." She wished to make much of him, sensed he would find it discomfiting, and fed him a tea sandwich of ham instead. "Is this bed a usual feature of this place?"

"It is not. I arranged it." He looked delighted with himself. "Had the lads carry it up and install it in good time."

"And the clothes in the other cottages? I presume they are for those who have shifted and are in need of covering?"

"So clever," he murmured, holding out another tasty morsel.

"I could not even think what they were for only days ago," she said. "How all has changed."

His eyes flickered away, and she held up a petit four. He nipped it whole out of her hand and grinned, but she grabbed his chin. "Changed for the better," she said. "Changed for the best."

"I have another apology," he said.

"Would this be my bridal gift?" She brushed his hair out of his eyes again. She could become accustomed to touching him whenever she desired.

He lay down, head on one hand, the other warm on her belly. "I regret I was more brusque than was wanted, when we first met," he said. "I've realized I had forgotten what little say women have in their lives."

"How radical, Your Grace."

He smiled, an expression that was gone almost before it turned his lips. "I would tell what I know of such things, if it does not bring down the tone."

"Alfred." She moved the food and curled into his side. "I seek to know your heart as well as your body. And your mind, of course."

"Vixen." He ran his nose around her face, and she laughed, to please him. He sighed, and she rested a hand over his heart.

"I was seven in human years when I was sent off to foster with Matthias. My sister had been born one year after I. We were at loggerheads much of the time, not that our parents were aware. The nursery was very much separate from the Hall. It was how I thought things were until I arrived at Matthias's family home. The place was stuffed to the rafters with pups, rambling all over the place at will. His parents were as loving toward me as they were with their own, and I perceived the lack Phoebe and I had experienced. Matthias's mother and father were *vera amorum* and I didn't understand until then that my parents were not."

"How could they mate if they were not?"

"Choice." He pulled her closer, his hand straying to his new favorite place—her bottom. "Because they both embraced it, and because they both declared themselves in front of witnesses in much the usual way, it was accepted. It was a *ton* marriage in every sense, with the addition of Shapeshifting."

"Knowing the little I do of your kind," she said, "I cannot imagine how it succeeded."

"It ultimately did not. They did not cherish us as pups, and so their ability to multiply ceased. I was unseen but for my status as heir, and Phoebe was a chess piece to be put on the board when it was time for her marriage." He reached up and twined a lock of Felicity's hair around his fingers. "My sister had no idea I was more than someone to torment until I was gone. I had no idea how much I loved her until I was parted from her, and she was all I looked forward to on my visits home."

"A bright spot. She was well named."

He kissed her forehead and rested his head against hers. "She dutifully wrote to me, her letters contained in my mother's own missives to me, but she constructed an elaborate network to smuggle me her true thoughts."

"So clever," Felicity said. "Very resourceful."

"You and she would get on well. Years passed, as they do, and I became a chess piece myself. It was time for me to mate, and my mother had several likely ladies in mind. Except I had decided I would not settle for less than my *vera amoris*. I was also a young buck and was in no rush."

Felicity leaned back. "How old are you, I'd like to know?"

"You have been told that we do not age as humans do?" She nodded. "I am eight hundred years old."

"What!" Felicity shrieked.

"No, I'm only ninety-seven."

"Are you joking?"

"It translates as thirty-two in human years." He rolled until she was atop him. "May I continue?"

She propped her chin on her hands. "You may."

"Elbows." He pulled her up to set her head on his shoulder. "My parents, much like your uncle, disdained the Quality but clung to their aristocratic status and their aristocratic ways. They mocked my desire for my *vera amoris*, yet agreed to leave me be and let me believe they would allow Phoebe the same pleasure. They said there was no rush to wed either of us, and that I should be off again to sow my wild oats. I had done my duty, I had been fostered, I was building my inner circle, I had graduated from Oxford with a first in classics."

"Classics! Unfair advantage," Felicity murmured, rubbing her hand over his heart.

"I was about to head off for India." The whole of his body quivered with suppressed rage. "Phoebe had warned me that something dire was brewing, but I was certain I had succeeded in negotiating with my parents. They would give me one more year, and Phoebe would not be bartered off to a disgusting lord of our kind who had been through four wives already—given our longevity, you cannot even fathom how old he was. He was also from that generation which did not think beyond keeping the lines pure. He was as good as feral, and he was to take my sister next.

"A letter caught up to me midway back to Dover, thanks to a tireless kestrel. The betrothal had been announced, my parents had declared them *vera amorum* to all and sundry, the contracts were drawn up, and all that remained was the meeting at the conclave rock."

"They lied to you."

"They lied to us both. They lied to our upper echelon, one of whom you may have met at our wedding. I made it to the conclave stone in the very nick of time. I invoked the *disputatione*, which was my right as a family member to object to the pairing, giving Phoebe a chance to deny the mating and refute that they were true mates. Those highly placed individuals who were present went on a rampage. It is against our laws to force a mating on any who do not wish it, even by their guardians."

"Unlike our human society," Felicity observed.

"And due to said rampage, my parents were removed from their position of power and sent to Australia. It's the usual place we banish our less-than-savory characters."

"Let us hope they never meet my cousin." She sat up. "And Phoebe?"

Alfred took a fortifying breath of Felicity's fragrance. "Did what many a maiden who has been brought to the altar and declined must do. She, too, had to emigrate, thus America, to keep up appearances before the human members of the *ton*, to appear to be ashamed of having led on one of their number. Her only recourse was to stay with human acquaintances when she found the society of the local pack unacceptable. This is not ideal in countless ways, for wolves cannot survive for long without the security of the pack, and I cannot think how she is able to Change under such circumstances—"

"Can we not bring her home, Alfred?"

His eyes glistened, and her heart trembled. The strength of emotion that would bring a being such as he to show his tears humbled her. "We can," he said. "It is time to fetch her home."

"You will set Mr. Bates on it, of course," she said. "He could find a needle in a haystack."

"Enough about him," Alfred growled. "Let us see about creating the first Baroness Templeton, shall we?"

She wiggled against his unyielding flesh. "Mrs. Birks said—"

"No. Your propensity for invoking our pack mates at inopportune times is dismaying."

"She said we can have as many babies, er, pups, as we wish." She looked worried. "I am not young."

"*I* am not young. I'm two thousand and three, if you'll recall." He lifted himself off her. He pulled away the covers and considered her body. "Now where shall we…" She felt an instant of self-consciousness that fled when she met his gaze, the intensity of it revealing the depths of his desire. "Shall I let you choose?"

"Where you will take your bite? But Mrs. Birks said Alfie must choose."

He blinked at her. "You did not tell Mrs. Birks you call him Alfie."

"No!" She laughed, gleeful and joyful. "But she said—"

"*I* say." He looked down at her, and his power gathered around him. "I say you must give me permission to give you my wolf's bite. As you felt you had no choice but to marry me—"

"Alfred, that is no longer relevant."

He dropped a finger to her lips. "You will have the choice of where the bite will fall. We insist."

She kissed his finger, fluttered her lashes, and ran a hand over her neck. "Here, perhaps? But then everyone would see."

"It is only to be between us." His eyes tracked her hand as she traced her shoulder.

"Not here, then," she said. "My ribs…" Both her hands joined the exploration. "They are not as bony as some, but nevertheless. It wants somewhere softer, does it not?"

"Soft. Yes." Her hands traveled over her breasts, and her nipples strained for his touch. His eyelids drooped, and he smiled; she saw a flash of teeth that were not the man's. "I might, there."

"Let us investigate every possibility." She bent her legs and presented him with a calf. "I am proud of my strong legs," she said. "Might I interest you in one?"

His grabbed her foot. "These little toes," he crooned, nipping the smallest. She tried to pull away, and he leaned down and dragged his nose from ankle to thigh. "A glorious leg, tiny toes and all." He dropped a kiss on her hip. "I like this exceedingly well."

"I do not."

"But I do. And all in between." He nestled between her thighs and dropped his chin on her belly. "Now, this. This is a wonderful site for my tribute." He ran his face all over her belly until she laughed, and he raised himself on his arms. "But it must be your choice."

She parted her thighs and took his hand. "It is very soft here. And very private. You did say it is meant to be shared only between ourselves."

"So tempting," he growled. "And delicious, as I well know." He raised up to kneel over her. "May I suggest?"

She was becoming accustomed to being moved with expedience—only just. She found herself on her belly, and he on all fours over her back. His tongue traced her spine, and she shuddered at the new sensation. "I adore your waistline." He gave a nip on either side. "This part here, right here." He squeezed low on her flank but high on her hip. "I have held myself back from this." His mouth ran back and forth, over and over, his hands cupping her bottom, and she dissolved in want and desire. "This is like nothing I have ever touched, so lush, so warm. I do not even think this has a name. It is not your hip, or your waist, or your heavenly bottom…"

"Heavenly!" She gasped. His fingers slid up and commenced caressing her very sensitive place. "It is too large."

"It is perfect," he retorted. He took a breath, and his fingers slowed in their movement. "This place of no name is the epitome of perfection." His fingers moved with swiftness now, and Felicity moved against them. One finger parted the depths and entered her, then another. He flipped her onto her side, and the palm of his hand hit that special place, and she moaned.

"The first time…" she said.

"The first time?" he whispered into her flesh.

"When you kissed me, in the Bassett Room, you touched me there." And she moved against his hand as he stroked that nameless yet delicious spot. "And I thought I might give you anything you asked for, just then. That is the place I choose."

"Then so it is." He leaned over and breathed onto that spot, that odd spot, a spot no one would ever regard, and kissed it, caressed it with his face even as his hand pleasured her. A tingle sparked, a warmth gathered beneath his mouth. He kissed it, suckled it, and as his fingers brought her close, closer, closest, his teeth ran across her body, once, twice, thrice, and as she came, as her body shook with release, she felt his fangs, felt the bite in her side, the pain that mixed with her pleasure. Her skin gave to admit him, much like her body had done the first time they'd joined. An energy meshed with her release, as if his breath were entering her body, as though his very essence were entering it, and she called his name, over and over, until he licked the spot, healing it, bathing it in kisses, murmuring against it, before she whispered, "My love, my love," and he pulled her into his embrace, and they rocked each other in sheer bliss.

———————

Alfred set about stoking the fire and replenishing the candles as Felicity lazed about, exerting herself only to watch the light from both sources dance along the delicious flesh on display.

"I would say I am happy to help," she said, "but it would be disingenuous."

"It is the job of the Alpha to tend to his mate." He set the last candle and clattered the tea things about.

"What is the job of the Alpha's mate?"

"You have been fulfilling it from the start," he said. "Supporting the staff, intervening on their behalf, identifying the shortfalls in the household, negotiating between factions. Your general demeanor exuded strength and compassion, your vitality in standing up to me..."

"Does that not undermine your authority?"

"It does not. It presents the picture to the pack that I am balanced by a strong feminine."

"I was compelled to right the wrongs I saw, whether or not it was my concern." She plumped the pillows, which had become disarranged. "When I told you everything that day in the meadow—"

"You did not tell me everything. But I was able to take the few details you disclosed and put them to use." Alfred shook out the duvet that had slid off the bed onto the floor. "I marveled you spoke so freely, but knowing your views on the intelligence of common beasts..."

"Not so common." She rose, wrapping a sheet around herself, which she then lost in a light tussle. They each took a side and spread it over the mattress. "How do you interact with non-shifting creatures of the common sort?"

"Simply and directly. Through tone and the position of the body. Much in the same way you do with horses, to be honest. We are also able to use language with them, to a limited degree, in our shifted forms."

"Do they fear you?"

"They cede to us and often welcome the strength of our presence. They recognize us, as we ourselves recognize one another." His wolf peeked out at her through his eyes. "Alfie recognized you as our mate from the start."

"I was so happy to see him, despite how large he seemed." She returned to her original thought. "When I told you almost everything that day in the meadow, I hadn't realized that I was missing someone to confide in. Yes, even a so-called mere animal. How cross I was with you that evening."

"How impressed I was with you." He smoothed the duvet over the top of the bed; they exchanged a glance acknowledging the uselessness of the endeavor. "I have had Matthias as my Second since we were boys. I cannot imagine being without him to talk to."

"I would very rarely see Jemima outside a *ton* event. Her aunt is quite strict. When at Templeton House, Delilah was my confidante, and I her only champion. Although," Felicity laughed, "once, Mama turned her ankle, and Father had to fetch Delilah back. They fought the whole way but came to an agreement in the end."

"She was his confidante as well." Alfred lounged onto the bed, at home in his own skin, in both his skins—muscular, beautiful, raw, vigorous, steadfast. "The jewels and the will were hidden in her stall."

"Oh, Papa." Felicity let a wave of sadness move through her. "Perhaps he forgave my mother's obsession with the horses, and my own, in the end."

"Do you forgive him?"

"I understand the pain of his loss now." She joined him atop the freshened bedclothes. "It will go some way to forgiving his behavior in the last years of his life."

"We believe in the continuity of our ancestors," he began.

"Ghosts?"

"Not as such," he replied and rubbed his big, warm hands on her arms. "We believe in their essence prevailing through time and space. Perhaps we can leave that thought for the moment," he said as she wilted in his arms. "You have taken in more than one new idea these last few days. I will say that the continuation of the title will be a fine tribute to him, and it will gratify his spirit."

"Where will that leave our second daughter?"

"Perhaps you will make another decree and we can confer one of my many titles upon the next daughter, and the next, and the—"

"Now see here, Your Grace. As many as we desire does not mean progeny without number." How peremptory she sounded. How confident she was that she would be heard.

"I desire twelve."

"I desire six. Three and three."

"My duchess has spoken."

"But not all at once."

"We do run to twins, hence the myth. No more than two at a time."

"I shall feel rather the spare part. Being the only member of the family who cannot Change." Felicity worried the edge of the duvet. "Are you disappointed that I am not a wolf? Or even a fish?"

He tickled her toes with his. "Are you disappointed that I am not simply a man?"

"Of course not. You are…you."

"Well, then." He howled as she managed to get her fingers on his ribs.

"You are not impervious then, to ills and such." She laughed as he once again subdued her, this time wrapping his arms around her from behind.

"There is no ill we cannot recover from up to death," he said, rubbing his cheek against hers. "And we are difficult to kill. If ever we are in need of speedy recovery as a human, we shift into our essential selves and can mend a bone in a matter of hours, for example."

"So you needn't wait for the full moon? Nor keep humans safe from your presence?"

"I have a few words to exchange with Lady Coleman," he grumbled. "Those novels are nothing but trouble for us, near to undoing all the good we have done in keeping our secrets."

"They are foul creatures, werewolves," she agreed. "It seemed as though the Change was painful. And accompanied by pain and blood and the sound of cracking bones. And copious amounts of saliva."

"While not as dramatic, the Shift is not without its physical challenges," he allowed. "The bones and sinews undergo a complete transformation. Matthias's father helped us through our first Change, and it was difficult, as it must be seen in the mind before the body can conform to the wolfskin. And until one has achieved it at least once, it can be almost impossible to form a picture. It makes sense, somewhere in the psyche, but the initial mental effort is unlike anything I'd ever known. Or known since. So, no, if we waited until every full moon, then we would not take on the speed we achieve with practice. The strongest among us can change in a finger snap. Matthias has yet to beat me."

She thought of their children. "And yet you are born with this need. How do you know when it is time?"

"We trust our instincts." He rubbed himself against her. "You are already acquainted with another benefit we enjoy…"

She felt said benefit growing hard against her back. "This did not feature in any of the stories."

"We attract the interest of more than one predatory human woman," he murmured. "Did they know what our abilities entailed…"

"Hmmmm." Her wandering fingers threatened another round of tickles, but she could tell he was becoming inured to her teasing touch. "There was a moment in *The Beastly Baron Bardolph*—"

"Good Goddess, woman. Do not torture me with such foolishness."

"It wasn't foolish," she said as she stroked his now quiescent ribs. "He controlled the lovely Ethelinda—"

"Ethelinda!" He howled into her neck.

"With his mind," she continued. "He made her do the most dreadful things to herself."

"Did he?" Alfred drew Felicity onto her back.

"Have you the power to make me do dreadful things?" She lowered her eyes. "Baron Bardolph compelled Ethelinda to use his hands to touch her body as though it was her will."

"I have already caused you to touch yourself," he said. "Was it against your will?"

"It was not," she sighed. "But it was lonely, in that great bath, with only the sound of the splashing water and my breath." She took his hands and ran them over her shoulders and down to her breasts.

"I am amazed," he said, as she encouraged him to plump her silken flesh and then flow over her ribs to her hips, "that the author of *The Beastly Baron Bardolph* was so explicit as to pollute the minds of young ladies."

"Oh," she sighed as his fingers found her honeypot. "Mrs. Anchoretta Asquith did not express the corrupting coercion— oh—" They found an especially sensitive spot. "Ahhhh, in plain speech, but the hints were rather broad in an effort to warn young ladies against such sin." His breath expelled in a rush as she turned eyes lambent with pleasure up to his. "It was only a matter of reading between the lines and following one's, uh, instincts."

He reclined next to her, and one hand caressed the mark he'd made on her skin. The heat of their bodies reached out to one another as Felicity's skin turned rosy, her lips parted, her legs fell away from one another, and her head dropped back, eyes closed. "Open your eyes," he ordered, and she obeyed. "Watch me watch you."

"Say please," she demanded.

"Please," he whispered in her ear. "Oh, please, don't stop."

"In this instance," she managed, "I am all that is obedient, Your Grace."

The rings of the bed-curtains sang as Alfred whipped them open; he stood in all his glory, hands on his hips as Felicity buried her face in a pillow. "You are grumpy of a morning, for a horsewoman." It was the third day of their mating retreat, and sadly the last. He set a piping hot cup of tea on the bedside table, which garnered her interest, as did the plate of eggs and toast.

"Have you made me tea?"

"Our desire to break our fast has once again been anticipated."

"To what degree does the pack anticipate all our desires?" Felicity lifted her head from the pillow, alarmed.

"Not to that degree." He handed her cup and saucer. "Although…"

"Oh, no."

"No. But our bond serves to strengthen our connection to the pack and within the pack."

"O'Mara said you were like a spider, or its web."

"A spider?"

"That you were the center of a web that spins throughout the community." She snorted and drained her tea. "A virginal spider."

He took the cup from her, set it aside, and pounced. He was as silent as the predator he was, and she struggled against the sheets, blankets, and the large, muscular male. Her hands were over her head in an instant, and she squirmed until she saw, and felt, evidence of his enjoyment in her struggles. She squirmed some more, but with intent.

"You will be sore." He lowered her arms and laid his palm over the bite. "Here, too, still."

"It is, a little," she said. He inhaled her new fragrance: the notes that had led him to her with the overlay of his own marking scent and the addition of something unique to them alone—the product of their joining and of his bite.

She wiggled once more. "I would not waste the food it took someone's labor to make and to carry here." He released her and rose.

"I would not waste it as I am ravenous. For food, also." Alfred grinned, his entire body euphoric. He had known there would be a change in himself, but not to such a degree. Soon his people would know this joy, as they were free now to be fruitful and multiply.

"When you smile…" she began and trailed off, shy once more.

"When I smile…"

"I cannot reconcile you to the man who dragged me off into the night." She patted his face, and he nuzzled her wrist. "So stern, so unyielding."

"So burdened, so unhappy." He linked his fingers with hers. "So afraid that my plans would not meet with success."

"And yet all here stood with you and trusted you." She looked down at their joined hands. "I, too, had a plan, and now I understand that while I had help, I did not have support. There is a difference."

"I had no way to describe us without revealing what we were," he said. "No way of explaining what you would gain, which is all the support in the world, without my people's blessing."

"O'Mara explained that as well." Felicity ate her eggs and drank from her refilled teacup. "I am astonished that you would ask permission for anything."

"We are a delicate system dependent on all observing their places." He filled his plate again and ate with gusto. "Those at the top have the greatest responsibility, as we must keep the equilibrium for those at the bottom. So, in their way, they are the most important since they require much of the energy and attention of the so-called upper echelons."

"And yet their very sense of well-being depends upon that echelon being at its fullest strength." He nodded, and she continued, "I understand, then, why you were so adamant that our marriage not be like those of the *ton*. It is important that you are true in all things."

"The pack requires a genuine mated pair to look upon, to know they are held by both a masculine and a feminine power, balanced in love and strength. It goes back to that blasted myth, of course."

"Mary Mossett told me rather a different version than you did."

"About the vengeance of Venus?" He shrugged. "I suppose anything is possible."

"This from a being of two natures who physically changes, one from the other? I suppose anything is possible as well!"

He rolled out of bed and stoked the fire. She snuggled up against the headboard and pulled the sheet up to her chin...then threw it aside and rose to join him, naked as the day she was born. "I suppose," she said as she leaned into his chest and slid a leg between his, "that the true meaning of the story is that when strength and love cannot be found within both man and woman, then one or the other will stray, seeking to draw what was lacking from outside the bond, thereby endangering it. Therefore, whether it is strength of thought or muscle, of spiritual love or carnal love, if all do not meet in each heart and soul, then betrayal and pain soon follow."

"I see no need to acquire the services of a tutor," he said, backing her toward the bed. "You have discovered an interpretation no other has before you."

She blushed and lifted her chin, defiant. "I insist that my marriage articles be honored to the letter, Your Grace."

"It will be as you dictated, Your Grace." He lifted her up high in his arms and tossed her down onto the rumpled bed linen.

She laughed and bounced and smiled up at him. "As it should be, else I would have taken you as a lover and not married you at all."

"You are the one who refused to be my mistress."

"Well, it would have been different had it been coming from me."

"Ah, yes, your 'bit o' trousers.'" She gasped, and he laughed. "I heard you discussing that scheme with Jupiter."

"I entertained that notion for no time at all," she admitted. "Even then, I couldn't fathom not falling in love with you."

"I would never have accepted less than what we have." He tickled her, to no avail. "I expect you would have been terribly expensive to keep, but rewarding in so many ways."

"It's not just about bed play." She pushed him away, returned fire to his still-vigilant ribs, and sulked.

"It is not," he allowed, running his nose along the side of her arm. "It is about all the other things that Bates likely read in that Goddess-forsaken book about how well-born men may best court women."

"Book?" She looked thoughtful. "I believe I owe you a groom's gift, Your Grace."

"You are all the gift I'd ever hoped for. That I'd ever prayed for." The laughter fell from both their faces. "I have gained a mate in more ways than I could have imagined. You have gained a stalwart, ferocious defender of your dreams."

"And you have gained your *vera amoris*, who will stand with you as we keep our people safe and raise our children secure in both their natures."

They held each other, wordless, needless of speech, as they embraced one another and these new vows, their pattern for the days and nights to come, full of love and joy and challenge and acceptance, the like that neither would ever take for granted.

Epilogue

IF FELICITY FOUND THE STATEROOMS OPULENT, THEY WERE AS a poorly lit reception room in comparison to the ducal suite. It boasted luxuriously appointed rooms double in number to those set aside for visiting dignitaries, and while the duchess's bedchamber would likely go unoccupied, the accompanying dressing room was immense and the lady's bath even more so.

The bed she woke upon—alone, alas—was double the size of that which graced the honeymoon cottage and draped with heavy satin-lined curtains suspended from an ornate canopy. The sheets and pillow slips were of the usual Lowell standard, but these were imbued with her and Alfred's essences, a fragrance she thought she may have been mortified to enjoy as a maiden when one did not speak of personal scents by any stretch of the imagination; as a married woman, it was part and parcel of the realities of her new status.

Little less than a week had passed since the bonding ceremony and with it their return to the Hall and quotidian life. How her life could ever be considered prosaic was beyond her, and yet, as Felicity wove more deeply into the unique fabric that was the Lowell Pack, she further understood its similarities to life lived anywhere in England and its employment of many of the structures and strictures of human society. Whether or not this was beneficial remained to be seen, but she appreciated the *versipellian* conundrum; to paraphrase Mr. Coburn: in order to remain free to be their essential creatures, they needs must conduct themselves with the utmost civility.

She mused over what she wished to accomplish in the day and wondered if Jemima would fashion her a night rail with pockets that she may keep pencil and paper on hand, and then she rejected

the notion—it was not as if she wore a night rail. She cuddled
Alfred's pillow to her breast and sighed like a tweenie mooning
over the boot boy. If they continued apace, she would be up the
spout in no time. Her heart leapt, and thoughts of her stud and the
need for her own steward ran side by side with wistful imaginings
of pups capering around the park under Alfred's watchful eye.

The curtains were pulled back briskly and with a familiar lack
of formality. "Oh, Your Grace, you are awake," Mary Mossett
chirped as she proceeded to open the hangings all around the bed.
"Although I'd say you earned your rest." She giggled.

"Mary!" Mrs. Birks's scolding rang out, as was customary.
Felicity sat, wrapped in the top sheet, and a perfectly prepared
a cup of tea was placed in her hands. "Here you are, Your Grace,
here you are." The housekeeper raised a brow at the clothing
strewn about the floor, and Felicity strove not to blush. "Mary
will draw your bath and then consult with you regarding today's
accoutrements."

"I truly am keen to apprentice her to Lady Coleman," Felicity
said, hoping the distance to the lady's bathing room and the sound
of the rushing water would combine to act as a buffer even against
Shifter hearing. "I have not devised how that may be achieved as
yet, but let us keep it between us for now, even as we discuss her
replacement as my lady's maid."

"Very good, ma'am. I understand this was a stipulation in your
marriage contracts." With the speed of her kind, the room was set
to rights in a trice, and Mrs. Birks lay Alfred's dressing gown at the
foot of the bed.

How like her first morning in Lowell Hall, yet how unlike it
was! She wrapped herself in her husband's scent and passed down
the connecting hall, through the duke's dressing room, and into
the duchess'—hers—and on to the bath. The water was redolent
with vanilla and vetiver, a canny compromise on Mary's part as
to each of her and Alfred's preferred fragrances, and the maid's

chatter was a homey, comforting accompaniment to her bathing as the mouse browsed her wardrobe.

Attired in one of her walking habits, Felicity made her way to the breakfast room, greeting the staff as she went, accepting their obeisance, which she had to admit she still found strange, then chatting with those cheeky ginger footmen whom she greeted at the top of the stairs. Mr. Coburn awaited her in the corridor near the breakfast room.

"Good morning, Mr. Coburn," she said. "I trust this day finds you well."

"Morning, is it, ma'am? Not for my kind it is not, I assure you." The rooster bowed, and they both blushed.

"Oh, dear," she smiled. "I plead the tardiness of the newly wed."

"We would have it no other way, ma'am, no other way," he assured her as he saw to the doors himself.

Alfred rose as his blushing bride entered the room.

"Your Grace." She curtseyed to the amusement of the footmen. "I do apologize for my lateness." Mr. Coburn rushed to pull out a chair opposite Alfred, who shook his head and indicated the seat to his left.

"I had business in the farthest field," Alfred said as she took her place. "I am only lately returned myself."

The usual complement of footmen ringed the wall, and Coburn tended to the couple's needs, freshening pots of tea and keeping a weather eye on the sideboard's offerings, taking his responsibilities as ducal butler seriously indeed. As Alfred's mate pushed eggs counterclockwise 'round her plate and failed to conceal another yawn, he opened a letter weighed down with Royal seals and made himself familiar with its contents.

"Osborn has wed the Marchioness of Castleton," he announced.

"Beatrice?" Felicity made to freshen her tea but was unequal to their butler's attentiveness. "Oh, thank you, Mr. Coburn. I was unaware she was being courted."

"No one knew I was courting you." He smiled at her and leaned an elbow on the table to gaze at her. She reproved him with a mere glance, and he sat up properly.

"No less a personage than myself knew you were courting me," she countered, and the footmen snickered. "Who is Osborn?"

"Still not up on your *Debretts*?" Alfred buttered half a scone and put it on her plate. "Arthur Humphries, Duke of Osborn. I knew him growing up, he lived in Court with Georgie, big lad, always on the fringes," he said. "He was present at our nuptials."

"I did not notice, I regret to say." They exchanged a fulsome look, and Alfred considered convincing her to delay attendance upon her duties at Templeton Stud.

"Did you not? What held your attention, I wonder?" The footmen giggled, and even Coburn cast aside his dignity enough to crack a smile. "His Highness demanded Bates's company once our vows were said," he continued. "Perhaps he had been called upon to witness theirs. I, too, had my attention elsewhere." He reached back to stroke the spot at the top of Felicity's hip that carried his mating mark.

She batted him away with her napkin. "Does he enjoy a similar, er, status beyond his ducal duties?"

"He is an Alpha," Alfred said. "Although he is not doing his duties. His father was challenged for primacy over their clan and lost. It is past time Osborn took up his mantle."

"Challenged?" Felicity warmed up his tea and administered the requisite two spoonfuls of sugar.

"A rogue of his species fought for the right to command the Osborn holdings. It is an old, old custom of *versipellis* life. George's great-great-grandfather upheld such hidebound notions, but it has largely been abolished." Alfred waved away the kippers proffered by Coburn at his mate's minute flinch.

"Largely?" Felicity added jam to the scone, cut it half, and put the larger piece on Alfred's plate.

"Veritably completely. As our kind have become civilized, so have many of our ways, but not all." Alfred applied himself to his meal.

"I do not think Beatrice will countenance violence," she said. "In fact I know she will not. I am not apprised of the details, but I can say with confidence her first marriage was not harmonious."

"I have no doubt it was not." He knew only too well what marriage to Castleton would have entailed for the unlucky wife.

"If she were wed to such as he without being any the wiser…" Felicity worried her eggs with her fork.

"Humans have unknowingly wed Shifters and remained in ignorance for the whole of their lives," Alfred said. "I am certain the new duchess is informed regarding our kind, however. As you are now aware, one can tell if one knows what to look for. She held herself aloof to all and sundry, but when sundry was *versipellis*, she was very much on her guard."

He perused the rest of the letter. "Ah. Yes, here, Bates was likely required as a witness, for they were indeed wed directly after we were, in Carlton House."

"Oh! But—" Felicity rose before a footman or three could pull out her chair. "This has every hallmark of an unwanted alliance. I shall write to her straightaway." She threw her napkin down and then picked it up and folded it. How like her, ever striving to make less work for the staff. "Have you their direction?"

Arthur rose and took his *vera amoris*'s hand. "I suspect they have taken up residence in Arcadia, the Humphries homeplace."

"Arcadia. How beautiful it sounds," said Felicity as she ran her hand along his arm to stroke his biceps.

Alfred shrugged. "If it has been uninhabited since his father's time," he said as they left the room, "I suspect it is in a state far less beautiful than its name."

Acknowledgments

It's been such a pleasure and an honor to bring this book to life with the help of so many others. Thank you, Julie Gwinn, for your effervescent support of me and this series. Thank you, Deb Werksman, for your belief in the work, as well as to everyone at Sourcebooks: design, copy, production, and marketing. Dream team!

The number of blogs devoted to all matters Regency was breathtaking, and an absolute gift. Spending forty-five minutes researching something that was an off-the-cuff mention was rather a challenge for this previously contemporary writer, but the hard work of those who came before made chasing facts a true pleasure. When I suddenly needed to know the difference between a drawing room and a parlor, the answer was there. Did fancy Regency people wear underpants? Someone out there knew. There are too many to name, but I am so grateful to the authors in this genre, whose generosity in creating and maintaining their websites made me feel part of a community.

Many innovations in Lowell Hall were ahead of their time; equally, Lady Coleman's fashions would become common in the decades following the one in which this is set, and, well, someone had to set the trend. My favorite find were acrostic rings, which were in fact a thing, coming to England from France around 1811 and remaining fashionable well into the early twentieth century. Liberties were taken about some of the "modern" inventions, such as unlimited running hot water (although the first shower in England was a Regency shower, 1810!); bequeathing the Templeton title to the females of the line are my invention.

Thanks to Caroline Tolley for her eagle eye and beta edit, and massive, heartfelt, endless gratitude to the Greystones gang, who have had my back and cheered me on from the very first draft and all along the way.

About the Author

Susanna Allen is a graduate of Pratt Institute with a BFA in Communication Design and counts *The Village Voice*, *New York Magazine*, and *Entertainment Weekly* as past design experiences. Born in New Jersey, she moved to Ireland for twelve months—in 1998. Writing as Susan Conley, she is the author of *Drama Queen* and *The Fidelity Project*, both published by Headline UK, and *That Magic Mischief*, via Crimson Romance. Susanna is living her life by the three Rs—reading, writing, and horseback riding—and can generally be found on her sofa with her e-reader, gazing out a window and thinking about made-up people, or cantering around in circles. She loves every minute of it!